MW01167354

Black Magic
&
Serendipity

Volume One:
The Blood Witch

Black Magic & Serendipity

Volume One:
The Blood Witch

Love Shack Books

www.loveshackbooks.com

Black Magic & Serendipity: Volume One--The Blood Witch
Copyright © 2023 Christopher P. Schmehl

All rights reserved. No part of this book may be reproduced in any form or by any electronic or mechanical means, including information storage and retrieveal systems, without written permission from the author, except in the case of a reviewer, who may quote brief passages embodied in critical articles or in a review.

This is a work of fiction. Names, characters, places, and incidents either are the product of the author's imagination or are used fictitiously, and any resemblance to actual persons, living or dead, events, or locales is entirely coincidental.

Published by Love Shack Books

Edited by Senojor

Cover Art by Angela Bagenstose

ISBN: 9798852995193

Love Shack Books

For Jeremy,
Thank you so much
for reading! I hope
you enjoy the book!
Sincerely,
Chris Schmidt
2023

Praise for *The State of Oz*

"I really enjoyed it! Exciting story."

Ken Perod, *Fifth Street Reviews*

"Don't miss this talented author."

Pasquale Q. Micklemack, author of *Diners Great and Small*

This book is dedicated to Paul and Linda Schmehl.

Also By Christopher Schmehl

The State of Oz

Acknowledgments

I could never have written this book without....

My parents Paul and Linda Schmehl.
I held them up in the bookstore for years! They also took me to the
library and made sure I went to college. A million thank yous.

My cover artist Angela Bagenstose
for her beautiful, provocative painting.
You are one talented woman! Thank you.

My professors at Kutztown University for the knowledge they shared.
I thank you all. Especially Harry Humes, William Collins, Jim Nechas,
Sam Keiser, Karen Blomain, Betty Reagan, and Patrick Duddy.

Scott Powers, Kenny Perod, and
Eileen Murphy-Schmehl for being first readers.
Thanks for your interest and your invaluable feedback.

A shout-out to the people who encouraged my writing.

Kathleen and Cullen Murphy

Sean Szmal

Matthew Szmal

Barbara and Ronnie Klee

Duane, Chris, and Sarah Keinard

Melisa and Steve Snyder

Bob and LouAnn Blankenbiller

Earl and Suzie Blankenbiller

Kelly and Steve George

Mike George

Eric Heim

Michael and Tanya Kleffel

Pam Tourangeau

Lisa T. Wojenski

Joy Gerhart

Kathi Fritz

Barbara Nagle

Gina Cavanna

Melissa Weitzel

Veronica Smith

Michael Massie

Sue Ciletti

Henrik Neilsen

Matt Funk

Eric Winter

Robert Choiniere

Lehman Fastnacht

Patrick Schiding

Jere Williams

Steve Spease

Jen and Damon Franks

Dan Heim

Rob Reeder

Jim Steranko

Steve and Elodie Witkowski

Courtney Thompson

Table of Contents

"I don't wanna live here no more,
I don't wanna stay
Ain't gonna spend the rest of my life,
Quietly fading away"

--Alan Parsons, Eric Woolfson
"Games People Play"

The
Blood
Witch

Part One

Chapter One

I f Moeera had followed the path her parents wanted, her goddaughter would have grown up with loving parents in the capital. This was not to be. Moeera's parents expected her to marry a farmer or tradesman. They thought she'd make a suitable housewife. The girl Moeera had other ideas. None of these involved settling down.

Why be dull?

*   *   *

Everywhere you looked somebody was having fun. The fairground was filled with tents and temporary stands. The townswomen entered in the baking contest looked on as the judges examined their masterpieces. Children danced around a Maypole and played a wide array of games.

"What's your name, little girl?" a man in bright colors asked. Sleigh bells jingled as he spun in circles.

The wide-eyed girl looked at him from between her mother and father. The five-year-old only came up to her mother's waist.

"It's okay," her mother said. "You can tell him your name."

"Moeera," the girl said. Her hair fell around her the color of sunset.

"Oh!" the man said. "A lovely name for a lovely girl. Do you like magic, Moeera?"

She shrugged her shoulders.

"You don't know? I'll let you in on a secret, Moeera--everyone likes magic. That's right. And you can see Wecks the Wizard perform all his best tricks in just half an hour!"

Moeera's mouth opened wide. A real live wizard doing magic tricks. She couldn't think of anything more exciting than that.

The man smiled again and then rose to his full height.

"I've never heard of Wecks the Wizard," her father said.

"He's come from far and wide, sir," the gaudily dressed man said.

"Why should I believe anything a jester tells me?"

The man grinned sheepishly. "Only a jester for today, sir. Wecks says it attracts attention. I'm really just manager of the caravan he travels with. He's our main draw."

"Can we see the show?" Moeera asked.

"I suppose," her father said. "Maybe this Wecks will change iron into gold."

"Perhaps, perhaps. You never know with Wecks!" the man exclaimed. "Moon Theater; half an hour." He wandered off to tell more people about the magic show. Moeera watched him waving his arms and pantomiming sawing something.

"Wecks's show sounds exciting, doesn't it?" Mallory said to Kor.

"I guess," he said, watching a chubby woman win first place ribbon for her blackberry stack pie. "Magic's all a bunch of silly parlor tricks."

"Maybe …," Mallory said.

"Course it is," Kor said. "It's all done with smoke and mirrors."

"Alright, dear," Mallory said. "Moeera will enjoy it, I bet."

"Sure," he replied. "You want to see the wizard trick everyone?"

"Yes!" Moeera said, adamantly. She smiled, clinging to her father's legs. "I want to see magic!"

"Let's have dessert first," her father said. "Pie would be nice … or fritters."

"Fritters," Moeera agreed, nodding.

They strolled through the throng of people to the bake stand. Moeera saw jugglers entertaining in front of the Moon Theater. A sound to the right drew her attention to two thin men on towering stilts, their arms outstretched to help keep their balance.

Kor and Mallory each chose a piece of pie. Moeera held her hands out for the hot apple fritter.

"Careful, dear," the baker said, handing it across, "it's very hot. Don't let it burn ya!"

Moeera nodded. She did a bit of magic of her own making a pocket handkerchief appear in her hands. The man lowered the fritter into her hanky.

"Thank you!" Moeera said.

2

"You're welcome," he said. "Next!"

Kor found them a bench to sit on at the big social tent. Luckily, it was toward the edge where Moeera had a good view of the people outside. There went Vaughn who farmed the land next to her father's. There was Wad who worked for her father at the smithy. She saw several girls she'd met at Sunday School ….

A shout interrupted her thoughts. More and more people outside the tent looked to the sky in the town hall's direction. She stood up, trying to search the sky, but her view was completely blocked.

"What's all the hubbub?" Kor asked.

People exited the social tent in droves.

"What's happening?" Mallory asked. She had a couple bites left on her plate.

"I don't know," Kor said, "but I'm going to find out. Wait here."

"I wanna go with you!" Moeera said.

"Fine, Moeera. Let's go see."

He took long strides from the tent into the crowd outside, Moeera hurrying after him. She watched him excuse himself to a dozen people as he searched for a good vantage point. Moeera pushed her way between legs, legs, and more legs to keep up. She reached up and took her father's hand when he stopped.

Around them people were whispering in hushed voices.

"What is he doing?"

"He'll be killed!"

"Do you see that!"

Moeera felt her father's hand stiffen in hers.

He muttered, "The fool--what in God's name does he think he's doing?"

She squinted through a gap in the crowd and saw the town hall's roof. A large man in a shiny, golden cloak stood right at the roof's edge. He waved to the crowd in over- exaggerated swipes. He looked tall, confident, and … wait. What was he doing? He stood tall, spreading his arms wide like a preacher or … a bird?

He leapt up and dove forward!

If the crowd hadn't been yelling quite so loudly, or if she wasn't so certain that the man would plunge to his death, Moeera would have found it beautiful. The cloak caught the air looking for all the world like an enormous eagle's wings. Down the man fell; fast at first, but more and more slowly until he floated the final few feet. His cloak swirled about him as his feet touched the ground. He stood up tall and then took a deep bow.

The magic show of Wecks the Wizard had begun.

$$* \qquad * \qquad *$$

Moeera and her parents found spots in front of town hall to watch the magic show. Wecks strode before them in his golden cloak across the wooden bandstand.

"Ladies and gentlemen!" he called in a booming voice. "It's fantastic to be in Bucktry! Thank you for being here today! You saw me levitate down from the rooftop. More awesome magic waits to be shared. This for instance."

He produced a large, red handkerchief from his jacket pocket. Waving it back and forth he pulled a bright yellow one out of nowhere to join it.

"Anybody ever lose their laundry on a really windy day?" he asked.

The red handkerchief leapt away from the stocky wizard of its own volition. It flew in circles, but whatever Wecks tried it evaded his grasping hands. The audience roared with laughter as Wecks overshot the handkerchief, hitting the deck with a thud.

He rubbed his elbow as he climbed to his feet. "It's got a mind of its own, doesn't it?"

At this point the yellow handkerchief came to life and started pulling away from Wecks's hand. "Not you, too," he said. The yellow hanky moved up and down and up and down as if nodding. He tightened his grip.

The red hanky flew over his head, dropping over his eyes. The audience laughed hysterically.

Wecks grabbed at the red hanky which slipped away to resume its whirling. The yellow one slipped from his fingers and joined the red one.

Wecks gestured toward them with both arms and waved in despair. "Oh, I give up!" he cried. "There's only so much hanky-panky a wizard can stand." He watched the swirling handkerchiefs with an annoyed look on his face. He tapped his foot. Still, they swirled.

Finally, Wecks turned to the audience and said, "Well, while they're having their fun how about we move on into the theater?"

He passed the renegade hankies and descended the steps to the ground. He motioned for the onlookers to follow him the short distance to the

Moon Theater. Golden cloak swirling Wecks strode into the theater. Silence ruled the crowd until he vanished from sight. Then it went berserk. It surged forward, a stampeding herd of bachukkas.

Money flashed in hands as people got to the doormen. The admission prices were swiftly paid, and people poured triumphantly into the place. As seats filled folks discussed the feats they'd seen. Moeera sat up straight between her parents ready to see Wecks perform more wonders.

When the theater had filled Wecks strode confidently onto the center stage. His shiny, golden wings were gone, replaced by a black ensemble.

"Welcome again, everybody!" he called. "I'm the Wondrous Wecks, and good ladies and gentlemen, you've seen my show opener--the descent and the wash trick. I'm pleased to be here at the Moon Theater with you all."

"I'm sure you all know a certain somebody you just don't get along with. You understand? Someone who walks up to you at market or always crosses the church to greet you on Sunday morning? You know the person I mean? Or maybe they always win when you're playing tiddledywinks or tag? The fastest runner, the meanest bully, the smelliest know-it-all? They make the hairs rise on your arms and legs. You know the one I mean. Me? I hate the barber."

"What do you do? Grin and bear it? Give them a slap on the back? If you know magic, you can do other things--like this!"

Wecks leaned over the stage front and waved his hands at a tall man wearing a purple slouch. A flash of light burst forth and a cloud of smoke obscured the man. When it cleared a bit, the man was gone. A cry of astonishment escaped the crowd.

"Don't you wish sometimes you could do that?" Wecks said. "Make a person fade away as if they'd never been there. Maybe it's occurred to you."

A cackle went up somewhere in the seats followed by laughter.

"You don't want to hurt them," Wecks continued, "you merely need a break."

A similar puff of smoke and flash burst on the stage behind Wecks. There was the man! He walked out of the thick smoke shaking his head and smiling. Wecks turned to him and offered his hand.

"I don't even know you, sir, but thank you for your assistance. You're not a barber, are you? No?"

The man left the stage looking no worse for wear than when he

5

disappeared from the audience. The audience clapped; Wecks took a bow.

"Thank you, thank you!" Wecks said. He pulled a brass candelabra to center stage and lit the twelve candles of various colors. Once all the candles were lit, he folded his hands behind his back.

"I know many of you wonder about the nature of magic. Hmm? You wonder how it all works and why it lets a certain select group of people do what seems impossible."

There was much nodding and murmuring from the audience.

Wecks circled the candles, passing his hands closely around them. As he did each flame became the same color as its respective candle.

The audience oohed and ahhed.

Wecks reached his arms toward the ceiling and the audience began applauding. He took a quick bow. Then he waved his arms sideways at the candelabra in a pulling motion; the flames returned to normal.

"Some of you believe in magic; some don't. That's all right--it's the way of the world. To quote the Wondrous Wam: 'It's all connected, every last bit in some way.'. You're probably thinking to yourself 'What does he mean? How am I connected to the constable in Slippakanu? Or the queen in Catty Corners? How am I--a person; a Gillikin--connected to the spiny sea urchin in the great, big Nonestic Ocean? Or the starfish? Or the stars in the sky for that matter?' Folks listen to me. Close your eyes for a moment and picture it …."

"The tide causes the waves to wash up soil on the beach; this contains miniscule creatures; little, tiny animals eat these miniscule creatures; a seabird eats a fiddler crab; the seabird becomes injured and is consumed by an orca; the whale is then attacked by sharks. One of the sharks lives a long time, but eventually dies. Its remains are deposited on the sea floor. This begins the cycle again and is repeated in various iterations. Life affects life; nature affects life."

"Every living thing has an aura. This is the energy it possesses. Magic happens when you tap into this energy …." Wecks became very still as if lost in his own thoughts. He came out of his reverie with a jerk. "Enough babbling, eh? You all paid to see magic."

At this point two men wheeled in an immense wooden barrel. Water spilled from the tip top as it splashed over the edges. The men put chocks against the wheels and left the stage.

"You're wondering about the wine vat here!" Wecks exclaimed. "Well, to be a successful wielder of the magic arts one must be ready for anything. Problems may arise that you simply have no foreknowledge of."

The men who had brought in the barrel now returned with a rolling gantry they pushed against the barrel. It banged the barrel with a thump. This was similarly stabilized. Wecks climbed the ladder and was soon joined by his helpers.

"Imagine if you will that you have an incident by the shore! For sensation's sake pretend that I'm a merchant on my way to trade my best wares. Desirable items indeed! A robber accosts me and throws me into the drink, but not before I am bound up thusly!"

The men wrapped Wecks in thick rope, pulling it tight and knotting it behind his back. One separately tied his hands while the other tied a rope from his neck to his crotch to his ankles. Wecks teetered on the platform. One of the men gave him a careless push and he disappeared into the water!

Murmurs and gasps rippled throughout the crowd. Moeera watched the giant barrel with wide eyes.

"He must be braver than Strifego's knights," Mallory said.

"Or else just plain crazy," Kor commented. "He's sealed his fate, the bugger. No more trickery for him!"

Whispers flowed like water throughout the theater. A clock--the one within the town hall's tower--began striking the hour. The two stagehands stood with hats held firmly to their chests, looking at the water's surface.

Dong!

Dong!

Dong!

Dong!

Dong! And suddenly a miracle! A hand leapt from the water to grasp the barrel's edge!

The crowd roared. The sound filled the theater louder than any cacophony ever heard before! Men and women rose from their seats waving arms and chanting the name Wecks! Moeera's father seized her under her arms and hoisted her up to see Wecks's head pop up beside the gantry. The wizard sucked in air greedily as his assistants took him by the arms and pulled him from liquid demise. He plopped onto the platform.

In seconds he was up and waving to the cheering crowd, blowing kisses, smiling. He bowed several times. The thunderous applause drowned out any words he might've said, but there were those close enough who could see his lips mouth the two words "thank you" again and again. Finally, he walked down the stage to retreat to his dressing room. The stagehands were joined by two more who followed Wecks with the gantry and the barrel.

*   *   *

The audience was informed shortly after that the show would be concluded with that escape trick. The disappointed crowd was assured it would receive markers on its way out ensuring free admittance to any future performances.

Moeera grabbed the wooden token as if life depended on it. She studied the stylized "W" carved into the pine round and embellished with charcoal. Wecks's display of miraculous tricks and his daring escape filled her mind with longing.

Magic was real. It was a part of life, created by life. She must learn to wield it, too.

Chapter Two

That night Moeera's thoughts raced around her head refusing to quiet down. She readied herself for bed and sat down studying the small, round token. It was a rather plain little thing with the inscribed "W" traced in black. Ordinary.

Looks could be deceiving. Wecks had proven that by cheating death not once but twice!

She placed the token under her bed by the wall.

Mallory entered Moeera's tiny bedroom to bid her good night.

"Get into bed, honey," Mallory said.

Moeera obeyed, but as her mother moved to tuck the covers around her, she sat up and said, "Wait!"

"What, dear?"

"I want to learn to use magic, Mother! Just like Wecks."

"Oh. I see. We can talk of such things tomorrow, Moeera."

"But why not now?"

"You know why. It's late. You need to sleep now."

Moeera yawned despite her enthusiasm. "I suppose."

"Right," Mallory said, tucking her in. "That's more like it."

"A story ...," Moeera said.

Mallory looked at her young daughter. "A short one."

"The Ballad of Eileen!"

"A short one, I said."

"Please? Tell me that story."

"Fine," Mallory said, "but you must calm down and sleep."

"I will."

"Alright. Once upon a time there was a princess named Eileen who sang like an angel from Heaven. She grew up in a far-off place by the sea with her mother and father and her two sisters. That made three princesses in the kingdom of Corbeck."

Moeera smiled.

"Eileen and her sisters were taught all the things about being proper ladies because one day they would marry handsome princes and rule over kingdoms. One of them would inherit the kingdom of Corbeck from her father King Cullen."

"Life in Corbeck was happy, but as with every bright light there comes a contrasting darkness. So, it was in Corbeck …."

Moeera slept.

Mallory got up and quietly extinguished the lamp.

*   *   *

The next day while she was to be doing her daily chores Moeera ran off to the fairground to visit The Wondrous Wecks. It was late in the morning when she arrived to find most of the fair tents taken down. Her face broke into smiles when she recognized the jester from the day before. His clothing today blended in with that of his companions who were disassembling the rolling gantry.

"Hello, sir," Moeera said to the man. "How are you?"

The man turned to the five-year-old and paused.

"Don't tell me now," he said. "Your name is … Moeera!"

"Yes! Is Wecks here?"

"He is, indeed, young Moeera. Right this way."

He left the takedown to his fellows and led Moeera to a large wagon. Wecks was loading crates and boxes onto the back with the help of several other men. Moeera looked at one and thought he bore a striking resemblance to the man that Wecks had made disappear.

"Wecks the Wizard," the man called.

Wecks turned from the wagon and looked. "What is it, Paul?"

"You have a visitor," he said. "This little girl--Moeera--saw you perform yesterday."

"Oh! Well, in that case. Excuse me fellows."

Wecks walked over to Moeera and Paul. "Now what could I do you for, little lady?"

Moeera felt like she could fly at that moment. "How did you learn to be a wizard?"

10

"How did I learn to be a wizard? Oh, well, the usual way, you know." He ran his fingers through his short, dark hair.

Moeera watched him expectantly.

"Let's find a place to sit down, shall we?" Wecks said. He led Moeera to a bench.

"It was kind of by accident, really," Wecks told her, frowning. "I was apprenticing at the apothecary in my hometown when a strange lady came to the counter one morning asking for moon dust. She was chagrined to learn that of course we had none. We didn't sell moon dust."

"Then what happened?" Moeera asked.

"She left," he said, "but lo and behold who should I see the next morning asking Mr. Flanders for cricket kidneys--the same lady! We didn't have cricket kidneys either. Mr. Flanders made a comment about it being an apothecary, not a witch's closet. The lady didn't much care for that and she touched him on the nose with a wand. His nose turned a nice shade of violet. Then she left again."

Moeera giggled.

Wecks laughed. "It was like that all day long. Poor man hid in the back till it faded to normal. Long story short, Moeera, I followed her out to the road. Turned out she was a fairy doing a little traveling. I told her I wished I could do magical things, so she taught me some tricks. Then she said to keep practicing and learning. Then poof! She disappeared, and I never saw her again. But she started me on my magical journey."

"That's wonderful," Moeera said. "I want to learn magic, too."

Wecks regarded her for a moment.

"How old are you, Moeera?"

"Five and a half."

"That's a little young to be an apprentice," Wecks said, "or I'd bring you with us."

"Where?" she asked.

"On tour. It's prime fair season. We're visiting as many towns as we can."

"How can I learn magic then?" she asked.

"Learn about being a person first," Wecks said. "It might not be as exciting, but there are things that everyone should know before they learn magic."

"What?" she asked with tears in her eyes.

"How to be a good person for starters. Listen to your mother and father, be a part of your family and household, learn how things work. Learn to be a woman."

"That will take forever."

"It won't. There will be time enough for magic. And believe me, magic's tiring!"

"If you say so."

"I do. I know so. I want you to have something, Moeera. Keep it to remember me by until we meet again."

Wecks reached into his pocket and pulled out the yellow handkerchief from his show. "You take care of this for me, you hear?"

"Okay."

"Okay! Thanks for being such a great girl, Moeera. M-waah!"

Moeera smiled at the thought she'd just received a kiss from a real live wizard.

*   *   *

She was still thinking about the kiss when she got home. Noon had come and gone. She dove into her outside chores to get them all done.

"Where have you been, Moeera?" Mallory asked when she found her at the chicken coop.

"I walked to town, Mother," Moeera answered.

"All that way! Alone?"

"Yes."

"Why would you do that? You know you're not supposed to go off on your own without letting me know first!"

"I thought you'd say 'no'."

"You're right about that," Mallory said grimly. "What possessed you so?"

"I wanted to talk to Wecks."

"I see. And did you?"

"Oh, yes, Mother. I asked him how he became a wizard, and he told me!"

"Moeera," her mother said. "The magic show was wonderful. It was thrilling, even. But you must follow the rules. You're not a baby."

12

"No, Mother."

"No more running off."

"I won't."

"Are your chores finished?"

"Outside they are. The chickens are eating."

"You're going to have an extra one today. I want you to collect wood for the stove. Kindling and the like. As much as you can before Father gets home. Pile it by the logs."

Moeera reluctantly collected forage in the woods. She carried it home and piled it up. It was totally unfair! She doubted Wecks ever had to spend so much time collecting wood. He probably had a spell that made the branches line up at his door to help build the fire.

She thought about this over the next couple hours. A few times she went over the food chain in her head. Then she began subbing in woodland creatures for the seaside ones. She pictured each animal in her mind, over and over. Then she would point her fingers at the dead branches and twigs on the ground.

"Get up and march!" she commanded the wood.

Of course, the wood didn't so much as quiver.

This frustrated her but didn't dim her desire to use magic. She would have to wait for Wecks to return with his caravan. He would, too. A year seemed like a long time, but she was sure he'd be back for the fair. She had his marker, and he'd kissed her. Five-year-old Moeera would wait.

Chapter Three

Moeera's childhood wasn't easy. Her parents worked hard to eke out an existence in the Gillikin Country. Their tiny house sat on a tiny, countryside lane amidst the purple-hued foliage.

Moeera's father was a blacksmith. This was an important, but hard occupation. Gillikin Country was amongst the rockiest places on Earth. The farmers made short work of their plows which would always break and need repairing. Bachukka shoes were in constant demand. All manner of ironwork was in demand. Kor labored long in the heat to keep up.

This left it up to Mallory and Moeera to do the household chores and work their small vegetable garden. Mallory patiently taught her daughter to keep house, to sew and weave, to do many things that a country wife did. Moeera for her part wanted nothing to do with marriage. She was still waiting for Wecks to return for the fair and take her with as an apprentice.

During Moeera's eighth year, she heard stories of disappearing livestock on nearby farms. This wasn't overly surprising. Hungry predators lived in the forests surrounding the farmland. They found ways to get into the pens and paddocks so they could make off with farm animals. Lions, tigers, and bears were the most dangerous.

Then a farmer disappeared, and the others mobilized to hunt down the responsible predator.

Kor laid two long hunting knives on the table. One was a couple inches shorter than the other. Otherwise, they looked identical. He carefully picked one up in an oily cloth and rubbed it over, polishing it, cleaning the dust off. He stared down its upturned edge and held his finger to it. A tiny cut appeared on his finger.

Satisfied, he placed the knife on the table and picked up the slightly smaller one. He repeated the process with that one until the blade shined and did the same test with his finger.

"What are you doing, Papa?" Moeera asked.

The eight-year-old had paused at her needlepoint to watch her father.

"Just checking my blades," he said. "Making certain they're ready in case I need them."

"For what?"

"Hunting," he said. "A group of us are going on a bear hunt this evening."

Kor next brought out his quiver so he could inspect his arrows one by one. He ran his fingers over the shafts, feeling for cracks; looked closely at the fletching; made certain the bladed tips were secure.

"Be careful," Moeera's mother said, not happily.

"I will," he said. "Besides, I believe there are a dozen of us going. I should be perfectly fine."

Mallory frowned but nodded her head in agreement. "Just don't do anything half-cocked," she said.

"Not me," he said, smiling, and kissed her on the forehead. She slid her hands around his waist, holding him next to her until he pulled away.

Kor slid the quiver's strap over his shoulder, letting the cylindrical, leather pouch hang behind him. He picked up both knives, sheathing them in his belt. Last, he doffed his hat and grasped his bow.

He stepped out the door into the gathering twilight and walked toward Edward's farm. Shadows covered the road and paths, making the way there especially gloomy. Stones crunched under Kor's boots, and the pungent smells of rotting wood, moss, and organic decay filled his nostrils.

Eyes peered at him from a tree branch. Upon closer inspection they revealed the outline and feathers of a long-eared owl. It hooted quietly from its vantage point.

Kor breathed easily but a shiver ran through his shoulders. The wind blew lightly, rustling the leaves on the trees.

He eventually arrived at Edward's house. Edward Caomhanach was a boisterous and outspoken man who had grown up alongside Kor. The farmer wanted to move to take care of whatever beast was menacing the local farms. His animals could be next, after all.

A lantern burned at the gate to the barnyard. He bypassed the house, entered the barnyard, and walked into the old, stone and wood barn.

"There's a good man," Edward said when he saw Kor.

Kor smiled despite the darkness falling and danger swirling. He clasped hands with his friend.

His eyes searched the room. Pask the hunter and Freedy Guy leaned against a manger. Both had bows and quivers slung over their shoulders.

In addition to his bow, Pask had a broadsword slung over his back. If the arrows proved to be unreliable, then the sword—which Kor's own father had forged—would get the job done. Pask was a man who liked to be prepared. He wore leather armor of brown and green and a wrist guard of silver.

Freedy was the complete opposite. He wore his normal work clothes and carried no other weapon beside his bow. The young man was barely more than a pup. He leaned there fiddling with a carving knife. Pask stared at him emotionlessly.

Freedy looked up from playing and nodded hello. He was oblivious. He was utterly enthralled by the knife.

"Who else is here?" Kor asked.

"This is it," Edward said.

"I thought I'd be late," Kor said.

"You're fine," Edward assured him. "Brought your arrows I see."

"Of course."

"I'll be bringing this," Edward motioned to a long spear with an eight-inch wrought iron head. The steel edges on the head glinted in the lantern light. It looked safe enough propped against the wall.

Kor glanced at the wickedly sharp point on Edward's spear.

"Do you think it's truly a bear or is it something else?" Kor asked.

"Like what?" Edward asked.

"It could be a wolf," Pask said quietly. He had an intense quietness about him.

"Maybe," Kor agreed, "or a lion or tiger."

"They're around these woods somewheres," Edward admitted, "but this thing—whatever it is—has carried off some very large sheep. Mrs. Piondar at the Circle Green said she heard grunts, growls, and moans in the night. That sounds an awful lot like a bear to me."

"It does," Pask nodded. "The river's been especially low these long months. Bear might be having trouble filling its belly."

"There you go," Edward said.

"Not necessarily," Pask said. "Bears don't live on fish alone. They forage for honey, berries, bugs, grain, carcasses…."

"So, you're going somewhere with this line of thinking?" Edward asked.

Pask shrugged his shoulders and looked at his boots. Then he looked up. "It could indeed be a bear doing this," he said, motioning toward Edward and Kor with his hand. "Or it could be another predator. A lion could carry off sheep easily. We won't know for certain till we scout the area."

"All right then," Edward said. "Let's get movin'. What's your preoccupation with that knife, Freedy?"

"Hnnh," Freedy mumbled. "Oh, it's new it is. Muh lady gave me it."

"Truly?" Kor asked. "It looks like a nice little knife."

"Yuh," Freedy said, nodding. He finally looked up.

"Come on then," Edward said. "None of the others care enough to protect the town's livestock."

"I care," Kor said, thinking to himself that so many might have declined because they didn't want Edward ordering them around.

"Good!" Edward exclaimed, clapping him on the shoulder. "And you're not even a farmer!"

"Neither is Pask," Kor pointed out.

"Nope," Pask said. "But when a predator steals sheep from Bucktry farms … it seems to fall upon my skills to do something about it."

The four men left the light and warmth of Edward's barn. They trudged along the wagon road one by one, following Edward.

They soon became merely four more shadows in the dusk.

Edward's plan was simple. Keep a lookout amongst the farms where this creature might appear looking for food. It had hit Circle Green, George's Forty, and Craigle. Nundle had disappeared from his orchards, not far from the river that ran past Craigle's exit. The river seemed to offer a possible place to find the beast too. Lots of wilderness encroached between the river, the farms, and the town proper.

Whatever it was that made off with Nundle was most likely the same thing that was stealing sheep.

Edward took them into the woods where they headed Southwest. They

17

were skirting the land next to Circle Green. When the trail got along George's Forty they'd be close to the river.

Every now and then, Pask would stop to check the ground for scat, check the bushes for possible hairs, or scan for tracks.

After walking for an hour, they stopped to rest. Weapons were set down and the companions sprawled on some huge boulders. George's barn and house were visible across the fields. They could see a lot from their vantage point in the elevated foothills of the Lucan Mountains. The moon lit the scene, making it easy to see the outlines of George's immediate house and barnyard. The only thing the men saw moving was a small animal, probably a fox.

"Certainly, that's not the thing we're hunting," Edward said with disgust.

"Aye, too small," Pask said, stating the obvious.

"Let's keep moving," Edward said. "All seems quiet here."

He had wanted to divide their numbers—have someone watching each farm overnight. Alas, four men just weren't enough. If their suspicions were correct and it was indeed a bear, then everyone would need at least one partner watching his back. They could split up, two and two; or they could stick together. Something made Edward want to keep the four together.

"Let's stay together and keep heading toward the river."

"Alright," Kor said.

Pask nodded.

Freedy said nothing.

"Ya back there, Freedy?" Edward asked.

"Ah-huh," Freedy murmured from the rear.

"Good."

He led them down the gently rolling hill along the edge of George's pipple field. The tall plants stood silently in the night, their purple stalks reaching high as a buppus' eye.

Kor watched the farmhouse off to their left. Not a light or sign of life shone anywhere.

"Fast asleep," he said, pointing.

"Yuh," Pask agreed.

They had to pick up their pace to keep up with Edward who walked quickly with purpose. Pask glanced back at one point to make sure Freedy was behind them.

18

At the other end of George's yard, they re-entered the woods.

It wasn't long before Kor said, "It's quiet, Edward, too quiet."

"No night insects, eh?" Ed said. "Probably because of us being here. Be alert, though."

They didn't encounter anything in the forest, not a bear, nor a bird, nor any other beast for that matter.

Pask could see no indications that any large animal had come through lately. He relaxed.

"Maybe whatever we're chasing has already moved on to greener pastures," the hunter said.

"I don't think so," Edward said. "It hasn't eaten everyone's livestock yet."

They wove back into the woods, the trail Edward followed was clear and free of obstacles. It took a sharp descent, cutting through a ridge.

"We seem to have found the river," Kor said.

"We'll be able to see better then, I reckon," Freedy offered.

It was the first time that he'd talked of his own volition for the entire trek.

"I hope so," Kor said.

In fact, moonlight cut through the break in the trees ahead. The quartet strode along the path to the moonlit clearing as if Heaven itself waited for them.

"That's better," Edward said upon emerging. "Maybe we'll sight the bear when it comes to drink."

The sound of running water was quiet as the river was low for the end of summer. The water lazily meandered on its way between the random rocks and boulders scattered throughout the riverbed.

"Anything can happen," Kor said, hopefully.

He stepped into the light, feeling his muscles relax. Even with a large animal running amok, the moonlight provided a feeling of safety.

Pask inhaled sharply just ahead of Kor. Kor looked up, alertly. Edward's hand closed tightly around his wrist.

"What!" Kor sputtered.

"Shh ... look!"

He spotted her then, lounging on a big, flat rock extending from the shore. She was twirling her long, black hair in her fingers absentmindedly.

Her eyes were closed; the midnight bather had not a care in the world.

The men were dumbfounded. They were searching for a bear, not a moonlight bather. Hadn't she heard the stories? There was danger lurking about. They approached her with more than a little urgency.

Hearing the men's footsteps approaching, her eyes flipped open to take in the sight of the hunters.

Kor was breathless. The greatest statues of ancient Greece would welcome this woman as an equal. Her plain, white dress that came down somewhere above her knees showed off her smooth shoulders and her long, supple legs.

She was young and nubile, but her eyes were a hawk's. Her hooded gaze seemed to take the measure of the men. Drops of water slid down her arms, her skin still wet from submerging in the river.

Kor felt instantly attracted to her. She was easily the most exotic woman he'd ever seen. A pang of guilt stabbed him for his unclean thoughts. Mallory was his one and only. Still, he couldn't stop gazing at those long, wet legs under the white dress.

"Oh!" she said, surprised. "I didn't realize anyone else came here at night."

"Neither did we," Edward said. "Why are you here, Miss? You're in danger."

"Danger?" she asked. She sat up a bit further. "What sort of danger?"

"We think it's a bear coming around," Edward said. "It's already killed a farmer nearby."

Her face grew serious. "Oh, my! It's good you're here to protect me then. Big, strong men and …."

Her voice trailed off. She scrutinized the party's fourth member. "Why, Freedy, darling!"

"Freedy, darling?" Kor asked.

Her lithe, pale form jumped up from the rock. Her white dress flowed in the air around her. Her pale, white feet pattered over to the young man.

"Muh girl," Freedy said, matter-of-factly.

She caught him in a tight embrace, clutching his cheek in her thin fingers. Then she looked up and planted a long, passionate kiss on the fool's face. Somehow he seemed less foolish now.

"Murh!" Edward cleared his throat.

The nighttime bather smiled a guilty smile and moved back from her beau.

Freedy's cheeks were a dark shade of red. He glanced down at his shoes.

"You men must be very brave to be out hunting a bear at night," the woman said in a husky voice.

"We only do what has to be done, Miss?" Pask stated.

"Brave of you, nonetheless," she said. Her dark eyes twinkled wetly. They had both clarity and depth. She was young of body but seemed mature in spirit.

Kor couldn't help thinking that Freedy was in over his head. Still, if he was courting a beauty such as this, he was due a measure of respect.

"Freedy showed us the knife you gave him," Kor said. "It's nice. He's been keeping you a complete secret otherwise."

"That's because I asked him to," she said. "I was betrothed to a man of my village. Alas, he died when some excruciating malady sucked the life from him. I was marked as a jinx. Then I found Freedy. He swept me off my feet."

Kor couldn't imagine Freedy sweeping anyone off their feet. He was clumsy and scatterbrained. Yet here was the proof, and quite beguiling proof she was.

"I'm afraid we can't let you stay out alone …."

"My name's Izzy," she said.

"Well, Izzy," Edward said, "where do you live? We should escort you home."

"Freedy knows," she said softly. "He could take me there in practically no time at all."

"Mm-hmm," he nodded, murmuring.

"Can you, Freedy?" Edward asked. "Can you walk her home and get yourself back here to help us watch for the beast?"

"Yes," he said.

"All right," Edward said. "Take your lady home then. We'll wait here."

"Sure," Freedy said. "Come on, Izzy."

They departed along a narrow trail, holding hands. She oddly went barefoot.

Then the three men were alone.

21

"Where should we hide to be out of sight but still be able to see?" Edward asked.

Pask was already glancing around the riverbank.

"That's really what you're thinking about?" Kor asked.

"Yes, sure," Edward replied.

"You're not wondering how in the world Freedy—of all people—is able to court a stunning lady like that?"

"The thought did cross my mind," Edward admitted.

"There," Pask interrupted, pointing to some small trees with rocks all around. "That should be okay, should keep us downwind."

"If you say so," Edward said.

"It's the best hiding place to observe from," Pask said. "And if the bear comes from that direction, then we'll be downwind."

"And if it comes from the other direction?" Kor asked.

"What are the chances it will show at all," Pask muttered. "If it comes from that direction, then it will undoubtedly smell us."

"Then we wouldn't be able to sneak up on it," Edward said.

"Nope," Pask said. "You better get that spear of yours ready."

Edward held the shaft of his spear tightly. He spun it absentmindedly. "It's ready," he said.

"Good," Pask said. "I hope you've prepared yourself to fight."

"Of course, I have," Edward said. "I'm here, aren't I?"

"You are," Pask said, nodding. "But you're a farmer; not a hunter. You nurture life."

"I'll be fine," Edward said. "In this case, we have to take a life if I am to continue my farming."

Kor listened, patiently. Pask was treading on Edward's nerves. It was that kind of night. Everyone was tired and on edge.

Quiet settled in once more and so did they. They crouched behind the trees and waited. The moonlight gave them an illuminated view.

They waited there for quite a while. There was no sign of the bear and no sign of Freedy returning.

Time stood still, lagging the way it does when you are bored and trapped.

The moon, partially visible through some tree branches, moved slowly, languidly across the heavens.

Finally, Kor needed to speak lest he go mad.

"Everyone awake?" he asked.

"Yes," Edward said.

"Yes," Pask echoed.

"Just checking," Kor said. "Anyone's legs cramping up?"

"Certainly are," Pask said.

"Where in the world is Freedy?" Edward demanded.

"Lost?" Kor commented.

"Probably," Pask chuckled. "That kid is as dense as granite."

"We should be worried about him," Edward said, "but he is a dunderhead."

"What do you think that woman sees in him?" Pask asked.

They thought about it for a few moments.

"I don't know," Edward said. "A potentially successful farmer? Maybe she just hasn't gotten to know him well enough yet."

"He's more scatterbrained than ever," Kor said. "It's a mystery that woman even wanted to talk to him."

"Then he must be lucky is all," Edward said.

"Shh!" Pask hissed. "Something's coming."

The other two froze. Was it Freedy returning or the bear they were seeking?

They watched from behind their makeshift blind as a massive, dark shape strode to the water. The moonlight filtered through different trees than when they had arrived, but it shone brightly enough to see that it was indeed ....

"Told you it was a bear," Edward whispered.

The bear was enormous. It stood in the silt, dipping its head to lap up water.

"But is it the bear?" Pask countered.

"It's awful huge!" Edward said. "What else would be taking those sheep?"

"Good point," Pask said.

"No Freedy," Kor said.

"No," Pask said. "Up to us three. On the count of three, then."

"One."

"Two."

Sweat trickled down Kor's back.

The bear turned its head to glance in their direction.

"Three!" Pask shouted.

They leapt up from behind the bushes and trees, grasping their weapons!

Chapter Four

The bear snarled, retreating from the river's edge. It pumped its mighty leg muscles, coming their way! Kor and Pask both let arrows fly at it. Kor's arrows glanced off its back. Pask's extruded from below its left ear.

"Hurry!" Edward screamed.

Pask sent another arrow into the beast's neck. Kor loosed an arrow that sped past the bear's head, lodging itself into a fallen log.

Pask and Kor scrambled to back up, the bear coming straight at them. Edward, face gone white, hurled his spear full force.

And missed.

The bear roared, batting him to the ground with its massive paw. Then it fell upon him, tearing at his clothing with its great teeth. Lunging at his neck.

Another arrow hit the bear in the face. Pask's fingers flew for another shaft from his quiver.

Kor sent an arrow into the bear's side that seemed to have little effect.

Edward screamed. The enraged beast knocked his outstretched hands aside and clamped down on his neck. The screaming ceased.

Kor pulled his long hunting knife and lunged for the bear's head. It moved aside, Edward still in its mouth. Kor stumbled, falling into rocks.

Kor felt pain in his hands, right knee, and right arm. He struggled to get up. The bear was just beyond him, mauling his friend.

He sensed Pask move on the bear with his sword.

Chaos raged near him as he flipped over and forced his way back up again. He grabbed his knife. It was broken in half.

The bear had Pask's sword arm in its teeth. The blade hung limply in the hunter's hand. Pask's other hand grasped for the bear's neck.

Kor stood up. He reached for an arrow. Where was his bow?

Then he saw Edward's spear lying among the leaves and rocks. Letting the arrow slip back into his quiver, he scrambled to the spear.

Spear in hand, Kor whirled to see the bear biting what was left of Pask's sword arm. The hunter fought less strongly now. He flailed his left arm wildly in the air.

Kor fought the urge to cry out. He hefted the spear, running directly at the bear.

The spear entered the bear's chest, piercing its heart. It cried out in pain. Its guttural bellow changing to an almost human shriek.

Kor pushed the spear into the bear with all his might. He could smell the creature's stink all around him. Oddly, the bear seemed somehow less giant. It's black, furred shape shrank away before him, melting into the forest floor.

Kor looked away for a couple seconds, coughing. When he looked back there was no sign of the bear. A young woman, just a girl actually—naked as at birth—stared into his eyes helplessly. Her breathing came in ragged little gasps. Her chest and abdomen were scarlet with blood, the spear lodged in her heart.

Kor let go of the spear, crying out in surprise.

The girl fell onto her back, the spear still lodged in her chest. Kor moved to her side.

"How can this be!" he yelled.

Life passed from her eyes as he gazed upon her. He was bewildered. There was no sign of the bear anywhere. No fur. Not even its stench remained. He leaned down and pulled the spear from her body. Its silvery tip was covered in crimson.

He leaned the weapon against an oak and hurried to Edward. The farmer was dead, his jugular severed.

He moved to Pask.

Pask was covered in blood and missing his right arm below the elbow.

"God!" Kor exhorted. He clasped his face with his hand.

"No," Pask sighed. "Pretty sure that bear came from the Devil."

Kor looked at Pask. "You're alive!"

"Just … barely."

"The bear disappeared," Kor said, numbly.

26

"You killed it," Pask mumbled. "You did it."

"I don't know," Kor said, as he let his quiver fall. He stripped off his shirt and wrapped it around Pask's stump.

Pask spit up some blood. He stared at the blacksmith questioningly.

"I ran the bear through its heart with Edward's spear," Kor said. "I looked away for just a moment ... when I looked back the bear was gone. There's a dead girl on the ground over there. A naked, dead girl."

Pask grimaced as Kor twined a branch in the makeshift bandage and twisted it around his severed limb. Blood soaked the shirt. "'Twas a changeling then. Witchcraft."

A fearful thought entered Kor's mind.

"Then it may not actually be dead," he said.

"Edward ... told me his spear was part ... silver," Pask coughed. "'Tis in the legends. Silver can kill ... bewitched."

"Part silver?"

"Head was iron ... steel edges," Pask said. "Said there was ... silver melded with the steel."

"I'm going to fix you a sledge to bring you to Craig's house," Kor said. "Hang on."

"I will," Pask said. "Take my sword, cut off her head ... should make it final."

"I have to get you somewhere safe."

"Cut the head off. Now! While it's still night!" Pask's eyes stared into Kor's. They had a wildness Kor had never witnessed before.

So, Kor found the old sword forged by his father and stepped cautiously to the girl's side. Other than the blood, she appeared to be sleeping. He raised the sword over his head and brought it chopping down across her neck. As the head was severed from the body he heard a scream of pain in his mind.

He dropped the blade amongst the rocks and returned to Pask's side.

"It's done," he told him.

Pask made no reply. He was still and silent.

Kor knelt beside him and listened for breath.

Nothing.

"Pask," Kor said. He grasped Pask's remaining hand and gave it a good squeeze.

27

"Pask!"

The hunter didn't respond.

"Dammit, Pask! Wake up! Don't die here!"

Kor patted the man's face, trying to rouse him. He checked his breathing again.

Pask was gone.

Now that the fighting had ended, emotions washed over Kor. Pask, the great hunter, had died fighting the bear that wasn't a bear. So had Edward. His friend who decided something must be done to save the area farms was dead. Only he was alive. Him. Why had he survived?

It was too much to absorb. He crouched above Pask's body and burst into tears.

Then he remembered Freedy. Where on God's green Earth was that blockhead? He decided to find him so the two could report how Edward and Pask had died. He wasn't going to their widows alone. He stood up, picked up Pask's sword, and headed in the direction that Freedy and Izzy had gone.

She spoke as if her home wasn't far. He ought to be able to find it, especially since Freedy should be coming toward him anytime now. The farther he walked, the angrier he became. Where was Freedy? Had he abandoned them to stay with his girlfriend?

Kor squinted in the darkness. The trail was barely there. In fact, he was just about certain he'd lost it when Freedy popped out of the branches.

"Where have you been, Freedy!" Kor demanded. "We needed you! Edward …."

Freedy reached out with both hands and grasped Kor's shoulders, falling into the older man.

"What's the matter?" Kor asked. "Are you hurt?"

He let Freedy slide to the ground and sit against his legs.

"Freedy! What's going on?"

Freedy didn't say a word. Kor felt his knees protest as he crouched down to check the young man.

Freedy's skin was pale, extremely pale. He looked as if he was sick as a dog. He was just fine earlier, Kor thought. Kor grabbed him by the arms and shook him roughly.

When he let him go, Freedy slumped over sideways. His body crushed

28

the wildflowers and sticker bushes by the trail.

No, Kor thought. Not him too!

He knelt over Freedy's lifeless form. The life had gone from his eyes.

"Don't do this to me, Freedy!" Kor shouted. "What the blazes is wrong with you!"

Freedy's head was turned to the side. Kor saw something dark on his neck. He leaned closer, touching the pale skin below the ear. Two bloody holes marred the skin. He felt them with his fingers, bringing back a bit of crimson.

"What ..."

A twig snapped just down the trail and Kor nearly jumped from his skin. It was Izzy.

"Hello, again," she said in a strangely melodic voice.

Kor looked at her and gasped. She stepped beside him in the semi dark, leaning down to place a hand on his bare shoulder. Her touch was warm. She seemed different but he couldn't decide how.

"Something's wrong with Freedy!" he blurted out. "What happened?"

"Nothing he didn't wish to happen," Izzy said.

"He's not breathing!"

"That's because he's dead, silly."

Kor felt his last nerve snapping. He jumped up.

"How could he be dead?" he demanded. "He didn't even fight the bear. He was with you."

Izzy's hands moved across Kor's chest and shoulders. He was still in disbelief as she embraced him. He realized that the something different about her was the smearing around her mouth. A tiny drop of dark liquid fell upon the white breast of her dress.

Kor shuddered. "He was with you!" he exclaimed, pushing her away.

She hissed like some wild animal.

He took two big steps back. She watched him, her eyes glittering.

"Did you fight the bear then?" she asked. Blood dripped from her chin.

"Yes!" he retorted. "Fought it and lived!"

"Bravo," she said. "Where are your other two friends?"

He was silent.

"Oh, they're dead too, aren't they?" she asked.

"They are," Kor said, "but so is the bear."

29

Izzy glared at him. She sighed, "that's what you think."

"She won't be ravaging any more farmers," Kor said. "That's for sure."

"You'd be surprised at what she can do," Izzy countered. She moved toward Kor.

"Stop," he said.

She ignored him.

He glanced at the sword. It was on the ground next to Freedy.

"The blade won't help you," she said into his ear, wrapping him in her arms.

Kor felt her hands sliding over his chest. He was simultaneously exhilarated and repulsed. He moved toward the spot where the sword rested.

He didn't get more than an inch. Her arms held him to her. She seemed to be rooted to the spot, and her hold was incredibly strong.

"Didn't you hear me?" she asked. "The blade won't help you."

She reached for his face; her fingers squeezed his chin. Then her lips fell upon his.

Her kiss was electric. A metallic taste assailed Kor's taste buds. He stared at her closed eyelids.

Kor's mind raced. Thinking beyond the sensation, he slid his left hand toward the remaining hunting knife tied by his hip.

Izzy seemed not to notice. She moved her wet, sticky lips to seek purchase on his neck.

Kor seized his small knife and drew back to plunge it into her chest. He thrust inward seeking her heart.

Suddenly, Izzy's right hand grasped his so tightly that he cried out in pain.

"Stupid," she cooed. "Just give in. That isn't so hard, is it?"

She squeezed harder and he dropped the knife.

"Now we've run out of distractions…."

Kor felt Izzy's mouth close over his neck. He felt a sharp, hard pressure as her teeth bit down, breaking the skin. The last thing he remembered was her tongue lapping at the wound. Then all was confusion and nothingness.

Chapter Five

The next morning, Mallory feared the worst when Kor didn't return home. She hitched Dot to their small wagon and lifted Moeera into the back. She "yah"-ed the bachukka and they took off for town hall.

"What's the matter, Mama?" Moeera asked.

Mallory had a look of grim determination on her face. She kept her eyes on Dot as she trotted to the tie-up post.

"Where is Papa?" Moeera asked.

"I don't know," her mother said. "You don't see him, do you?"

"No."

"That's right. We've come here to ask if anybody has seen him."

"I wonder if he caught the bear," Moeera said.

Mallory squinted her eyes as she pulled the reins tightly. She took a rapid breath, her head sinking forward. She imagined the bear might have caught Kor.

Dot lazed obediently in place as they climbed from the wagon.

*   *   *

"What do you mean you don't know?" Mallory demanded.

Mayor Moylan stared at the distraught woman with the clinging child. Mallory's eyes blazed with cold fire.

"Edward Caomhanach did tell me his intention to flush out whatever has been hunting our livestock," the mayor said, "but he didn't share his specific plans."

"That blockhead," Mallory grated through clenched teeth. "My husband left last night to assist Edward and a gang of farmers in an overnight vigil. They expected they might kill a bear."

"It makes sense," Mayor Moylan said. "Killing the bear that's been terrorizing the countryside."

"Problem is," Mallory continued, "Kor never came home. Where are these other farmers who needed him to help?"

"I don't know who else went," the mayor admitted. "Ed said he had Pask the hunter's promise to help. Dony Berns is around back right now, delivering something or other. We'll ask him if he knows."

Mallory, with Moeera in tow, followed the mayor down the hall which bisected the town hall's first floor. They found Dony stacking cases of vegetables by the back door.

"That's all of them, Mayor," he said.

"Thank you, Dony. Thanks for all you do," the mayor said. "Mallory here has a question for you."

"Oh?" the farmer said, standing up and rubbing the dust from his hands.

"Who went on the hunt last night? My husband went to keep vigil last night. He isn't back," Mallory said, fighting back tears.

"Edward's party isn't back, yet?" Dony asked.

"No, it isn't."

"Dear me. I see why you're looking then. Ed said he would take everyone willing. I turned him down because my arthritis is bad. He planned to do a lot of walking, and I didn't think I'd make it all the way."

"So, who was going?" Mallory asked.

"Pask was going. I don't really know who else."

"Where were they going?"

"Toward Craigle where the last incident was… Nundle's orchards. If they didn't see anything on the way, that is. They would be passing Circle Green and George's Forty. Livestock at all of them; potential targets."

The mayor squinted and looked down. He clasped his hands together.

"I'll tell you what, Mrs. Robin. If you have room for me on your wagon, I'll ride with you to Craigle's exit and the Whispering River if need be. Dony, round up some men and send them after us."

"Certainly," the farmer said.

"What about the girl?" Mayor Moylan asked.

Wide-eyed Moeera clung to her mother's long skirt.

"There isn't time to leave her with anyone," Mallory said, frowning. "She'll have to come with."

"Very well."

"Come along, Moeera," Mallory said. "You're coming with to search for your father."

*   *   *

As Mallory chucked and clucked to get Dot moving, Dony Berns rang the copper bell out front. Mayor Moylan climbed up beside Moeera's mother, his good shoes hastily replaced by a pair of boots.

They set off for Circle Green, the farm of Bumper and Holly Piondar.

An excited feeling surged through eight-year-old Moeera. There was urgency in the actions of the adults, but she wasn't yet aware how serious it was that the hunting party wasn't back yet. She contentedly and curiously watched the country go by outside the wagon. She was a part of all this fuss, and it exhilarated her.

It was a dreadful ride for the adults. Mallory and the mayor may as well have been on a wagon ride through the wretched land of Purgatory.

What would they find when they caught up with the hunters?

Mallory was distraught but she tried to force that worry to the back of her mind. She would drive the wagon to the Cliffs of Eternal Despair to find Kor.

Where was he? she wondered. And what had been the outcome of the search for the bear?

Only time would tell.

Along the way they added Jenk Quickens and Tully Goess to their search party. The two farmhands waved them down as they drove along the rough road. They agreed to help beginning with their workplace at Circle Green.

*   *   *

"Don't go in there," Jenk said, his face gone pale.

The farmhand had looked for his boss in the farmyard to no avail. After much rapping on the farmhouse door, he and Tully forced it open to find a horrifying scene.

Mallory frowned in the driver's seat. Mayor Moylan looked pensive.

"What is it?" the mayor asked.

Jenk walked to the front of the wagon, looking up at the two behind the bachukka.

He spoke in low, steady tones. "It appears that Bumper and Holly had a nighttime intruder," he said. "Bear by the looks of it. No survivors."

33

This revelation blew Mallory's mind. Her eyes were saucers as she swallowed and asked, "It killed them inside the farmhouse?"

"Yes," Tully said.

"Begorrah!" the mayor exclaimed, just loudly enough to register on Moeera's curiosity meter.

The girl scooched as close to them as she could.

"What is it?" she asked. "Has anyone here seen Papa?"

"No, dear," her mother said quietly. "We have to keep looking."

"What are we waiting for?" Moeera asked.

"Oh," Mallory said, "just for Jenk to climb in."

Jenk complied and they were on their way. Mallory drove Dot harder now.

Moeera watched the fields fly by as the wagon flew along. They hit quite a few bumps which made the ride much more uncomfortable. Tully held onto his hat to keep it from flying into a ditch.

George was harvesting beans when they skidded into his yard. He smashed his hat down and strode over to the wagon. Moeera sat up as tall as she was able to pay attention to the conversation.

"Morning!" George exclaimed. "Mr. Mayor, what brings you here?"

"Trouble, I'm afraid," Mayor Moylan said. "We're looking for a group that went hunting last night."

"Caomhanach, hmm," George said. "No, I haven't seen him."

"I was afraid you'd say that. We're off to Craigle then."

George glanced at the farmhands and the little girl in the back of the wagon. He nodded.

"Tully, Jenk," he said.

"George," they said.

Before Moeera could introduce herself, Mallory stirred Dot to action. They pulled away from George's farm, heading in Craigle's direction. The bachukka ran like Quicksilver.

Moeera had grown tired of taking in the sights. She huddled in the wagon with her hands clasped around her shins. She felt the wagon bump when its wheels hit more rocks. Luckily, nothing too big interfered with their journey.

*   *   *

They came upon an incline that rose ever-so-gradually. In no time at all,

Dot began breathing hard. Mallory urged her on. They plodded onward and upward.

A scene of absolute wonder awaited them when they crested the rise. Craigle, or Craig's Land, surpassed the most exquisite of paintings. The farmhouse was there, freshly painted and in the best repair possible. It had quaint little windows with quaint little shutters. It was the traditional dome shape that most houses in those parts were. A skinny, red chimney reached straight for the zenith. The house was trimmed in green, the color of pine trees. The rest of it was a pristine egg white color.

That wasn't all. The barn was a pretty orange and violet affair off to the rear of the house, just visible to the left.

Dot was very tired, but she hauled the wagon down the hill's other side to the house.

Craig came walking from the front door, wringing his hands. He glanced at the wagon in a startled manner.

"Mr. Mayor!" he exclaimed. "It's good you're here."

"Oh," Mayor Moylan said. "What makes you say so, Craig?"

Craig's face darkened. Well... truth is... there have been deaths right near to here."

"Deaths!" the mayor snapped.

Mallory's face went whiter than the farmhouse.

"Yes, sir," Craig said, looking from the mayor to Mallory and back. "Ed Caomhanach, Freedy Guy, and Pask. They look like a bear mauled them."

"What about Kor?" Mallory breathed.

"I'm sorry?" Craig asked, obviously confused.

"My husband!" Mallory yelled. "What about my husband! Is he alive?"

Chapter Six

Craig looked at the mayor, then back at Mallory. "We only found the three men," he said. "They're in the woods by the river where it slows up amongst those rocks. What a fight it must have been."

"Kor," Mallory said quietly. She was caught up in turmoil. They hadn't found him dead. But they hadn't found him.

"Jack," Craig said, "those three fellows are in awful shape."

"Where are they?"

"Still by the river," Craig said. "I was trying to decide on the best way to move them here. They're a real mess."

Mallory slid down to the ground.

"Take me to them," she said firmly. "Come along, everyone. We must search for Kor. Mayor, you and Craig can gather anyone you can to bring those bodies here."

The mayor glanced from man to man.

"Sounds like a plan," he said. "You have anybody around to help, Craig?"

"Yes," the farmer said. "I'll go round them up."

Mallory helped Moeera to the ground.

"Which way must we go?" she asked.

Craig pointed to a spot amongst some trees. "Through there," he said. "Careful going down the hill."

Mallory took Moeera's hand and pulled her along the path to the woods. Tully and Jenk jogged behind.

Upon entering the woods, Mallory said, "Mee, you need to be my brave girl. We're going to find your father now. Stay close to me."

"Okay, Mama," Moeera said, spinning a pipple flower in her fingers.

They descended the hill and followed the path, cutting across the ridge. Sunlight filtered through the canopy.

Tully passed by Moeera and her mother. He came to the bloody, ravaged form of Edward.

"Here they are," he said. He took his face in his hand.

Mallory, Moeera, and Jenk came to a stop around him.

Edward's throat had been torn out. A pool of blood surrounded his head, neck, and shoulders.

"Oh, Lord," Mallory said. She picked Moeera up and held her awkwardly.

It was a pointless effort. Moeera had seen Edward's bloody corpse, its eyes staring into oblivion.

Jenk and Tully walked over to Pask. His severed arm lay several feet from his body. Kor's shirt was wrapped crudely around the stump.

Mallory set Moeera back on her feet.

"Are you all right?" she asked.

Moeera nodded her head. Her eyes widened when they saw Tully set Pask's arm on top of his chest. She shuddered.

"I'm sorry, dear," her mother said, pulling her close and hugging her. "I wanted you to help find Papa—not to see this."

Moeera clung to her mother, her hands wrapped around her back. Her face buried itself in her mother's chestnut locks, the smell comforting the girl. She tried to blot out the visions she had of Edward, battered and bloody. The fact that he was dead and blood-covered wasn't the only disturbing thing to her. He was missing his throat. He was incomplete.

She thought about both men as her mother set her down. Both were incomplete now, and not merely because of a missing throat or arm. They both lacked their souls or whatever the thing was that made them people. She'd never met Pask, and now she never would. Not in this lifetime.

Moeera went to worship whenever her parents took her. She didn't know much about what happened to you when you died. She knew of the All-father who watched over all people everywhere in the world. She knew of the light place and the dark place. Everyone wanted to go to the light place.

Edward and Pask were gone. Their bodies could no longer see, hear, walk, or talk. She shut her eyes and tried to forget. She couldn't. But she could push it away behind thoughts of....

"Papa!" she cried.

"Moeera?" Mallory asked.

"Over there," she said, pointing to a dry part of the riverbed.

Tully and Jenk hustled to the man lying there.

"Dead," Tully said morosely. "Just like Craig said. Three dead men."

Mallory pulled Moeera after her. She walked up to the corpse and gasped.

"Freedy," she said.

Freedy Guy was on the silt and gravel, face up. He was chalk white, as though he'd been there for days. A crimson halo radiated from his head.

"I don't get it," Jenk muttered.

"What?" Mallory asked.

"No wounds," Moeera said quietly.

"Right," Jenk said. "Ed and Pask are mutilated, the way a person might look after a bear attack."

"Maybe the bear knocked Freedy down and he hit his head on a rock," Tully suggested.

"Sure," Jenk said. "But it must be completely under his head. Must be some rock."

"Some rock," Moeera repeated.

"Shush," Mallory told her. "I'm going to keep looking for Kor," she said to the men. "Craig must not have gone any further than here."

She and Moeera looked for signs of which way Kor or even a bear might have gone. Then she spied the trail that Freedy and Izzy, and later Kor, had taken.

"This way," she said.

They followed the trail away from the water into the woods. After what seemed like a very long time, they found Kor curled up on the ground. Pask's sword was close by where he had dropped it.

"Papa!" Moeera exclaimed.

"Kor!" Mallory shouted. She knelt by his head and stuck her ear over his mouth.

"Is he all right, Mama?"

"He's alive! Thank the Lord!"

Mallory examined her husband as best she could. Dried blood was caked over a gash made by some sharp claws. It seemed like it would keep till they could get him home.

Curious, she thought. *Blood on his neck, just a tiny patch. Did it land there as the bear mauled Pask or Edward?*

"Kor!" she exclaimed, trying to rouse him.

He came to when she shook his arm and shoulder.

"Kor Robin! You had me scared out of my mind!"

"Oh, I feel lousy," he sighed.

"You're lucky you feel anything at all!" Mallory said.

"What happened, Papa?" Moeera blurted out.

"The bear came to the river where we were waiting," he whispered.

He coughed a nagging, twisting kind of cough.

"We guessed that," Mallory said. "We found the others."

Kor coughed again. He began to speak but his voice was strained.

"Easy," Mallory said. "Take your time."

Kor cleared his throat. This time his voice came forth stronger.

"We attacked the bear, but it was too much. It killed Ed and Pask."

"How did you get away?" Moeera asked.

"I managed to kill the bear," he said. "Too late for my friends though."

Mallory kissed him.

"You must have wounded it badly," Mallory said.

"Sure," he said. "Fatally."

Mallory studied his face. Her husband looked utterly exhausted.

"I hate to be the bearer of bad news," Mallory said, "but you didn't kill it."

He struggled to sit up straighter but failed. He coughed.

"What do you mean?" he asked.

Mallory frowned. "We found your friends' bodies. They're all dead. But there was no carcass; the bear must have run away."

Now Kor did force himself to sit up.

"It couldn't have," he said. "It was stone dead."

"Then how do you explain it?"

"I... I don't know."

"Rest, honey," she said. "You've earned it. That bear will never bother us again, I'm sure."

Mallory held Kor in her arms, rocking him gently.

"My brave, fool of a husband," she said softly. "The lengths you'll go to just to impress me."

Moeera watched her mother and father. They seemed almost like two strangers to her, lost in their private, little world. She felt the importance of the moment, and she knew that things may not have turned out so well if her father hadn't been strong. She felt new respect for him at that moment.

*   *   *

"Here's our hero," the mayor said.

He watched the exhausted and ragged form of Kor Robin as Mallory and Tully helped him walk to Craig's front stoop. Moeera brought up the rear, awkwardly carrying the late Pask's sword.

The mayor pushed a rocking chair to the porch entrance. Kor collapsed into it, his hands gripping the armrests. They were covered by crusted blood; two strange crabs with five legs each.

"Mayor Moylan," Kor gasped. "I'm sorry."

"Sorry? Sorry about what?"

"I let the bear get away. I thought it was dead, decapitated it and all… so I thought."

The mayor rested a hand on Kor's arm.

"It's fine, Kor," he said. "You must have missed. Thanks for all you do."

"He looks like he lost a fight with a thresher," Jenk said.

The mayor nodded. "Who can blame you for being confused? You lost some blood."

"I'm alive though," Kor said.

"I'm glad you are!" Mallory said. "Scared me half to death when you didn't come home."

Moeera grabbed her father around the neck and hugged him.

"I'm glad you're okay too, Papa!"

"So am I. So am I," he said.

Kor rested on Craig's porch for a while. He was exhausted but happy to be alive with his loved ones. Craig's wife brought him juice to drink and a plate of cookies.

Before long, Mallory and Moeera took him home on their wagon. They passed the big wagon of men that the mayor had called for. Wouldn't the men be surprised to find the bodies of Edward, Pask, and Freedy.

40

Kor sat in the back with Moeera, his back resting against the front of the wagon. Moeera held him the best she could. The girl willed him to be well and for his cuts to be healed. In her heart she knew only time would erase his wounds.

"I'm all right, Moeera," he said. "I feel a lot better knowing you and Mama came to rescue me."

She smiled up at him. "You're so brave, Papa."

"Almost got killed, dear. Perhaps I was brave but wasn't using my head."

"How scary was the bear?"

"Very scary. It was huge, the biggest I've ever seen. And it was stronger than anything."

"Where do you hurt?"

"All over. I think my right knee hurts the worst; the bear knocked me down."

"Wow," Moeera said, surprised he was in as good shape as he was.

*   *   *

The rest of the day was an easy one for Kor. He spent most of it propped up on the bench on the front porch.

Mallory did her best to nurse him back to proper strength. She covered his legs, arms, and neck with salve. She served him soup and tea and biscuits. She covered his legs with a comfortable blanket. She spent a lot of time talking with him, always keeping the conversation far away from the previous night.

Moeera had her hands full with her chores. She managed to grab some time with her mother and father between washing and scrubbing and preparing things for the evening meal. She also did her regular, daily chores.

Chapter Seven

Several weeks passed. Kor was hale and hearty once again. Life for the Robins went back to normal, mostly. Kor was a town hero. No one lost any more livestock. There were no murders, or anyone gone missing.

On the other hand, fear and superstition surrounded the name Kor Robin whenever he was spoken of. Why had he, and only he, been spared? How had the blacksmith escaped but not the hunter?

What started as admiration changed into something less friendly. People would whisper and grumble whenever they noticed Kor around. What exactly had happened that fateful night? What happened to the bear that Kor had driven away? No carcass or blood trail was ever found. These were troubling details that no one could properly answer. Even Kor couldn't explain why he thought he'd decapitated the bear with Pask's sword after running it through the heart with Edward's spear.

It bothered Kor but he tried not to show it. There wasn't much to be done about it. Once a rumor made it around the community, the people believed what they wanted.

Some believed the truth that he had waited with the other men until the bear appeared at the river's shallows. They fought it, and by dumb luck he was the only survivor.

Others thought there was no bear. They whispered and gossiped that Kor was the murderer all along, that he had murdered his fellow hunters.

Then there were a few people who took the "Kor the murderer" or "Killer Kor" tale and ran with it. They posited that Kor was part of a witch coven, and that all the missing livestock was part of ritual sacrifice and spellcasting.

The make-believe gossip that people can invent is truly staggering. So is its power to hurt people.

Unfortunately, in this case, the gossips weren't far off about the witch at all.

*   *   *   **

"Do you ever regret your life here?" Kor asked Mallory.

They were spending a quiet moment on the porch swing. Moeera was asleep in bed. Locusts and crickets serenaded the nocturnal creatures that were just starting their nights. A lone candle illuminated a lantern hanging by the front door.

"What do you mean?" Mallory asked quietly.

"Is this life in Bucktry… on the outskirts of Bucktry a dull life?"

Mallory turned a bit to look directly into her husband's eyes. Their depths were shrouded in shadow.

"Now, Kor," she said, "are you serious, or is this some jest born of a tired mind?"

"Serious. I mean to be serious. I haven't quite thought it out."

"What?"

"Just that you could have had an exciting life… if you wanted to."

"Exciting life? We share our lives. What could be better than that?"

"You know what I mean."

She inhaled sharply. Then she let her breath out and sighed.

"You know very well that I was firmly set on my decision to marry you and live my life here. You're the blacksmith. I'm the homemaker. And a farmer. And most importantly a mother."

A silence momentarily hung. The insects did their best to fill it with distraction.

Mallory moved closer to him, trying to get comfortable.

"What brought this up?" she asked. "How long have you been thinking this?"

"Maybe a week. I don't remember exactly. Just a stray thought that sprang up because of the witchcraft rumors flying around these days."

"Oh, those."

"Yes. You've heard them then?"

She nodded. The flickering candlelight created a halo around her head.

"It's countryfolk looking for answers where there are none," she said.

"I guess," he said. "They need something bigger than a perilous fight with a big, scary animal to explain three deaths, six counting Nundle and Holly and Bumper."

"That thing almost killed you too! The fools ought to look to you as a hero for making it out alive."

"I guess they haven't anything better to do," Kor said. "At least they still bring me work to do."

Mallory cuddled him. "Sure. I bet they'll forget all about these baseless rumors soon."

"I hope so," Kor said.

"Nothing odd or supernatural about it," she said, and giggled.

"Just dumb luck."

"Luck. Nothing dumb about it."

"No."

"And as far as excitement?"

"Yes?" Kor asked.

"I enjoy my quiet life. I like the same ordinary stuff."

"If you say so."

"I do say so. I hate surprises. Give me the dull, drudgework-filled life any day."

"Alright," Kor said. He gave the stone patio a push with his foot, sending the swing rocking ever so slightly. "No need then for the Mojo."

"Shh."

The candlelight wavered in the lantern, bathing the patio in ever-shifting eddies and currents of yellow. The couple held one another with contentment.

*   *   *

Deep in the Gillikin woods, an old shack sat by an even older lane that was all but forgotten. The dwelling stood as if by some miracle; it needed major repairs. A hole in the roof had been getting larger for quite some time.

Inside, sitting cross-legged on a worn pillow, was Izzy. A crystal orb sat before her on a wooden stand. Clouds swirled within the ball.

She focused her gaze at the clouds, willing them to clear away so she could see the inside. Soon the clouds parted, revealing an image of Mallory and Kor sitting together on the porch.

"There's my new servant," she said softly. "At home with wifey no doubt."

She resumed her silence and listened closely to hear their conversation.

What a boring pair, she thought.

She listened, thinking that this new slave wouldn't be any more valuable to her than that last buffoon.

Then Kor said, "No need then for the Mojo."

The Mojo? What?

Izzy scrutinized the woman on the swing. She was hard to see in the partial darkness.

"Shh."

Could it be?

She strained her eyes, murmuring a charm to give her sight beyond that of mere mortals.

The woman's features sharpened. Izzy could now see her clearly.

Yes, there was some resemblance between this woman and the spritely imp she'd known as "The Mojo". Faint as it was… could that truly be….

That was so many years ago. Izzy bit her lip in contemplation.

The husband had uttered "the Mojo", hadn't he? Or had she imagined it?

Izzpalin, blood witch extraordinaire, gnashed her teeth.

By the lost lands! This servant may prove to be more useful than I could have imagined!

Her eyes widened.

And if that's really my old nemesis, The Mojo; I'll have so much fun indeed.

Izzy laughed her witch's laugh, and in their burrows and hidey-holes the forest creatures shivered.

* * *

That very night Kor awoke promptly at three in the morning. Of course, he wasn't truly awake. Izzpalin had fed of his life's blood. Now she tugged the invisible chain that bound him to her.

He rose from bed, a somnambulist seeking what he knew not. Mallory slept soundly on. Kor left the house and shuffled down the lane. His bare feet tread on soil and rock alike, he didn't notice. It barely registered that he was walking.

His walk took him beyond the sight of home into the woods. Eventually, he knew on some level that he was walking but he didn't know why or where he walked to.

He pushed his way through some vines and entered a small clearing. His gait slowed until he was standing still.

"Fancy meeting you here."

He snapped out of his trancelike state. There was Izzy, standing next to a large oak tree.

"You," he said, surprised. The forgotten memories of the hunt night flooded back. He grasped at his head.

"Me," she said. "I'm sure you remember me... now."

"Where am I?" he asked, noticing his bare feet.

"The woods, dear. With me"

She moved closer to him.

Kor's mind raced.

"You bit me!"

"That I did," Izzy said, smiling. "One of my little endearments."

"Who are you? You killed Freedy, didn't you?"

"Tsk tsk," she said. "Don't get annoying on me."

"You killed him."

"He was a complete twit, so of course I killed him."

"He was courting you."

"So."

"Did he love you?"

"He thought he did," Izzpalin said icily. "I guess we'll never know for certain."

Kor was incredulous. "Why'd you kill him then?"

"It suited my purposes."

"What purposes? Who are you?"

"You ask a lot of questions, Mr. Mojo."

Kor did a doubletake.

"What did you call me?" he asked.

Izzy grinned. "You're not admitting that the former, infamous Mojo grew up, married you, and settled down?"

Kor frowned, shook his head.

"I don't know what you're talking about," he said. "I certainly don't know anyone named Mojo."

"If you say so," she said. "We can play it your way."

"My wife's name is Mallory. As for this Mojo person, I haven't the

46

foggiest idea who that is."

Izzy reached out and touched Kor's nightshirt over top of his chest. She idly traced his contours with her finger.

In an absentminded tone of voice, she said, "I don't think she exists anymore. What I can't figure out is why she retired here with you, Kor."

She moved even closer, uncomfortably so. Kor moved back the way he'd come.

"Stop," she said, quietly. "Hold still."

He could no longer move away. The magic chain was stretched to its limit.

"Don't you remember that night that you killed the bear?" she asked.

"What about it? You killed Freedy and you bit me."

"What else? Do you remember what you told me about the bear?"

"I killed it," Kor said. He could remember the details, and they were back with a vengeance. He felt like retching. "But…."

"But what, darling?" she cooed. She had started to gently nibble his ear.

"That was no bear! Not truly. It was a girl."

"That's right. She was my moppet and a quick learner. She would have been a cunning blood witch…."

Izzy held Kor's head in her hands and stared into his eyes.

"…. if you hadn't cut her head off."

Kor shifted uncomfortably. Izzy reached down and took his hand.

The shock he felt traveled like electric current over his body. He wanted to pull away, to run; but he couldn't. The blood rushed in his ears so loudly he couldn't hear the words she said softly as she pulled him to embrace her.

He sat upon the ground, the yarrow and the lace crunching down underneath him. She followed him down into the weeds. Her face changed from that of a woman to one as feral as a wild beast. Her eyes became vicious and predatory.

Kor was terrified. He wanted to scream out, to run away. He couldn't move a muscle.

Izzy fell upon him. She plunged her sharp teeth into his neck and bit down. The healed wound was replaced by a fresh pair of holes from which the blood poured forth.

Izzy lapped at the flowing, crimson stream. The lapping gave way to sucking as she greedily feasted on her victim. She pushed him onto his back, her bloodlust taking over. She lost control. She perched on Kor's chest, a raptor atop her prey. Her back arched forward, stretching muscles so she could feed.

Life was leaving Kor as surely as it had his friends on the night they met the bear. His mind drifted in a sea of confusion.

With the last bit of humanity left in her, she pulled herself off him. Blood covered her mouth, neck, breast. She inhaled deeply and let it back out in a shriek of exhilaration.

Kor stayed on the ground, his breath coming in ragged gasps. He was too weak to move a muscle.

Izzy snarled and growled, half kneeling in the weeds. She stood, feeling strong again.

Kor looked up at her in frightened fascination. He still couldn't move but thoughts raced through his head.

She had to be a witch, there was no doubt about it. And because of the bloodlust and the thought that she could no doubt drain him dry if she wanted he knew what type she was. Blood witches fed off the life's blood of the living!

Izzy breathed in rough gasps which gradually gave way to even breaths. Her skin was the pinkest it had ever looked. Her eyes lost their ferocity.

"Delicious," she purred. "Such life and vitality in that unassuming frame of yours."

She moved beside him and began stroking his face lightly with her fingers. She peered into his eyes.

"You're wondering what happens next," she stated.

He saw shadow and light within her eyes. They went on forever, two bottomless pools.

"We're going to have to be careful not to let that imp wife of yours know about us."

Kor wanted to jump up and shake her. What did she want with him and Mallory? How did she know who Mallory was?

"It should be easy to keep our secret," she said genially. "You're going to be forgetting our tryst until next time."

He felt an acute panic. *Hold onto this memory long enough to warn Mallory. Any shred of knowledge will do it.*

Izzy smiled lustily and held Kor, leaning in, kissing him passionately on

48

his mouth....

*   *   *

...he came to in his bedroom.

Kor ran his hand over his face. He peered into the darkness.

I must have been walking in my sleep, he thought.

The groggy blacksmith felt tired as could be. He shuffled to the bed and got under the covers. Next to him, Mallory mumbled something unintelligible.

Kor Robin slept.

Chapter Eight

Not long after Kor's nocturnal visits to Izzpalin began (of which he had no recollection), he began to feel tired every day by midday. His ailment combined with the summer's hottest days made him feel awful.

He didn't know the true reason for his constant fatigue, and so he chalked it up to his busy smithing schedule. That, and the sorrowful thought that perhaps he'd gotten old.

Moeera and Mallory both noticed the change in Kor. The only real origin for this change seemed to be its near coincidence with the bear encounter. Despite what seemed like a full and speedy recovery, Kor's health plunged deeper and deeper into weariness.

He slowed down notably at the blacksmith shop. Customers complained about how long it took for him to do his work. Wad did his best to pick up the slack.

When Kor got home from work he spent more and more time sleeping in his chair.

Mallory made him see the doctor. The doctor was perplexed. He advised Kor not to overdo it.

Moeera turned nine that fall. She got a new pair of shoes, a book about a hero who met a dragon, and a new Sunday dress.

Her mother baked her a yummy cake decorated with flowers made from frosting. She blew out a candle for luck. Her wish was for her father to have his magnificent strength back again. Each year before it had been for Wecks to finally return to Bucktry and teach her to do magic.

The next day she was playing outside. She'd been to school, her chores were done, and the animals had been cared for. She ran around the yard, sprinting here and there. One moment she would touch the side of the house, the next she'd be tagging the side of the chicken coop.

Behind the house and the large yard were the fields. Mallory had a variety of fruits and vegetables planted. As she ran and goofed in the relatively short grass of the yard, Moeera spied something in the whisket stalks.

At first she thought it was a person. It appeared to be coming up almost as tall as the stalks. Then it ducked down and vanished for a bit.

"Hello there!" she called out.

The shape appeared again for a brief time, but then it vanished once more. She couldn't see it well at all from where she stood so she walked toward it.

It popped up again. To Moeera's eyes it appeared dark as if whomever this was wore black. Then, just as quickly, it was gone again.

Someone's playing peekaboo with me, she thought. *But who?*

She stopped short of the crops by about six yards. She didn't want to go in there if this was a bad person. One never knew, and if they chose wrong; well, that was it for them.

The shape popped up again. It was an animal she decided. Hmm.

She continued watching, a smile covering her face.

Popped?

More like hopped.

Moeera lost all sense of caution and darted into the whisket.

It was a rabbit, a midnight black rabbit with the most vibrant red eyes she'd ever seen. The rabbit noticed her and stopped its high hopping. It put one paw out in front of it as if to run in her direction. Then it twitched its nose and wiggled its ears.

"Oh, you're beautiful," she said in awe. "And cute."

The rabbit stuck its neck out as if to reply to her remarks. It twitched its nose some more.

"I don't want to hurt you, no," she said softly. "May I pet you? Would you like that?"

The rabbit looked at her with its grandiose eyes and bobbed its head up and down. It hopped closer until it could stretch and touch its nose to Moeera's leg.

Moeera laughed. She knelt in the dirt amongst the whisket stalks. The rabbit moved itself next to her leg, sitting close to the ground. It yawned.

She began stroking it from its ears to its fluffy tail. "You're so pretty and soft," Moeera told it.

The rabbit was quiet, only its nose moved ever so slightly. It stretched out even more and flattened itself into the grass.

"Where did you come from?" she asked it. "I'd remember if I'd seen you before."

Still quiet, it relaxed while she petted it.

"Do you have a family somewhere on the other side of the field?"

The rabbit looked at her as if contemplating an answer.

She stroked its back for a few more minutes, and then she got up and dusted herself off.

"I'm going home now," she told it. "I live right over there."

The rabbit scrambled up. But it didn't leap into the depths of the whisket. On the contrary, it hopped after Moeera into her yard.

"Coming with, are you? Sure! It will be nice to have you visit."

She leaned down to pet the rabbit some more. It hopped toward her house.

Moeera directed the rabbit to her house's back door with a combination of coaxing and stepping in its way when it strayed.

"Now, I'm going in to tell Mama about you, Mr. Rabbit," she said. "Will you please wait here?"

The rabbit stretched out its body and laid down nearby. She watched for a moment as it munched the clover.

"Good," she said, going into the house.

Her mother was mending a pair of her pants that were torn on one leg. The needle and thread moved deftly in her fingers as she concentrated.

"How did you tear this pair of pants?" she asked.

"On a sticker bush," Moeera said.

"A pox on that sticker bush!" Mallory said. "This tear is a mile long."

"Sorry, Mama. I'll be more careful."

"You do that. Remind me that we're going to be practicing sewing together from now on."

"Yes, Mama," Moeera said.

"Good," Mallory said, looking at her daughter. "Now tell me what you're up to."

"Playing outside."

"Mm-hmm. Then why did you come in?"

"Um...."

"I knew I recognized that look in your eyes. What's going on?"

"I made friends with a rabbit!" Moeera blurted out.

"Friends, huh?"

"Yes!"

"Most rabbits hop away really fast."

"Not Mr. Rabbit, Mama. He likes me."

"Where is he?"

"At the back door."

Mallory set her sewing on the table and said, "Let's see him."

"Yay!" Moeera exclaimed with joy. "He's pretty. Not brown like most bunnies. He's the color of soot."

Moeera opened the door and there was her friend, contentedly munching clover.

"See, Mama!"

Mallory walked out the door and looked to her daughter. She saw the black rabbit and its shining red eyes. Her smile warped into a dread-filled frown.

"Oh, Moeera," she sighed wearily.

"What's wrong, Mama?"

"I think your rabbit friend is a puca."

Moeera looked at her blankly.

"What's that?"

"It's hard to explain. It's not just any ordinary rabbit though."

"See how nice he is, Mama?"

"Yes, and I hope he stays nice."

The rabbit appeared totally oblivious to Mallory's statements. It munched a bit, and then it hopped to Moeera, nuzzling her under her chin.

"Can he stay here?"

"If he wants to, I suppose he may. You'd better be extra special nice to him."

"I will. Where will he sleep?"

"In the tool shed next to the chicken coop. You can make him a bed of straw to sleep in. I'll find him a water dish and a bowl for vegetables."

"Thank you, Mama."

"You're welcome. You're responsible for taking care of him. And remember what I said about being nice to him."

"I will! Thanks, Mama."

"You are going to have to take care, Moeera. If he's a puca, and I'm pretty sure he is, then don't make him angry. And don't shut him in at night. Let the shed door open."

"Okay."

Moeera sat down next to Mr. Rabbit and petted his furry back.

"You hear that?" she asked. "Mama says you can stay, you can sleep in the shed."

The rabbit looked content as could be. It nodded its head and relaxed.

"What do you call it?" Mallory asked.

"Mr. Rabbit," Moeera said.

"He looks like a Soot to me."

"Soot?"

"Yes, like his fur color. You're right about that. He looks as if he rolled in the fireplace."

"Hmm. Soot. Do you like that name, Mr. Rabbit?"

Mr. Rabbit looked quite indifferent about the whole name thing.

"I have to finish mending your pants," Mallory said, and went in the house.

"When you're ready, Mr. uh Soot, I'll show you where you can bed down for the night."

The rabbit finished eating the clover it had just pulled. Then it sat up expectantly as if preparing to salute.

"Right this way," Moeera said. She led it the short distance to the tool shed.

She slid the wooden bolt to the side and pulled open the door. Rakes, pitchforks, shovels, hoes, and a large broom hung along the rear wall. Several barrels sat inside to the left. A spare bag of chicken feed sat atop a wooden box of tools.

Soot came to the doorway, dipped its head till its chin touched the threshold, and lifted it again to peer at the girl. Then it quickly continued moving side to side, looking every which way and probing with its nose.

"I'll go fetch some straw," Moeera told it. "That way you'll have a nest."

The rabbit continued its inspection.

54

It supervised her shaking the straw over the bare wooden floor, creating a nice, little pile.

Finally, after the rabbit nuzzled Moeera in approval, she said, "I hope that's enough. I must go inside now and help with supper." Moeera walked to the small barn where Dot and Bahb's stable was. She found the hay bin and the pile of straw bales. She grabbed an armload of loose straw and carried it to the shed.

The rabbit nodded in its bobbing sort of way.

"I'll bring you some carrots in a little bit."

*   *   *

Kor came home tired as ever. He washed up and came in to join his family at the supper table.

"Moeera made a new friend today," Mallory said.

"Who?" Kor asked.

"I made friends with a rabbit, Papa."

"That's nice," he said. "It didn't make a beeline for a rabbit hole?"

"No," Moeera said. "He likes me."

"Why wouldn't he?" Kor laughed.

"He might spend the night in the tool shed," Moeera said.

"That sounds good," Kor said. "You'll be in charge of cleaning up any mess he makes."

"Okay."

Chapter Nine

Soot spent the night in the shed. He found the small pile of straw to be comfortable enough. Nevertheless, something woke him up in the middle of the night. He sprang from his bed, heart beating wildly.

Peering from the shed's open doorway, he spied Kor walking from the house in his still sleeping state.

Curious, he thought.

Without a sound, the black rabbit hopped from the shed to follow in the shadows. It was a new moon and very dark.

Kor found a pale lady among the trees. Soot watched the blood witch drain some of Kor's blood.

No good can come from this. The puca stayed out of sight in the blueberry bushes.

Before long, Kor was sleepwalking home. The witch slipped away into the darkness as her kind was apt to do.

Soot huddled under some shrubs, pondering what he'd seen. Then he began hopping home to get some more sleep.

*   *   *

The next morning, Moeera rushed outside to check on her new friend. He was awake and munching away on a patch of pig ear leaves. He bobbed his head at her in greeting and began demolishing another leaf. She thought about how she would never mix him up with another rabbit because of his red eyes.

She sat next to him and stroked his furry back.

"I'm going to school today, okay?" she said. "It's way down the lane, and then I go in the schoolhouse."

Soot kept munching as he listened.

"It only lasts part of the day, and then I'll be home."

The rabbit gave no indication that he understood her. He stopped munching and relaxed as she petted him several more times.

"I gotta get ready, Soot," she said, leaping up.

She went in the house.

*   *   *

About fifteen minutes later, Moeera walked onto the dirt lane at a jaunty pace. She had a book in one hand and a black rabbit hopping behind her.

When she noticed her companion, she turned to him and said, "Soot, you don't have to come with me to school."

He gave her an innocent look, raised and lowered his head. His nose twitched.

"All right, if that's what you want to do."

They arrived at the schoolhouse. Moeera left her friend outside to forage for food and do what rabbits do.

Mr. Court called the children to order. There were students of different ages in his class, so his lessons often covered a broad range of activities and assignments related to one subject.

"I'm glad to see so many of you today," he said.

He called the roll and paused after the last name. He turned to his small writing desk, snatching up a book.

"Today's reading and writing will center on this," he said, holding the book out for the students to see.

The kids looked at the book curiously.

"Which book is it?" Maria asked.

"Which?" the kids asked.

Mr. Court grinned. Now that he had everyone's attention....

"It's an old favorite of mine," he said, excitedly. "I doubt that any of you have ever heard of it, much less read it."

He flipped the green book back and forth in his hands. There was a title embossed on the cover in thin, gold script. He read it to the class:

Corbeck by the Sea

Moeera's heart leapt in her chest. Corbeck was the kingdom in the stories that her mother told her. The stories she told her about—

"Princess Eileen is the main character in the book," Mr. Court said. "She is the youngest of three sisters. One of them will grow up and rule the

57

kingdom in her father's place."

"Which one?" Maeve asked.

"The oldest," Wilbur said. "It's the oldest that always takes over."

"But Eileen is the main character," Fenta said. Fenta was the oldest girl in the class at the age of fifteen.

"Well," Mr. Court interjected, "it's true that the oldest child of royal parents, especially if male, often inherits the throne. In this case, there was no male heir. But... it isn't always the oldest who becomes leader."

The children watched their teacher expectantly, waiting for a clue about the story's outcome. Mr. Court, not a man who was apt to spill the beans, merely smiled and turned to the first page.

He began reading:

The land of Corbeck lies amongst the waves of the wild sea, a kingdom of mystery and delight. Its rocky shores overlooked the churning waters and foam. Coastal dwellers gazed at the horizon looking for signs of life.

Most days the rolling billows were the only movement the eyes could see. Sometimes a sailing ship would approach, and the birds would cry welcomes and circle looking greedily for signs of food.

Corbeck was a pretty, green land. Shepherds kept flocks of sheep and goats. Small farms dotted the rocky land. In places where docks could be built, boats were moored. The people fished for the myriad aquatic creatures frequenting the surrounding waters.

Life in Corbeck was merry.

The High King Robert ruled from his hillside castle for years. Life was peaceful. When Robert became old and feeble, he passed his throne to his son Cullen. King Cullen was tall and strong and wise. He enjoyed music and games, and he was known for hunting from time to time.

Cullen's wife Queen Kath had the task of raising their three daughters: Maeve, Caitlin, and Eileen.

*   *   *

"How art thou on this lovely morning, Queen Kath?" Emeria asked.

"Fine, I suppose," Kath said. "But there is pain."

"Oh! My queen," Em gasped. "Art thou in distress?"

"No, no I don't believe that I am," the queen said. "This child insists on kicking my innards."

"I see. Soon it shalt be out, my queen."

"Thank God in Heaven above for that!"

Every mother feels her baby move around as it grows inside the womb. Every baby kicks. Kath's baby kicked morning, noon, and night.

Then, a few days later, oh, happy day! The child was born. A princess!

How the king and queen celebrated! So happy were they. The entire kingdom rejoiced to hear they had a pretty, little princess. Many came to court over the following days to pay their respects and see the baby.

One such visitor was a woman named Deidre, tall and talkative. She wished the king and queen well at court and found many topics to ramble on about. She only left that day because the castle supper hour was nigh. Right in the middle of commenting on the war occurring in Balsadad, she was escorted out.

Baby Maeve grew into a curious toddler. The girl soaked in the attention of the court, the castle servants, and her extended family. Her father spent more and more time afield, making a dedicated effort to drive away the monsters and beasts that were laying claim to the forests and the cliffs of Corbeck.

Cullen's cousins, Duncan and Sean, aided him on many a fight with werewolves, trolls, goblins, and even worse things. For every creature they dispatched, another was certain to appear. They even crawled from the sea to do battle with King Cullen and his brave warriors.

Maeve learned more and more in her beginning years. She talked a lot. She also watched and listened. She began imitating her mother and any other high-born lady at court. If imitation is the sincerest form of flattery, then little Maeve was a natural.

Mr. Court lowered the book and looked at his class.

"That's enough for now," he said. "I'm afraid you must come back tomorrow to find out the answers to your questions about the sisters three."

"But you just started," Ham whined.

"I know," Mr. Court said. "But there's something I want you all to do before I tell you the rest."

"The alphabet?" Maeve asked.

"No, not that. What I'd like you to do now is picture the story so far. Imagine with your mind's eye the setting, the kingdom of Corbeck. It sits high above the sea, above the cliffs. What does it look like? What do the rolling waves look like? And the castle and the cliffs? The royal family…

Cullen is tall and strong, but what color is his hair? What do his clothes look like?"

"What's a wave, Mr. Court?" Tom asked.

"It's a body of water within the sea... the ocean... it's long and moves toward the shore in a curling shape like so," the teacher said, demonstrating with his hand and his arm.

"The sea moves?" Sara asked.

"The water in it moves, yes," Mr. Court said. "It's always moving, sometimes slowly; sometimes quickly. That's why the ships that sail the briny sea move up and down, to and fro."

Many of the children looked confused. A few faces lit up, signaling that ideas were forming.

"Legends often spoke of gods and monsters who blew with tremendous breath upon the ocean to cause the waves," Mr. Court said. He grabbed a rolled paper from under his desk.

"This," he said, unfurling the paper. "This map. That's where this head over here comes from. Legend." He tapped a small character on the map.

The kids stood to try to get a better look. Mr. Court walked to each, letting his students see the floating head of a man with long hair who blew the air into a cloud above the sea.

Some mouths dropped open as they contemplated the head. Some glimpsed the phrase further down which declared "here there be monsters".

"Back to your assignment," Mr. Court said, rolling the map. "There are plenty of things for you to write about or draw. You could describe the monsters that Cullen and his cousins and knights had to fight. What were their names? Were they smart? Were they dumb? Could they talk like people, or did they merely snarl and growl like animals? I want you to read between the lines."

"What does that mean?" Maria asked.

"It means that I want you to use your imaginations. Choose something from the beginning of the story and draw a picture of it. If that's not to your liking, then write a poem or your own story about it."

"That's all we have to do?" Moeera asked.

"That's all. You might find that it's a bigger prospect than you expect. Anyone nine and older needs to write something about Corbeck. You can draw too but I want to see you put words down."

60

The rest of the school day was spent in a flurry of writing and thinking and drawing. The children peppered Mr. Court with question after question. His lips were sealed about a great many things. "What do you think?" was the question he put forth the rest of the day.

Moeera wrote about the castle with its great hall and many visitors. She wrote about the little girl from the story and the many things she saw day after day.

*   *   *

Moeera enjoyed the lesson that day at school, but when it was time to leave she was ready. All that thinking made her head hurt.

Soot was sitting on the ground between the little schoolhouse and the road. He yawned and hopped over to Moeera to greet her.

"Ready to go home, Soot?" she asked.

Then Moeera heard Ivy and Bevan talking.

"I can hardly wait!" Bevan shouted.

Moeera, Bernadette, and Tanta went up to Bevan. What was he so excited about?

"It will be so much fun," Ivy said. "Only a few more days till my parents take me."

"What will be fun?" Moeera asked.

"The fair is on until Friday," Bevan said. "Didn't you know?"

She hadn't. Somehow the week of the fair arrived, and she was oblivious. Maybe it had been her excitement over Soot's arrival. Maybe it was something else.

"There are wagons from all over at the fairground today," Ivy said.

Moeera started on her way home with Soot hopping along at her side. Thoughts of her day at school had been replaced by memories of Wecks the Wizard. Wecks and his magic.

About halfway between school and home, Moeera and Soot passed the fairground. The rabbit paused.

"What do you see, Soot?" Moeera asked.

He made a small hippity hop to the lane's edge, his long ears pricking up.

"You hear something. Let's go see!"

The girl stepped over some rocks along the roadside. She and Soot lit out across the meadow at a fast clip. She saw wagons lined up in the distance.

By the time they got close to the wagons, Moeera was running short on breath. She and Soot stopped to rest. She counted the wagons. One, two, three, four, five, six, and more hidden behind those.

"They're here for the fair, Soot," Moeera said, excitedly. "Maybe, just maybe, he's returned!"

Soot looked at the girl questioningly. He began sampling the clover and grass which grew thick and lush at the fairground's edge.

"Come on!" she whispered with anticipation.

She didn't wait to see if Soot followed her or not. She'd been waiting for him to return for three years. Now she wanted nothing more than to see if he was here.

She zipped between the wagons. The first she saw was there every year, the red coach of the pretzel maker. A plain, brown coach had a sign on its side proclaiming it belonged to Popay Wimton, the owner and trainer of a flea circus.

She grimaced, running past the light blue trailer of the flower girls. A red trailer belonging to Jock Ardoo, Leatherworker, was next. And so on, and so forth. White trailer, Goodie's Bake Shop. Yellow coach, Ardelle Teppis, Trained Beavers.

Where in the world was....

Then she spied a vaguely familiar trailer, gray with black trim. A golden "W" reflected the sunlight on the side. Her breath caught in her throat.

He's here! she thought. It's been three years, but he made it back. He's here.

She felt that she could cry.

A soft shape bumped her ankles. She reached down to softly pet Soot's back. She could hardly take her eyes off that trailer.

Her memory of it was hazy. Three years gone by and all. But there was no doubt—she would know it anyplace. It was freshly painted and in good repair. Wecks must have visited many places and performed many, many shows.

Moeera took a deep breath and approached the door on the side of the trailer.

Rap, rap, rap!

Her knocks broke the silence of the quiet field. Soot sat up high on his haunches, looking at her.

She turned to the rabbit. "Maybe nobody's home. Where do you think they are?"

Soot twitched his nose and dropped to all fours. He began inspecting the surrounding grass and wildflowers for snacks.

"Are you looking for someone in particular?" a voice asked suddenly.

Moeera whirled around.

A man was standing nearby, watching her. Did he seem familiar?

"Miss?" he asked.

She shook her head as adrenaline shot through her.

"I saw the wagons gathered here for the fair, and I wondered if Wecks was here," she said, forcing a smile.

"Oh," he said. Then he seemed to look her in the eyes a bit harder. "Moeera?"

"That's me!" she exclaimed, shaking all over. "You're the jester, aren't you?"

"I'm Paul," he said. "Yes, I remember you. You saw the show and wanted to learn magic."

"Yes!"

"Wecks is at the watering hole near the town hall," Paul said. "He should be here soon. We're going to talk to the man in charge about where to set up."

"Great!" Moeera exclaimed. "I must go now. I'm on my way home from school."

"I'll tell Wecks you asked about him," Paul said. "It's nice to see you again, Moeera!"

"Likewise!" Moeera said with a big smile. "I'm so glad that you're here."

Paul waved as Moeera turned to leave. She collected Soot from his explorations and carried him along. The rabbit seemed nonplussed but didn't object.

He's here, she thought. Wecks the Wizard is in Bucktry.

Her heart sang. This time she would convince Wecks to make her his apprentice. She would learn magic, and she would leave Bucktry behind to travel the world.

Chapter Ten

Papa, Mama!" Moeera shouted. She ran from the lane to the path which led to her house. She scrambled up the step, her face red from running. Soot scampered up after her, plopping down on the flagstone.

"What is it, dear?" Mallory asked. She and Kor sat on the swing enjoying the bright afternoon sun and the shade provided by the porch roof.

"Wecks is back! He's back! For the fair. He's finally back."

Moeera was so excited that her face beamed happiness. Soot watched the girl as her parents tried to figure out what was going on.

"Wecks is back, you say," Mallory said, her brow furrowed. "Who is Wecks?"

"Mama, you must be joking," Moeera said.

"Wecks," Kor said. "Are you talking about that magician we saw?"

"Yes, but he's a wizard, Papa! And he's here once again for the fair."

"Oh. Well, that's very nice."

"We'll have to see the show," Mallory added.

"I'm counting the days!" Moeera exclaimed. She pirouetted around the porch, narrowly avoiding knocking over a lantern.

"Moeera!" her mother admonished her.

"What?" she asked, freezing in place.

"You know better than to spin around without looking first! Settle yourself."

"Yes, Mama," Moeera said.

She dashed into the house to swap her long skirt for a pair of dungarees. Then she reappeared in the doorway.

"I'm going to do my chores now," she said.

"Sounds good," Mallory said.

She and Kor watched their daughter skip off energetically. Soot scampered off the porch to disappear into some weeds.

Kor sighed.

"You sound troubled," Mallory said.

He smiled. "You know, it's just odd to see our girl with that much pep in her step."

"You didn't think she'd forgotten about magic or the Wondrous Wecks, did you?"

"No," he said. "Maybe. Er… I guess I thought just that. I forgot about him."

"Moeera didn't," Mallory said.

"It's not even real magic."

"She doesn't know that. It doesn't matter."

"No, I guess it doesn't."

*   *   *

The next day Moeera popped out of bed at the crack of dawn. She dressed and went to the shed to check on Soot. He was just waking up. She watched him stretch his fuzzy body and yawn, his pink mouth and tongue a contrast from his dark fur.

"I'll check on the animals, Soot. See you in a little bit."

He watched her scurry off to check water buckets and check in with the farm animals.

Dot greeted Moeera with a customary neigh. The bachukka was awake and ready as always. Moeera opened her stall and led her into the small barnyard. Dot happily left the barn and meandered around the yard in the brightening morning sun. Moeera filled her water bucket using a smaller bucket she could fill in the spring house.

She latched the barnyard gate and dashed to the chicken coop. The chickens were still bundled in their little cubbies. Moeera checked underneath the birds for eggs, finding a few. She placed the eggs in another bucket. The rooster strutted around the enclosure. He rose to full height and crowed his "cock-a-doodle-doo" at Moeera.

"Good morning, Donald," she said. She went to the part of the enclosure with the water trough and fetched a couple buckets to add to it.

Donald rushed at her as her second bucket went empty, and she decided to get out of the pen. They had enough feed to tide them over.

*   *   *

At school, Moeera and her classmates spent most of the day on the basics. Mr. Court drilled them on their spelling words, addition, subtraction, measurements, grammar, and reading.

Moeera was called upon to read aloud from the book of the natural world. She read:

"The potato bug is a beetle with a bright yellow/orange body and five brown stripes along the length of each of its... I'm sorry, Mr. Court, I don't know this word."

"Sound it out, Moeera," Mr. Court said.

"E – lie – tra."

"Good," Mr. Court said. "That's correct."

"But whatever is an elytra?" Moeera asked.

"It's one of the two matching coverings over a beetle's wings," Mr. Court said. "When the beetle wants to fly, it pops its elytron—that's both of them—forward toward its head. That way its wings are free to flutter."

"That's nice," Moeera said. "Should I read any more?"

"Yes, please continue," Mr. Court said, "right where you left off."

"Yes, sir. Potato bugs are about 3/8 inches in length. The female can lay up to five hundred eggs in one four-to-five-week period. The eggs are attached to the undersides of leaves. If the weather is right, the eggs hatch into tiny larvae."

"The larvae begin as reddish-brown with humped backs and two rows of dark spots on either side."

"Potato bugs can be quite a pest to farmers. They eat plants including black nightshade, potato, and haremma."

"They are occasionally mistaken for wogglebugs which resemble potato bugs in coloration. However, if one looks closely they will observe that the colorations, marking patterns, and heads are markedly different. After all, the potato bug is a beetle while the wogglebug is not."

"That will be enough for now, Moeera," Mr. Court said. "You did a fine job with that passage."

"Thank you, Mr. Court," Moeera said.

"Next up, Bernadette," Mr. Court said. "Read us your passage, please."

Bernadette turned to the pages in her book which held her assignment. She had a passage from *The Ancestors of Llyr*.

She read:

"For more than a generation, the Tuath de Danaan fought the invading Fomorians. As they themselves had come to the green isles from overseas, now came the Fomorians."

"The new invaders were monstrous in appearance and strength. They too had those amongst them versed in magic. They posed a challenge and an opposite force to the Tuath de Danaan and their heroes."

"This especially delighted the Morrigan, she whose very essence thrived on warfare. She led armies into battle after battle."

"The Morrigan fell in love with a warrior-hero named Cu Chulainn. Despite her power and cunning, he spurned her many attempts to win his love. Besides being able to transform into any living creature, she could predict the future."

"The Morrigan predicted Cu Chulainn's death."

"Thank you, Bernadette," Mr. Court said.

The rest of the morning passed in the same fashion. Each student read from one of five books. If they stumbled, Mr. Court guided them along. The other students listened. They learned new vocabulary while they listened about nature, the green isles, the sky and weather, the peoples of the continent, and passages from the Big Book of Limited Elaborateness.

After lunch, Mr. Court had the class continue work on its Corbeck by the Sea project. Before they got to work, he read some more.

Beyond the thick forest which separated Corbeck from the rest of the land, another forest existed in a westerly direction. This forest was full of magical folk. There were gnomes and brownies and fairies. The fairies had strong magic that they used to help other people.

One day, King Cullen sent Sean and Jimmy on a mission to traverse the forest and visit the fairies. Maybe the fairies could tell them why so many monsters were in the forest and causing trouble for Corbeck's farmers and peasants.

Sean and Jimmy rode their animals into the forest. The first person they met was a woodcutter named Josh. He greeted the brave knights and set down his ax.

"That ax," he told them, "is what deters the giant from bothering me."

"Giant?" Sean asked. "You say there might be a giant about?"

"Most definitely," Josh said. "The very same giant that steals sheep from their grazing pastures in the hills. He lives in these woods."

"Makes sense," Jimmy said. "He'd loathe to attack us with our long, sharp swords."

"Perhaps," Josh said. "Perhaps not."

"Oh?" the knights said.

"He's really big," Josh said.

"I suppose he'll be hard to miss," Sean said.

"You can bet your buttons on that," Josh said. He asked the knights if they had time to stop at his house for a drink.

Sean and Jimmy reckoned that well, yes, they believed they did have time to stop in. They helped Josh load his wood into a wagon for transport and accompanied him home.

At Josh's house, they met Mrs. Josh and their daughter Sara. Mrs. Josh put the stew in the pot, put the pot over the fire, and took some bread out of the bread oven. The three men sat down in front of the house to toast the King and Queen over a whiskey.

"So, what brings you brave knights to the forest?" Josh asked.

Sean swirled his drink in his cup and said, "We're looking for the magical folk."

"The fairies," Jimmy added.

Josh looked a bit surprised. "Looking for fairies. I see."

Though he did not see. He'd never heard of that kind of thing outside of childish fantasies.

Josh took a drink. Then he said, "Why must you find fairies?"

Sean hiccupped. Jimmy slapped him on the back.

"Simple," Jimmy said. "King Cullen is curious about the abundance of monsters. He thought the magical folk might be able to explain why there are so many of late."

"Oh," Josh said.

"Have you ever met any fairies?" Sean asked.

"Me? Nah," Josh said. "Monsters, now, that's a different story."

"Do tell."

"The giant is just the biggest danger I've seen lurking around. And believe me, there are others that come close in size."

Sean's eyebrows raised.

"I mostly see goblins, gnomes, gryphons, hobs... I've seen a werewolf once."

"A werewolf," Jimmy said, "and alive to tell the tale."

Josh scratched the back of his neck. "Yes, sir knight. That was a lucky one for certain."

"What happened?" Jimmy asked.

"I was tying a load of wood to my wagon to deliver the next day. The full moon was shining bright. I happened to look out toward the road. There, in the cut in the forest, I saw it!

The beast walked with a crouching posture as if he would drop and walk on all fours. He was moving toward me!

He had horrible yellow eyes that reflected the moonlight. He was covered in dark fur. He wore pants that hung loosely as if not quite the right size for his legs.

Those yellow eyes watched me, and the monster's clawed hands pointed to me in the night.

I don't know how I resisted wetting myself. I climbed off the wagon and tried to run away. There, next to me, the creature blocked the way. His claws reached for me and....

SMACK!"

Josh had clapped his hands together, hard. It startled the other men to attention.

"And what?" Sean asked.

"That's when the wyvern swooped down out of nowhere!" Josh exclaimed. "What a sight to see! So big it blocked out the moonlight."

The two knights watched Josh in anticipation. Surely he jested! How else could he be alive to tell this tale?

"I thought I was a goner," Josh continued, "but those giant, scaly claws seized the wolf-beast and flew away with it!"

Sean and Jimmy's mouths hung open.

"You should have heard the noise it made when that thing grabbed it. Screamed and howled."

"Are you telling us true?" Jimmy asked.

"Yes," Josh said. "The wyvern might have been bigger than the giant I told you about. Luckily, I haven't seen the beast since it flew away with the werewolf."

"Good Lord!" Sean exclaimed.

Josh grimaced. "I know all about the monster problem hereabouts. I found out the next day that the werewolf was probably my neighbor Adams. He went missing the very same night I saw the werewolf and the wyvern. His wife found his shirt and vest all torn up on the lane by their property."

"Could be," Sean said, "or the werewolf may have got him before it came after you."

"Oh, I'm pretty sure it was him," Josh said."

"Why?" Jimmy asked.

"He got bit by a wolf one night the month before. At least, he said it was a wolf. Now I know better."

"What else did he say?"

"That he clubbed the wolf off him with a digging bar. Then he rode away on his animal."

"Hmm."

"But you've never seen a fairy."

"No. Maybe they exist. I guess they could."

The three men went inside and had stew and bread. Mrs. Josh, whose name was really Jenny, asked the knights about the King and Queen. Sara asked about the princess.

After eating, the men thanked Josh and Jenny. They saluted Sara. Then they said farewell.

But before they could mount up again, Josh approached them with something shiny in his hand. He held it out to them, a silvery metal amulet hanging upon a chain of tiny links.

"It's pretty," Sean said. "What is it?"

"My grandmother believed in the fairy folk," Josh said. "She said that one gave this to her mother when she was younger than my Sara."

He held it out.

"You should take this with you for luck. It might help."

Sean accepted the shining disc, nodding. "Thank you, Josh. Mayhap it will bring us luck." He slipped the chain over his head and tucked the amulet between his tunic and his sash.

"Safe journey!" Josh called after them as they rode further into the woods.

"Do you believe that artifact comes from the fair folk?" Jimmy asked.

"Who can say?" Sean answered. "Time will tell."

"True enough," Jimmy said.

They rode until the sun had dipped quite low. Seeing no signs of civilization, they found a spot where they could tether their mounts and set up a small camp.

They erected a small tent and built a fire ring in a spot not far from the lane. Sean gathered kindling for a fire while Jimmy fed and watered the animals.

Once the fire was going and their supplies from the saddlebags were retrieved they sat on a couple of fallen trees and discussed what they had learned.

"The forest is definitely the source of the monsters," Jimmy said.

"If what Josh told us was true, then there are some new ones here," Sean said.

"So many!" Jimmy said.

"Cullen was right to send us looking into things," Sean said, digging at the tree with a small dagger.

"Right," Jimmy said. "I only hope we make it through and back alive."

"So far, so good," Sean said, smiling.

"You're an optimist, Sir Sean."

"I thought we all were at the court."

Jimmy chuckled. "I guess we mostly are," he said. "Tales of lycanthropes and giant, flying reptiles… they give me a bad feeling."

"I wasn't expecting to hear about either of them," Sean admitted. "Werewolves, though, present quite a danger in regard to their fast-growing numbers."

"Did you bring any silver?" Jimmy asked.

"As a matter of fact…," Sean began. He pulled a chain out from under his tunic. A silver crucifix dropped over his chest, settling against the amulet.

Jimmy smiled. "That'll do it," he said.

"And you?" Sean asked.

"Well, mine is gold," Jimmy said ruefully, tugging out his own chain and cross. "But I have this."

He drew out a silver locket from inside his vest. "Caroline's token," he said. "It always brings me luck."

After a time, they began to roast a couple of forest critters they had caught, killed, and skinned. That, along with a horn of ale, would be their evening meal.

The forest was dark, but the fire cheered the two knights. It could have been a simple campout.

During supper, Sean's horse Fitty made a noise.

The hair on the back of Jimmy's neck stood on end.

CRACK

"Halt! Who goes there!" exclaimed Jimmy, rising from his seat.

The snapping branch had both men standing with swords prepared to be drawn in seconds flat.

"We come only to barter," a voice said. It was high-pitched but masculine.

"So, you say," Sean said. "Who are you?"

The light from the fire only illuminated the woods about ten feet in every direction.

"Merely denizens of the forest," the voice replied.

Two short figures—shorter than the men anyway—emerged from the shadows. They had ashen faces, pointed teeth, and pointed ears.

"Goblins!" Jimmy exclaimed.

"Again, sir knight," the first goblin said, "we mean you no harm."

"Let us see your hands!" Jimmy commanded.

Both creatures held out their hands, palms up.

"Any weapons?" Sean asked.

"Yes," the second goblin said. "I have a knife concealed in my boot."

"How about you?" Sean asked the first one.

The one who had spoken first carried a large sack that appeared to be stuffed almost full. He lowered it to the ground, a tether stretched from the tying cord to his cloth belt.

"My wares," he said. "As for weapons, I have my wits and cunning."

"And if wits and cunning aren't enough?" Jimmy asked.

"There are rocks," the goblin answered.

"Hmm. True enough," Sean said. He reached out a hand to the goblin.

The goblin hesitated.

"Shake?" Sean suggested.

The creature took his hand and shook it awkwardly.

72

Jimmy shook with the other one.

They sat down around the fire.

"We didn't expect to encounter you here, good knights. Most of your kingdom and those who visit take the southerly road through the rocks."

"Yes, that's true," Jimmy said, "they take the good road."

The road he spoke of began at Corbeck and ran west into the inland. It took a much more southerly course through boulder-laden lands. The view was substantially free of trees, the road solid and unbroken.

"The king gave us leave to explore the forest," Sean said. "We plan to see how far we can get to the West Marches before the next full moon."

The goblins exchanged glances, and the one with the sack said, "Next full moon, eh? Just you two...."

"That's correct," Jimmy said.

"You're brave men," the other goblin said.

"We try," Sean said.

"Of course," said the other goblin.

Introductions were belatedly made. The sack-lugging goblin was Grahk. His companion was Eert. The two seemed calm, cool, and collected—not at all the way you often heard goblins described.

"I'd really like to trade with you," Grahk said, "or, at least show you my wares. First, though...."

He paused.

"What's the matter?" Sean asked.

"Be warned!" Eert interrupted, displaying the first sign of aggressive behavior.

"Tell us!" Jimmy insisted. "Warned of what!"

"Darkness spreads throughout this forest," Grahk said.

"Werewolves," Jimmy said.

"Werewolves; and yet so much more than their accursed lot."

Eert took up the tale. "There is a unifying voice behind the dark things that dwell within the forest, a single person."

"Who is this person?" Sean asked.

"She of the raven," Eert said. "She who crosses the sea."

"Forgive my ignorance," Jimmy said, "but does she have a name?"

"We do not know it," Grahk said. "She has befriended our king and the leaders of others. The hobs, the trolls, the gnomes, even some gryphons

73

agreed to wage war on the kingdoms of the isle at her behest. But she has given us no name, merely the sign of the raven and the picture of the sea."

"Hmmph," Sean said.

"We thought you might want to know this," Eert said.

"Oh, yes," Sean said. "Thanks for the warning."

"Why would you warn us?" Jimmy asked. "Aren't you breaking the commitment you have with this Raven lady?"

"Yes. No. How would you say, 'someplace in between'?" Grahk said, cheerfully.

"How's that?" Sean asked.

"Our king made this agreement with the Lady of the Raven to be part of her army, not us."

"When will she wage her war?"

"When she's ready to wipe out her enemies, of course—"

Eert raised clawed fingers, silencing his peer. "Many of our brethren don't agree with this. We don't agree with it."

"Why not?" Sean asked. "Our peoples have had differences in the past."

"They have," Grahk said, smiling. "We don't all hate humans though. Eert and I are just two who seek humans out to trade with."

The knights relaxed a bit. This was comforting news. Both had suspected a trap.

"So, no ambush then?" Sean asked.

"No!" Grahk exclaimed.

He turned his bag upside down, dumping its contents on the ground in front of him.

Sean and Jimmy beheld a plethora of tools, implements, jewelry, food stuff, and bones.

"Remember," Eert said, "the Lady of the Raven has designs on your lands, all of you humans."

"We won't forget, I assure you," Jimmy said. "Thanks for the warning."

"You're welcome," Grahk said. "What catches your eyes?"

"Hmm," Sean responded, looking amidst the jumble. "That braided lanyard looks useful. What would you want for that?"

"Wise choice," Grahk gushed. "High quality piece, braided by my other half. Well, sir knight, have you a tinder box to spare?"

"Tinder box," Sean said. "Yes, I do."

He pulled the small box from his boot and tossed it to the goblin.

"Look it over, see if it meets your approval."

Grahk snatched the little box from his lap and popped it open. He nodded and smiled at the contents.

"Yes, yes," he said. "This should be very useful."

"What about you, Sean?" Jimmy asked.

"I'll just have to depend on you, Jimmy."

"So be it," Jimmy said. "Looks like you made a decent trade there."

"Yes," Sean said. He reached down to retrieve the lanyard. "Thank you, Grahk."

Grahk made an odd trio of quick nods, reminding the knights that these were not human beings they were dealing with.

"I have to say," Sean said, "that you fellows are the most agreeable goblins I've ever met."

Eert laughed, at least it sounded like a laugh crossed with a giggle. "And how many goblins have you met?"

"Not many," Sean said.

"It's true that we are very different," Eert said. "Most often our peoples come to blows and worse."

"Yes," Jimmy agreed, "but it need not be that way."

"Not at all," Grahk said. "We could try harder... to get along."

"We should," Sean agreed. "It would keep the fighting from getting the better of us."

"Here, here!" Eert said.

"Enough worrying," Grahk said. "See anything else you want to trade for?"

Sean and Jimmy scrutinized the array of goods. Jimmy traded his pocket knife for a seven inch long hammer made of rock.

Sean examined a few of the truly obscure objects, a gryphon feather here; a dragon's scale there.

"Quite the collection, Grahk," he said.

"Yes," Grahk said, proudly.

"How'd you get some of these?" Sean asked.

"Trade, mostly. Some I found."

"What's this for?" Sean asked. He picked up a stick that was gnarly and cold to the touch.

"The stick? You know, I'm not certain. But it's important, more than any of the other tools or tokens."

"How do you know?" Jimmy asked. "I mean, if you don't even know what it's for?"

"I just do. I won it in a game of chance."

"So, you don't really know."

Grahk looked irritated. He made some choppy, nodding motions and frowned.

"Do you feel the coldness?" he asked.

"What?" Jimmy asked. "Should I add more wood to the fire?"

"No," Grahk said, taking Jimmy's hand to stop him. "I'm referring to the stick."

Sean held the stick in his hands. "It feels cold, but I really can't tell why."

Grahk nodded. "It feels cold to me as well. Pass it to your friend."

Sean handed the stick to Jimmy. "Yes," Jimmy said, "it feels cold. So what?"

"Most people would agree with us, goblin and human alike," Grahk said.

"Most?" Jimmy asked.

"The gnome who lost to me in a game of pick'l d'lesper swore to me that this stick was greater than any of the items you see here. To a select few, it should feel warm—even hot—to the touch."

"Grahk accepted it as payment from the gnome," Eert said. "No gems, no precious metals."

"He was surprisingly lacking in such things," Grahk said. "But this gnarled twig is imbued with great magics."

"Magic?" Sean said. "You're joking."

"It was used by a great sorceress! And it can be used again by the right person! It retains remnants of its master's magic."

"What do you want for it?" Sean asked.

"Hmm," Grahk mused. "One of a kind item. Powerful. How to put a price on that?"

"Name it," Sean said.

"Your boots?"

"I can't give you my boots," Sean said. "I'm going to need those!"

"Yes, yes," Grahk nodded. He snapped his fingers, the claws making an

76

odd sound.

"Have you a spare cloak?" Grahk asked.

"No, and again, my cloak is something I'll need. I can't part with it."

"Worth a try, eh? It gets chilly at night. Hmm. What's that chain around your neck?"

"You mean this?" Sean asked, pulling the crucifix from beneath his tunic. "My cross. It's pure silver."

"Not exactly my thing," Grahk commented.

"Then how about this?" Sean asked.

He pulled the fine chain and amulet so that it fell out of his tunic. Curious, he pulled the chain over his head.

"Want to see?"

Grahk caught the amulet and inspected it. He held it close to his face, scrutinizing it.

"Silver," he said. "A higher quality silver I doubt you'll ever see again. Where did you get this?"

"A woodcutter gave it to me," Sean said.

"Odd," Grahk said. "I would swear it was fey made."

"Really?"

"Yes, the luminous quality of the silver is a clue. Such luster! The dead giveaway is the inscription though."

"I didn't notice any inscription," Sean said.

"The lettering is so tiny that it probably looked like marring to you."

"Oh."

"Let's see if I can read it," Grahk said. He held the amulet close to his face.

"Life circles… life cycles… beginnings, endings."

"How were you able to read that!" Jimmy exclaimed.

"I've known a few fairies," Grahk replied. "This would be an acceptable trade for the stick."

Sean thought about the two items. The amulet seemed like a lucky item to possess, especially since they sought fairies. But there was something about the goblin's tale of the stick that rang true. The stick could be more important than a good luck charm. Yet, it was cold to his touch, so was it important?"

"Done!" Sean said.

"Very good," Grahk said, smiling. Perhaps you will encounter another human who will feel warmth from the stick."

"Perhaps," Sean repeated. "I'll hope for it. Seeing the wand, if that's what this is, helping to unlock magic…. That would be a thing to see."

*   *   *

Mr. Court lowered the book. The children contemplated the part of the story they'd just heard. Werewolves, an enormous wyvern, friendly goblins (how weird that was!), a magic wand, and a warning about a mysterious woman…. These things all seemed fantastic, not at all like things they encountered in their day-to-day lives. And all they had to do to experience these things began with the turn of a page.

Mr. Court put the book down on his desk and discussed the knights' journey with the class.

Chapter Eleven

Moeera sauntered up to the men who were setting up the rain fly between the trailer's side and the space between it and the next trailer. She checked to make sure that Soot was with her and reached down to reassuringly pet his back.

It was Paul, two men she didn't remember, and the Wondrous Wecks himself.

"Tony, do you have the eye over your upright?" Paul asked.

"Yes," the tall, dark man wearing the purple slouch hat said.

"How 'bout you, Dave?" he asked.

"It's on there, Mr. Plum," Dave replied. The bearded man held the wooden post toward the top, his other hand holding the canvas.

"I'm hooking my end of the awning on the roof here, Paul," Wecks said.

"Very good," Paul said, pulling his end to make the canvas taut.

"Got it," Wecks said. "It's on there."

"Alright, I'm hooking mine now," Paul said, straining to keep it taut. He stepped onto a boulder to get closer.

Paul hooked one of several eyeholes which had been reinforced at the canvas edge.

"Any time you fellas are ready to get the tie-out lines tight is good with me," Dave said.

"Yes, sir," Wecks said. He went over to Dave, grasping a rope that was already secured to his upright and pulling it outward at a forty-five-degree angle.

Paul did the same with Tony's line. Then they tied the ropes to stakes and hammered them into the ground.

The ropes pulled tight when taut line hitches were adjusted.

Dave and Tony dropped their arms. Dave huffed quietly and rubbed his aching arms.

The poles were up, and the awning was taut. Wecks and Paul staked out two more tie-out lines to prevent the poles from going down sideways.

"We have an audience," Wecks said, straightening up.

He looked at Moeera standing there with the red-eyed bunny.

"Can I help you, Miss?" he asked.

"I'm glad you've come back, finally," she said.

"Moeera!" Wecks exclaimed. "You're much taller than I remember. Who's your friend?"

Soot scampered about, sniffing the ground cover with his twitchy nose. He checked every nook, cranny, and corner that he found. He would inspect some grass and then back up as if committing that specific clump to memory.

"This is Soot," she said. "He's my friend from the field behind my house. Mama says he's a puca."

"She might be right at that," Wecks said. "He's black as the night with those red eyes."

"He seems like any other bunny," Moeera said, "except he likes me and isn't scared of people."

"I think most everyone likes you, dear," Wecks said. "What have you been doing with yourself?"

"Helping with the animals at home, going to school, chores, and wondering about you."

"Well, wonder no more," Wecks said. "We've traveled near and far, but now we're in Bucktry again. We have quite a show in store for you."

"I missed you," Moeera told him. "Nothing exciting happens around here."

"I'm sure you're exaggerating."

"I've waited for you. I want to help out, and I need you to teach me magic."

Dave looked over from a trunk he was searching through.

"You've got a serious volunteer there, Wecks," Dave said.

"Is that right?"

Moeera nodded.

"I did what you told me," she said. "I was good. I helped with the work

80

and my chores. No complaining. Ever."

"Not ever?"

"No, of course not."

Wecks looked straight into Moeera's serious eyes. He paused a moment. She stood before him, and her countenance was as unwavering as stone.

"I'm very impressed, Moeera," Wecks said. "I'll tell you what: if your parents are accepting of it, then you're welcome to help us out while we prepare for the show."

Moeera's eyes lit up with joy.

Wecks raised his hand. "Now, now," he said. "This is a trial offer only, if you do well and like it, then we'll keep it going."

"Thank you, Wecks! Thank you!" she exclaimed, dancing a little jig.

"You're welcome," Wecks said. "I believe introductions are in order. You've met Mr. Paul Plum. He's our manager and keeps track of our earnings. You could say he's the brains behind it all."

"Hi, Mr. Plum," Moeera said.

"Hello, Moeera. 'Paul' will be fine."

"Yessir," she said.

The two other men stepped up.

"This tall, strapping man is Tony. And this man with the beard is Dave. They handle all our construction work. If we need a new set piece or prop, they make it happen."

"We're always building something," Dave said. "You'll see, if you come around before the shows."

"Pleased to meet you, Moeera," Tony said, proffering his hand.

Moeera shook it.

Soot, for his part, continued searching around the trailer. He sniffed here, he sniffed there.

"All right," Wecks said. "You discuss it with your mother and father. We'll see you soon."

"I will," Moeera said. "Come on, Soot! We gotta get home."

"Bye, Moeera," Dave said.

"Bye!" she exclaimed.

*   *   *

The rest of the walk home was a quick scurry. Moeera was out of breath when they got there.

81

Mallory watched her daughter and Soot catch their breath in the front yard.

Now what was that girl up to?

She continued hanging wash on the wash line and clipping it with long, wooden pins.

"How was your day?" she asked, as the two meandered her way.

"Good, Mama! The best!" Moeera said, energetically.

"How's Mr. Court? Did he read your story yet?"

"He's fine. I don't know if he read mine yet. Gotta get my chores started."

The girl began huffing away with the puca in tow.

"One second, please," her mother said.

"Yes?" Moeera asked, stopping in her tracks.

"You're going to take care of the animals first?"

"Yes."

"Give Dot a carrot and an apple."

"Yes, Mama."

"And make sure you talk to her."

"I will."

"Gather all the eggs."

"Mm-hmm."

"After the animals, gather wood for the stove. I ran out of time, and I think it will be cold tonight."

"You got it, Mama."

"One more thing."

Mallory looked at Moeera intently. Moeera knew that look meant something important.

Mallory clipped up a shirt and paused.

"Your father's home early today, Mee. He got sick at work."

"Oh," Moeera said. "Poor Papa."

"He's resting in bed. Keep quiet when you go in."

"Sure, Mama."

Moeera raced off with Soot hot on her heels.

The house was quiet.

Papa is sleeping, she thought.

In no time, she was out of her school clothes and in some chore clothes.

82

"Alright, Soot," she said to her pal. "Let's go back out."

Soon she was having a one-sided conversation with Dot who munched the carrot hungrily. When done with that she inhaled the apple.

Crunch, crunch, crunch, crunch!

"Yes, you like that," Moeera said. "You sure are hungry, Dot!" She petted the bachukka with her hands making long strokes down the animal's back.

When the other animals were done, Moeera poured some bachukka feed into Soot's shed bowl. He seemed to enjoy it.

Next, Moeera found the wheelbarrow and wheeled it to the corner of the property with a stand of trees. There were hundreds of branches in the dead leaves. She picked them up, one by one, and loaded them into the wheelbarrow. Some were heavy. Other branches were too big to load up without being chopped up. Many branches were of the size of kindling. Whatever she could fit went in the barrow.

After she wheeled the load of wood to the covered rack on the front porch, she transferred each piece to the rack. Then she returned to the trees to gather more. After the second load was stowed, she and Soot went inside.

The delicious smell of shepherd's pie filled the kitchen. Before long, Moeera and her mother sat down at the table.

"We'll let Papa get up when he's ready," Mallory said. "Lead the prayer, Mee."

Moeera folded her hands and closed her eyes. "Blessings be with Mama and me and Soot, and especially with Papa. Help him to get well again."

"Thank you, Moeera," her mother said.

"Yes'm."

Mallory served the shepherd's pie from the large serving bowl. When they both had some on their plates, she looked at Moeera.

"Tell me about your day," she said. "Did you talk to Wecks?"

Moeera nodded. "Yes, I did."

"How was it?"

"Oh, good."

"Just good? You've been waiting to talk to him for... how long?"

"Three years, Mama."

Chapter Twelve

Once again, Soot followed Kor into the dark woods in the third hour after midnight. Once again he was filled with trepidation, and so he hid himself well from the sight of both Kor and the blood witch.

He saw the pale witch greet the blacksmith, flirting with the man. Soot saw that Kor appeared surprised to be there, at first. Then the witch laughed and made a flicking at him with her fingers. Kor's demeanor changed to that of familiarity. Soot sprawled in the dirt beneath a laurel bush, stretching his long ears forward for all he was worth. He'd seen this same episode before—now he wanted to hear every detail. And word spoken between the two may reveal a weakness the vile witch had. He wanted that knowledge.

The small creature watched intently as the blood witch toyed with her plaything. She alternately used her mind power to frighten Kor, anger him, and even make love with him.

After the lovemaking, and the feeding, was over Izzy sat on the dry weeds holding Kor in her arms. She was about to release his mind one last time before hypnotizing him and sending him back home, but she tarried there. She stroked his back with her fingertips and blew on his neck. Goose pimples formed on his skin.

She held him close wondering what life would be like if this man was truly hers. A love, a partner, somebody to be there for her... to complement her.

Oh, but that was absurd! She wanted no man to hold ownership over her. She was an entity complete unto herself. Weaklings like the Mojo (apparently) took consorts and lovers and ran off to blend in and lead normal lives.

She relaxed her mental chain on Kor's mind, then with a blink of her eyes she relinquished her hold completely.

"Still alive," he choked out. He was groggy and exhausted.

"For now," Izzy said. "You'll see another day to play house with your wife and daughter."

"Do what you will with me but leave my family in peace."

"Darling, peace is a word that can have a variety of meanings."

Her words stung him. He was trapped and Mallory and Moeera along with him.

"Leave them alone, I beg of you."

She studied his face intently. The worry clung there, dirtying this visage which she now had to admit had an attractiveness to it.

Izzy sighed.

"Don't hurt them," he pleaded. "My loves. My sweet Mallory and our little—"

"Yes, the brat," Izzy interrupted. "What's her name...?"

"Moeera."

"Moeera, hmm," she repeated thoughtfully. "Means 'far-seeing', doesn't it?"

"Visionary."

"Hmmph. Well, Kor, I'm lacking something important. Do you know what that is?"

"No."

"Someone to do my bidding, but not like you. Someone who will do what I tell them of their own free will."

"Oh," he said.

"Since you murdered my apprentice," she said crossly. "Witches don't grow on trees, you know."

"Thank God!" Kor muttered.

"Why, whatever is eating you, dear; besides me, of course."

Kor was silent. He was exhausted, and he felt powerless. He felt that way just about all the time now.

"This wasn't supposed to happen," he said.

"What?"

"This," he said. "We live just like everyone else. Mallory doesn't even use a spell when the crops are dry. You weren't supposed to...."

"Find you? Prey on you? Hunting down my enemies is my specialty. In all fairness, blame this on fate."

"Fate?"

"I had no idea Mojo was here. I thought she found a lost stronghold somewhere, and they were pooling their talents to hide."

"Why did you come to Bucktry?"

"Why anything? I came for the blood! I haven't seen another true blood witch in years. I worked my way across the countryside sucking the necks of the plentiful country bumpkins."

"You're awful," Kor accused.

"I'm a realist, you fool. Eventually, I'll either find more of my brethren, or I'll find those I deem worthy to share in my exceptional gifts."

"Mallory will beat you."

"She's so out of touch with her abilities that she'll never see me coming."

Kor was at a loss for words. When he met Mallory she was finished with her witchcraft. The world had moved on, leaving a lot of magic users dead and gone. She walked away from her birthright, swearing off magic and witchcraft completely.

"Yet...," Izzy mused, "her daughter would no doubt be as formidable a witch as her mother, with the proper guidance of course."

"What do you think?" she asked. "Could the visionary find me a new apprentice?"

"You leave my Moeera alone!" Kor choked.

Izzy snapped her fingers in front of his face, and Kor fell into a trance. He got up and dressed. Then he set off for his house.

Soot watched from his vantage point in rapt consternation. Not only was the blood witch bad news for everyone, especially Kor and Mallory, now she had her sights set on Moeera.

Izzpalin wanted to train Moeera in the ways of evil. If his friend learned magic from the blood witch, then Soot had no doubt that she would be corrupted by power.

Soot was one puca who wasn't about to let that happen. He waited until Izzy departed on another trail. Then he scampered home as quickly as he could.

Chapter Thirteen

When Moeera arrived at the fairgrounds Wecks was helping Dave paint a tall cabinet a bright shade of red. Soot inspected the bucket of paint quizzically, and then retreated to the tall grass to munch.

Wecks asked Moeera if she'd like to see the list of tricks in the act. Would she ever! He wiped his hands on a rag hanging from his overalls pocket.

"Come inside the trailer, and I'll show you the list," Wecks said.

"Sure," Moeera said.

The trailer was an enigma to the girl. How could there be so much space inside?

Wecks noticed her mouth hanging slightly open.

"We spend a major portion of the year traveling from town to town," he said. "All this is the result of Dave's careful planning."

She walked into the miniature house. A tiny kitchen made up the very end past the side door. Before and to her left a living room made up an ample section with enough room to seat eight people. A large table, about two feet by six, dominated the space between two couches. To her far left, the trailer's rear end was a wall of closets and shelves.

The whole place was neat and clean.

"What will the act be like?" Moeera asked.

"That's what I want to discuss with you," Wecks said. "I'd like to perform some spectacular tricks that I don't often do."

"Wonderful!" Moeera exclaimed.

"Having you as my assistant will make it possible. Would you be willing to perform in the show?"

"You mean go on stage and do magic?"

"Absolutely."

"Oh, yes! Yes! I want that more than anything in the world."

"Good. Here's the list."

Wecks pulled the sheet of paper from a pigeonhole in a neat, little desk. Moeera took it, holding her breath.

"If you're willing to participate in the actual show, then we'll be able to step up the variety of illusions from the last time I was here."

"Basket trick," Moeera read.

"That'll really get the audience's attention," Wecks said. "We put you into a big basket. I stick swords through the weaving and out the other side. We'll probably have you scream to really get people's hair on end."

"I should say I'll be screaming, if you run swords through me!" Moeera cried.

"That's why we practice ahead of time, so you don't get hurt," Wecks said.

"If you say so," she said, doubtfully.

"Ah huh," he said, looking at Moeera carefully. "There's something I need to speak to you about before we do any more stuff. Do you understand the difference between real magic and the kind of magic I do?"

"Difference? What difference? You're a wizard! You do magic. Real magic!"

Moeera's eyes were wide and fearful with the feeling that Wecks had gone crazy.

Wecks closed his eyes and shook his head. "No, Moeera, I'm not a true wizard. I perform stage magic.

Moeera didn't know what that was. A memory flashed in her mind from out of years past. In it, her father was commenting about magic "done with smoke and mirrors". That was what he'd said though she'd been distracted and barely listening.

Wecks offered Moeera a chair. She sat down, dreading whatever he had to tell her. He pulled a chair opposite her and straddled it backward.

"Moeera, dear, the last thing I want to do is upset you," he said. "You're my biggest fan!"

He searched within, trying to choose the exact words to explain.

"I know that you want to learn magic," he continued. "If you're to help me with my show, then I need to be up front with you. The magic that

I perform—with no small help from my friends—is done by sleight of hand and distraction. I get my audience focused on one thing that diverts their attention. Then I make things happen where they're not looking."

"Trickery? Your magic is just trickery?" Her face fell.

"Essentially, I suppose you could say that. It's more than trickery to me, Moeera. There's an art to it."

"What about the fairy you told me about, the one who turned the man's nose purple? Just a story."

"No!" Wecks said. "That really happened. I wouldn't lie to you, Moeera."

"You really met a fairy?"

"Oh, yes. I mean, I believed her. She turned Mr. Flanders' nose purple for a day for suggesting her shopping requests were for witchcraft."

Several tears ran down Moeera's face. She giggled.

"You said she taught you a magic trick...."

"I embellished that a little bit," he said. "Every act that I perform, I repeat something that she told me about magic and how it's related to life. I may have changed it a bit here and there, I met her years and years ago."

"Mmm."

"She gave me a keepsake to remember her by," Wecks said.

"What?"

"A magic wand," Wecks said. "Silly thing—it's just a gnarled, old stick. I've never seen it do anything out of the ordinary, and I have tried, believe you me."

"Just like the wand that Sean got from the goblin," Moeera said. She marveled at the similarity to the story.

"What?"

"Sean of Corbeck traded an amulet for a gnarled stick like that in a story from school."

"You see," Wecks said, "the fairy was right. Everything is connected."

"I want to learn magic," Moeera stated.

"I know," Wecks said. "You shouldn't give up hoping either. Maybe someone will teach you someday."

She was quiet. Her gaze drifted to the floor.

"I can still teach you how to amaze an audience. It's just a bit unorthodox. Would you like that?"

Moeera's lips sagged into a frown.

"If you don't want to, I'll understand. I hope you understand the service we provide though."

"What service," Moeera said, dully.

"We offer ordinary people, living ordinary lives, the opportunity to believe in something larger than their everyday world."

She frowned.

"Oh, it's true," he said. "Part of it is escapism. What they see thrills them. It makes them believe more is possible… like it did for you."

Her mind opened a bit at his referral to her.

"You saw the show, even an incomplete show, and now your dream is to wield magic."

"Yes." She nodded.

"Magic is real, Moeera. It's as real as you or I."

She relaxed.

"As far as anybody knows, I'm a powerful wizard with magic coursing through my veins. And I'm going to give the town of Bucktry one hell of a show so that they keep believing that. Every miracle I perform is an illusion."

"Good," she said. "I just don't know what to do now. I wanted you to take me away with you and teach me to cast spells. You're the only one I knew who could do that."

"If it's meant to be, it will be."

"I hope so."

"So…, are you in or out?"

"As long as you don't run a sword through me, I'm in," Moeera said.

"Wonderful!" Wecks said. He stood up. "I'll fetch the basket from the cupboard and show you exactly how to situate yourself in it to avoid death."

Her eyes popped, but she smiled. "Oh, goody."

"And Moeera."

"Yes?"

"Thank you for understanding."

*   *   *

Moeera and Soot barely made it home in time for supper that night. Mallory let the rabbit in to eat some vegetable peels and carrots near the table where they ate.

"I know I don't let you eat in the house often, but you're a nice friend to Moeera, aren't you?" Mallory commented.

Soot munched contentedly. Mallory was certain she saw him bob his head in agreement.

"Soot's a good bunny, Mama," Moeera said. "He deserves to eat with us."

"Yes, well, tonight he does," Mallory said.

More and more, Mallory had the feeling that Soot followed Moeera everywhere to keep an eye on her. Or was it just the animal's desire for companionship?

She still believed him to be a puca. Though she'd never found any evidence of him transforming into a creature with hands. Puca were known to help out in various ways. The rule to follow was not to let on or thank a puca for its helpful deeds.

She stressed to Moeera to be polite and kind to Soot. It was a slippery slope: don't offend a puca, but at the same time don't thank it or give it gifts. Soot wasn't doing chores, and so none of them ever thanked him, yet they fed him and provided shelter and companionship for him. Either Soot was merely a rabbit, or he was an odd sort of puca.

That feeling of him watching Moeera persisted. It was almost like he was guarding her from something. But what in the world would she need his protection from?

"You know," Kor said, "I feel much better today."

"That's good, dear," Mallory said, giving his hand a squeeze.

"That's great, Papa," Moeera said. She ate her supper with gusto. Stage magic training was hard work!

"Yes," Kor said, "I really do feel better. My strength is back again. I can get my lazy self back to the forge tomorrow."

"You shouldn't rush it," Mallory said.

"I know," he said. "I just feel inadequate when I can't get my work done."

"It'll be fine," Mallory said. "You need to take care of yourself."

"What did you do today, Moeera?" Kor asked.

"A lot!" she said. "Mr. Court read us more about Corbeck today. Two knights named Jimmy and Sean went into the forest to search for fairies."

"Did they find any?" Mallory asked.

"No, but Mr. Court stopped reading while they were still looking."

"You'll have to tell us what happens," Mallory said.

"I will," Moeera said.

"How was practice for the magic show?" Kor asked.

"Good," Moeera said. "We're going to be doing some spectacular tricks!"

"We, huh?"

"Yes! I'm Wecks' assistant in the show."

Mallory's eyebrows lifted. "Well! Congratulations!"

"Thanks, Mama," Moeera said. Her cheeks reddened.

"I can't wait to see the show," Mallory said.

"Me too," Kor agreed. "I'm glad you're enjoying yourself."

"Wecks is a great wizard, Papa. He's going to show me how to perform magic that will have Bucktry reeling."

*   *   *

Alone in her wreck of a house, Izzy stared at the girl she saw inside her orb. She had just observed the exchange at the supper table.

She's kind of pathetic. A hopeful, young girl, filled with positive thoughts and happiness. We'll soon change that!

At least she desires magic. That means I was right. She'll be a suitable replacement for Joria.

Izzy gnashed her teeth at the memory of her fallen protege.

The Mojo picked an adequate man to run away with. He's strong of body and spirit. Too bad for her that his spirit belongs to me now.

So… this daughter, this… Moeera. She should have the strength and the prowess of the Mojo, if trained properly. And more.

Izzy suspected that the child just might have the right parents to be a magical powerhouse. It was possible. The Mojo came from a long and storied line of forebears. Troublesome family line!

No more! She would punish the parents and take the child. The young one would bend to her will once she began offering her lessons in true magic. Her own mother had denied her the birthright that was rightfully hers.

The thought that such a potentially gifted girl should be performing parlor tricks among charlatans disgusted Izzy. What was the world coming to!

She would act decisively to prevent her world from eroding any more.

Chapter Fourteen

The next day Mallory drove Dotty and the wagon to the fairground. It was a beautiful fall afternoon, the sort that reveals summer's last embrace on the land. Bright sunshine made everything look beauteous and cheerful.

It was Thursday. The fair unofficially began that day. The magic show was scheduled for Saturday after the supper crowd ate their fill.

Tents of every color dotted the field. Buggies and wagons and carriages of all sorts accompanied the trailers. And there was more. Pavilions outnumbered the tents. Tailors displayed their latest dresses, shirts, and pants. Cobblers had shoe racks filled with the results of their labors. Metalsmiths and jewelers had come from hither and yon to sell their wares.

Mallory smiled. She liked the fair very much. Some years were better than others, but they were all pretty good.

Being out amongst the combined citizenry of the surrounding countryside made her feel that she belonged. She didn't stand out, other than being pretty enough to turn a few heads. She blended in with the people here.

Growing up, she spent most of her time around the mages and witches. Her parents had wielded magic; they'd been among the powerful movers and shakers. Perhaps not the strongest, or even the leaders, but they'd both been well known. Naturally, she'd learned from them a wide array of spells, charms, and the rest of the magic arts.

She became famous too. The Mojo was witch-child and hellion. Her name brought fear to evil witch and sorcerer alike. She did the Sea Council's bidding for years. She never lost a duel, and she never left a mission unfinished.

As she grew older, she wondered what it would be like to fit in among the common folk. She couldn't go anywhere without someone recognizing her. When that happened the people always felt suspicious toward her.

Then she met Kor by a complete happenstance, and she fell in love. When that happened, her entire worldview changed. It was only right that she should settle down and find a place of her own in society which didn't require her to constantly risk her life to protect it. She'd done that for years.

Mallory accompanied Kor back home to Bucktry with nary a backward glance. They married, worked, and had Moeera. And nobody ever recognized her again. The forces of darkness cared not for out of the way, little Bucktry.

She doubted that the Sea Council ever missed her at all. They probably had plenty of young witches and wizards to stem the tide of darkness.

Moeera wanting so badly to be a magic-wielder was something she hadn't counted on. How could she ever expect it? None of the children hereabouts knew about magic other than the tales they heard from storytellers.

Her instinct was to shelter her daughter away from it. Witchcraft led to a dangerous life. But she remembered learning from her mother. They had truly bonded as mother and daughter, master and pupil.

So, was she truly looking out for her daughter's best interests? The question vexed her.

She relegated the doubt she had to the simple fact that someone had to raise Moeera. She had been raised by magic-wielders. But neither Kor nor she wielded magic—not anymore. That made her course of action very simple indeed.

Mallory found Wecks's trailer and parked Dot and the wagon nearby. She found Dave and Tony assembling a contraption that resembled a drying rack for black walnuts.

"They're inside practicing, ma'am," Dave said. "Go right in."

"Thank you," Mallory said.

She climbed the steps and knocked on the door.

Wecks opened it. "Yes? Can I help you?"

"Mama!" Moeera exclaimed. "We're practicing the basket trick!"

"Mrs. Robin!" Wecks said. "It's very nice to meet you."

His smile was disarming. She had to give him that. He was tall, dark, and knew how to engage an audience. The man was the size of a bear, but

Mallory expected she had more magical prowess in her little finger. Yet here he was entertaining her daughter and teaching her his trade to boot.

"Likewise," she said, beaming. "Moeera talks about you and the show constantly."

"Not too much, I hope," Wecks said, winking. "There are trade secrets to guard."

"She tells her father and I how much she likes being your assistant," Mallory said. "Moeera, how about we take a break," Wecks said.

"Sure," Moeera said. "But not too long; the show is almost here."

"That's right. If you want to practice while I talk with your mother, then work with the handkerchiefs."

"Yes," the girl said.

"Now Mrs. Robin, was there anything in particular you wished to discuss?"

Mallory shrugged her shoulders.

"Oh, sit down, sit down," Wecks said, motioning to the chairs.

"Thank you," Mallory said. "I wanted to meet you, sir. And I wanted to thank you for indulging Moeera in her love of magic."

"You're very welcome. You have an incredible daughter. I'm sure you know that already."

"She's a pip," Mallory said.

"She certainly is," Wecks said. "I have to tell you I half expected her to run out of here and never speak to me again when I revealed to her that my magic is built on tricks and illusions."

"I get your thinking on that," Mallory said. "Ever since she saw you perform she's wanted to learn magic."

Wecks nodded. "Yes, but not stage magic."

"She never knew there was such a thing. She saw a truly wondrous wizard make a man disappear and reappear somewhere else. And bring life to ordinary handkerchiefs, and swoop from a rooftop to land safely on the ground. And escape a watery death."

"The vat!" Wecks exclaimed. "That one gets them every time! They go crazy about it."

"They certainly should," Mallory said, "if it's as dangerous as it looks."

"You got me," the magician said. "Of all my tricks, that one leaves the least margin for error. If I'm not in the right mindset to do it, then I could drown."

"It raises the stakes higher to the audience though, doesn't it?" Mallory asked. "It's real and they sense that the danger is great. Less trick than escape."

"You're very intuitive," Wecks said. "Now I see where Moeera gets it."

"Indeed," Mallory said. "Well, I'm really just a housewife, a farmer, and a mother."

"Do you have any concerns?" Wecks asked.

"No," Mallory said. "I don't. As long as none of Moeera's involvement requires her to bellyflop into a vat of water while restrained."

"Absolutely not," Wecks said. "No escape tricks for assistants. Those are all on me."

"I look forward to seeing the show then."

"I'll save you and your husband a spot in the front."

"Thank you," she said, standing up. "I should let you get your practice time in."

*   *   *

Mallory decided to sightsee a bit while Moeera finished rehearsing. She left the wagon and Dot where they were and walked between the wagons and carriages to the row of pavilions.

She hadn't gone far when she realized that someone was following her. A dark shape rubbed up against her ankle.

"Soot! How are you?"

The rabbit nuzzled her ankle. Then he sat up on his haunches.

Despite her wariness that a puca has a temper, she reached down and stroked his head and ears.

Whatever you do just never thank him!

"You're waiting for Moeera, correct? Me too. I'm going to see if I can find any goodies to buy."

The red-eyed creature bobbed his head.

It's uncanny for sure. Mallory tried to hide her surprise but didn't quite make it.

"Come along with me, Soot, if you like. We'll be back to Moeera soon."

The rabbit answered by hopping a few yards ahead of her.

"Lead on, Soot."

They strolled by a hatter's pavilion, a hawking tent (for his part, the sight of a red-tailed hawk perched on its master's gloved hand didn't faze Soot one bit), and a violinist. The latter sat atop a high stool playing an emotional solo. The music cut the air with its high-pitched tone. The hawk stared raptly at the gray-haired violinist, whether in like or dislike wasn't apparent.

When they were past the hawking tent, Mallory took the lead.

"This way, Soot," she said. "Let's see the baker's tent for something to eat."

They followed their noses down the cobblestone pathway until the food tents were visible.

"There we go," Mallory said.

They were almost to the first food stand when a disturbing voice to the left said, "Your fortune, Miss, for a bagus. In the Mojo's case however, I'd hardly call it a fortune."

Mallory stopped in her tracks. She stood with Soot close to her feet. Then she slowly turned her head to look at the thin, emaciated woman wearing the jeweled baldcap, just inside the flap of the drab tent.

"If you're talking to me, then you've made an error," Mallory told her. "I'm neither called the Mojo, nor am I interested in a preview of future happenings."

"Fine," crackled the woman. Her voice sounded forced as if her throat was very sore. "Have it your own way, Mallory."

Mallory took a deep breath. "Look, I don't know who you think you are," she said pointedly. "And I don't know who you think I am, but you can—"

"Buzz off? Certainly. Interesting metaphor you have there."

"Arregh!" Mallory growled. Now she had lost her temper.

"How much?" Mallory asked. "A bagus? Here you go!" She strode over to the woman, plunking a thin coin into her wrinkled hand.

"Thank you. Come into my tent."

Mallory entered to find a small table covered in silk. A stool and a plethora of soft pillows surrounded it, all atop a fancy rug. A wisp of smoke rose, curling itself into the air from a tiny incense burner.

"Make yourself—yourselves—comfortable, please," the thin woman said. She wore an outfit of mostly translucent mesh that provided ample view of her dainty arms and long legs. Mallory guessed the woman would be quite stunning if she wasn't hopelessly thin.

98

"I am Madame Richardson," she said, sitting on the stool. "You think I look hungry, do you not?"

"A little," Mallory said. Soot snuggled close to her as she lay down among the pillows. She felt odd, he was extremely cozy as a bunny. How long would he remain that way?

"An unfortunate reality I must face," Madame said. "I was normal enough until recently, but I now have to be quite careful that I don't wither away."

She stirred the water in a bowl on the table. Then she got up and dropped onto another pile of pillows.

Mallory rolled her eyes. "Don't you need to focus on the space of water to direct your sight?"

Madame made a face. She held a pillow to her breast. "That doesn't sound like something most people would know."

"It's true, isn't it? Though many tellers use a crystal ball."

"You have no idea who I am, do you?"

"No. Should I?" The hairs on the back of Mallory's neck stood straight up.

Madame smiled. "You taught me a spell that saved my life once...."

Curious, Mallory asked, "Which spell?"

"The juxtaposition."

"Hmmf, I'm sure this 'Mojo' of yours taught 'the juxtaposition' to many other white siders."

"I don't know, but then I wasn't a white sider."

Mallory studied the skinny face. Wisps of blond hair from beneath the skull cap. Exquisitely arched eyebrows. Glinting, black eyes. Wait... black eyes?

"Hold out your palm," Mallory said.

"Very well, but I'll remind you that that's my line!"

Mallory studied the thin, dainty hand. She turned it upside down to reveal a patch of bright scales somewhat like a serpent. Mallory took hold of the wrist with her other hand and forced the mesh sleeve back. There were more of the fragmented scales along her arm.

"Erica?"

Madame Richardson smiled and nodded. Mallory embraced her and held her.

"It must be…."

"Twenty years, I believe," Erica said. "I always wondered what happened to you."

"Couldn't you see what happened? A few minutes ago, you were offering to tell me my fortune. And you called me by name… your farsight must be exceptional."

"It is strong," Erica said. "It seemed like you didn't wish to be found or looked in on."

"Yes," Mallory said. "That's true. I broke from my previous life and duties when I married my husband. We decided to raise our children as common folk. No magic, sorcery, witchcraft, you name it."

"Oh," Erica said. "That doesn't sound like the Mojo I knew. She never seemed like she could get enough!"

"I changed," Mallory said. "I realized I wanted things beyond adventure and magic."

"What did you want?"

"The safety that being normal could give me. I wanted a man who wasn't a wizard or sorcerer. I was tired of magic. The war made it an all-encompassing part of my life, so I left."

Erica nodded. "Well. I had only to look at you to get a strong sense of yourself and your surroundings. There is imminent danger around."

"What?" Mallory asked. "Do you mean him?" She pointed at the listening rabbit.

"No," Erica said. "He gives me no sense of threat at all."

"Then what?"

"Let me focus," Erica said. "Perhaps we'll find out."

She held Mallory's hand in hers, palm side up, and closed her eyes. She convulsed suddenly.

"Someone very powerful is nearby," she said, keeping her eyes closed.

"Who?" Mallory asked.

"Shh!"

Erica made a couple of passes with her free hand.

"Someone who knows you. Someone from your past as the Mojo."

Erica focused on her divining, switching back and forth from farsight to innersight. "She is stalking you, watching you."

"What about my daughter!" Mallory cried. "Is Moeera in trouble?"

"You are all in trouble," Erica said, "but there is a hidden factor watching over your child. Your enemy doesn't know about it."

"Hidden? How?"

Erica strained to see what wasn't there. "Ugh. Whatever this protector is, it's far better at hiding than you are. I can see a shadow's edge, nothing more."

"What about this enemy?" Mallory demanded. "Another witch?"

"Yes! A witch you have fought. That much I know. I cannot see her face."

Erica continued searching within and without to no avail.

"I'm sorry, Mojo," she said, breathing hard. "This witch has her own spells guarding against the seeing. She's stronger than I."

Mallory held Erica in her arms again. "It's a fine warning you've given me, sister. One I can never repay."

"You saved my life," Erica said. "I aspired to be like you. If I helped you now, then consider us even… sister."

Mallory hugged Erica tightly. "You're wiped out."

"Yes, I don't think I'll be doing much seeing the rest of the day."

"You'll be right again?"

"Sure. After I rest a bit."

"I'll be going then. I have to figure this out and find who is watching me."

"Fare thee well," Erica said.

"Till we meet again, Dragoness."

Mallory left the fortune-telling tent with Soot in tow. Her thoughts ran wild, food was the last thing on her mind. She closed her eyes for a moment and breathed in through her nose and out through her mouth.

Then she said to her companion, "Let's not show up empty handed. There must be something good to be had."

Chapter Fifteen

Moeera and Wecks were outside the trailer helping Tony and Dave with their building project. Mallory and Soot approached with puzzled looks upon seeing Moeera strapped to the "drying rack".

"That should be alright," Dave said. "She fits along there nicely, and the straps aren't working too hard because of the slant."

"I would say it's a good design," Tony said.

"What in the world is it for?" Mallory asked, eyeing her daughter. Moeera was on her back on a board that ran the length of the rack. It was held between the top and bottom at an angle of about forty-five degrees. One leather strap was buckled above her chest, the other around her shins.

"That's where Moeera will be when I make her disappear," Wecks explained. "The audience will love it."

"I bet," Mallory said. "You understand what's happening, Moeera?"

"Yes, Mama. It's all part of the illusion."

"It's mostly so that more of the audience can get a good look at her, Mrs. Robin," Dave said. "Instead of her lying flat on a table."

"That makes sense," Mallory said. "Are you almost done with her for today?"

"Yes, indeed," Wecks said. "I'm going to undo the straps, Moeera. Wait till they're both open, then you can roll off."

"Got it," Moeera said.

Tony held his arms out below the girl just in case she rolled too much. But she did it just right and landed on her feet.

"Perfect," Tony said.

"We're all done for today, Moeera," Wecks said. "See you tomorrow."

"Goodbye!" Moeera said.

She went with her mother and the rabbit to the wagon for the ride home. "I really like learning to do stage magic," she said.

"That's good," Mallory said. "Wecks thinks you're quite good at it."

"He does? All right!"

"That's what he told me."

Mallory lapsed into silence for the ride home. Where was this other witch? And who was she? Most importantly, how would she protect Moeera and Kor?

* * *

That night at bedtime, Mallory looked in at her sleeping daughter. Soot was tucked comfortably under an arm (not the first time he had spent the night in the house). Mallory had little doubt about this arrangement. Perhaps the puca was the x-factor that Erica sensed.

Mallory shut the door and entered her own bedroom. Kor was on the bed. He slipped under the covers. Mallory picked up her nightgown.

She set it on the maple dresser and unbuttoned the front of her blouse.

"Kor?"

"Hmmn?"

"I heard some disturbing news today."

"What did you hear?" he asked. He expected that someone's crops might have caught a blight, or that wild beasts had destroyed a garden.

Mallory sat down on the bed and looked at him.

"There's a witch here in Bucktry—an evil witch. She knows me from the past, and she's been watching us."

"What! How can you be so sure? You don't use magic. How would someone like that find us?"

"I don't know," Mallory said. "I didn't think anyone would be looking. But I met a fortune teller at the fairground."

"That's who told you this?" Kor asked. "Sounds like a trick."

"She knew who I was," Mallory said. "She has the seeing."

Kor frowned. "Let's say she's right…."

She is right! he thought, within his compromised mind.

"…what do we do? Where do we go?"

"I don't know," Mallory said.

Far from here! And never stop running!

"Kortar, I don't know what an evil witch would want with me anymore.

103

I haven't been the Mojo in forever!"

She wants revenge! She wants Moeera! Kor wanted to tell her, but he could not.

Mallory teared up. "God, Kor! I'm sorry. This is all my fault! We're in danger because of my past."

"We'll think of something," he said. "We'll find a safe place to hide."

"Yes," she said, "but this witch will follow us."

"We'll sleep on it," Kor said. "Tomorrow, we'll load up the wagon and leave."

"I think the Mojo must return," Mallory said.

"You talk as if she and you are different people."

"We're not, but we are. I was very different when I went by that name."

Kor drew her to him and kissed her on the forehead.

"It will be all right," he said.

We're in horrible trouble! Moeera's in danger!

Mallory got off the bed. She let her clothes fall to the floor. She picked up her nightgown and let it fall over her head and envelope her body. She pulled the bow open that held her hair back. Her brown tresses fell upon her shoulders. She slid under the covers and pressed her body against her husband's.

They settled in, but neither slept for some time.

*   *   *

Izzy skipped the lovemaking that night when she drew Kor into the woods. She pounced on him and fed on just enough of his blood to sustain her for the next day or two. She sat up, throwing her head back and sending her hair flying.

After allowing Kor a few moments to catch his breath, she yanked on the invisible chain.

"I have a job for you, slave," she told him.

"What do you want?" he asked.

"You're to visit a certain fortune teller at the fairground and lay her low. Go home and fetch that sword you used on my girl. The seer sleeps all by herself in a tent behind her show tent. Enter that tent and cut her throat. She's told her last fortune!"

"I don't want to kill anyone!" Kor exclaimed.

"You'll do as you're told!" Izzy snapped. "Get going!"

"Yes, your greatness," Kor murmured.

And off he went.

*   *   *

At home, Kor went to the barn and used a pitchfork to move a pile of straw. He knelt by the long, wooden box on the floor and slid a brass key into the lock.

Inside, the sword of his father gleamed in its cloth dressings. He pulled it out, marveling at the long, shiny blade. He exited the barn and the moonlight fell upon the weapon. Now it shone with a luminosity both beautiful and deadly. He paused and caught sight of his face on the mirrored surface. He resembled his father, the man who had forged this very sword.

And he stopped dead in his tracks.

He struggled to reassert control over himself. He wanted to break free, to smite the blood witch and save the day.

No matter how hard he tried, her invisible hold kept him a prisoner. He gave up struggling, his head pounding with pain.

He stole away into the night.

*   *   *

Soot stirred in Moeera's room. He resolved to stay by her side. His fact-finding excursions were over. He knew that his friend was in terrible danger, and he would wait for any and all comers. Anyone who tried to hurt her had to get through him first.

And that wouldn't be easy.

Chapter Sixteen

Kor moved silently through the shadowy fairground. He found the fortune teller's tent quickly, Izzy's vision guiding him. He was seeing one fairway overlaying a second; one that was directly in front of him and one through Izzy's farsight.

Skirting the show tent, he crept up on the small tent's front. He thrust his free hand between the flaps to spread them apart.

The tent was pitch black inside. He entered and stood still for a few moments. Izzpalin was attentively following his every move. He heard her voice in his mind, crystal clear.

Your eyes may or may not adjust well enough to see. She's lying on a cot straight in front of you. Take two steps and her head will be on your left.

He wished he could turn and go. He didn't want to kill anyone, but he pressed onward. He took the two steps.

He almost jumped out of his skin when a hand took his wrist in the dark. While he clamped his mouth shut to avoid screaming, the hand let him go. A tiny oil lamp erupted into brilliance, showing Kor the thin lady sitting on the side of the cot directly in front of him.

"I know who you are and why you're here," Madame Richardson said. "Any seer worth her abilities can anticipate the moment of her death."

Kor stared at her speechless.

"After Mallory left, I had the vision of this. I was too tired to do anything other than wait for it to happen."

Kill her now, slave! Izzy shouted in Kor's head.

"She's directing you now, isn't she?" Madame asked. "Izzpalin, I suspect. She held a grudge against your wife. Now she's come for her."

Kor looked her in the eye. "I can't help it," Kor muttered. "She controls me."

"I know," Madame said. "Blood witches do that."

Don't talk to her, Kor! Kill her!

Kor could no longer speak; the invisible chain prevented it.

The seer laid down on her cot. "Do it," she said. "Please make it quick and clean."

Kor's eyes widened. He raised the sword above his head.

Do it! Izzy shrieked.

Kor brought the sword whizzing down upon the woman. At the last second she reached out to block his blow. The sword connected with her forearm, slicing to the bone.

Madame cried out in pain. As Kor raised the sword to strike again, she grabbed the blade with her other hand and spoke the following:

> The son honors the father.
> The father instructs the son.
> He watches and wanders
> and open his eyes shall be.

The sword blade shined brilliantly for a moment, but faded as Kor brought the edge down to Madame's throat.

Kor stole quickly out of the tent and headed for the road. He heard people stirring to see where the scream of pain had come from. He faded into the shadows.

*   *   *

Morning came and chased the darkness away. Moeera and Soot dashed around the farmyard. Moeera did her usual chores and ate some muffins for breakfast. She yelled a quick goodbye to her mother and father, and then she and Soot headed out for school.

Upstairs, Mallory and Kor were discussing what there was to do.

"I want to pack up the wagon and depart," Mallory said. "I know this witch will come after us though."

"What if we stay here and track her down?" Kor asked.

"I don't know," Mallory said. "If this witch has been practicing magic all these years that I haven't been... she'll probably be stronger than I am."

107

"Then we have to be smarter than her," Kor said.

"I suppose so," Mallory said. "Maybe Erica can help us too."

"Who's Erica?" Kor asked.

"The fortune teller at the fair," Mallory said. "She's not just a seer, she has borrowed abilities."

Had, Izzy crowed in Kor's mind.

Kor ignored her.

"What do you mean 'borrowed abilities'?" he asked.

Mallory frowned. "How do I explain it? She was hurt badly during the Magic War. She probably would have bled to death, but she used a spell to trade certain body parts with a newly dead dragon. I'm not sure what abilities she gained from that, but if she breathes fire or flies or even has the thick hide of a dragon—she might be quite some help indeed."

"Sure," Kor said. "You're messing with me, right?"

"No," Mallory said. "She's part dragon. Therefore, she very well may be tougher than me and the evil witch put together."

"Gosh!" Kor said. He felt sick to his stomach with the knowledge that he had dispatched her living spirit to the afterlife.

"Kor!" Mallory said. "Pay attention! How can we get the upper hand against this enemy?"

"I'm thinking, I'm thinking," he said.

Inside his head, he sensed Izzy grinning. *Tell her we need to set a trap.*

"We could set a trap," Kor said.

"Alright," Mallory said. "A trap. I'm listening. What else have you got?"

"We could lock her up somewhere," Kor said.

"Maybe. If she doesn't figure out what's going on first."

Tell her to ask the girl's "wizard" friend to help set the trap.

"We could ask Moeera's friend Wecks to help us set a trap," Kor said.

"I don't know if that's the mother of all bad ideas, or if it's a really smart idea," Mallory said.

"He's at the fair; the fortune teller is at the fair," Kor said. "We could have help from both of them."

"How do we get the witch to the fair?" Mallory asked.

"How do we get her attention?" Kor asked.

Magic. Kor felt Izzy chuckle from inside his mind.

Kor cleared his throat and looked at his wife.

"The magic show," he said.

"What about it?"

"We can get her to turn up for that."

"Kor, she knows it's just illusions and such."

Tell her that she'll make the best bait. Wecks can let her perform a magic trick with Moeera.

"She'll be there for it if you do a magic trick in the show."

"Yes. With Moeera. I guess so. How will she know about it?"

Tell the gossips at The Cork and Kettle, Izzy said in Kor's mind.

"We'll stop at The Cork and Kettle. As long as Shirley is there, word should get around."

"That's true," Mallory agreed. "We have a plan then—not the greatest plan—but a plan nonetheless."

"Maybe we can beat this witch at her own game," Kor said.

"I think we're going to need a lot of luck," Mallory said, tugging her lip. "I'm going to visit Wecks and then, rumor pending, stop by The Cork and Kettle."

"I'll go to work then," Kor said. "I better get a move on. I'm late already."

"Sounds good."

Mallory and Kor got dressed and had breakfast together.

As Kor mounted Bahb, Mallory said, "Watch yourself out there, dear."

"I will," he said. "You do the same."

"Alright."

She waved as he left for the smithy. Then she watched him until he disappeared around the bend.

Her shoulders slumped. She needed the Mojo, but could she really become that person again? It remained to be seen.

Chapter Seventeen

Twenty years ago, she could have easily and giddily defeated any of them: Myra Moonbeam, Amara Dolores, the Eris, Izzpalin. She bit her lip. Izzpalin... no, it couldn't be, could it? She'd fought against her the most.

Trounced her too. Is that what this was all about? She hoped not. A shudder ran through her body.

She had to pay Wecks a visit. First, though, there was something to do. She trudged around the house to the small herb garden. Amongst the herbs growing there were several large rocks that were too much of a hassle to move. They resembled a trio of gray islands.

Mallory grabbed a trowel and a digger and stepped through the garden to the point equidistant from the three boulders. She knelt in the dirt and pulled the digger through the soil. Once there was plenty of loose dirt, she scooped it out and to the side with the trowel. Then she resumed loosening with the digger.

It took her five repetitions with the digger and the trowel until she hit something solid. She eagerly scraped dirt and pebbles away with the trowel to reveal the lid of a small kettle. She yanked on it with the digger's prongs. After some great effort, it popped up and off.

She thrust the lid aside and it crashed against one of the rocks. She peered into the hole and into the little, black kettle to see an old sack.

Smiling with satisfaction, she grabbed the sack and dashed to the barn to get Dot.

*   *   *

Wecks opened the trailer door to find Mallory waiting.

"Good morning, Mrs. Robin," he said. "Moeera won't be here for a while yet."

"I know she's at school," Mallory said. "I wanted to talk to you before you started rehearsing with her today."

"Oh, sure. Won't you come in."

"I didn't see any of your friends outside today," she commented.

"That's because they're helping to take the body to the undertaker. There was a murder last night."

Mallory's blood froze.

"What! Who?"

"A fortune teller named Madam Richardson. I hadn't met her, but I hear that she was clever as they come."

"Oh, no!" Mallory said. Dread filled her, a tightness spread through her chest.

"Someone tenting near her heard something strange last night," Wecks said. "When they started poking around they discovered the bloody mess that used to be Madam."

"But no look at the killer," she surmised.

"No," he said, sadly. "I never would've expected something like that to happen here."

"Nor would I," Mallory said carefully. "Except that Bucktry is the eye in the center of a storm now."

"Come again?" Wecks asked.

Mallory exhaled, took another breath. She looked at the magician.

There's something vulnerable about her, he thought.

"I've kept a secret for the last twenty years, and now it's coming back to obliterate my life."

"Oh," Wecks said. "Must be some secret."

"Only my husband and I know. But now there's an evil witch about, so I'm going to have to tell others."

"Me?" he asked.

She nodded. "You're Moeera's friend. She's in danger along with Kor and I."

*　　　*　　　*

"Let me get this straight," Wecks said in his naturally loud voice. "You grew up among witches, wizards, and others who wield true magic. You're a witch, but you hid all this from your daughter."

Mallory slowly nodded. "That's the gist of it. Before I gave it all up

111

two decades ago, I was a witch. The Council of the Sea sent me on assignments before the War of the Powers started."

"Assignments?"

"They were gathering information about the covens who used black magic. I infiltrated around a dozen of them; Sisters of Sorrow, Moon Daughters, blood witches."

Mallory's face darkened. "Then the war happened. Witch versus witch. Wizards too. I watched everyone I knew and loved at their worst. I saw my parents protect a lot of people. I also saw them duel shocking opponents."

"I loved what I was, at first, but I couldn't deal with the fighting anymore. So, I left."

"Excuse me for saying this, but I'm absolutely stunned. Your daughter is a delightful girl. She's curious, willful, ambitious, and good-natured. Why have you kept this secret from her?"

"To protect her."

"What would a witch among witches need protection from?"

"The other side," Mallory said, eyes flashing. "Evil witches, ghouls, demons, warlocks, ... everyday people."

"What danger do ordinary people pose to witches?"

"You must ask? Do you know how well I fit in around here? Pretty well. But I look just like everyone else. If they saw me practicing magic, casting spells... then what?"

"I don't know," Wecks said, quietly. "When I was a boy, the magically inclined were revered and celebrated."

"Sure," Mallory said. "The good ones. The ones that the people liked. There are all types of witches though. Good. Bad. It doesn't take much at all to get people hating each other."

"Right," Wecks said. "Isn't hiding all this from Moeera just as bad as lying to her? You kept her hidden away, living an ordinary life. Still, you say there's a witch lying in wait somewhere. How did any of what you did protect her?"

"I protected her by keeping her away from a lifestyle of danger and conflict, Mr. Wecks!"

Wecks paused. He didn't realize the effect his words would have on Mallory.

"Venable," he said.

"What?"

"Wecks is my first name. I'm Mr. Venable to anyone who knows me outside the magic shows."

"Oh," she said. "Mr. Venable, I've come to you for help. I don't know that I truly need to perform a trick to lure the evil witch out of the shadows, but if the word spreads around town that I'll be assisting you to do that, I think it's our best bet."

"Hmm. I want to help you. I'm perfectly willing to help catch an evil witch from your previous days."

"But?"

"I can't figure out what will happen about Moeera."

"If we capture Izzpalin, I could neutralize her," Mallory said.

"How would you 'neutralize' her?" Wecks asked.

"There are several ways I might do it, short of killing her," Mallory said.

"Can you successfully stop her? Without a doubt, I mean."

"Nothing's a certainty," Mallory admitted. "I'll tell you this, I feel my connections to Mother Nature's energies strengthening. I could do anything to keep Moeera safe."

"Right, but when will you tell Moeera the truth? More troubling than that, how will she react?"

"I don't know," Mallory said, "but there isn't a choice anymore. One way or another the truth will come out."

"Alright, Mrs. Robin," Wecks said. "I'm going to read off all the illusions in the act for Friday night. Ask me anything you like about them. Then we have to work you into the show someplace."

Wecks read her the list and they got down to work.

*　　　*　　　*

After they had an idea of what Mallory would do in the magic show, she went to the edge of the field. Moeera would be a little while yet coming from school. She sat cross-legged, facing the forest. The little sack rested beside her.

Before her lie four tiny dolls. The poppets had been in the sack buried by her house for two decades. Now she needed them again.

One had red ochre smeared across its blank face. That represented the blood witch Izzpalin. Another poppet had a crescent moon shape marked on the front. Myra. Amara Dolores had a poppet with charcoal tears

113

running down its face. Lastly, the Eris held a twig fashioned into an itty-bitty sword.

Mallory marked them up to be the witches she thought might be stalking her. Now she sat on the grass, meditating. She was no longer the housewife and farmer known as Mallory.

Once again, she was the Mojo, scourge of evil in any form it took.

She was extremely weak just now. The voice inside her head, the voice of her younger self, urged her to reach out and find this assuming beldam. Any witch who knew her should know that to threaten the Mojo was to court death!

But the part of her who'd spent the last twenty years living without communing with the natural world in the witch way needed to reconnect with the Earth.

She breathed in, held it a few seconds, and exhaled. And again, and again.

The forest and the field jumped to life, a tapestry of living things, in her mind's eye.

She saw ants marching on their purposeful errands, playing follow the leader. To the ants it was the furthest thing from play. They transported food and water to their tunnels beneath the ground. Flycatchers, sparrows, skylarks, and gold finches clung to tree branches all around the woods. Here they flew, there they swooped. The delicate little creatures alighted on the forest floor, examining nooks and crannies for food. Their songs traversed the trees in a network that connected them. They called to one another, high pitched whistles and warbles and trills piercing the spaces between.

Squirrels dashed and scurried, munched nuts, chased each other. Pairs spiraled upward in the trunks of maple, oak, and mahogany trees.

The trees stood fast, motionless, except for the small movements that reminded one that they too were living. Leaves waving in the breeze, branches bending under the weight of squirrels and other small animals.

Mallory felt the energy of all these things and more. She continued her focused breathing, in and out, and concentrated on being part of the whole lifeforce around her. She emptied the fear and worry from her thoughts. Calm overtook her.

The feeling that permeated her body was incredible. She felt all those other living things. They all made up a whole being, and she was a part of that being. The sun shone down, finding her at the field's edge. It bathed her in its radiance. The sun was the beginning, the physical core of this whole living world.

Circles came from it. Mallory was a part of one of those circles. Her circle was but one of an inconceivable number of interlocking rings.

It was a good feeling, being complete after such a long period of being apart. She felt whole.

Energy flowed into her, waking muscles she hadn't used in years.

An involuntary shiver ran through her body. She closed her eyes and shook her bones.

Once more she relaxed herself. Then she let her mind wander out methodically. She encountered human beings, at work and play. Nothing out of the ordinary so far. The thought occurred to her that whomever this was plotting against her and her family, that she'd been stronger than Erica.

Dragoness, she thought curtly. *I'm back to witchcraft. I might as well use the correct aliases.*

She decided to stop searching person to person with her mind and try her original idea. The poppets lie in a row in the grass. She reached down with her right hand and held her palm above them.

"Cas guhl nik va senan!" she said, speaking the words of a very old spell.

If the poppets had all had eyes, they'd have taunted Mallory with their stillness.

"Fine, fine," Mallory bit out. "I'm a bit rusty. That's all."

She tried again, paying close attention to the nature around her and channeling the life adjacent to her into her task.

The little dolls rose off the ground, tilting forward to face Mallory. The Mojo opened her mouth and shouted. Three of the dolls gave off wisps of smoke and burst into flames.

She withdrew the power from the simulacrums which promptly fell to the ground. The fires devoured the three poppets of the witches who weren't involved. The doll with the ochre smudge across its face was the only one remaining.

I should have known, the Mojo thought, *once a bitch, always a bitch.*

The angry feeling passed from her as she continued her meditation.

She was out of practice. That was a certainty.

She was far from weak, however. She needed to awaken her sleeping muscles. Her surroundings would provide the energy.

Her book of magic would hold all the review she needed.

Still… she felt very tense about engaging Izzpalin. She couldn't fathom why. How good could the blood witch be?

It remained to be seen. The Mojo smiled. She'd defeated Izzpalin more than once in the old days. This time would be no different.

Wouldn't it?

She frowned, lining her forehead with creases. She focused on her breathing and banished all thought of Izzpalin from her mind.

Chapter Eighteen

When Moeera arrived for dress rehearsal, she and Soot found Mallory scrubbing the bars of a bamboo cage. It was taller than a person with room inside to hold one adult.

"Hi, Mama," Moeera said. "You're early. Why are you doing that?"

Mallory stopped and dropped her washcloth into the water bucket.

"Hello, Mee," she said. "I'm helping with the show too."

A frown etched itself onto the girl's face.

"Huh? Why?" Moeera asked.

"Well...."

Mallory wanted so much to admit the truth to her daughter right this very minute, but her trepidation held it back.

Wecks watched from nearby. He stopped working on the filaments he'd acquired from several marsh flowers and bounded over.

I knew this was going to be awkward, he thought. And Mallory is freezing up like a pond in mid-winter.

"Moeera!" Wecks said, grinning. "Your mother's going to help us with one of our illusions."

"She doesn't like magic like I do," Moeera said sulkily.

"Now, really, dear," Wecks said. "I haven't met anybody who likes magic as much as you do."

"How do you even have time to help?" Moeera asked. "What about the farm?"

"It's only for two days, Moeera," Mallory said.

"It was my idea," Wecks lied. "I thought we could use another set of hands for a tricky illusion I've created. What do you say?"

"What's the illusion?" Moeera asked.

"I call it the 'Which Witch Switch' trick. I'm going to start with you in the bamboo cage. Your mother will help me to cover the cage so that no one can see you. Then we spin the cage a couple times."

"Then what?"

"We rip the cover away to reveal an empty cage. Then your mother will enter the cage. I'll have Tony and Dave come out to recover the cage."

"They'll spin it around twice, and as they're doing that I'll exit stage right. Then they'll pantomime 'where did he go'. They'll shrug and tear the cover off the cage, revealing that you're back in the cage and that your mother has disappeared. They'll let you out of the cage and throw the cover back on. You'll wave your hands in the air, shout 'Eureka', and whip off the cover. It'll be me in the cage this time. Then your mama strides in from stage right and we all take a bow.

"That sounds spectacular," Moeera said, her eyes bright again.

"It certainly does," Mallory said.

"Now let me tell you how we do it," Wecks said.

Moeera and her mother listened as the magician explained how the trick worked.

*   *   *

Shirley was on her break when Mallory walked into the Cork and Kettle an hour later.

"Greetings, Mallory, I haven't seen you in here for a Hip-po-gy-raf's age."

"You know me," Mallory said. "I like to keep busy."

"I imagine you're overwhelmed with the harvest right now," Shirley said.

"Slow and steady wins the race, Shirley. I've been picking and threshing and harvesting for weeks now. Plus, I've got Moeera to help me."

"Yes, that delightful Moeera!" Shirley said. "I hear she's made quite an impression on the wizard who's visiting."

"She's his shadow whenever she has free time," Mallory said. "She's curious about the illusions that he performs."

"Isn't that nice," Shirley said. "Every girl needs a hobby; I hear tell she's part of his weekend show."

"Well, yes, actually we both are," Mallory said nonchalantly.

Shirley's eyebrows shot up.

Bullseye! Mallory thought.

118

"Both of you? How in the world do you have time to waste at the fair with performers, Mallory Robin!"

"It's not such a big waste," Mallory said. "I get to spend some time with my daughter doing what she likes and learning new things about her and her 'hobby'."

Shirley's face twitched. "Good for you, Mallory," she said with as much conviction as she could muster.

Mallory knew that Shirley was itching to get this news circulating. So much the better if it got Izzpalin's attention.

"Thank you, dear," she said. "After I wet my whistle, I'm going to go practice magic at the fairground."

"Good for you," Shirley said. "Well, I best be getting back to work."

"Always a pleasure, dear," Mallory said.

As soon as Shirley disappeared behind the kitchen doors, Mallory got up and left. She was terribly thirsty, but she had more important things to be about than lounging in the Cork and Kettle.

She mounted Dot and urged her toward the fairground. The bachukka galloped off at a speedy clip.

$$* \qquad * \qquad *$$

At work, Kor pounded away at an iron ingot. He hammered and hit and smashed until the molten metal flattened and elongated into the proper shape.

What began as a bar shaped for transporting took on a new form.

Kor grabbed an edge of the hot metal with a large set of tongs. He held the tongs fast with his left hand while he rained down blows upon the iron. A piece of the metal broke off.

Kor set the big piece of iron down. He traded the large tongs for a smaller pair and seized the small shard. This he hammered into a thin bar and put it against a small, round protrusion on his anvil. Smacking it again and again against the anvil, he bent it into a half circle shape.

Satisfied with the shape of the iron, Kor placed the semi-circle on the work surface and began to add fine detailing, including a groove that ran the length of the bend and straights.

"Kor!" Wadow said loudly, interrupting him. "There's a stranger here. She wants you to repair something."

"Oh," he said, putting his hammer and tongs down. "I'll go talk to her."

119

He left the forge and walked into their front area.

Izzy stood on the other side of the counter smiling at him.

All the trouble he'd been trying to hold at bay with his hammering roared back to the front of his thoughts.

"What are *you* doing here?" he asked.

He felt a slight tug at his mind—a not so subtle reminder of the invisible chain.

"Such fire in your tone, blacksmith," Izzy said. "Is that how you speak to everyone who visits here?"

Kor spoke in a faint voice. "I'm at your mercy, but I don't have to like it. Mallory has gone to entreat the magician to help with the plan. *Your* plan."

"Good," she said. "It's all falling into place quite easily."

Kor stared at her across the counter.

"Cat got your tongue, darling?" Izzy asked.

"I stopped by to see you," she continued, "so that you could have a choice."

"Choice?"

"Yes, Kor, and understand that I offer very few people this choice—ever. You'd be the first male."

A cold feeling of unease shot through the man who up till then had been sweating.

"I'm offering to make you as I am."

"A witch?"

"No, not that," Izzy said. "How to explain… we blood witches exist separately from the rest of humankind. We are immortal."

"That's hard to believe," Kor said. "No one is immortal."

"I am," Izzy said. "And you could be too, if I wish you to be."

"A strange thought," Kor said.

"You could live forever," Izzy said, softly. "Think of it. Never grow old. Never get sick. You'd have your strength back, sixfold."

"Hmmph," Kor said. "I can answer your offer right now: I'm spoken for."

Her face stayed expressionless but there was ice in her voice.

"Are you certain? You'd turn your back on the chance of a lifetime. I'll destroy you, or perhaps leave you so dry that you never walk again."

"You can force me to do your evil, but you can't kill the love I have for

120

my wife. My life, long or short, is with her and Moeera."

"Fool," was all she said.

She made a tiny jerking motion. Kor lurched up and forward as if a giant had grabbed his shirt collar.

"I offer you never-ending power and longevity by my side, and you pass it up for a pointless demise. The Mojo certainly has her claws in you!"

"What can I say?" Kor asked.

She released her physical grip on him, and he settled back to standing position.

"It won't be long now till I defeat your Mojo. No doubt she's preparing for our showdown, reestablishing her symbiosis with the natural world. It won't do her any good. I'll have the last laugh."

"I better get back to work," Kor said. "Those bachukka shoes won't make themselves."

"Short though my wait may be, I'll still have time to play," Izzy said.

"Just leave me be," Kor said.

"I can worm my way around that mind of yours," she spat. "You'll wish you had accepted my offer."

And then she was gone. Just like that. She didn't turn and walk out. She was simply gone.

Magic, he thought, blinking his eyes. He half expected a dust mote to fall and her to be still standing there.

No, she had gone. She had caused herself to vanish.

He returned to the forge, vexed, and feeling the impending doom closing in.

Chapter Nineteen

Back at the fair, Mallory once again pitched in with the magic crew to get the show ready. She was in the Moon Theater with Dave and Tony. Several toolboxes were set about the stage. Dave stood with his hands on his hips, staring at a trap door set into the stage.

"I thought so," Dave said, triumphantly. "This stage has a trap door center stage. This should save us a lot of time, not to mention not getting into trouble with the stage manager."

"Let's try it out," Tony said. He took a metal rod with a hooked end and reached for the metal ring pull set into the wood.

The hook slipped under the ring and caught hold. Tony pulled at the door, but it refused to move.

"Well!" Tony said. "This trap door seems to be stuck."

"Oh, boy, I wonder if it's been nailed shut," Dave said, shaking his head.

"Why would they do that?" Tony asked.

"I guess if they didn't want to use it anymore," Dave said.

Mallory had an idea. Dave was looking at their assortment of prybars and putty knives. While he and Tony discussed what to do, she searched her memory for an old spell.

She closed her eyes and recited the spell in her mind. Then she opened her eyes and said, "Gleeto beeto narya."

Dave and Tony watched her walk to the trap door and lean down to take the ring. She grasped it firmly and pulled.

The door opened smoothly. Mallory smiled.

Some things you never forget, she thought.

"How in the world did you do that?" Dave asked.

"Tony must have loosened it for me," she said.

"I wasn't even sure that was a real door," Tony said. "I thought some joker might have played a trick making it appear there was one."

"It's real enough," Mallory said. "Some time ago, somebody painted the stage. The paint seeped between the door and the door frame and sealed it shut."

"Hmm," Dave said. "And you know that how?"

She knelt and pointed to the framing. "See, right here. The paint ran all along there and dried in the gap."

"Uh, huh," Dave said. "But how did you know before you saw it? How did you open it?"

"Oh," she said, quickly. "I'm a witch."

"No kidding," Dave said.

"I thought so," Tony said. "You said a spell just then before opening that."

She nodded. It felt strange to tell people, but this had been easier than telling Wecks.

"Does Wecks know?"

"Yes, but Moeera doesn't."

"Why not?" Dave asked.

"It's a long story," Mallory said.

"I guess we better examine this old thing, huh?" Tony said.

"Sure," Dave said. "I believe having Mallory here may make this easier."

Dave lit a candle and lowered the lamp into the darkness under the stage. The light didn't go very far. It revealed a set of wooden steps descending under the stage.

"Now we need to figure out if these stairs are sturdy," he said. "Can you do anything about the dark?"

Mallory squinted. "Let me see…"

She felt the familiar energy coursing through her veins. Even though she was indoors she could sense the trees and flowers that weren't too far away. She felt the living creatures among those plants and underneath. She pictured the sunlight in the blue sky above.

"Light visible and bright!" she exclaimed.

The candlelight from the lamp expanded as if the sun was rising in the sky.

"*That* is a neat trick," Dave said, handing the lamp to Tony.

123

He took a mallet from the largest toolbox and leaned over the side of the opening.

Thump! Thump! Thump! Thump!

"The top two steps seem sturdy enough," he said.

"Don't forget," Tony said. "Wecks is a big guy."

"Sure," Dave said. "I'll lean into 'em as I climb down."

He descended into the narrow space, placing his full weight on each step.

"You good down there?" Tony called down.

"Sure," Dave said, reappearing at the top of the steps. "The stairs seem fine. Wecks shouldn't have any trouble, or Mallory. I'm going to look around a bit."

Dave passed his mallet to Tony and took the lantern.

*   *   *

Izzy watched from her cabin.

A dark cellar; lots of potential there. The Mojo was remembering some spells. Hah! A lot of good two simple tricks would do her.

How many others did she remember? The wench might pose a serious threat. She thought about it shortly, but of course, nothing was ever certain, was it! Certainly not when witches were involved.

The Mojo had grown into a dull woman. She was playing right into her waiting hands. When Izzy sprung her trap and seized her that would be it. The grand finale to a career of trouble would be cut short prematurely.

She pondered. The lightsider had done that herself. Izzy would make it permanent. If anyone had told her that the Mojo would give up her witch's heritage and opt for a plain and simple life, Izzy would have laughed herself silly. What bullocks!

Yet here she was watching her old nemesis play stagehand with a couple of vaudeville fops. The truth was stranger than fiction.

The handyman went back down into the cellar. She listened to the Mojo talk to the other man.

"You see," Tony said, "the stage is high enough that the audience won't know about the trap door. Or that the cage has no bottom either. You and Moeera will be able to switch places when the cage is covered."

"And so on and so on," Mallory said. "I hope the passageway is the way Wecks expects it to be."

124

"I hope so too," Tony said. "That many switches will knock the socks off the audience. They'll love it."

"Absolutely," Mallory said.

What a bunch of rubbish, Izzy thought. *They think they're so smart. Their ignorance is going to leave them in a sad state.*

Chapter Twenty

Finally, the day of the big performance dawned. Moeera had a bit of trouble getting out of bed. She was so excited about her big debut as part of Wecks' magic show that she'd had trouble falling asleep the night before.

Mallory woke up feeling strong and refreshed. She opened her mind to the life surrounding her. Then she bowed her head and prayed to the Earth Mother, giving thanks for the environment that supported every living thing.

She got up and dressed.

"May your beauteous world thrive, Mother," she said aloud, walking to Moeera's room.

She laughed a pleasant laugh born of surprise at what she found. Moeera snored loudly while Soot stepped carefully around her arm. He bobbed his head up and down, then nuzzled Moeera's ears, her nose…

"Uhrn!" the girl snorted. "What are you doing? Soot!"

Mallory smiled. Here was a happy moment she would remember forever—even with all the uncertainty going on.

"Moeera," she said.

"Mm."

"Moeera, it's morning. Time to get up. It's your big day."

"Uhhhhh…," Moeera mumbled, loudly.

"Come on, sleepy head," Mallory said. "Get out of bed."

Moeera sat up and rubbed her eyes.

"This evening you can show the entire town what a good apprentice you are to the Wondrous Wecks!" Mallory said.

"Yay!" Moeera cried, tumbling from her bed.

Soot leaped to the floor.

"After breakfast and tending to the animals, we'll take the wagon straight to the fair."

"Wonderful, Mama," Moeera said.

*　　　*　　　*

After breakfast, Kor took Bahb to the blacksmith shop. He was so nervous that he couldn't stop his body from trembling. The sword of his father bounced across his back in its sheath.

He and Mallory were planning to flush Izzy out at the fair tonight. After that, he knew very little about the plan. The Mojo, Mallory as witch trained and formerly part of the "Whitesiders", would do the rest.

The problem was the whole thing was a setup. The Mojo was playing with fire, and the fire was already burning.

He wanted to ride back home, to tell Mallory everything. Alas, he could not. Izzpalin had a firm grip on his actions.

The most that Kor could hope for was that Mallory was still as powerful as she used to be. If she was, then there was a chance they could survive this.

*　　　*　　　*

"Here's what we're going to do," Wecks said.

He, Moeera, Mallory, Dave, and Tony stood on the theater's stage. All the trappings and equipment were scattered around them.

"We're going to arrange the props and set pieces by order and block the big things. Someone painted the stage black since we were here last. Chalk should do the trick to mark out our blocking. Then we're going to rehearse each illusion here on the stage."

The rest of them nodded their agreement. They moved each big piece to its position on the stage. Mallory manipulated a piece of chalk via locomotion charm to draw outlines, angles, and instructions on the stage. It didn't take much time at all.

Wecks walked into the backstage area. A second later he strode onto the stage with his right arm outstretched. He stopped when he got to center stage.

"Ladies and gentlemen! Boys and girls! It is great to be in Bucktry tonight! Do you believe in magic? If not, you will by the end of tonight's show."

"I'm the Wondrous Wecks by name, wizard by game. Please let me introduce my assistants, Magnificent Moeera—you walk over and greet the audience, Moeera, give it a flourish."

Moeera walked over to Wecks and curtseyed at the non-existent audience.

"Perfect. And… The Mojo!"

Mallory followed suit, traipsing to center stage and taking an exaggerated bow.

The hairs on the back of Moeera's neck stood on end. Why did Wecks call her the Mojo? What does mojo mean?

"Then I give my little speech about magic," Wecks said.

"For my first illusion, ladies and gentlemen, I'll require a basket—a rather large basket," Wecks said.

Dave carried the basket and placed it on the stage next to Wecks. Tony wheeled in a cart of implements.

Wecks picked up the basket and held it for the audience to see.

"You'll notice there's nothing special about this basket whatsoever. It's big, it's woven, it's not particularly heavy at all."

So went the dress rehearsal. Kinks were worked out. Blocking and placement of the set pieces was finalized. The show was rehearsed from beginning to end, three times.

After that, Mallory and Moeera got a look at some costumes. Beautiful, extravagant clothing that the quartet had stowed away from times in their more than twenty years of working the traveling performers circuit.

"We don't have much in the way of feminine accoutrements," Wecks said, "but we have a few things."

He opened a closet door in the trailer to reveal silk, sequins, mesh, and other flashy materials.

"If you're going to play the part, you have to dress for the role!" he said. "Everything in the closet is fair picking. Most of it belonged to jugglers, tumblers, and assistants who worked with us at one time or another."

Mallory pulled out a bright, blue gown that looked like it would hug every curve.

"I'll try this one," she said. "If it fits, and I can climb stairs with it, then I'm set."

"What about me?" Moeera asked, doubtfully.

"Yes, what about you," Wecks echoed. "I seem to remember a couple of sisters who helped me for a while. They were rather short."

He looked at various outfits, moving them apart to look at them. He touched the sleeve of a green costume with yellow and black detailing and yanked it from the clothes rod.

"This may work," he told Moeera, winking.

Moeera took the costume and stared at it hard. "It's amazing," she said.

"Most importantly, it might fit," Wecks said.

"Definitely," Mallory said. "You're going to be a star, Mee."

Chapter Twenty-one

Everything has its time. The curtain rising in the Moon Theater that night marked a turning point in Moeera's life, as well as in the life of her mother. Moeera was embracing a life of magical possibilities, and the Mojo was renewing hers.

The audience saw the Wondrous Wecks standing tall in the stage's center.

"Greetings, ladies and gentlemen, boys and girls! Welcome to the show! I'm the Wondrous Wecks!"

"Thank you, thank you! It's fantastic to be back in Bucktry again, here in the Moon Theater. My colleagues Dave, Tony, and Paul were pleased when we realized we'd be close by as your fair commenced."

"Bucktry is quite a place. And, to make this show even better, I found not one, but *two*, new assistants to help me perform magic onstage."

Mallory and Moeera entered respectively from stage left and stage right. They each walked to the center, waving to the audience as they went.

"Let me introduce you to the Mojo!"

Mallory stepped to the front edge of the stage and bowed.

The audience went wild. Most of them recognized her even if they didn't know her personally.

Mallory stepped back.

Wecks stepped to the very edge of the stage, and said, "Last but not least, my apprentice, the Magnificent *Moeera!*"

Moeera approached the stage edge. She curtseyed and gave them a quick bow.

When the clapping died down Wecks stuck his arms out to the left and right. "Let's have some magic!"

He and Moeera stepped back to find Mallory dragging the basket to center stage.

"For our first illusion," Wecks called out, "the Magnificent Moeera will submit herself to the Basket of Destiny!"

He stepped to a nearby table of instruments and selected a long, menacing sword. He turned it in the lamplight so that everyone would see it gleam. It was the same sword that they had practiced with. Wecks and Moeera were very familiar with it.

So was Paul, but that didn't stop him from coming forth from his seat in the third row to inspect it.

"A volunteer from the audience," Wecks boomed.

Hands went up.

"You, sir, there in the third row with the red bandana."

When Paul was standing beside him, Wecks looked at the audience. "Would you please tell us, sir, if this blade is indeed sharp?"

Paul took the sword, turning it over in his hands. He pretended to touch the edge with his finger. He quickly jerked his finger away.

Handing it back to Wecks, Paul nodded emphatically.

"Yes, ladies and gents," Wecks said, "it's very sharp."

Wecks lifted the lid from the basket. Moeera climbed inside.

"Now ladies and gents, my apprentice has placed her life in my hands! I will now drive this sharp sword through the basket and through my assistant!"

With no further explanation, Wecks plunged the sword into the basket. Its tip pierced the basket's other side. The basket remained silent but somewhere in the theater a woman screamed. Meanwhile, Mallory mimed horror, shock, and dread at the sight of such an undeniably fatal action.

"Do not be alarmed," Wex said, picking another sword from the prop table. "My magic is great."

That remained to be seen, of course.

Without another word, Wecks plunged the second sword into the basket from another angle. Once again, the tip of said sword exited the basket's other side.

Gasps came from the audience.

"You sound concerned, my friends!" Wecks exclaimed. "Worry not, the power of magic protects my young protégé."

Wecks drew a third sword from the table. He held it out horizontally, a hand on each end.

"One last sword. If anyone here is faint of heart, then cover your eyes!"

He plunged the sword through the basket. Mallory dropped to her knees, holding her head in her hands.

You could hear the person next to you breathing. A thousand eyes focused on Wecks.

Wecks shook his arms and wiggled his fingers. He leaned into the basket, pulling the third sword back out. Mallory, back on her feet, took the sword and returned it to its place on the table.

When all three swords were once again on the table, Wecks pulled the lid off the basket, reached in, and offered a hand to the girl inside. Moeera climbed out none the worse for wear. She stood up straight and raised her hands in the air. Then she took a bow. The audience went nuts.

Wecks grinned warmly as the sun.

"There she is, Moeera the made-to-last magician!"

Wecks leaned into a half bow.

Tony and Dave wheeled the curious construct resembling a drying rack onto center stage. They chocked it in place and stood at each end.

"For my next trick I'm going to make Moeera vanish into thin air!"

The audience went "oooooo and ahhhh" upon hearing this.

"Won't you come over here, please," Wecks said to Moeera.

She stood in front of the curious-looking contraption.

"Have a seat on the board, dear, and Dave will strap you in place."

Moeera sat down and then reclined on her back while Dave tightened two canvas straps.

"Ladies and gentlemen, I'd be remiss if I didn't introduce Dave and Tony."

Dave waved and stood up again. Tony waved.

"These two men build all my fancy props. This wooden apparatus that they're presenting now is to help you all to see this reclining girl disappear. When Tony turns the little crank on the side there, the board will turn up so you can look upon her as you would view a portrait."

Tony did just that. Moeera looked at the audience in the dimness of the seats. They watched her back in rapt silence. Would Wecks really make her disappear?

Well, of course he will, Moeera thought. She flashed the people the biggest smile she could.

Wecks produced a large black sheet as if from air. He threw it over the rack, obscuring Moeera from sight.

"Zizzo!" Wecks exclaimed.

"Zazzo!" he shouted, waving his arms in the air.

"Zappo!"

Wecks whipped the sheet off the rack.

The board Moeera was strapped to was empty.

There came a great "Huhhnn" from the audience.

"Poof!" Wecks exclaimed. "She's gone, yes indeedy!"

"Now," he said, "let's get her back! Shall we?"

On went the sheet again.

This time Wecks said the magic words in reverse, ending with zazzo. He whipped the sheet away, and there was Moeera, grinning away.

"There she is!" Wecks exclaimed. "There you have it!"

He bowed once more.

A few seconds later, Dave and Tony had Moeera free again. They wheeled the big rack off stage left.

"Now my assistant and I would like to show you the disappearing bandana trick!" Wecks said.

He and Moeera performed that and several other illusions. They all landed well with the audience.

Wecks performed a couple more by himself.

After that, Wecks stood at the stage edge.

"For my final illusion tonight, I'm enlisting the help of your own resident witch The Mojo! We call this one the 'Which Witch Switch'!"

Tony and Dave brought the cage out, carefully placing it on the marked part of the stage over the trap door.

Wecks approached the cage and pulled open the bamboo door. Moeera waved to the audience and walked inside. Then Wecks made an obtrusive display of locking the door. He and Mallory covered the cage with a huge tarp, obscuring all view of Moeera.

Inside the cage, Moeera crouched down. As Dave and Tony started spinning the cage, tarp, and all, Moeera pulled the trap door open and climbed onto the steps.

No time to waste! She pulled the door down again.

She descended the steps of the wooden stairway. In just a couple minutes, her mother would be joining her. Then Wecks would come down the cellar stairs down the hall.

Once Mallory was off the narrow steps, Moeera would have to climb up into the cage for the reveal.

Then Wecks would appear, and Mallory would appear again from stage right. Moeera hoped the stage switcheroo wouldn't reveal the trick's secret. Hopefully, everyone would just be amazed and befuddled by all the changes.

The trap door flipped up allowing Mallory to climb onto the steps. She carefully descended next to Moeera.

"Empty cage," she said. "Now they need you back, Mee."

"On my way," Moeera said, smiling.

She grabbed the handrails and hoofed it up through the door into the cage. And not a moment too soon. The trap door was barely closed before Dave and Tony removed the tarp.

Moeera stood triumphantly in the cage, her arms outstretched.

The crowd cheered. Dave unlatched the cage door and ushered her out.

Moeera took a deep bow. She stood aside for Dave and Tony to recover the cage.

Chapter Twenty-two

Down in the cellar, Mallory walked the hall toward the stairs. The way was dark, lit by only the occasional oil lamp. She was beginning to feel like the Mojo again. Wecks met her in the middle.

"Good luck," Mallory said.

"Break a leg," he replied.

Mallory giggled.

* * *

On stage, Moeera was watching the two men turn the cage. They were purposefully counting their steps to keep things slow and measured.

Moeera addressed the audience as loudly as she could.

"Around the cage goes," she projected, "and the spell reaches out… searching… searching. Where are you? Return to us… now!"

Dave and Tony tore the tarpaulin from the cage, revealing the Wondrous Wecks.

The audience burst into applause at the sight of the wizard. Most people were doing doubletakes. Where was Mallory?

Wecks emerged and took a bow.

* * *

Mallory felt good, genuinely good. Izzpalin was out for her blood, and she was trying to flush her out. But right at this moment she was happy. The show was going off without a hitch. Moeera was enjoying herself, and she was a part of that.

If their lives weren't in danger, she'd be genuinely enjoying herself. Magic, real or illusion, brought out the wonder in everyone who witnessed it. It felt good being a part of that again.

She came to the room at the hallway's end and hurried to the stairs.

There was somebody standing beside the bottom step. Whoever it was wore a long, dark cloak with the hood up. The muscles tensed in Mallory's neck and shoulders.

"Excuse me," Mallory said. "I have to get by. Part of the show."

The figure turned and the hood fell back revealing pale, almost translucent skin and a wavy mass of dark hair.

Mallory let out a gasp. "Izzpalin," she said with dread in her voice.

"Mojo," she said, grinning. "So, it actually is you. I knew I was right, but I constantly found myself doubtful."

"Yes, it is I," Mallory said. "Will you let me pass, please?"

"I suppose I could," Izzy said, "but that would give you the upper hand."

"Then I'll just have to go through you."

Mallory was reaching out to every living being for strength. The flicker of a fireball was sparking into existence above her open hand.

"Can you go through yourself?" Izzy asked.

"What?"

Mallory glanced at Izzy's face. Every bit as harsh and cruel as she remembered. Izzy's self-confident grin hadn't changed either. She was older now, wrinkles taking over her face.

Then the wrinkles began shrinking away as if the face absorbed them. Mallory felt something cold on her hand. Glancing down, she noticed that the fireball had become ice. It fell off her hand, shattering on the floor.

She concentrated on a different spell to solidify Izzy's feet and root them to the wooden floor, but she was suddenly freezing. Frost covered her face and blocked her vision. She tried to summon a heat of the heart spell, but it was too late.

Mallory was incapacitated, her body stiff and her breath coming in ragged little gasps.

"No challenge at all," Izzy said, rushing up the steps.

Not only did the blood witch look younger, but she also bore an uncanny resemblance to Mallory. Her black dress rippled like the ocean at high tide.

When she rushed onto the stage she wore a blue gown indistinguishable from the Mojo's. She raised her arm toward the cage and the now present Wecks. Then she took her turn bowing with the others.

Wecks took center stage. "Thank you all! That's it for our show. Thank you for coming to see us perform! It's been wonderful to have you all here!"

The curtains closed. Izzy joined Moeera and Wecks behind them.

"You ladies were terrific!" Wecks said in a more subdued version of his excited voice.

"You're a fine teacher!" Moeera exclaimed, rushing to embrace the large man.

"Thank you," Wecks said. "You're an exceptional student."

"I feel so happy!" Moeera exclaimed.

"A good show will do that for you," Wecks said.

"What a rush," Izzy said from behind Mallory's face.

"Exactly," Wecks agreed. "There really is nothing like the high one gets performing for a good audience."

Dave and Tony were moving the bamboo cage into the backstage area.

Dave said, "Cork and Kettle, Wecks?"

Wecks nodded. "Yes, that sounds good. Would you ladies care to celebrate with us at The Cork and Kettle?"

Izzy looked at Moeera. The little girl was liable to lose her eyes when they popped out. Of course, Izzy's will was immune to such trifles. But... it might just make spiriting the brat away that much easier.

"Count us in!" Izzy said. "Will we have time to change clothes first."

"I believe it," Wecks said. "We'll walk back to the trailer, get changed, and accompany you over there in your wagon. Is that acceptable?"

"Certainly," Izzy said.

They helped Dave, Tony, and Paul to set all the props and pieces by the theater's back door. Then they walked across the fairground to the trailer. With the curtain dividing the space in two, the performers changed out of their flashy garb.

Izzy found Mallory's hick town clothes atop a chair. This presented her with a conundrum. It looked like she was wearing the blue dress from the trailer closet, but she really had her slinky, black number on. Moeera was right there with her.

When Moeera was involved enough with her own clothes and not looking, Izzy "changed" from blue dress to dull, provincial garb. She hid Mallory's clothes beneath a large pillow.

"Mama?"

"Yes, dear?" Izzy asked.

"Do you think Papa will come to the Cork and Kettle with us?"

"I don't see why not," Izzy said.

"I hope he does," Moeera said. "I want to ask what he thought of the show."

"You'll see him in a moment. You can ask him then."

"Yes, Mama."

Izzy was trying to size the girl up now that they were finally in the same place together. She really seemed quite insignificant to the blood witch—a young, naïve girl no different than most. Her redeeming qualities were her curiosity and her love of magic. She might provide a better apprentice witch than Joria given time.

Chapter Twenty-three

K or was waiting by the wagon. The blacksmith could hardly contain his excitement. Smiling, he embraced the disguised blood witch. He kissed her ear, saying, "Fantastic show, darling!"

"Wasn't it?" Izzy replied. "Thank you."

"And you," he said, kneeling until he could see eye to eye with his daughter. "You were absolutely amazing! Magnificent Moeera!"

She hugged him then, clinging tightly. "Thank you, Papa! You liked it, huh?"

"I loved it," he said, kissing her cheek twice.

"We're going to the Cork and Kettle to…"

"Celebrate!" Wecks finished for her. He descended the steps from the trailer, smiling.

He looked completely ordinary now in a plain, midnight blue suit.

"Indeed," Kor said. "Sounds good to me."

He helped "Mallory" up to the driver's platform and climbed up beside her.

The fool, Izzy thought. *He suspects nothing!*

Moeera and the showmen piled into the back. It was a nice load for Dot and Bahb.

Kor drove them all from the fairground to the Cork and Kettle.

"I'm thirsty enough to drink a jade tea," Dave commented.

"Well," Moeera boasted, "I'm thirsty enough to drink a fizzy scrapper."

"Oh, my," Wecks said.

The others laughed good-naturedly.

Wecks felt both exhilarated and uneasy. Kor and Mallory didn't seem the least bit on edge. Yet, none of them had seen hide nor hair of the blood witch. Mallory had been so darned sure that the magic show would flush her out....

"Wecks!"

Mallory was turned around in her seat, looking at him.

"Sorry, Mrs. Robin," he said. "My thoughts took flight for a bit there."

"I was just asking how long you've been performing your show."

"Hmm... I've been learning my trade since I was about twelve," he said. "I toured with another wizard for about a year. Then Paul and I started a small show, more of a side-act. We met Tony and Dave a couple of years after that. To answer your question, I've been doing this show for the last eighteen years."

"That's a long time that the four of you have been working together," Mallory said.

"Definitely a while," Dave said.

"Yes," Tony said. "All good years too."

Paul chimed in, "They certainly weren't all easy. The entertainment business has given us a fair share of lean times."

They arrived at the Cork and Kettle. Wecks and his partners entered the doorway with Kor and his family close behind. Moeera was rushing after Paul to get inside and enjoy every moment of her success.

Mallory was at the threshold when someone in the dark shouted.

"Stop!"

She and Kor turned to see a figure in a bright, blue dress. The woman ran toward them.

"What? Mallory! But...," Kor trailed off as realization sunk in.

He looked at his wife who was tensing beside him.

Izzy looked back with Mallory's face, wearing an uncharacteristic smug look.

"God!" Kor exclaimed. He took a step away from the doppelganger.

"It's her, the blood witch," the real Mallory said. Kor thought he detected an underlying snarl there. He suddenly felt weak.

"So, Mojo, you got free from my trap," Izzy said. "Show me what else you can do that won't matter at all."

Mallory felt a scream rising in her, but she forced it down somewhere into her gut. She thought of the good life she'd led since Moeera had been born. All the time they'd spent together as her daughter grew up. She with

140

Moeera as a toddler visiting the chickens, Moeera clapping her hands together and laughing as if they were the height of hilarity. Walking along a field's edge on a sunny day collecting blackberries. Teaching Moeera to collect eggs from the henhouse, teaching her how to spot ripe vegetables to pick.

Mallory hovered between memory and the present, remaining calm and centered. She drew strength from the environment around her as anybody would draw breath from the air.

Izzy, always striving to one-up even herself, waved a finger at Mallory's feet. The ground opened, swallowing Mallory and forcing Kor to run for cover. Izzy waved her hand and closed her fist, causing the chasm in the ground to close.

She smiled, but before she could so much as gloat, root-like tendrils sprang from the soil, wrapping around her ankles!

"Aaah! No!" she screamed in vain.

She was yanked down on her knees. More roots came forth to snag her wrists. Immobilized, she glared at Kor. He felt the invisible chain pulling him toward her to help her get free.

A burst of light between them knocked Kor on his butt. Mallory materialized next to Izzy.

"Why can't you just pass on by and leave us alone!" she demanded.

Izzy struggled against her bonds. "Because I want you dead! Whitesider!"

The roots holding Izzy fell slack. She sprang to her feet. Then a curious thing happened. Before she could attack Mallory, a small, dark shape darted between her legs.

"Soot!" Kor exclaimed.

He and Mallory watched as the rabbit seemed to run like spilled ink. Its shape changed and grew, catching Izzy atop itself.

Then the rabbit was gone, and in its place was a magnificent black horse. The horse stamped and blew. It neighed once, and then it rocketed off carrying Izzy on its back!

Mallory watched the two disappear completely into the night. Her shoulders slumped.

She looked at Kor who was on his feet once again and said, "I knew he was a puca."

They embraced. Each held the other tightly. When they were able to let each other go, Mallory looked at her blue stage gown. She snapped her fingers. Lo and behold, she was wearing her own clothes again.

Chapter Twenty-four

Mallory and Kor went in to join the others. They found them seated at several tables that were pulled together. Tony was telling Moeera about a trick Wecks did during his early days as a traveling showman.

"Finally!" Paul said.

"Mama, Papa! What took you so long?"

"We were just talking, Mee," Mallory said.

"Moeera thought you two had somehow got lost at the front door," Wecks said.

"We just needed a moment alone," Kor said.

"We took the liberty of ordering you each a drink," Wecks said.

The bartender brought their drinks. "Heidi will be over to take your orders," he said.

"Thank you," Dave said.

"You know," Moeera said, swirling the contents of her magical mystery tempest with her finger, "that was a less dangerous show than the one where you escaped from the water vat."

"It certainly was," Wecks said.

"Moeera, that escape always went a bit differently," Tony said.

"It did?" the girl asked, then took a gulp of the tempest.

"Escapes are like that," Wecks said. "Escapology is a science unto itself. If you're under the water, you have a limited time to complete your task before you run out of air and drown."

"So why do escapes at all then?" Kor asked.

"The audiences eat them up," the magician said. "They see you do something like that... you must be powerful. Capable of anything."

"What'll you have?" Heidi asked. The waitress loomed over them with a notepad.

"I'd like the gypsmacks."

"The winklesmoot."

"Whole wheat and kooble."

"Corn schwink."

"Grilled cheese."

"What do you want, Moeera?" Mallory asked.

"Well… I'll have grilled cheese too."

"And I'll have the striped bean curd."

"Ya want dill swickles with that?" Heidi asked.

"Sure," Mallory said.

"Alright," Heidi said. "Will that be everything?"

"Yes, ma'am."

"Good, cause the kitchen's closing real soon. Ya know what I'm saying?"

"Mm-hmm."

She hurried off to put the last orders of the night in.

"Back to escapes," Wecks said. "I'm glad I didn't have to do one this time—less chance of dying that way."

"Exactly," Mallory said. She lifted her glass and drank.

"Whiskey!" she said, eyes slitting. "Not what I would have ordered, but I think I could use one about now."

"Good," Wecks said. "We weren't sure. Thought you might want something strong."

"Mine the same?" Kor asked. "Good."

Dave and Tony were drinking the local Gillikin Ridge Ale. Paul was having a freeplesneak. Wecks nursed his purple vavoom.

Then the question came. The question on Moeera's mind.

"Where did you come up with that name that you called Mama?" Moeera asked.

"Probably in the trailer while I was reviewing the equipment list," Wecks said matter-of-factly.

"Very funny," Moeera said. She wasn't about to be put off.

"Perhaps I'd better answer this one, Moeera," Mallory said.

Moeera shifted her gaze to her mother.

"You see," Mallory said, feeling very self-conscious, "Wecks called me

The Mojo because that's the name I went by when I was your age. It was my witch's name, given to me by the Council of the Sea."

Moeera's jaw dropped almost to the tabletop.

"You? A witch? How – how can that be?" she stammered.

Mallory took a deep breath. "Magic has been intertwined with this land for a very long time. There have been countless beings to practice the magic arts. At the time of my birth, our land had factions everywhere. Two of those were the Council of the Sea and the Tobreeb Coven. My parents belonged to the former."

"My mother taught me to feel the magic around me and to use it to my advantage. When I turned eight, I became her official apprentice. That's how I became a witch."

"Then why are you a farmer?" Moeera asked.

"Because I realized after years of witchcraft and taking part in the ceremonies that I'd rather lead a simple life."

"You don't even use magic—at all!" Moeera screeched.

"That was true until a couple of days ago."

"What do you mean?"

"That's when I found out that a witch of the black arts was hunting for our family," Mallory said.

Moeera listened to this revelation in wonder. Not only was her mother not at all what she believed, but an evil witch was after them. Moeera was speechless for a few minutes. So was everybody else. Finally, Wecks broke the uncomfortable silence.

"That's an incredible story, Mrs. Robin," Wecks said, gravely.

"A witch, truly," Paul said. "I never would have suspected."

Heidi brought them their food on a big, circular tray. "I could only fit half on," she said. "I'll be back."

Moeera stared at her grilled cheese.

"Are you going to say anything?" her mother asked.

Silence.

"Surely, you'll have some questions you want to ask Mama," Kor said. "You don't have to right this minute unless you want to."

"Yes, Mee," Mallory said. "I realize this is a lot."

Moeera nodded.

Heidi returned with the rest of the food.

"Thank you," Dave said.

"Thanks, Miss," Wecks said.

Heidi scrutinized the five men, woman, and girl. "So, are you from the fair?"

"Yes, indeed we are," Paul said. "It's hungry work, ma'am."

"Oh, yeah?" Heidi asked. She looked at Wecks. "You know, you look familiar."

"You probably saw me in here earlier this week," he said.

"No, I've seen you before someplace, you know what I'm sayin'?"

"Umm...."

"Now I remember! You're the wizard, aren't you? You did the belly flop into that big tub of water!"

"Guilty," Wecks said.

"I saw you do that! All tied up. How the heck did you get out of there?"

"I have a knack for knots, Miss Heidi," he said.

"I'll say you do! I thought for sure you were a goner. Barry did too!"

"Sometimes the thought's crossed my mind while I'm under water that it might be my final moment alive," Wecks admitted. "It gets a little scary."

"How do you do that, over and over again? I could never do that! I'd be so afraid."

"I'm a wizard, dear," he said with a twinkle in his eye. "I use magic."

"Well!" Heidi said. "I hope your magic stays strong!"

"So do I," he said.

She left them to their meal.

"This is great," Paul said. "Great show, great people, and now some time to celebrate."

"You can say that again," Tony said. "Let's toast your assistant."

"Here, here," Dave said, lifting his glass. "She survived the Basket of Destiny. To Moeera!"

"To Moeera," the others echoed.

Moeera's smile widened until the entire Cork and Kettle was bright.

They all clinked glasses and drank to the girl.

"What will we do about the evil witch?" Moeera asked.

Mallory looked at her daughter and said, "Soot arrived in the nick of time just before Papa and I came in here. He became a mighty creature and

146

carried the bad witch away."

Moeera dropped her grilled cheese on the plate. "What!"

"It happened just then," Mallory said. "That's what took us so long to come in. The witch wanted to kill us."

"What will happen to Soot?"

"I don't know. Who does know when it comes to pucas?"

"I'm betting that Soot will be fine," Kor said. "He was magnificent when he became that... that...."

"Horse," Mallory finished his sentence for him. "Though, now that horses are seen so rarely I wonder if he'll ever choose that form again."

"What if the witch hurts him?" Moeera asked.

Dave chimed into the conversation. "I wouldn't worry about him, Moeera. He's a magical creature. His kind are known far and wide for the mischief they're capable of."

"You really think so?" Moeera asked.

"Yes," Dave said. "He may have spent a lot of time as a bunny, but underneath that he's a very cunning puca. Most importantly, he was your friend."

"I doubt that witch was any match for him," Wecks said.

"I hope he comes back," Moeera said.

"We all do," Mallory said. "As for the witch, we will have to be on our guard."

"Does that mean you're going to teach me magic?" Moeera asked.

"I suppose so," Mallory said, smiling.

"Good," Moeera said.

"So, you'll get what you've been wanting," Wecks said. "You won't even have to leave home."

It seemed that the blood witch's machinations against the Mojo and her family had ended. If not for good, then for some undefined interlude.

After their meal and some light-hearted conversation, the group left. Wecks and company would be grabbing some sleep before an early start the next day. Everything needed to be packed up just right so they could travel to their next destination.

Mallory was very tired. She drew strength from the living world around her, but now that her spells were cast she felt weary. Moeera and Kor were tired too. Moeera had exhausted her excited energy and was ready for bed.

She fell asleep as soon as her head hit the pillow.

The little farmhouse was quiet in the night. It was a bit lonelier without the black bunny called Soot.

Chapter Twenty-five

The next day after dragging herself out of bed, Moeera looked around the house and the barnyard for the puca, but he wasn't there. She hoped that he would come back to them, bunny or not.

She fed the chickens and opened the coop door to their little enclosure. She checked everyone's water. Then she stole away to see Wecks before he left.

When Mallory and Kor woke up, Moeera was long gone for the fairground. Most Sundays they went to church, but this week they just slept in.

"Do you think Soot was able to beat the witch?" Kor asked.

"I don't know," Mallory said. "He certainly surprised her, but beyond that I wonder."

"She hasn't come after us again," Kor said. "That's a good sign."

"She could just be lying in wait," Mallory said. "She's devious, that one is."

"Yes," Kor said.

"Now, everything has changed. The word will get around town that I may be a witch. They'll treat us differently."

"It doesn't necessarily mean they'll treat us badly," Kor said.

"I suppose it doesn't, but..."

"But what?" Kor asked, curiously.

"It seems funny, you know, after your friends were killed by that bear... you wounded it, drove it away."

"Yes."

"And the town gossips started rumors that it must be witchcraft involved."

"That's right," Kor said. "They whispered that a witch or witches must have been involved."

"And they practically blamed you for being alive, of all the salacious ideas!"

"What are you driving at?" he asked.

"Those same nosy liars will be all over us...."

"Perhaps," Kor said. "How can we know for sure?"

"It's just...."

"What?"

"Just...."

Yes! Kor screamed in his mind. *Figure it out. You're so close!*

Even if Izzy was far, far away, her power still held him in silence about what she'd been up to.

"...witchcraft."

Mallory looked at Kor intensely as if seeing him anew.

"The only survivor," she said, looking at him with a wooden face. "The blood marks on your neck, they make perfect sense now."

"Don't be silly," Kor's lips mouthed. Against his will, his larynx produced the sound against his wishes.

"Izzpalin's been controlling you all this time—for months!" Mallory accused. "Oh, Mother! It's why you've been so weak! Oh, Kor...."

Kor didn't respond. Now that she knew, he should be free to tell her she was right, shouldn't he?

"It – it's...."

"Yes?" Mallory asked.

"It – it's – it's..."

She knows! I can talk to her about it, can't I!

"What am I going to do with you?" Mallory asked in despair. "Even now, she controls you."

"True," Kor said. He was sweating.

"We need to get the hell out of here," Mallory said. "Unless Soot dumped her in a bottomless pit, she'll be coming."

"Where will we go?" Kor asked.

"Somewhere," she said.

She dared not tell him for fear of Izzy finding out. All she could do was keep her lips buttoned.

150

"You were such a good assistant, Moeera," Wecks said. "I wish you were coming with us."

"That's what I've been wishing for since you left the last time," she said. "I'm going to stay and learn magic from my mother though."

"I understand," Wecks said. "Should your heart ever yearn for the stage, you have a place with us. Just find us."

"Thank you!" she said. She embraced the magician in a bear hug. Wecks was so much bigger than her that you might call it a bear cub hug.

"You're very welcome," he said. "We'll be back this way eventually. I look forward to seeing all the new things you can do."

"I'll be here," Moeera said.

"I have something for you," Wecks said. "Parting gift. I'll be right back."

He vanished into the trailer.

Tony and Dave walked over.

"Good luck, Moeera," Tony said.

"Yes, good luck," Dave seconded. "You'll be great. Who better to teach you than your mother."

"Yes," Moeera said. She still had trouble believing that Mama was a witch.

Wecks emerged from the trailer with something clutched in his right hand. He held it out to Moeera, wrapped in a handkerchief.

She took the gift and unwrapped the fabric. It was...

"An old stick?" she asked.

"Not just any old stick," Wecks said, proudly. "The wand of Murr."

"Wand of Murr...."

"Murr was the old fairy I met when I was not so much older than you, Moeera," Wecks said. "I never use it in my magic shows, but I thought maybe a true apprentice witch might find use for it."

Moeera turned the old stick over and over in her hands.

"I don't know what to say," she said in a hushed tone.

"No thanks necessary," her friend said. "Perhaps it will help you do magic. Perhaps not. Keep it as a memento of our time together."

"I will!" she cried, hugging Wecks again. "Thank you! I'll miss you."

"I'll miss you too," he said. "You keep smiling and never give up."

When Moeera returned home, she discovered that her parents were packing a lot of stuff onto their wagon. Not only were they packing vegetables, fruits, grains, and eggs for the market; they'd loaded clothes, blankets, lamps, tools, bachukka feed, water, and other things as well.

"What's going on?" she asked. "Why are we moving?"

"We're not," Mallory said. "We're taking a trip."

"To where?"

"Oh, here and there," Mallory said. "We're going to begin your instruction in magic."

"Why can't we do it here?"

"This will be better, believe me. There are aspects of the magic arts that we won't be able to study here."

"It sounds complicated."

"Not too complicated, Mee."

"Wecks gave me a gift to remember him by," Moeera said. She showed her mother the wand.

"What's this?"

"A wand he got from a fairy."

Mallory's eyes widened. "Really? A fairy?"

"Yes, Mama. Her name was Murr."

"Hmm." Mallory looked puzzled.

She stopped what she was doing and held out her hand. "May I?"

Moeera gave her the stick and watched carefully as she rolled it along her fingers.

"Does it feel hot?" she asked.

"Huh?" Mallory asked.

"Sean got a magic wand from a goblin in the book at school. It was supposed to feel hot if you had magic."

"You mean the book about Corbeck," Mallory said, realization dawning. "I remember now. There's truth to that line of thought, but it depends on several things."

"What?" Moeera asked.

"For one thing, the wand isn't magical itself."

"It's not?"

"No, a witch uses her wand to direct her spell—her focus. All it really is,

152

is an extension of your arm."

"Like a prop?"

"Not exactly. It's more of a tool, like a carpenter's guide for making cuts. Secondly, some wands have been imbued with residual magic from longtime or powerful users."

"Has this one had magic rub off on it?"

"I don't know," Mallory said. "I'll have to examine it further."

She handed it back to Moeera.

"In any case, you have a memento of your time with Wecks. We'll get to wands and their usage soon enough. You can use that one."

"Great!" Moeera exclaimed.

And so, Moeera helped her parents prepare for the journey. She helped pack food for the road, wondering if it would be enough. Where would they go? Where would they stay? What would they see along the way?

Arrangements were made for their home and farm. They weren't sold, but they were left in the care of the closest neighbors. The chickens and the goats would be looked after. The land and the bounty were theirs to reap until the Robins came home again.

Dot and Bahb were hitched to the wagon, now sporting a set of hoops to hold a canvas cover.

They went to Wadow's house so Kor could say goodbye.

He gave his assistant the keys to the lockbox in the shop.

Then they left.

Chapter Twenty-six

Moeera spent a good portion of that day staring out the back of the wagon. That, and thinking. Even though she wasn't on the road with Wecks and friends, here she was on the road. Sometimes life confused her.

She wished that Soot had come with them. She missed him being there. Ever since she'd met him he'd been around. Almost her perfect shadow. She wondered what had happened to him after he ran off with the blood witch. Was he still alive? Was the witch?

They traveled all day long. The only time they stopped was to deliver some produce and eggs to the farmer's market in Breezetown.

The rhythmic clopping produced by the bachukkas' hooves ticked away the time as it passed. Moeera pulled out the copy of Corbeck by the Sea her mother had packed. She wasn't even aware she had that book until she saw it being carefully tucked in the wagon.

She began reading where Mr. Court left off in class....

Sean and Jimmy continued through the woods. After their palaver with the trolls, they met many other interesting folks. No one threatened them or spoke at all about the Lady of the Raven.

Until they met the giant, that is.

They were far past Josh's house when they heard a thumping sound. The sound got louder and louder. The ground shook. The trees creaked. The birds made a racket.

"I think the giant we've heard about is coming this way," Jimmy said.

"You do, do you!" Sean exclaimed. "And what do you propose we do about it?"

Then the giant saved Jimmy the trouble of answering by bounding into their midst.

He was more than one hundred feet tall with legs big around as tree trunks. He had dark hair and eyes the color of pitch. His face was pasty white with a dopey look that became one of triumph when he saw the two knights.

"Ho, ho!" he said, in a voice that could split rock. "I reckon you two will make a satisfying lunch!"

"I'm afraid you're mistaken, chap," Sean called to the brute. "We're both lean and gristly. You'd have a better lunch if you ate your shoes!"

"Well, I'll be the judge of that!" the giant snarled.

"What's your name?" Jimmy asked.

"Why?" the giant asked.

"I just make it a point of knowing who it is I'm dispatching to the underworld."

"The name is Sant," the giant said, grinning. "Side Sant. Go ahead and dispatch me."

"With pleasure," Jimmy said. He drew his sword and urged his horse forward. "Yeeah!"

Sean's eyes were dinner plates. The giant was the size of Griffin's Peak back home. What could Jimmy possibly do with his sword against such a mountain? He exhaled and drew his own sword.

"Gimme strength," he muttered.

Sean charged his horse toward the giant. The giant seized Jimmy, horse and all, in his hands. Try as he might, Jimmy couldn't reach the giant with his sword. The enormous man used one hand to hold the horse and the other to pinch the sword between two tree-sized fingers.

"Ouch," Side said, pulling the sword from Jimmy's grasp.

Jimmy looked up, horrified.

Side Sant stuck the sword into the side of a tree as if it was a flagpole. Then he reached down for Jimmy.

Jimmy leapt from his saddle, but the giant caught him anyway. He felt the giant's fingers grasping him by his shoulders. Then he was pulled up, up, and away as the giant held him aloft.

"What were you saying again?" Side Sant asked. "You're going to dispatch me?"

He began laughing, but stopped short when Sean rode up behind him and thrust his sword into the giant's posterior.

155

"Ouch!" Side, said. "Fierce li'l mosquito."

He lumbered around to face Sir Sean.

"We have no quarrel with you," Sean said. "Let us go on our way in peace."

"I'm too hungry to let you go!" Side exclaimed. "I'm hungry as hungry can be!"

"We could help you hunt for your lunch!" Sean called up to the giant. "Jimmy and I are old hats at hunting!"

"It would have to be a pretty big lunch!"

"That goes without saying," Sean called. "We'd rather have lunch with you than be lunch!"

Side Sant regarded the two knights, curiously.

"I have to admit you have an interesting proposal," he said. The knights shuddered as they would during a loud crack of thunder.

"Then take us up on it!" Sean shouted. "We're trustworthy."

"Are you?" Side asked. "Probably are. Where do you call home?"

"Corbeck," Sean said. "The kingdom ruled by my kinsman King Cullen."

"Corbeck, eh," the giant said in a tone that made the hairs on Sir Sean's neck stand up.

"That's correct," Jimmy added from where he hung. He had a considerably uncomfortable view of Side's gaping mouth.

"I'm afraid I can't spare you then," the giant said. "I'll have you fellows for my repast."

"What!" Sean cried. "What's Corbeck got to do with this?"

The giant didn't answer. He scooped Sean up and put him and Jimmy into one hand. Then he drove the horses ahead of him.

"This is a fine pickle we're in," Jimmy muttered. He was pressed against Sean in Side's enclosed fingers.

"Keep your fingers crossed and your eyes open," Sean said.

*   *   *

After what seemed like a very long time, the giant opened his fist and deposited Sean and Jimmy into a huge bowl.

"Hum dee dum dee diddle," the giant sang.

Wherever they were, they could both see again.

"Good lord!" Jimmy said. "We're in a giant mixing bowl!"

156

"Ugh!" Sean said. "Where are the horses?"

A telltale neighing revealed the steeds' presence somewhere else in the great kitchen.

Jimmy stood up and said, "We've got to get out of here."

"Hoist me up," Sean said. "Let's see how far I can reach."

Jimmy hoisted Sean up against the bowl's side and onto his shoulders. The concave shape made keeping his balance harder the closer he moved to the side.

Sean balanced as best he could. He reached tentatively upward for the top. His fingers grasped as far as they could.

"Drat," he said, breathing heavily. "Stretch I may, but I can't touch the edge!"

"Let's get you down on your feet," Jim said. He bent at his knees, allowing Sean to slide along the wall.

Sean jumped off his cousin's shoulders. He landed with a thud.

"What can we do?" he mused.

"Let's think of a plan," Jimmy said.

"Hmm," Sean murmured, looking at the bowl's smooth sides. "Too smooth to climb, even the way we tried."

"Could we flip it over?" Jimmy asked. "Even better, on its side?"

Sean ran from one spot to another. "I should think so. Join in. Together now."

They ran across the flat bottom and up a couple steps, then back and two steps up the other side.

"Repeat," Sean said.

They kept at it. Inertia helped them get a bit higher up the curve on their next couple tries.

The bowl began to wobble.

"That's it!" Jimmy exclaimed.

Finally, they built up enough momentum that the bowl rolled onto its side. They leapt out onto an enormous table, and the bowl rolled over the side. It hit the floor with a clatter.

"Oh, boy," Sean said. "I'll bet he heard that."

Jimmy scanned the surrounding tabletop in all directions. "Oh, well."

"Fitty!" Sean called.

An answering whinny brought his gaze to the two horses. They were far below on the vast floor. Each was tethered to a ring in the wall.

"They're unharmed, at least," Sean said.

"There's no way down," Jimmy declared.

He was right. A fall from this height would be lethal.

"Get that stick out," Jim said. "You still have it, don't you?"

"Sure," Sean said, digging for the stick. "If it hasn't broken, that is."

He produced the stick he'd received from Grahk.

"It won't work for either of us," Sean said.

"According to his story, which I never really believed anyway," Jimmy said. "Thing is, all we can do now is pray or die."

"Do you think praying will help?" Sean asked.

"It might," Jimmy said. "You believe in God, don't you?"

"Yes, but I—"

"That's really all we need. Faith."

The horses were braying now.

"He's coming!" Sean cried.

"We're going to both hold the stick in our hands," Jimmy said.

The table shook ever so slightly.

"Dear Lord in Heaven," Jimmy said, "we are about to be eaten by a giant. Please help and guide us. If ever this stick was a magic tool, let us defend ourselves now."

Sean nodded. "Help us, great Lord. We vow to follow your teachings for as long as we may draw breath."

They both concluded by saying, "In your name we pray."

"Hah hah!" Side laughed from the doorway. "Trying to escape? You two are hilarious!"

He stomped to the table and reached for the knights.

Sean waved the stick in his hand and shouted, "Abra kadabra!"

The giant laughed again, scooping the two up.

"You have no swords and are as mice to me," he said. "Now you seek to assail me with gibberish!"

He picked up the bowl and returned them to it. Then he snatched away the magic wand.

"Hey!" Sean shouted.

"Hay's for horses," Side muttered. He examined the stick, then threw it on the table.

"Your time is up," he said. "I'm famished. Too bad you aren't a little bigger."

He grabbed a bag of cornmeal and dumped some in the bowl.

Sean and Jimmy danced about in the rain of meal. It slid off their clothes and fell from their heads and shoulders. As they brushed the meal off, they kept bumping into each other.

"Hey!" Sean said. "The bowl edge is getting lower."

"No, we're getting taller!" Jimmy exclaimed. "Look!"

Suddenly they could see over the bowl's edge and beyond. They scrambled out of it, Sean's foot sending it back to the floor.

Side looked at them aghast.

"What is happening!" he uttered in a high-pitched whine.

Then they leapt from the table—just as big as the giant!

What a round of fisticuffs ensued between Jimmy and Side! Jimmy caught the brute with a solid right hook to his jaw. Side stepped backward into the wall.

"That'll make you think twice before trying to eat anyone," Jimmy huffed.

Side yelled and exploded forward. He caught Jimmy by surprise, pushing him against the table.

Sean stepped in, grabbing Side's right arm and pulling it behind him.

"Whoof," Side breathed.

"Why did you react the way you did when we mentioned we were from Corbeck?" Sean demanded.

"I don't understand," Side complained. "Corbeck is supposed to be full of little people."

"What do you know about it?" Sean pressed.

"Giants lived there, along the coast, a long time ago," Side said. "Then you little people came and multiplied like rabbits!"

"Corbeck has been there for generations," Jimmy said.

"Maybe so," Side said, "but we giants live a long time. We remember when it was our country."

"So… what are you planning?" Sean asked. "An attack?"

"She plans the attack," Side said. "She didn't say your people had any quick-growers though."

He seemed annoyed. Sean couldn't help thinking about one word.

"She who?" he asked.

"Oh, the ancient one," Side said. "She of the raven."

Sean's blood ran cold. It had to be the same woman the goblins warned them about.

"When will the attack be?" Jimmy asked.

"Why would I tell you?"

"Because it's two to one," Sean said.

"You haven't got the guts to kill me," Side said.

"Don't you think so?"

"No, that's why it will be so easy to squash your kingdom to dust."

Sean resisted the urge to belt Side in the chops.

"This is completely mad!" Sean said.

"We could find a common ground to work this out," Jimmy said.

"I truly doubt it," Side said.

"You don't have to mow us all down...."

Jimmy stopped speaking.

Side Sant stood as still as a statue. He no longer struggled in Jimmy's hands. Not one bit. His mouth was frozen, his eyes stared into space.

"What happened?" Sean asked. "Hey!" He snapped his fingers in front of Side's face.

Nothing. No reaction.

"That's strange," Jimmy said.

"So is growing to giant size," Sean said. He picked up the wand and held it gingerly in his hand.

A flash of white light appeared in front of them, and a woman's voice said, "Be still, brave knights."

The two men now experienced the staggering sensation of shrinking down to their true size. One moment they fit the kitchen around them, the next they once again felt like mice. The giant loomed above them.

"Who are you?" Sean asked the voice.

"I'm a friend," she said.

The white light moved downward. It slowly drifted toward the floor in front of them.

A beautiful woman dressed all in white and silver stepped from the light. It faded from sight and left her standing before them, smiling.

"Greetings," the woman said. She lifted the silvery hem of her dress

160

and curtseyed.

Sean and Jimmy were dumbfounded.

"My name is Angela," she said in a friendly voice. "Yes, I am a fairy--I sense you were wondering that."

"That's wonderful!" Sean said, grinning. "King Cullen sent us to find you."

"Me?" she asked. "Whatever for?"

"He wondered if there were fairies in these woods anymore," Sean said.

"I'd say that question has been answered," Angela said.

"There's more," Sean said, "but tell us, did you freeze the giant like that?"

"Not only that," she said. "I made you both big enough to stand up to him."

Sean and Jimmy exchanged glances. This woman, this fairy, could defeat all three of them if she were so inclined. King Cullen was right in seeking out her kind.

"Will you help us defeat the giants?" Jimmy asked.

"This is the only giant nearby," Angela said. "He'll be still like that long enough for you to get away."

"Thank you," Sean said. "Is there any way that we can repay you for saving our lives?"

"Yes, there is," she said. "I want you to keep using your brains. You tried talking your way out of that predicament."

"It would have been preferable to fighting," Jimmy said, "and being eaten."

"Absolutely," Angela said. "And not all giants are like that... cannibalizing people who are smaller than they are. Some of them aren't bad."

"King Cullen was hoping to enlist your help," Sean said.

"Help with what, Sir Sean?" she asked.

"Our countryside and the coastal lands have been plagued by monsters," Sean said. "We didn't know why there have been so many recently. Do you know why? We've heard twice now about a mysterious "Lady of the Raven".

"I see," Angela said. Her smile became a look of indifference.

"I'm sorry if I offended you, bright lady," Sean said.

161

"You haven't," she said, smiling again.

She's forcing it, Sean thought.

Angela looked him straight in the eye and said, "It just isn't known to me how much we fairies should involve ourselves."

"Oh," Sean said.

"I shall have to discuss it further with the others in the Forest of Burzee," she said.

"What can I tell King Cullen?" Sean asked.

"The woman you have heard tell of... she is the Morrigan."

"The Morrigan?" Jimmy asked.

"Yes," Angela said, a millisecond of fear in her eyes. It was so quick as to have nearly not happened. Yet, it had.

She cleared her throat. "She is known by other names, but the Morrigan is her true appellation. She is very skilled at the art of war, and she is very dangerous."

"The Lady of the Raven is the Morrigan?" Sean said. "The Morrigan is legendary."

"A couple of goblins we met warned us that she's raising an army to wipe out our kingdom," Jimmy said.

Sean's eyes widened. He raised his hands in frustration. "Why would she want us dead? We've never even met her!"

"I know not why she sets her sights on Corbeck," Angela said, "but that is what I have heard also."

"We must ride home and warn the king," Sean said. "Forewarned is forearmed. We can muster up defenses, contact allies."

"If this is the same being from the legends, then most men would lay odds on her victory," Jimmy said.

Determination dominated Angela's face. "Let's prove them wrong," she said.

"Yes, my lady," Sean said.

"Corbeck will stand," Jimmy added.

Angela smiled. "Now," she said. "You know there are still fairies, not just fairytales. Time to return home."

Before either of them could utter another word, there was a blinding flash of light.

Sir Sean and Sir Jimmy opened their eyes to find they were no longer in

162

Side Sant's kitchen. They sat atop their steeds on a grassy road. The road led to an orchard and beyond the orchard....

"Corbeck!" Jimmy thundered. "How in the world?"

"Angela, no doubt," Sean answered. "She gave us a speedy shortcut home."

"Right," Jimmy said. "It's altogether unbelievable just the same."

Sean shook his head and blinked his eyes. "Magic!" he said, stashing the stick he was holding in a saddle bag.

Then they rode the short distance home.

*   *   *

Moeera closed the book and set it aside. Sean and Jimmy found the fairies—a fairy. She hadn't expected them to get home the way they did.

She was glad to have the book with. It entertained her and allowed her to keep practicing her reading skills.

Chapter Twenty-seven

When the sun was getting close to the treetops, they stopped for the night. The next town was still miles away. Moeera's parents seemed to know where they were though. A clearing by the roadside provided a campsite.

Soon the bachukkas were unhitched from the wagon and grazing amongst the tall grass. Kor set to work felling a tree by the woods edge with his ax. Mallory organized the wagon and went through the cooking gear.

"Moeera, take the kettle to the river and get water," Mallory said. "Be careful."

"Where is it?"

"Through the woods there and down the hill," Mallory said, pointing.

"Yes, Mama," she said.

Moeera found the kettle and turned in the direction of the river.

"Wait," her mother said. "Come here first."

Moeera went to her. She watched her mother close her eyes and seek a memory.

"Ah," Mallory said. "Of course." She grasped the kettle by the mouth and spoke some words.

Moeera looked at her.

"Just a simple charm," Mallory said. "It should keep the pot from getting too heavy." She smiled. "Go ahead."

Moeera couldn't wait to see if her mother's charm worked. She hurried away to the river.

It was after this that Kor felt the tugging.

No! he thought.

Your anguish makes this sweeter.

Once more, he could hear Izzy's voice in his head.

Tut tut, Kor. Aren't you overjoyed that I've found you again?

He dropped the ax he was chopping firewood with and grasped the makeshift chopping block.

Don't resist. You're fighting the inevitable.

"NYEEARGH!" he screamed.

"What's wrong, Kor?" Mallory called from the wagon.

When he didn't answer she jumped down and ran over to the woodpile.

"Kor! Are you all right?" She came to the spot where the ax lie.

Kor wasn't there.

"Kor? Kor? Honey?" she called.

A twig cracked behind her.

Mallory whirled, barely ducking the swinging blade of Kor's sword!

She touched the ground briefly before rebounding and ducking again.

"Fight her, Kor!" Mallory yelled. "Fight her control!"

Kor sweated profusely. He slowly got up from where he'd fallen when he lunged and missed.

Mallory watched from about eight paces away. Kor struggled against his puppeteer. He stared into the shining blade of the sword and saw himself. He thought back to what the fortune teller said when she grabbed the blade.

The son honors the father.

The father instructs the son.

He watches and wanders and open his eyes shall be.

Why had she said those things?

She was trying to set you free, Izzy muttered from his mind. *Too bad I'm stronger.*

Kor felt the invisible chain pull taut. His struggle was done.

Mallory watched him standing there, staring at his reflection.

"Kor?" she asked. "Are you all right?"

"I think so," he answered. "That woman at the fair—the fortune teller. She did something to the sword."

Mallory's breath caught and she thought she might retch. Of course, it was Kor who killed Erica. Why would Izzpalin bother when she could make him do it.

Her eyes teared up. She danced back even farther and wiped them away.

Kor called out, "It's tearing me away from her grasp."

Mallory breathed deeply and summoned a truth-seeing spell.

Kor repeated the words that the Dragoness had spoken.

"The real, the true," Mallory said.

Kor finished his recitation and lowered the sword.

"Vision beyond frontiers," Mallory continued.

He stood there breathing evenly and slowly.

She watched her husband as she recited some old words. "Tre noh supvi diak…"

He looked like he was pitching forward.

"Kor!"

Her mind cut from her truth-seeing to helping the man she loved.

"Kor, I got you!" she exclaimed, rushing to him.

She grabbed him around his broad shoulders, easing him onto her knee.

"It's all right," she said. "I've got you."

"Thank you," he said.

She relaxed. Her hand felt for his back, sliding upward over his shirt.

You're going to be fine; she was about to tell him, but the words wouldn't come out. She felt a blinding pain in her chest, her throat wanting to close on her. A pressure was pushing into her back. What?

What was happening?

Despair seized her as she dropped her gaze downward and saw the reddened point of Kor's sword protruding from her chest. Her blouse darkened as blood exited the wound.

Oh, Kor, Mallory thought.

Then he stood up, letting her crumple to the ground as he pulled the sword free of her body. She landed on her back.

Mallory stared upward at Kor. She couldn't move. Nor could she do anything about the jagged wound in her chest.

She tried to speak but began gagging on the blood that welled up from her throat.

Somewhere deep inside Kor's mind he could see this happening, but he was powerless to stop it. Izzpalin had possessed control of his body from wherever she was. She was there in almost every sense, and he was locked in a box—lost in his own mind.

The life faded from Mallory's eyes as she died. Running away, falling in love, giving up her magical roots—none of those choices had prevented her from dying violently.

Izzpalin gloated. The Mojo was dead by her hand. Revenge had been won. Now to set other matters right.

She guided Kor's body in the river's direction.

I'll take your girl now, dear.

No, Kor thought. *You aren't even here.*

I possessed you, love, Izzy's voice said from his mind. *I had to borrow your body until I can be there myself,* she thought.

No, Kor thought. He felt around for his hands, his legs. How did he lose control of his own body?

Where are you? Kor mused.

On my way. That equine friend of yours was quite a nuisance! But no match for me.

Kor's thoughts inhabited his grey matter like specters. Nothing worked the way it was supposed to.

I'm going to enjoy training your daughter in the ways of magic, Izzy told him. *We'll begin easily, naturally. Before she knows it, we'll be using magic to slaughter any and all lightsiders we encounter. Then, when she's a bit more mature, we'll make her a true blood witch.*

Izzy walked Kor toward the river, dragging the bloody tip of the sword in the dirt. She swung it upward, playfully.

The blade reflected Kor's image and shimmered. Kor discovered he was no longer trapped in a box. He heard Izzpalin's surprised reaction as he heaved the sword into a dense patch of woods.

She howled in fury. Kor shivered to hear it in a faraway corner of his mind.

That's when he noticed Moeera walking up to him carrying the kettle of water as if it was still empty. She took in the frightening sight of him: bloody hands and sleeves, disheveled and sweaty, and a look of utter despair on his face.

"Papa! What's wrong? What happened?"

He dropped to his knees before his daughter.

"Moeera, my heart," he said. "Mama is gone. The blood witch returned and killed her."

Moeera dropped the kettle to the ground and said, "No! That can't be true, Papa!"

"I'm sorry," he said. "It's true."

167

She clung to her father, shaking like an autumn leaf. Then she started crying.

Kor sobbed in her arms. They continued like this for a spell, and then Kor extricated himself from her grip. He struggled to his feet; his legs having fallen asleep.

"Moeera," he said, taking her and lifting her into his arms.

"Papa?"

"This seems like the worst possible thing to happen," he said. "And it is. But the witch is coming for you. You have to get away from here."

"Yes, Papa!" she exclaimed. "We should go. We aren't safe here."

"I can't come with you, Moeera."

"Why!"

"The blood witch will catch us both if we stay together."

"No, I can't go on my own!"

"You have to!" Kor exclaimed. "You must run very fast and very far."

"What about you?"

"The witch is going to find me no matter what. She put a spell on me."

"How do you know?" Moeera asked, wiping her eyes with her sleeve.

"I know because she told me, and I can feel the magic lurking on me like a cloud."

"Papa, we have to get away," she insisted.

"Moeera, the witch will be back soon, sooner than is safe. I scared her off for a little, but she'll just summon stronger magic to catch us."

Moeera began sobbing.

"Be my brave girl and run. Run for your life. Find the white witches—the good witches. They must be out there somewhere."

Moeera looked at her father. Then she turned and ran back toward the river.

Kor watched her flee. When he couldn't see her anymore he trudged back to their camp. He found Mallory where he had left her. Her eyes were glassy as he looked upon her. He bent down and slid his arms beneath her lifeless body.

After setting her on the floor of the wagon, he pulled out a shovel and pick. He found a place by the forest edge that looked pretty, and he began to dig.

The shadows were long on the ground when Kor had a hole large enough to bury his wife. He left the tools embedded in the dirt pile while he retrieved her from the wagon.

Kor carried Mallory across the meadow and put her down gingerly by the grave.

He sat down and swung his legs into the hole. Then he pushed off the surface and dropped in.

The rough outcrops of dirt lined the grave's edges. It felt to Kor as if he was in some nightmare, and he willed himself to wake up. Silence surrounded him. Not one bird chirped, nor did any animal stir. All was calm.

Resigned to his task, he pulled his dead wife into his arms. She almost seemed ready to awaken from a nap. But the blood from her wound covered much of her clothing, and his dirty hands felt the wet stickiness adding another layer to his caked palms.

He laid her down in the hole and said a prayer. Before he'd finished, he was crying. He climbed out and grabbed the shovel.

*   *   *

Kor was in the wagon sleeping when he felt something prodding him. He awakened with a start, looking up to see Izzpalin poking him with a big stick.

"Get up!" she screamed. "Get up, you useless maggot!"

He pushed himself up with his elbows and looked at her.

"What do you have to say for yourself!" she continued. "Where is Moeera?"

"Long gone," he said, his throat dry. "She turned into a bird and flew away."

"You idiot!" Izzy exclaimed. "How dare you!"

"I made sure to tell her how craven and inept you really are," Kor croaked. "And that you murdered her mother out of jealousy."

Izzy shrieked and used her magic to seize Kor and force him down flat on the wagon bed. She rushed to him and snapped her teeth into his neck. He could do nothing to protect himself as he was paralyzed and chained.

Kor's blood poured from the punctures and Izzy sucked it down madly. He'd tried to thwart her, and she would have all of it now. Before she was finished, Kor was dead. She swallowed the last drop and climbed out of the wagon.

Served him right, she thought.

As she calmed a bit though, she realized the mistake she had made. Kor's death left no one to bait the girl with. Beside that, Kor as a blood servant could have tracked his daughter.

She spat a curse on his name.

In the end, he'd outsmarted her easily. He knew exactly what playing on her rage would get him.

She would find the girl anyway. It was just a matter of when.

Part Two

Chapter One

The passing years saw Moeera grow into a beautiful, young woman. Her lithe figure and flaming red hair turned many a young man's head. She pretended not to notice them, spurning their advances. Wherever she wound up, word got around that Moeera was too much trouble to bother with. After trying to find a home or place to fit in, she disappeared into the Gillikin wilderness. She thought often of her parents and her friends from Wecks' Magic Show.

Moeera spent the next years of her life learning to survive in the wild. She built a simple shelter in a pine barren. The soil was sandy and didn't grow any sort of smorgasbord, but it grew a lot of pitch pines, orchids, and blueberries. She subsisted on a diet of blueberries, black huckleberries, sweet-fern, curly dock, and purslane. Sometimes she would find chickweed, dandelion, and other edible plants.

The barrens had its animal community, too. She often noticed birds, mammals, reptiles, and amphibians watching her curiously. It was fun watching them back. The black bears she saw once made her quite nervous though.

Life was calm there. She would repair her shelter when necessary, and she avoided boredom by taking long walks on the twisting paths. She encountered all manner of birds, including the one she nicknamed the long-legged spooner. She set traps to snare small game, and she taught herself to fish in the local streams.

On one of her lonely walks, she discovered someone else living in the barrens. It was a hot, sunny day. Summer had dried the forest to the point where the tree trunks sprouted needles and branches snapped like matchsticks.

Moeera wandered along a ridge overlooking a cliff. As far as the eye could see there were pine trees, fallen needles, rocks, shrubs, and leaves. The sun lit up the scene like a picture book's pretty page.

The needles lining the trail cushioned the ground under her worn out shoes. She hadn't come this far before. She'd just concentrated on other directions and trails. Chickadees scratched around beneath the scrubby brush, darting in and out as it pleased them.

Moeera began humming a tune her mother taught her when she was a little girl. She was so relaxed she didn't realize the harmonies joining her melody came from someone else.

Then it struck her, frightening the loner.

"Who's there?" she demanded.

Silence. No answer: no humming. Whoever it was stopped when she did.

"Who are you!" she cried.

A crow's hoarse, throaty caw was the only reply.

"Who are you?" she asked.

Was she going crazy? How long had she been by herself?

"Follow your nose," a woman's voice finally said. "I get so few visitors. Perhaps you'd care for some mint tea."

Moeera was scared, but glad that there might be an answer to this other than her own insanity. She kept walking the path. The ridge descended from the hilltops, melting back into the forest. There amidst the pine trees stood a tiny shack cobbled together from fallen logs and pine branches.

"Come in," the voice said. "Don't be afraid. I heard you humming with your pretty voice."

"Who are you?" Moeera asked.

"Fair question," the voice said, "but I believe the true question is 'Who are you?'."

Moeera summoned her courage. It took every shred of it to keep her from fleeing into the barrens.

"I'm just a girl," she said, stepping up to the door.

The wooden door appeared to be the most solid component of the haphazard little lodge. Moeera wondered where it had come from.

"Let me give you some advice," the voice said. "No one is 'just a girl'."

"I am," Moeera said. "My name is Moeera."

"Come in, Moeera. I won't hurt you."

"That's the oldest line in the book," Moeera said.

"Ha! Right you are. Let me come out to you."

Moeera stepped back. The sound of shuffling led to the door being pushed open. It banged against a boulder.

"Hello, Moeera," the old lady in the doorway said.

"Hello."

She stood about five foot four with a slight build and strawberry blond hair sticking out from a wool beret. She had a pleasant smile that lit her face along with her twinkling eyes.

"Why, you're no girl," she said, animatedly, "you're a young woman!"

"I guess I am," Moeera said, blushing. "I lost track of time."

"Sheesh! I'll say you did. How old are you?"

"Seventeen," Moeera said. "Now, what is your name?"

"Carrie," she said, grasping Moeera's hand. Hers was slender and wrinkled.

Moeera pulled her hand away instinctively.

"Oh, don't worry," Carrie said. "You didn't come by to steal my goose, did you?"

"What?"

She heard a honk. A snow goose of all things came running around the shack.

"Honk!" it exclaimed.

"I didn't come to steal anything," Moeera said. "I like walking in the woods."

"Really?" Carrie asked.

"Sure. It's quiet. I can hear myself think, and I see all sorts of interesting things."

"Like what?"

"Your house. I never expected to see it when I took that ridge and followed the path this way."

"It's nice, keeps the rain off; but I never thought of it as interesting before. It needs a lot of fixing." Carrie winked at her. "What other things do you see?"

"Deer sometimes, laurel bushes, oak trees, acorns, squirrels, thistles, countless pine trees, thrushes, jays, sparrows, chickadees, worms, grasshoppers, toads … pine trees mostly."

175

"Ha ha. Those sound like some good walks."

"They--

"Honk!" the goose honked.

"Oo! Let her talk, Charles!" Carrie admonished.

"Honk!"

"Shoo! Go guard the back of the house."

The goose stretched its neck out uncertainly.

"Go on. I'll comb your feathers later, I promise."

"Honk."

The goose waddled back around the house.

Moeera watched it curiously. "Don't you worry that a fox or wolf will get him back there?"

"Have you seen some around?" Carrie asked.

"No," Moeera admitted.

"It's possible that one could come this way looking for dinner, but he's quite a tough bird. Any animal would have trouble capturing Charles. Plus, he's loud enough to call for help."

Moeera smiled.

"So where did you walk here from?"

"Beyond the ridge, back about three hills, followed the brook for a while. My place is up the hill from the brook."

"Oh, the brook."

"Yes."

"Was it babbling?"

"Was what babbling?"

"That brook, of course. Sometimes it does."

Moeera wondered if Carrie was kidding, but the woman looked serious.

"Yes, it was babbling a little bit," she said.

"I thought so," Carrie said. "I thought so." She nodded, staring through Moeera for a couple moments.

"It's nice to meet you, Carrie," Moeera said.

"Likewise, I'm sure," Carrie replied. She picked up a doormat to shake off the dirt and needles. "Would you like some tea? We can drink it out here if you like."

Moeera thought tea sounded nice. "What? Stand out here?"

"Mm-hmm," Carrie nodded. "Or we could sit."

"Where?" Moeera asked. "There aren't any stumps or rocks other than your doorstop there."

"Why are you saying that?" Carrie demanded. "There's seating for two right behind you."

"No," Moeera said. "I didn't see anything."

"Well, look there," Carrie said, pointing with a hooked finger. "Go on!"

Moeera spun around to find a table made from rough, sawed logs and two tree stumps that had been sanded and lacquered.

"Oops," Moeera said sheepishly. "I must have missed this. Sorry, Carrie."

Carrie waved her hand dismissively. "No problem. I'll get the tea. Do you like lemon? Milk? Honey?"

"Honey, please," Moeera said eagerly.

"Tsss," Carrie laughed. "You must really like honey. Good thing I've got some."

Moeera sat down on a tree stump chair while Carrie went into the shack. She appraised the structure. It was teeny-tiny--not much bigger she thought than her crude shelter. It did have a tiny chimney, though. And there was a diminutive wisp of smoke escaping the top. She didn't see any windows, maybe it had one on the side or around back.

Despite her reservations about other people, she decided she liked Carrie. She seemed a bit strange, but nice. She didn't trigger Moeera's sense of danger.

Carrie emerged after a short time with two steaming hot cups of tea balanced on a little, wooden tray.

"Yours has honey, dear," she said. "So, does mine. It's my favor-ite." She pronounced the end of favorite as if it rhymed with bite.

"Thank you!" Moeera said, taking the proffered drink.

"You're welcome, I'm sure," her new friend said.

Carrie sat on the stump opposite her and took a big sip of tea.

"So, what did you mean earlier when you said, 'no one is just a girl'?" Moeera asked.

"Oh, yes! I did say that, right after you hummed that pretty song. I meant just what I said."

"But I am just a girl. My parents wanted me to grow up, marry a good husband, and keep house. There didn't seem to be much else in the way of choices."

"What happened?" Carrie asked.

"I had my own ideas," Moeera told her. "I wanted to do something else. I finally ran away. After I worked up enough nerve, that is."

"Ran away? Oh. On the other hand, I'd say you 'ran to'. You ran to me."

"That's a coincidence."

"People cite coincidence because they're missing the big picture," Carrie said.

"What do you mean?"

"You met me for a reason."

"What reason?" Moeera asked.

"Maybe to be my friend."

Moeera stared down into her teacup. "You're saying I ran to you to be your friend."

"Maybe."

"You may be right."

"Of course, I may be right. I may be a lot of things."

Moeera finished her tea in one last gulp. "I had to meet some bad people first before I found you."

"You did?" Carrie asked. "Tell me all about it!"

Moeera sat at the tiny woodland table telling Carrie about the unpleasant crooks she'd encountered since her father sent her away.

Carrie listened and nodded and even seemed to recognize her descriptions of one group of thieves. She giggled when Moeera told of thwarting the fiend in the thicket with the knife.

"Served him right!" Carrie said.

"What about you?" Moeera asked. "How long have you lived here in the woods?"

"A few years now," Carrie said. "It's nice here; a lot of work, but nice."

"Do you ever get lonely?"

"I'm not always here in the woods," Carrie said. "I go into the closest town sometimes. I see a lot of people then."

"Oh," Moeera said.

"Plus, I'll never get lonely with Charles around."

"That's good," Moeera said.

"Other than an occasional passerby I expected I'd stay by myself," Moeera said. "Nicer that way."

"How can you spend your entire life by yourself?" Carrie asked.

"Easy. Just stay out of sight."

"No good," Carrie said. "That's no good. You'll go crazy for sure. I should know--I almost did."

Moeera chuckled. "I won't go crazy. I just spent my afternoon chatting with you."

"Promise me you'll visit me again soon and often," Carrie declared.

"Sure," Moeera said. "I will. My days are free anyway."

"Good. I expect to see you again soon."

"You will. I better get back home now. Best to travel by the sun."

"Goodbye, Moeera dear."

"Goodbye, Carrie. Thanks for the tea."

Meeting Carrie marked a milestone in Moeera's life. Carrie was both friend and safe person. She made Moeera feel comfortable.

Chapter Two

If Carrie surprised Moeera when they first met, then the opposite was true upon their second meeting. Just a few days later Moeera set out in the early morning to visit Carrie. In her hands she carried a woven basket of blackberries she collected the day before. She was quite eager to surprise Carrie with a gift.

Surprise Carrie, and herself, she certainly did.

The sun moved lazily into the sky above the pine barrens as Moeera walked with purpose. Soon she came to the tiny hut. She forced away a bit of random nervousness and knocked on the door.

Several minutes passed so she knocked again. Still no answer.

It's funny, she thought, Charles isn't coming after me honking.

She pondered this. Could Carrie have gone for a morning walk and taken the gander with her? She decided to sit down at the rough, little table to wait for her friend.

Here was another strange thing: it was nowhere to be found when she turned around.

That's peculiar, she thought. The table and stump chairs were right there.

All she saw now were pine trees and fallen needles.

First time I was here I didn't see it either. Not right away.

She pondered this odd discovery. Where could Carrie have put the table? Not in her tiny house. The lady didn't appear strong enough to move it, and there weren't any signs on the ground that it had been dragged.

She decided to be on her way, but she wanted to leave Carrie the blackberries. She pulled open the wooden door, letting it rest against the boulder.

The house was dark inside, too dark to see much at all. Somewhere ahead a lamp burned. She could just make out a pathway leading straight back into the house. Moeera had never seen the house's back, but she didn't

expect it could be very far. She felt around for a table to leave the blackberries on. The lamp sat on a very tiny end table--the kind that appear to just melt into the wall. She set the basket down next to the lamp. Then she turned to go. She moved carefully toward the open doorway.

Another door somewhere behind her slammed and she heard laughing. It sounded like Carrie.

She spun back toward the lamp but saw nothing new. The laughing continued.

"Carrie?" she asked.

The laughter stopped. There was a rustling sound. Seconds passed like hours.

"Is someone there?" Carrie's voice asked. "Who is that?"

Moeera felt tense as she said, "It's me--Moeera from the other day. I brought you some blackberries I picked."

"Oh, my stars!" Carrie exclaimed, suddenly appearing from the darkness of a doorway. "Moeera!"

She rushed up to the girl and grabbed her arms. Moeera noticed she was naked other than a robe that was falling off her shoulder.

"I love blackberries," Carrie said. "I can bake them in a pie!"

"I didn't mean to intrude," Moeera said. "I was going to sit at your table outside, but I couldn't find it."

"Oh! Moeera. Thanks for thinking of me."

"Who on Earth is that?" a man's voice came from the backroom.

"Who?" Moeera asked. "I thought you lived here alone."

"No, not exactly … my husband is here," Carrie said.

"Husband? I didn't realize you were married."

"Sure. It's just Charles."

"Charles? I thought your goose was named Charles!"

"Yes, … he is."

Then a naked man emerged with his hands placed strategically over his man parts.

"Hello, there," he said. "Nice to meet you. I'm Charles. You must be Carrie's new friend."

"Um, yeah."

Moeera covered her eyes with her hand even though the hut was still very dark.

"Sorry, sir. I stopped to visit, but no one answered the door."

"We were indisposed," he said. "Didn't hear you."

"Look, Charles! Moeera brought a basket of blackberries."

"Nice of her. I'd better go get dressed."

"But it's almost time, isn't it?" Carrie asked.

"Not quite," Charles said. I'll be right back."

He disappeared into the darkness.

"Is he gone?" Moeera asked.

"Yes, dear," Carrie said. "Would you like some tea? Fruit perhaps?"

Moeera didn't say anything.

Carrie said, "Here. Let me show you to the kitchen. There's a bench; you can sit down."

"Sorry I barged in on you," Moeera said.

Carrie shrugged. "I'm sorry, too. It's fine, though. I thought you were afraid to come in here."

"Just before I knew you. You're very nice."

Carrie laughed. "Let me fetch that basket," she said.

She left Moeera alone in the dark kitchen, returning in just a few seconds.

"Here they are," Carrie said, "and nice and ripe, too! Would you like some breakfast?"

"Sure," Moeera said. "Are you sure I'm not interrupting?"

Carrie turned to Moeera. "It's very nice that you're here. A nice surprise. The three of us can eat breakfast together."

Soon they were eating and talking in the small kitchen. Moeera dug into the blackberry pancakes Carrie made with delight. Charles had joined them; now fully clothed. He seemed nice, but not quite as nice as Carrie who for all Moeera's initial caution she would gladly trust with her life now.

"What brings you to our corner of the forest?" Charles asked. "Do you need a home remedy?"

"No," Moeera said. Now that her embarrassment was gone, she noticed the gray flecks running through Charles's brown hair. He was tall and slender. His arms had wrinkles but also their fair share of muscles. "I just like to walk and explore. I live a few hills that way." She pointed with her

182

finger.

"Oh," Charles said. "I thought maybe you came from Reeds. Carrie gets a lot of customers from there."

"Moeera's much more interesting than anyone from that village," Carrie said. "Aren't you, Moeera?"

Moeera shook her head. "I don't know; I don't even know anyone from that village."

"No big loss," Carrie said. "The most exciting they get from there is Lyle with his rash. He trades with me for jewelweed ointment. And maybe Mitch the Itch. He's in a similar predicament. Neither is very exciting."

"So, no need to visit Reeds. I'll remember," Moeera said.

"I only go there if we run out of something," Carrie said. "Maybe I shop there every week; maybe not. I keep to myself mostly."

"She has a friend named Dora," Charles said. "What about Dora?"

"Oh, yes," Carrie said, smiling. "Dora's okay. She and I like to talk."

"She gives Carrie all the gossip," Charles said.

"Mm-hmm. Mm-hmm!" Carrie said, shaking her head "yes".

"You make home remedies," Moeera said.

"Yes," Carrie said. "Cures for sore throats, soothers for fussy babies, ointments for rashes and itches and pox, aphrodisiacs, love potions, things to oil your joints, etc."

"Wow!" Moeera said. "That's really extraordinary."

"Oh, yes," Charles said. "Many seek out Carrie for her knowledge and skill making remedies."

"I learned most of it from my mother; and she from hers," Carrie said. "The people of Reeds and other nearby towns are easily impressed."

"No, they're easily healed," Charles said, grinning.

"Moeera and I were talking about the importance of being a girl the other day," Carrie said.

"We were?" Moeera asked.

"Don't you remember?" Carrie asked. "You told me you were just a girl ...."

"Right," Moeera said. "And you told me no one is just a girl."

"Exactly!" Carrie said. "It's true. Everyone is important in one way or another." She raised her arms toward the ceiling. "Everyone has their place--their role to play--in this living world."

"Yours is to heal people it sounds like," Moeera said.

Carrie nodded. "Yes, and to keep Charles happy and out of trouble."

Charles smiled. "She does quite well at it."

"What about you?" Moeera asked Charles.

"I'm her other half," he said. "I'm other things ..., too ..., but ... it's ... difficult ...."

"Charles!" Carrie exclaimed.

His face was very pale. Moeera wondered if he was choking on something, but she hadn't seen him eat anything. He'd already finished his breakfast.

"Oh, Charles!" Carrie yelled. She sprang from her seat. "It's time, and you waited too long!"

She rushed to him, grabbing hold of his spastic body.

"Help me, Moeera!" she cried.

"What can I do?"

"Help me undress him."

"What!"

"We have to get his clothing off!"

Moeera thought she might explode. What good would it do?

Charles was writhing and crying out as if he was in pain. He gritted his teeth and made a grating noise in his throat.

Carrie yanked his shirt off over his head. She pulled him by his shoulders, maneuvering him out of his chair.

Moeera grabbed his shoes and tugged them off. Charles began flailing about as if he would fly away. Moeera crashed to the floor.

"That might be good enough," Carrie said, "but I don't know--he's usually naked when this happens!"

"When what happens?" Moeera cried. "He's dying!"

"No!" Carrie exclaimed, pulling his trousers off. "He's--

Charles glowed as if lit by the sun. He faded--no, Moeera thought--he shrank into something white and feathery.

"Honk!"

"Yes, yes," Carrie muttered. "You waited too long. I'm sorry."

Moeera looked at the gander in disbelief. It ran at her hissing. She covered her face with her arms to protect it.

"Charles! Leave Moeera alone!" Carrie threw a dish towel at the bird who waddled off at a fast clip.

"You - you!" Moeera sputtered.

"What?" Carrie asked. "If you're trying to say: 'You married a goose'; well, yes, I did."

Moeera looked at Carrie with an expression somewhere between aghast and befuddled.

"You have to admit ... he makes a handsome devil of a gander," Carrie sighed.

Chapter Three

Once Moeera had recovered her senses she and Carrie followed the gander outside. He strutted around proudly as if the scene in the kitchen had never happened. He ignored them.

"Let's have a seat, shall we," Carrie said, motioning to the table for two which was suddenly there again as if it had never moved.

Moeera walked to the table and took the same stump as before. She frowned as she watched Carrie sit opposite.

"What is it?" Carrie asked.

"This table and the chairs," Moeera said.

"I don't believe it," Carrie said. "I thought you'd ask me about Charles."

"How about Charles then!" Moeera exclaimed. "How can you sit there so calmly on a chair that seems to disappear and reappear depending on what time of the day it is? You just told me in there that you married a gander! We both just saw your husband behaving as if he would die. But he didn't die! Oh, no! He changed into a gander!"

Moeera's heart pounded in her chest, and she breathed hard. She couldn't seem to breathe easy.

"It's my turn, correct?" Carrie asked.

Moeera nodded. A half-hearted smile crossed her lips.

"I'm sorry you found out about Charles the way you did," Carrie said. "I was going to explain it to you, but I hadn't thought I had to quite yet. We only met just four days past."

"Is he really a goose?" Moeera asked.

"Sometimes he is really a goose," Carrie said. She looked Moeera in the eyes. "And sometimes he is a man named Charles--my beloved. He usually changes into a bird about five hours past sunup. Then he changes back to a man at dusk. He can't help it--it's a result of the war he fought in."

"What war?"

"The Magic War," Carrie said. "The largest conflagration involving wizards and witches and others who manipulate magic the way a composer manipulates musical notes."

"So, he's a man."

"Yes. He's a wizard, too; or was. He doesn't do much magic anymore."

"How did he become a ...."

"Weregander? An evil wizard--sorcerer actually--cursed him on the battlefield at Lyte."

"Couldn't you reverse the curse?"

"No. Curses are more visceral than spells; they have a habit of sticking," Carrie said. "Besides, what makes you think I could do anything about it?"

"You're a witch, aren't you?"

Carrie stared at Moeera. She laughed a little, but it seemed forced.

"Aren't you?" Moeera pressed.

"What makes you think I'm a witch?"

"You know ...."

"Tell me what makes you think I'm a witch! It's the invisible benches, isn't it?"

"What!"

"This table and the seats; I make them invisible when I'm not using them."

"I thought somebody was moving them around behind our backs," Moeera said.

"No," Carrie said. "Why would you think that? I just don't always feel like cleaning them. They get so dirty in the woods."

"A-ha!" Moeera exclaimed. "You're a witch!"

"You got me," Carrie said a bit deflated. "Hmm hmm hmm."

She laughed.

"My mama was a witch too," Moeera said.

"She was?" Carrie asked.

"Yes, kind of."

"What do you mean?" Carrie asked. "How can you kind of be a witch?"

"She grew up with witches," Moeera said. "She left them and stopped doing magic."

"I see."

"I finally found out about it, and she said she would teach me…."

"Did she?"

"No," Moeera sighed. "An evil witch came along and killed her."

"That's terrible!" Carrie exclaimed.

"Yes, I didn't truly run away because I wanted to. My parents were coming around to my interest in magic. I ran away because my mama died, and Papa told me I needed to flee."

"Or the witch would get you," Carrie added.

"Yes," Moeera said, "but Papa wouldn't come with me."

"Hmm. This witch must have had a spell on him," Carrie said.

"Something like that. Not like Charles though."

"The curse on Charles makes for an interesting life, let me tell you," Carrie said.

Moeera frowned. "What about the sorcerer? Can't he dispel the curse?"

"No," Carrie said.

"But if he placed it on Charles …."

"Curses are very difficult," Carrie said, "and very dangerous. We're lucky Charles doesn't become something deadly when he changes, or I'd be dead by now."

"Isn't it worth asking?"

"No," Carrie said. "The sorcerer that did it is dead; Charles is alive. Long as he doesn't find some goose he likes better than me I think we're good."

"Why do you live here in the barrens? Who won The Magic War? Why did it start?"

"What?" Carrie asked, slightly annoyed. "Are you writing a book?"

"No," Moeera said.

Carrie exhaled.

"Would you like to hear a story?"

Moeera nodded enthusiastically.

Carrie tapped her fingers. "Where to start. Charles fought in The Magic War. I did, too. Carrie the Pip I was called. Now … why did we fight … think about it. You can tell me why it started, I'm sure."

"I don't know."

"Take a guess." Carrie looked at Moeera like she'd asked her a tricky

188

riddle.

"A dispute," Moeera said. "Over whom would rule the witches."

Carrie looked excited enough to explode. "You're so close. That's not exactly right, but you're close. I could pee in my pants!"

"Just tell me!"

"Oooo--no. Guess again."

"A war always has two sides," Moeera said noncommittally.

"What sides?" Carrie asked.

"Two countries ...."

"That's true, but this war involved witches and wizards from near and far."

"But they weren't all on the same side," Moeera said. "A sorcerer cursed Charles."

"Mm-hmm, mm-hmm," Carrie said emphatically.

"It would be so much easier if you told me straight out."

"Guess again," Carrie said.

"Fine. All the magicians went to war to decide who would serve Oz's ruler."

"No. You're fixating on who's in charge. That's not it."

"You said I was close."

"The way you said it sounded close. Oh, very well. We had a big war to see who was stronger; those who wield their magic by the light or those who wield black magic for their own selfishness."

"Good versus evil," Moeera said. "A war of good magic against bad."

"More or less," Carrie said. "More or less."

"How did it start?"

"I'm not sure. Ranga did something bad, course he was evil. We knew it. It might have been when he killed Jeffery with the banana dance spell. Or was it when Patrick the Wildman stole the glove of Ces? Maybe. Mystical objects were disappearing left and right. And the wicked Sisters of the Sorrows got up to no good. So, I don't know how it started. I only know that one day Charles told me we were at war and had to attend the meeting of the white magicians. We met with a forest full of magical folk."

Moeera creased her brow. A forest filled with magicians and witches and wizards! "And now he's a gander during the day."

"Yes," Carrie said with finality, "every day. We have the nights and mornings together as husband and wife. After that my companion is an irritable gander who guards me and our house like so much precious gold."

"It's horrible what happened to Charles," Moeera said, "but I'm glad you and he made it through alive."

"Me, too," Carrie said. "A lot weren't that lucky. As for who won the war--nobody did. Thousands of witches and warlocks and magicians died. It didn't prove that either side was stronger; just that many of us were stupid."

Moeera shuddered. Even magic was fallible. "Why do you live in the barrens?" she asked.

Carrie wrinkled her nose. "You do ask a lot of questions, dear."

Moeera didn't say anything.

"We came here to keep to ourselves, and to avoid trouble--witches aren't looked kindly upon since the war."

"Were they ever?" Moeera asked.

"Probably not, but witches are the same as anyone else."

"Really?"

"Sure. Some are good; some are evil."

"How does a person figure out which they are?"

"Do you like to kill people?" Carrie asked.

"No," Moeera said.

"People who like killing other people are evil."

"That makes sense."

"Good. Do you like hurting people? I mean torture--or being mean to others just to spite them. Same with animals."

"No."

"Good, dear, because that's evil, too."

"What about good?"

"Good people avoid evil. It sounds simple, but it's hard."

"Why? I avoid it."

"Do you?"

"Yes. I feel a certain way if I'm around bad people. I should know; I met some."

"Really?"

"Mm-hmm. Thieves and such. I started getting funny feelings when I saw them on the roads. I was extra careful to stay far away from them."

"What sort of funny feelings?" Carrie asked.

"Concern. Worry. I would begin to itch all over. A mere hobo or traveler wouldn't make me feel that way, but someone up to thieving would. I knew to be on guard."

"It sounds to me like you have magic abilities," Carrie said.

"I wish!" Moeera said. "Mama said I could learn magic, but I've never been able to cast a spell."

"There's an art to it," Carrie said, sighing. "Passed from master to novice. Perhaps you're a powerful witch behind that pretty face."

"What! No, I'm just …."

"A girl?"

"Yes."

"Moeera."

"Yes?"

"Every witch starts out as 'just a girl'."

"Oh. I guess they must, right?"

Carrie smiled. "That's how it works. I was a girl once."

She hummed a little tune. Moeera didn't recognize it.

"Now, Moeera, a big difference between good folk and evil folk hinges on temptation and how easily you cave to it."

Moeera nodded.

"Everyone makes mistakes," Carrie said. "Nobody's perfect. It matters that you resist dark thoughts and revenge. We all get judged in the next life."

"Okay, Carrie," Moeera said. "I can certainly strive to be a good person."

"That makes me happy!" Carrie said. "Would you like me to teach you witchcraft?"

"Sure," Moeera said. "Do you really want to?"

"Yes. You have an affinity for magic and a good heart."

So it was that Moeera discovered there was more to her intuition than she believed. Carrie was a witch; she would be, too.

Moeera made the trek to Carrie's each day for a week. She learned about relationships in nature and about the power that flowed from life.

* * *

A thunderstorm inundated the barrens at the second week's start. Moeera huddled in her shelter surrounded by darkness and the drenching rain.   Lightning flashed and thunder cracked.   The storm continued for more than an hour, and then moved slowly off into the distance.   The rain continued until nightfall.

Moeera was sad to not be visiting Carrie that day.   The weather did its best to dampen her spirits, but it aided her as well.   She learned that her construction technique had paid off.   The thatch roof she had put on her shelter of pine boughs had miraculously done its job.

The roof that started out as an interlacing of needled branches had gained branch after new branch during her stay.   She replaced anything that fell in or blew away, and she kept adding.   She'd suffered very few leaks during this mother of all storms; the water ran off onto the ground.   The buckets and buckets of water saturated the ground and formed enormous puddles, but Moeera's raised pallet of ground was just high enough to remain dry.   She felt pride in her handiwork and a great deal of gratitude to the trees for providing her with adequate shelter.

The rain finally ended.   She found branches down all around--some from her roof.   Trees had fallen, exposing their saucer-shaped root systems.   Moeera breathed in the smell of wetness and pine as she went about inspecting and refortifying her shelter.   It might be black as the night under her pine bough roof, but it was comfortable and camouflaging.   She worked on it for more than an hour.

When she finally rested, she wondered how Carrie and Charles were.   She decided to stay home and set out for the little house early the next day.

*   *   *

"How do you think Moeera has fared through this rain and noise?" Charles asked.

"I've been wondering that very thing," Carrie muttered, setting a crystal ball on the table. "Now that you have hands again light two candles."

Charles lit two candles arranged on two sides of the ball.   Then he and Carrie sat opposite one another; he facing East and she facing West.   The candles stood in the North and South positions of their square.

Carrie stared into the crystal ball with one thing on her mind, the girl Moeera.

Moments became minutes.   Carrie's expression of concentration became one of satisfaction.

"She's fine," she said. "The young spark has turned in for the night."

192

"So, she's all right," Charles said. "Good."

Carrie smiled. "Not so much as a soggy foot or wet hair. That's what I'm getting. She's hard to pinpoint, though. There's a natural invisibility to her--almost."

"Then you've found a worthy student."

"I guess," Carrie said.

"She reminds me of our Mallory," Charles pondered. "Same spirit, same determination."

"You took the words from my mouth, dear," Carrie said. "I think you may have something there."

"You don't think… could she be Mallory's?"

"Could be, though I don't know for sure."

"Imagine that."

"What?"

"Us as grandparents."

"Stranger things have happened."

*   *   *

Moeera was on her way when the sun broke through the cloud cover. She trudged up a hill to get a better look. Birds sang cheerfully from branches in every direction. She saw a woodchuck sniffing around some underbrush. It fled into the wet scrub bushes when it heard her coming.

When she reached a good spot with a decent view of the hillside and the surrounding land, she unrolled a small mat and sat on it atop a boulder. The sun lit up the land with a warmth and cheeriness that made her forget the long storm. She stretched her arms and watched the landscape for a while. Here and there she could see smoke from one of the village's chimneys. It rose from the tree cover in insignificant columns.

She stayed until the sun was quite low to the horizon, bathing the sky in dark colors.

Then she walked down the hill again to her shelter. Two squirrels were lurking about, searching for nuts.

"Don't you know the walnut trees are that way?" she asked, pointing.

The squirrels froze to watch Moeera for ten seconds. They bolted into the trees.

Moeera sighed and entered through the opening she'd covered with an enormous fallen pine bough. Two striped ground squirrels darted past her

193

like lightning.

"Is every rodent visiting today?" she wondered.

She dropped the bough over the opening behind her and snatched a candle out of its spot. She lit the candle with a crude match and jammed it onto a flat stone. This she placed on a rock that was away from her sleeping spot. Satisfied that no branches were poking out anywhere near it she plopped down and seized her coffer of nuts and berries. By now she was so hungry she ate nearly her entire supply. When she was done, she extinguished the candle and bedded down for the night.

*   *   *

"It only makes sense for you to come live here with us," Carrie said the next day.

Charles chopped wood in the morning sun. The staccato chop, chop, chop sound framed Carrie's words.

"Do you really think so?" Moeera asked.

"I know so. No worries, the place is bigger on the inside than the outside, you know."

"Yes," Moeera said.

"As long as you don't mind Charles running about naked sometimes," Carrie said.

Moeera grinned. "Beggars can't be choosy."

"No begging involved," Carrie said, hands on her hips. "You're my apprentice now, as well as my friend. Stay for as long as you like."

"Thank you." Moeera beamed with happiness. Finally, a place she could belong.

"You're welcome, I'm sure," Carrie said.

A loud squawk came from outside signaling Charles's transformation into his bird self.

"There he goes again," Carrie said, sighing. She laughed.

*   *   *

About a month later Moeera was learning spells with ease. She'd acclimated well to being a part of the household. Carrie taught her many things about magic and how to use it. She taught her other things as well.

"This is where we'll dig," she declared one day at the base of a sassafras tree.

Moeera knelt by the tree with her metal trowel and her digger and began

194

pulling at the topsoil. She cleared leaves and twigs away.

"That's good," Carrie said. She found a similar tree and got on hands and knees to begin digging.

"Pull up as many roots as you can," Carrie said. "When you have them out of the ground pick them up. Cut them if you need to."

"Sure," Moeera said.

When they both had an armload of roots they headed back to the cabin.

"Fetch some water," Carrie instructed.

Moeera took a pot to the nearby stream and filled it at a small waterfall. When she returned, she placed it on top of the wood stove.

"Good," Carrie said. "Thank you. I stoked the fire up; it should boil quickly."

She sent Moeera to the stream for a second pot of water. This Carrie used to rinse the roots of dirt. Then she laid them on the table. After a time, she brought the pot of boiling water to the table and set it down.

In went the roots. Carrie brought out a long spoon and gave them a good stir. Then she nodded.

"If I didn't know it," Moeera said, "I'd think you were making tea."

"Know what?" Carrie asked.

"It's a potion, isn't it?"

"Potion, smotion. It's sassafras tea! Or it will be after it sits awhile."

Moeera shrugged.

"What is it, dear?"

"Nothing."

"It must be something. Tell me."

"I mean no disrespect. You've been more than kind to me. You and Charles have made me believe there are nice people."

"But …."

"When are you going to teach me the good stuff?"

"What do you mean?"

"Nature and life and relationships are fine. They're important. Casting spells to heal the sick and injured is amazing. Learning about salves and remedies is fine. But when will I be able to do the truly wild stuff? Like fly and read minds and influence people and create living servants?"

"Oh," Carrie said. "Yes. We can explore those. I wasn't certain you were ready."

"I think I am. I want to be."

"Once we begin things like that there won't be any going back, dear. You'll be a witch truly and absolutely. People will fear you and the power you possess."

Moeera shrugged. "I really don't associate with very many people."

"Now you don't," Carrie said, "but the future has a way of bringing you surprises. And you'll have the same weaknesses as other magic users."

"Weaknesses? I thought you were … you know … all-powerful."

"Heavens, no! Do you want to pursue magic further? Therein lies the ultimate irony. The knowledge of magic provides tremendous power, but with it comes great weakness."

"When you put it that way I don't know," Moeera said.

"Listen close, girl," Carrie said. "Listen hard. What I tell you now you must vow to never tell another soul--not your friend, not your lover. Once I've told you the knowledge must be locked away in your head."

Moeera nodded. She looked at her friend. What dire warning was she about to give her?

"We magicians whether witch or wizard draw our special strength from nature as I have shown you. The world around you supplies your arsenal. It combines with your will to make spells possible."

"What I haven't told you is that the four elements of the natural world dig their claws into you. I say claws because it's the closest thing I can imagine to describe it. Just know that we witches can be killed by the very things we take advantage of--fire, water, air, and earth. You must always, always, always respect the four elements because any one of them could wind up being your executioner."

"You're saying that nearly anything can kill a witch," Moeera groaned.

"Yes," Carrie said. "I daren't sugarcoat it. Witches who reach my age and … you know … older are ones who stay vigilant, pay attention!"

"Even if you do," Moeera said, "danger could be just one step away."

"The price, I'm sure, of an exciting life," Carrie said. "I've known many such cases. Phyllis the Flesh bender deposed the ruler of La De Da. She practiced her spells in ways that marked it as black magic--very evil. One day she burned her hand with a hot poker. She held the correct end, but the fire traveled its length and gave her a bad burn. Three days later she died of infection and shock."

196

"Because she was burned," Moeera said. "People get burned sometimes."

"True," Carrie admitted, "but listen. Calamitous Caroline late of the Sisters of Sorrow was captured by Munchkins and tried and convicted of witchcraft. Her punishment was to be dunked under a pond until drowning. She only came up alive once. The water took her life swiftly."

"Oh, now that might happen to anyone. She could've died of fright. Or choked the first time under. Anybody would've died once they'd been under long enough."

"There's more," Carrie said. "Katie Kaw Kaw was a white witch. If she ever used her power to work the black arts, then nobody knew it."

"How did she die?"

"She answered the summons of King Onderto to help repel outlaws. The outlaws jumped her in the woods--eleven to one. She netted eight by spider-spin, and the others fled. She pursued only to be crushed by a falling tree."

"Another coincidence?"

"Perhaps."

Moeera frowned. "So ... how else did the elements kill witches?"

"Townsfolk with torches drove Fagooglen out of her house. One caught up to her and thrust a wooden stake through her heart."

"Why didn't she use magic against them?" Moeera asked.

Carrie shuddered. "That's just it, you see. I'm sure she tried, but the wood of the stake negated her spells. Almost as if the Earth turned against her."

"Mmm," Moeera mmm-ed. She ran all the unfortunate ends around her mind. It sounded crazy, but what if it was true? Did the very land in which they lived prefer some over others? How could it? The stones and rocks, dead wood and plants, sand and soil weren't alive. Fire wasn't alive either, was it? It acted like a living thing, but it wasn't. It was light and heat that consumed without discretion.

Carrie watched Moeera intently and nodded. "I see it in your face. The look of you wondering if such fantasy could be true. Somehow and someway, it is. Think about it carefully before you agree to be a witch."

Moeera nodded.

"So how about we try some tea?" Carrie asked.

"Sounds like a good idea," Moeera said.

Chapter Four

The next day Carrie and Moeera ventured into Leeds for supplies. It was a tiny town surrounded by farm after farm after farm. The actual center had very few roads and not a lot of buildings. They found the farmers' market easily.

The Night of Crack Blam festival occurred the next evening so most of the town residents were there whether buying, selling, or trading. The two women watched the people entering and exiting the market.

"They still hold the festival every year," Carrie told Moeera. She shook her head.

"Doesn't everyone?" Moeera asked. "Bucktry always celebrated. I think that's when the town was the most fun."

"That sounds good," Carrie said, "but tell me what it was all about."

"What?" Moeera said. "Good will, brotherhood, togetherness …."

"Right," Carrie said. "Why did it start in the first place?"

"I don't know."

"Almost nobody knows," Carrie said. "Its origins were forgotten. The name of the night says it all, though."

"Crack Blam?" Moeera asked. "Was he a famous person?"

"He wasn't a he at all," Carrie said. "Crack Blam is a sound."

"Really?"

"A sound heard by thousands amidst the largest earthquake ever known."

"An earthquake. Now I hear it. They do sound like loud noises."

"Exactly," Carrie said. "Mm-hmm! An earthquake that changed our world forever!"

"Okay," Moeera said, "but nobody seems to remember. How do you know about it?"

"Ancient writings put onto rocks. I have a diary with their scribbling copied down."

"How ancient?"

"I'm the only person I know who can read it. I could show you--it's mostly pictures really."

"Sure. To think that something so important happened and the knowledge is all but lost."

"Time, dear. Time moves mountains and heals the heart. Time is a distance."

"What's wrong?" Moeera asked. She saw the look on her friend's face.

"I was just thinking about my daughter Mallory, that's all," Carrie said, watching Moeera intently. "I haven't seen her in a long time."

Moeera felt as if she had been struck.

"Mallory was my mama's name," she said.

Carrie nodded. "I thought so, Moeera. I thought it might be."

"You did! How long have you thought this?"

"Since you mentioned that an evil witch killed your mother," Carrie said. "That planted the thought in my head. And you remind me so much of her."

"She had another name; she used it in the magic show we helped with…."

"What name?"

"The… Mojo," Moeera whispered.

Carrie nodded. "My little Mojo. She burned so brightly. I never expected she would leave us behind."

"I don't know what to say," Moeera said, the weight of it hitting her.

"You don't have to say anything, granddaughter," Carrie said. "Serendipity be praised for bringing you to me."

"I have a gramma," Moeera said, smiling. She started to cry.

"Oh, there there," Carrie said, taking Moeera into her arms and planting a dozen kisses on her. "I love you, honey!"

The tears of joy flowed down Moeera's cheeks until Carrie couldn't help herself and joined in.

"I wish your mama was here with us!" Carrie declared. "Charles and I always hoped she would come back to us someday. At least you made it to us."

The tears abated and Moeera laughed. "What do I call you now?"

"Oh!" Carrie exclaimed. "Hmm, hmm, hmm. Call me Mom-mom."

"I will, Mom-mom."

And just like that, Moeera officially had a family again.

They got in line at the butcher's stand. A man came by with a big sack. "Happy tidings to you," he said.

"And to you," Carrie said.

They were behind three other people. The woman up front was trying to haggle the price down on some nice cuts of meat. "Can't you slice it any thinner!" she sniffed to the lady at the counter.

"It's already less than one pigger," the butcher said.

"Humph. I should've gone to Zell's stand."

"Maybe I can trim it a bit more. If you aren't hungry for meat …."

The butcher worked a sharp knife into the already thin pork chops.

"I enjoy my meat same as anyone else!" the woman whined. "You just cut it too big!"

When they finally reached the counter, the lady smiled at them. "What can I get you?"

"Sausage," Carrie said. "You have any left?"

"Of course," the butcher told her. "None of the customers want to pay today. They're saving their money for whiskey and wine."

"Of course," Carrie said. "I can't forget to buy some more beer myself, but if you could give me a nice big portion of sausage …."

"Making stew?"

"Yes!" Carrie said, laughing. "Come by this week if you want some."

"I don't know," the lady said, "after all, you live way out in the sticks." Now it was her turn to crack a big smile.

"Oh, you're funny, you are," Carrie said. "Moeera meet Melissa; Melissa, this is my granddaughter, Moeera."

"Charmed," Melissa said, smiling. "Maybe you can convince your grandmother to visit the market more often."

"I suppose I can try," Moeera said.

"What have you been up to way out in the woods?" Melissa asked.

"Exciting stuff," Moeera said. "I didn't expect digging for roots and picking herbs could be so good."

"Hah, hah," Melissa said.

Carrie bought some poultry as well. Moeera couldn't help but wonder about Charles's thoughts on eating bird. Then they bid Melissa a happy Crack Blam and visited the dairy several stalls down. Carrie bought milk and cheese.

"You carry this," Carrie said. "Time to get the beer before they run out."

*   *   *

Not so long after their conversation about the elements Carrie was happy to accept Moeera's admonition of her to be an apprentice witch. Carrie agreed to teach her granddaughter that which she knew.

"Bring me the text on preserving oneself when faced with danger," Carrie said.

She was putting away the dinner plates one evening when she told Moeera this.

Moeera did as she was bidden. It sounded like this could be an invaluable lesson. About that much she was correct.

Her fingers touched the spines of half a dozen books before finding the one Carrie wanted. The name on the spine was torn away, but she saw the title on the worn cover. The book wasn't much more than a loose sheaf of pages bearing the name Magical Self Defense.

A much-read book must be an important one, right? Moeera thought. Satisfied she turned to leave.

Wait a minute. What was that? Movement!

She spun back to the dusty bookshelf. Something was moving inside a small jar sitting in front of a book on The Melodies. She moved closer leaning toward the jar to get a closer look. Its contents appeared black and soiled with inky liquid half-filling the jar. Something, things rather, scrabbled about inside the jar. Ants? No. They seemed too large and pale to be ants.

Carrie walked into the room. "Can't you find it, dear? Is it--"

When she saw Moeera staring at the bookshelf her smile vamoosed.

Moeera stood in front of the tiny jar, her hand outstretched to take it from the bookshelf.

"No!" Carrie commanded.

Moeera froze.

"Moeera!" Carrie said sharply. "Step back this instant."

Moeera barely heard Carrie. Her voice sounded very far away.

"Now, Moeera!"

Moeera shook her head in a bit of bewilderment. She felt startled. Had she been daydreaming?

Carrie went to Moeera and took her hands. The book was still clutched against her left side.

"You found the book," Carrie said. She relaxed. "Good. Let's study some defense spells together."

"Okay, Mom-mom," Moeera said. "I'm sorry; I feel as if my mind wandered for a bit."

"It happens, I guess," Carrie said. She led the girl by the hand.

Moeera stopped.

"What is it, Moeera?"

"I'm not sure," Moeera said. She frowned. "I noticed something. What was it?"

"This old place is full of oddities," Carrie said. "It could've been the brooms on the walls or the silver candlesticks standing on the mantle ...."

"I ... don't think it was either of those," Moeera said.

Carrie sighed.

"What's wrong?"

"I know what you were looking at."

She stepped to the bookshelf. "It's my fault for leaving it there. I was rearranging some things and silly me left it out in plain sight." She took the little jar in both hands and lifted it from the shelf.

"That's right!" Moeera said. "I remember now--the jar. What's in there? Termites?"

"No," Carrie said. "Something else; something very dangerous. Swear to me on your mother's life that you'll leave this jar be."

"Okay. I swear," Moeera said. "But what's in there?"

Carrie had her hands wrapped around the jar. "Let's say it is termites. I'm going to put this away out of sight. Believe it or not it's dangerous to look at."

"Oh."

Carrie stuck the jar inside a clay urn in the room's corner. She pushed a clay lid firmly into the urn's opening. Then she lit a candle and dropped hot wax all around the lid's edge.

"It's sealed," she said. "Not very strongly, but it should be safer. Out of sight; out of mind."

"They should die soon anyway, shouldn't they ... the termites," Moeera said.

"Yes," Carrie said, "but, you know--magic!"

"Why do you have them?"

"It's all Pandora's fault."

"Pandora?"

"Yes. Long ago ... when I was young, someone gave this girl Pandora a special box."

"What was special about it?"

"I take it you've never heard this story."

"No."

"Pandora was told that the special box was a surprise. Under no circumstances was she to open it."

"Then what?"

"As you can guess she got more and more curious. Time dragged on as time sometimes does, and her desire to know what the surprise was grew. One day when the box's true owner was indisposed she crept to the thing and lifted the lid to peek inside."

Carrie paused. She was looking down, not wanting to continue.

Moeera said, "You have to admit that wasn't the smartest thing to do on the part of the box's owner. Who's going to sit idly by when there's a mystery like that to uncover?"

"Uncover answers about the box; she certainly did that," Carrie said. "As soon as she lifted the lid a teensy bit to peek there came a fluttering and the lid was thrown back from the inside. Pandora watched terrified as scores of creatures flew out and circled her, filling the room. All the troubles and hardships that plague humankind came from that box."

"Nice story," Moeera said doubtfully. "Must've been an enormous box."

"No, just magic," Carrie said. "The Powers trapped those hardships to help humankind survive an overwhelming world."

Moeera grimaced. "But Pandora let them out. Did they kill her?"

"No, not then. They scurried away--or flew--so happy were they to be free of their prison. Pandora's friend woke up and found her just in time to see the last of the creatures leaving. He was sad."

"But then Pandora and Epimetheus heard a tiny voice coming from the box. At first, they were scared, thinking more bad things were still in there. The voice was comforting, though. It sounded meek and innocent. The box was opened, and one tiny creature flew out."

"'I am hope' it told them. 'Women and men will face many evils and difficult trials, but as long as I am free, they will have hope to guide them through life'."

"Hmm. That's some story," Moeera said.

"Yes."

"So, this jar of termites ...."

Carrie smiled. She looked confident for the first time since beginning the tale. "Contains one of the hardships that came from Pandora's box. Right now, it's trapped in the jar, thanks to Charles."

"He trapped it?"

"Mm-hmm."

"How?"

"He's a great wizard--when he's human."

"Why's it dangerous to look at?"

"Because it wants you to let it out," Carrie said. "Yes, it does. It isn't absolutely trapped in that jar. It has power... limited though it may be."

Moeera was silent.

"When is a door not a door?" Carrie asked.

"When?" Moeera asked.

"When it's ajar!" Carrie exclaimed, giggling.

She noticed Moeera's somber face.

"A-hem! You know, a jar!"

"I know," Moeera said. She sighed.

"Well!" Carrie said. "It's safe now! Let's review some magical defenses."

*   *   *

Another day they were tidying up the "yard" around the house. Sunshine filtered through the tree leaves brightening the woods. From the outer, scrubby barrens the townsfolk came--three men and a woman.

The woman wore a green dress and brown, crocheted shawl across her shoulders. She walked with a slight limp, leaning on the cane in her right hand. Her face displayed the lines of age, marking her as a septuagenarian.

The men were younger. Two were stocky, dressed in heavy boots and dirty work clothes. The third couldn't have appeared more different. He wore nice clothes; the kind that only an official or merchant could afford. His fingers bore gold rings and his cufflinks appeared to be gold also.

"Hello there!" Charles called.

"Hello," the wealthy-looking man said. "Might this be the home of Carrie the miracle healer?"

"It might well be," Charles said noncommittally. "That's my better half Carrie right there with the trimming scissors. You'll have to judge yourself her healing ability."

The man smiled a quick grin that seemed amused, but also hinted that he was used to getting right down to business.

"My name's Maxwell," he said. "This lovely lady is my mother. The two nice men who helped us walk the trails to get here are the Boash brothers, Doon and Skeery. Both brothers shook Charles's hand. The woman smiled.

Carrie overheard the last bit of introductions and jumped up from her grass-trimming endeavors. "Mr. Maxwell," she said. "Skeery. Doon." She shook each of their hands. She focused on the lady and said, "I'm Carrie. Who might you be?"

"Desiree," the lady said. "I've come here for your help. We heard you're a healer."

"I try," Carrie said. "What seems to be the problem?"

"My legs ... my feet ...." Desiree trailed off.

Maxwell stepped forward.

"My mother has developed a curious condition. She has the hardest time walking anymore despite having suffered no falls or injuries to bestow this malady on her. In her line of work this is even more frustrating than dealing with it day to day."

"Have you seen a doctor?" Carrie asked.

"Yes," the woman said. "He says it must be arthritis."

"What do you think?"

"It could be ...."

"But you doubt it?"

"Yes," Desiree said. "I've had the pain now for more than a month. It doesn't abate. I always thought arthritis came and went."

"It does, believe me," Carrie said. "The weather affects it; the moisture

206

in the air …. I can give you an ointment to rub into the affected areas."

"Will it help?"

"It helps arthritis and some other ailments. What line of work are you in?"

"I walk the tightrope in the Strong Jonathan Carnival Show."

"Well!" Carrie said. She chuckled. "Charles, fetch me potion number eight!"

"Okay," he said. He disappeared into the house.

"With all due respect, ma'am, my mother requires something stronger than an ointment," Maxwell said.

"But that's what I do," Carrie said. "Ointments, potions, creams, salves--remedies from nature."

"Yes, we were told that. The people in the town nearby said you're better than any doctor."

"Why do you doubt me then?"

"I thought that--"

"What?"

"I thought you might know some magic."

"Magic?" Carrie's eyebrows shot up. She smiled as if this was the greatest of amusements. "If you're searching for magic you've ended up in the wrong woods. I'm just good with plants is all."

"Money isn't an obstacle," Maxwell said. "We have performances to put on for the carnival. Without the Death-defying Desiree the show will attract far fewer paying spectators."

"Mr. Maxwell," Carrie said as she slathered a generous amount of ointment onto Desiree's legs, "I suggest you assist your mother in applying this twice a day for a week. Additionally, she can take a thimbleful of the potion daily to ease any swelling. She needs to try these for at least a week before attempting any tightrope walking."

"Thank you, Carrie," Desiree said, smiling.

"You're quite welcome!" Carrie said. "If this helps your problem you should be able to tell after a few days. Apply it in the morning and at night before bed."

"What if it doesn't help?" Desiree asked.

"Come back and see me again," Carrie said. "We'll try something else."

Moeera watched and listened to the exchange, raking oak leaves away from the table and chairs (which were visible). The woman seemed nice enough, but the men gave her the willies. The Boash brothers would fit in perfectly with a traveling show; both looked strong enough to lift an ox. They were the strong, silent type.

Maxwell struck her as odd and not in a good way. Could he be a barker or ringmaster? Perhaps. He seemed dishonest to her. Why that was she couldn't put her finger on.

Carrie collected her fee for the tin of ointment and the little bottle of potion number eight. Maxwell and the Death-defying Desiree thanked her and returned from whence they came.

Charles had gone into the house. When the quartet was out of sight Moeera told Carrie her feelings about Maxwell.

"Mm-hmm! He seemed to be hiding something," Carrie said excitedly.

"He wanted to know if you could do magic," Moeera murmured.

"Exactly," Carrie said. "What was that about?"

"A bad omen?" Moeera asked.

"Honey, all omens are bad," Carrie said. "So, yes!"

They continued tidying up. As Moeera finished with the dead leaves Charles the gander fluttered across the clearing, honking something at Carrie. What it was he honked Moeera didn't know.

*   *   *

In the ringmaster's wagon of the Strong Jonathan Carnival Show Desiree sat back as Skeery Boash massaged ointment onto her legs. She sighed.

Maxwell and Doon were there also, but they weren't watching Desiree's treatment. Their attention was focused sharply on the woman lounging on the overstuffed sofa.

"You talked with her," she stated simply. Her voice was water slowly seeping down an obstructed drain.

"Yes," Maxwell said, dreamily.

"Good," she said. "Did she admit to being Carrie the Pip?"

"No," Maxwell said, shaking his head. "She claimed to be just good with plants."

"Is this true!" the lady snapped. Her gaze bore into Doon's eyes.

"Yes," Doon said.

"Did you believe her?" the lady asked.

"I don't know," Doon said.

"You others?"

"No," Skeery said. "She was hiding something."

"We'll know if this helps my legs, won't we," Desiree said. She winced as Skeery massaged a tender spot.

Maxwell had a faraway look on his face. He frowned. "She wouldn't admit it, but I think she was a witch."

The mysterious lady sat back, smiling. "Yes … yes …. Exactly what I think, slave. She may keep a low profile living in the wilderness, but she can't hide the magic traces of her husband's curse. Carrie the Pip and Charles, Wizard of the Eastern Marches. At last, I have found them."

Chapter Five

That night, Carrie began talking about tools. Not tools for woodworking or repairing or harvesting. She was all about tools used in witchcraft. Poppets, cauldrons, broomsticks, crystal balls....

"Orbs such as crystal balls are often used to farsee," she said. "They can surpass or be not as good as a pool of water. It depends on your preference."

She set her crystal ball on the table between herself and Moeera.

"I've always had a soft spot for these," she said. "This is a small one. Isn't it cue-it?"

"Sure," Moeera said.

"Let's try an exercise," Carrie said. She took two candles from a sideboard and placed them on the table. "Light those, dear."

Moeera focused on the candles. She pictured them in her mind as having flames, and they did.

"Thank you," Carrie said. She sat down. "One can farsee by herself, or she can farsee with a friend."

"How in the world does one do that?" Moeera asked.

"Like this," Carrie said, reaching across the table and clasping hands with her granddaughter.

Carrie closed her eyes.

Do you hear me? the voice asked in Moeera's mind.

Mom-mom! I hear you, Moeera thought.

That's good. I hear you as well. Open your eyes.

Moeera opened them. Nothing was different. Was it?

We're attuned to each other. It will be easier to farsee together.

How did you do that?

It's not important.

Now what? Moeera asked.

Stare at the ball, focus your gaze.

What else, Mom-mom?

Keep staring. What or who would you like to see?

Wecks. Can we see Wecks?

I don't see why not. Focus. Say the words of the farsight spell.

Out loud?

Whatever way you like.

Moeera recited the spell in her mind. She repeated the words. The ball in front of her disappeared, replaced by Wecks addressing an audience in a darkened theater.

I see it too, Carrie thought. *Concentrate. Focus. Let yourself be calm. You'll hear what he's saying if we can make a strong enough connection.*

A few moments later, Moeera could hear the Wondrous Wecks speaking in her head.

"Did everyone have a good Crack Blam? Anybody do anything memorable?" Wecks asked. "I bet you all did a lot of pot banging, huh?"

Amazing.

The first time I farsaw with another witch was with Murr.

Murr. Wait. What!

The vision of Wecks terminated as if it had never happened. The crystal ball was right where it had been.

"What's wrong?" Carrie asked, giving Moeera's right hand a squeeze.

"Nothing, Mom-mom," Moeera said. "It's just that you mentioned the name Murr."

"Murr was one of my elders when I became apprenticed to my mother."

"I see. Wecks gave me a stick that he got from a fairy named Murr. He said it was a magic wand."

"Do you have it?" Carrie asked.

Moeera reached into her bodice and pulled out the wand.

"Is this a magic wand?" she asked. "Mama said it might be. She said the wand just directs the spells."

"Let me take a look."

Carrie took the wand and scrutinized it. She slid it back and forth between her fingers.

211

"I suppose it could have been someone's magic wand. It does make my fingers tingle. Why don't you put it on the mantle there?"

"Okay."

"We'll be practicing with wands any day now," Carrie said. "You're welcome to start with that one."

* * *

Three days later they learned what was so off about Maxwell. The house was dark. Dusk had fallen over the forest and the sun's last rays quickly vanished.

Carrie was clearing the supper table. Moeera's casserole had met with her approval and delight.

"Honk!"

"What is it, Charles?" Carrie asked.

"Honk!"

"Really!"

Carrie left the dishes stacked on the table and hurried to the front room. Moeera followed.

Carrie made passes in the air and pulled the air in front of the door aside creating a one-sided window.

Moeera gasped.

A crowd of more than twenty men with torches and clubs stood about twelve feet from the door. One approached the door and knocked emphatically with his club.

"Miss Carrie!" he called out. "Miss Carrie, open up! We want to talk!"

Carrie took a breath and called back, "It's Mrs.! And it looks like you have something besides talking in mind!"

"Carrie of the Barrens!" another shouted.

The magic window still hovered before the door. They recognized Maxwell who looked menacing tonight. His hair stuck out every which way as if he'd been zapped by lightning. He wore black from head to toe and held a fiery torch in one hand and a pitchfork in the other.

"I knew it!" Moeera exclaimed.

Carrie held a finger to her lips.

"I knew he was trouble," Moeera muttered.

"Are you afraid, Miss Carrie?" Maxwell called. "Or should I call you Carrie the Pip?"

212

Carrie straightened as if she'd just been shocked.

"What do you want!" she shouted. "It's late. We're closed!"

"We're not here for medicine!" he shouted back. "We want you and your husband the wizard! He's the same Charles who fought in the War of the Powers, isn't he?"

"What would a stripling such as you know about that?" Carrie asked.

"We know enough!" Maxwell yelled. "We know you're a witch and he's a wizard of the Old Guard!"

"Go away!" Carrie exclaimed. "You're all fools! We don't want any!"

The witch and her apprentice watched ten men move forward with a felled oak tree set as a battering ram.

"Toadstools!" Carrie cried.

She wiped the air with her hand and the magic window vanished.

"Moeera! Get the defense spell ready."

"Which one?"

"The Nebulous! Place it on yourself!"

Moeera held her breath. She'd never have it ready before they broke down the door.

"Do it!" Carrie hissed. "Like we practiced!"

Moeera relaxed a smidgen. How could one relax in the face of overwhelming odds? Focus. She needed to focus. She saw Carrie make a pass in the air. Suddenly the door and the front wall were made of the strongest iron.

Not a moment too soon. The men rammed the oak squarely against the door. The resounding "clong" was loud, but the door held firmly.

Moeera closed her eyes. She ran the magic words through her mind.

"Moeera!" Carrie exclaimed. She grabbed her arm, pushing something smooth and hard into her hand.

"What's this?" Moeera asked, distracted from the Nebulous.

Moeera's eyes snapped open to discover the forbidden jar in her hand.

"Guard that jar, Moeera!" Carrie snapped. "No matter what else happens--guard it and let none open it!"

Great! Moeera thought. *First, I'm not to even look at it; now I'm to protect it. Dangerous to look at.*

"At least Charles will be himself soon," Carrie said.

Moeera nodded. She noticed that the room was becoming steamy.

213

Wait! Steamy? What was happening?

A shriek pierced the air. Someone stood between the front room and the hallway.

"Huhn," Moeera breathed.

She was scared out of her mind now if she hadn't been before. She heard the battering ram slam again against the front door. She jumped. The noise and the figure she now saw in the room behind them appeared to have come from someone's bad dream.

It had to be a witch--how else had it managed to get in the locked house? But where Carrie was sweet and cheerful--this nightmare woman looked like a beast from Hell. Moeera could see it was a she but thought of the figure as an it--a creature with murder in mind. It had eyes to rival the most hideous of wolves, its skin was white as eggshells, and blood oozed down over gore-encrusted lips and chin. Long, dark hair swept back and fell, pasting itself to white shoulders as if washed in blood. It wore only white leggings and a bloodstained bodice ripped practically to shreds.

Calmly as if they were playing old maid, Carrie said, "Moeera, finish your spell."

A hideous gargling sound came from the blood witch, and she raised her oddly clean hands, clawed fingernails pointing.

Moeera watched awestruck as the blood witch approached them. Carrie made passes in the air, muttering to herself.

Moeera watched, terrified, until she heard Carrie's voice again in her head telling her to place the Nebulous on herself. She closed her eyes and chanted the words. She put the two witches out of mind, blocking their fight out with the words she spoke. Each word put her goal deeper into her train of thought. Carefully, ever so carefully, she made passes with her left hand. It traveled up the side of her body and topped the crown of her head. Then she brought it down the other side. Heel, palm. Heel, palm-- fingertips at each of the body's sacred chakras. Heel, palm. Heel, palm, fingers.

Her body warmed as if she stood next to a roaring fire. She repeated the procedure again and opened her eyes when she felt the change. There came an odd staccato beat--tap tap tap tap tap tap tap--from no visible source. Her eyes squinted, the very air surrounding her glowed as if every molecule was a miniature sun.

She looked to Carrie who now was locked in mortal combat with the blood witch. Carrie seemed to have the … creature on the ropes. A creature--a non-verbal animal--was all she was to Moeera.

Only it was so much worse. Fire engulfed the walls and roof above the iron door and front wall. The cottage wasn't large by any means. Without a monsoon it was lost. But what about Carrie and Charles?

Moeera paused in her ritual. How could she just leave Carrie to the fire and the blood witch? Charles, too. He was a goose. Maybe he was becoming human again at that very instant. Wouldn't he be able to stop the fire and the fiends outside?

She didn't know.

"Carrie!" she called out. Her words seemed muted as if she were closed up in a closet.

All around her the air was awash with different colors. They lit the very air, stronger than the brightest lanterns. The effect was strongest immediately around her, but the colored lights radiated outward.

Can I extend the spell to bring Carrie, too? Moeera wondered this, hoped this. She had no idea. They hadn't discussed it. But she could damned well try.

She resumed the charm, dancing her hands heel, palm, fingers. The lights coalesced into a rainbow pattern around her--indigo, blue, and green bathing her flesh. Yellow, orange, and red forming a corona which nearly blocked her vision of the cottage.

She could see silhouettes of red marking Carrie and the blood witch. Their fingers were laced as they struggled to overcome one another. Moeera took a step toward the combatants. The charm's effects made her feel as if she walked waist-deep through molasses. She saw the shape of the women through a blurry haze as she slipped from this world to another.

Two steps … three steps ….

She felt tired but continued to push to move her feet. The rainbow of colors blended to create white light, blinding white light.

She lurched forward hoping to grasp Carrie's shoulder. A roar came from directly above, sparks fell, burning pieces of the roof fell.

Suddenly her vision cleared, and she saw Carrie. The blood witch had her hands around Carrie's neck. Then the entire roof fell in burying everything with wood and flame!

215

Moeera blacked out.

*   *   *

She awoke to something nibbling at her ankle.

"Stop it," she said.

The nibbling continued, becoming more insistent.

"Rrrgh," she moaned. "Stop it!"

She tried rising, but pain wracked her head. "Uhhn!"

She turned over and stared at the fawn who nudged her with his nose.

"What do you want?" she moaned.

The young deer nodded its head, saying nothing of course.

"I hurt all over!" she exclaimed.

The deer stamped its front hoof.

Moeera groaned. She thought of a spell.

"Titter tatter witter watter laugh guffaw chitter chatter," she said, staring at the deer.

The fawn was surprised to see what it thought was its fellow deer at the pasture's edge. A large buck nodded to him and leapt off followed by several dozen deer. The fawn who had been off at play when he stumbled upon Moeera ran after.

Moeera smiled. He chased phantoms from his own memory. The spell should conclude quickly, and he'd realize he'd been seeing things before he went far.

A sharp pain lanced through her head.

"Ugh."

She was still for what seemed like an eternity. Her head still hurt when she forced herself to sit up. The memory of casting the Nebulous filled her with dread. She found herself in a field of wildflowers, the sun shone in the sky. There was no sign of Carrie and Charles or their house. It seemed she'd successfully fled. She'd passed out and slept all night into the next day.

Moeera wept until she'd exhausted her tears. She shifted on the ground and felt a hard, smooth object under her. She reached down and pulled from beneath her....

"The jar, of course," she said.

She looked at it a moment, but thought better of it, wrapping it in a kerchief. Then she rested a little while longer. The illusion she cast for the fawn had sapped even more of her energy.

216

Moeera thought about her situation. *I feel like a wreck! I guess that's why you don't see more people popping in with the Nebulous.*

After a while she felt a bit better. She was still miserable, but her head ached less. The meadow stretched for quite a way. To her right it kept going; a rolling hill blocked her extended vision. To the left she saw a line of trees marking a forest's edge.

An hour later she began walking along the forest's edge. The tree leaves all had a yellow hue. So did the grass. She'd never seen yellow grass. Purple, green once in a while, but not yellow. Most of the wildflowers were yellow, too.

Where on Earth was she?

Chapter Six

The rain fell steadily across the landscape, the yellow tree leaves looking sick in the gray sky. The road ahead had the sorrowful appearance of a creature expecting to never be dry again. Moeera didn't mind. The road was a welcome companion to her.

There had to be someone who would let her come in for supper. Perhaps they'd have a hayloft or floor to sleep on. She'd been nearly two days without food, and her stomach was growling terribly.

Luck is a tricky thing. It makes kings out of common men and beggars out of emperors. Always entwined with fate luck can be graceful or hard. Love is blind and luck is fickle.

She was turned away from the few houses she found. The seventeen-year-old girl met a mistrust amongst the back-wood dwellers born of a recent spate of burglaries. She walked on, the night descending around her.

The road she traveled stretched long and lonely amongst the trees, fields, and rocks. She shivered underneath her shawl which was soaked through.

How would she get out of this mess?

She clung to the hope that she had cast the Nebulous properly. She had chosen no destination, but the spell should have sent her somewhere pertinent. She just needed to find out where she was and why. Her feet slapped the water-slicked road, shoes coated brown with mud and slime. A scream built in her throat, but she kept it there not wanting to waste energy.

A light appeared ahead sending her heart into palpitations. A light surely meant a house and someplace to get out of the rain.

The darkness dissipated somewhat, and the shadows fell long on the road. Moeera saw a whole series of tree stumps alongside the road. But as she got closer she saw crosses: gravestones.

The cemetery stretched into infinity.

This must be where all of Gillikin Country buries their dead, she thought.

The light wasn't far from the road and the covered wagon gave reason as to why. A lantern burned, hanging from the driver's seat.

Moeera stopped at the wagon. The rain was coming down hard, preventing her from listening for the occupants. Perhaps they'd pulled to the side to wait out the rain. A poor, wet woobacus stood in front of the wagon making groaning noises.

"You poor baby," Moeera said, stroking the creature's hairy back. "It's definitely not your best night."

The woobacus wiggled its nose and wheezed mournfully.

"Hello?" Moeera called out. "Do you have room for a traveler to get out of the rain for a little?"

There was no answer of course; the wagon was devoid of people. Moeera didn't know what to expect, but she was soaked and miserable, so she climbed into the back.

"Hello?"

No answer. The light from the driver's seat cut in enough to show her some blankets, two trunks, and not much else.

She pondered this. Where were the owners? The lantern made her think they were someplace close by. She hopped back out into the rain wondering if they'd drowned.

Be serious, she thought.

From somewhere out in the gloom a voice came to her, barely audible. Someone talked to another in harsh, excited tones. Moeera blinked away the raindrops sliding down her forehead into her eyes. This must be it, she thought. My imagination has taken over. Now I'm ... mad. Mad, mad, mad.

A thunderclap sounded almost simultaneously with a lightning bolt. She felt the boom in her bones and her teeth.

But then ... voices, talking back and forth urgently in the stormy night. She did hear voices--real voices. She peered into the graveyard's depths; her hand raised to block the glare from the wagon lantern that swung to-and-fro in the wind.

219

Finally, she spied another light faint in the distance. She staggered toward its source, treading carefully between headstones and markers. The voices grew louder as the rain whipped this way and that.

Moeera could soon see two figures crouched down in front of a grave, digging side by side with short spades.

Grave robbers!

The girl now realized that the night could get worse than being drenched and homeless. The men digging up the dead didn't care much for their rest; she doubted they would care much to be witnessed by anyone living. There was no shelter for her here.

Nonetheless she was fascinated. What kind of lunatics would spend a stormy night disturbing the deceased?

She crossed herself and headed toward the excavation. There were a few trees invading the graveyard off to the left. She circled that way hoping to blend in with the coniferous sentinels swaying in the night.

When Moeera was about thirty yards away she stood against a tree trunk and watched. The two men's voices were lost in the storm, but their conversation went something like this:

"Come on, brother! Dig! It has to be here!"

"What does it look like I'm doing!"

They grunted and wheezed and puffed. The heavy rain took a huge toll on their work. Dirt became mud, sliding back down the dirt pile into the grave.

"Hey! I hit something!" one cried happily.

They set to work clearing the slab-like cover they'd found. Edges were felt out, mud and dirt were thrown by hand in clods. Now that they had something tangible they worked with manic glee.

Moeera watched amidst the rain and lightning as they stuck long prybars into the hole. They strained and pushed and hemmed and hawed until finally the taller one thrust out his hand. The other stopped.

The tall one bent down (to open the coffin lid Moeera expected). She saw the look on the other man's face. He was enraptured about something in that grave.

Then the first stood up holding something very small in his hands. Moeera strained away from the tree to try to see, but it was no use.

Then the man held it up to his face to see better, and the object caught

220

the light from the lantern.

Whatever that is he's got, Moeera thought, *I bet it's made of gold!*

The thought of gold excited Moeera. If she had gold in her purse or on her fingers people would invite her in. Gold took you places, didn't it?

Her earlier disgust of the grave robbers wavered. Maybe she could find something they missed. If the dead was disturbed to begin with would it still be wrong?

Both the men were crouched in the grave searching for valuables. Moeera noticed a large, blocky tombstone behind the grave they were searching. If she got behind it maybe she could see something.

She began stepping through the markers to get behind the men. As she made it even with the open grave a thunder strike hit close by and a flash lit the place up like high noon.

The taller man popped his head up looking like a humanoid gopher. He saw Moeera in the seconds the lightning bathed the cemetery in white.

"Dominic!" he yelled.

"What?" the other man bawled.

"There's somebody spying on us!"

"In this Hell shower? Not a chance!"

"She's right there!"

Moeera ran off as fast as her legs could carry her.

"Hey! Stop!" the first man yelled. He and Dominic climbed out of the grave.

Moeera's throat caught fire as she ran down a dirt lane that intersected the graveyard. She'd put a nice space between her and the grave robbers, but she knew from their shouts that they were coming.

Her feet started sinking deeper and deeper into the lane as she hit an especially waterlogged section. She wanted badly to catch her breath, but she didn't want to be caught. She darted into the cold darkness further off in the cemetery.

She could still hear their shouts.

She closed her eyes tightly, willing her pursuers to give up. Her thoughts ran the jungle of her mind. Let me get away! Just let me alone.

She ran until she couldn't anymore. She saw a mausoleum and ducked behind a row of large headstones to its left.

She crouched down against the cold, wet stone and the soggy earth. She

221

didn't dare peer around to watch for them. She tried to pull her body into as small of a ball as she could.

The shouting continued for a while as the two robbers called back and forth to one another.

Then they stopped.

Moeera breathed a sigh of relief. They were moving off in another direction. She could slip away soon and get out of this place.

She breathed freely and deeply. She might have to run again if ….

"Gotcha!"

A strong pair of hands reached down over the tombstone grabbing her by her shoulders.

"AAAAH!" Moeera shrieked.

"Hey, Dominic!"

"Yes?"

"I got her! Help me!"

"Okay," Dominic said. "Can't you handle a woman by yourself?"

"No, she's all wet! This mud's slippery, too."

Moeera thrashed and kicked and clawed and bit, but the next moment Dominic held her by the waist and her left leg.

"Let me go! Let me go!" she shouted.

"What do we do with her?" Dominic asked.

"Tie her up," his partner said. "We have what we came for. It's time to get out of here."

They herded Moeera unceremoniously through the tombstones to their wagon.

"Stop struggling!" Dominic said. He drew aside the wagon's covering.

"Looks like she was already here," the other commented, seeing the muddy footprints on the floorboards.

They pulled her into the wagon and sat her on one of the trunks. Then Dominic tied her wrists together with twine.

"Stand up," he said to her.

Moeera was scared, but at least she was out of the downpour. If these two meant her harm she would probably be dead already. She stood, trying to think of an escape plan.

Dominic opened the trunk and brought out a long coil of rope. The trunk's lid fell closed with a clank.

"Sit down," he said.

Moeera sighed and did as she was told. He tied a knot to the trunk's handle and wrapped her around and around, under, over, and through. She looked like a fly in a web when he was done.

"Now drive us away from here," his partner said. "The farther; the better."

Dominic left the dry space of the wagon to rein the woobacus. The beast was miserable but decided it might be happier if they found someplace to get under cover.

Chapter Seven

As the wagon lurched along the rutted country road Moeera observed her other captor carefully. He was tall, probably close to six feet, with short, brown hair and a slender build. Muscles rippled along his arms as he stripped off his shirt and vest. He toweled off and pitched the cloth to the floor. Then he pulled a stool from the shadows and sat down facing his prisoner.

"What's your name?" he asked.

She stared at him, wondering whether or not to tell him.

"If you don't tell me what will I call you?" he asked. "Girl? Wench? Spy in the rain?"

"Moeera," she said. "What will you do with me?"

"Fair question, Moeera," he said. "I'm Ben, by the way."

"Do you spend all your nights defiling graves?" she asked.

"No," he said. "This is a crazy night. We were hunting for something, and wouldn't you know the current owner happened to be dead and buried."

"So that makes sacrilege fine then."

"When someone offers enough money for said possession, yes," Ben said.

"What's worth disturbing the dead?"

"Ah, but you first: what were you doing in the graveyard tonight?"

"Watching you."

Ben raised his hand as if to strike Moeera. He lowered it.

"Why?" he asked.

"I was looking for shelter from the storm. I found your wagon by the lantern light, but you weren't there so I came looking. I saw the second lantern. I didn't expect you'd be grave robbers."

"We're treasure hunters," Ben said. "Not the easiest job, but lucrative.

This ring should fetch our best price, yet."

He pulled a ring from his pocket, and Moeera got a close-up look at the shining object she'd only seen from a distance in the rain. It was indeed a gold ring, beautiful to behold, with a tan stone mounted upon it.

"Pretty, eh?" Ben said.

"Yes," Moeera said. "What stone is that? Carnelian?"

"No, just a tiger's eye."

"That's why you dug up that grave?"

"Obviously."

"Hmmph," Moeera said.

Ben eyed her curiously.

"It's very nice," Moeera said, "but if that's your biggest find you need to up your game."

Ben nodded. "I see."

"What will you do with me?" Moeera asked again.

"Not sure," Ben said. "Who are you, Moeera?"

"A traveler out to see the world."

"You look a bit young."

"You don't look especially old either," she said. "We all have to start someplace."

"True, I suppose," Ben said.

"Where are we headed?"

"Little town called Trappe."

"Never heard of it."

"Our buyer will be there soon to exchange for the ring."

"You must have been pretty sure it was in that grave," Moeera said.

"The ring was very hard to find," Ben said. "We spent the better part of the last two years asking around and looking stuff up. Every clue led us closer to the name Carr of Stanton."

"You seem relieved."

"I'm very relieved. We'll finally get paid. We won't have to work for Mozik anymore. It's a lot of money, but he scares me."

"It's wonderful you found it then."

"Yes. There were times I thought we never would, and I almost stopped believing it even existed. I'm ready to go back to looking for lost gold."

Ben looked thoughtful. "Once we get rid of the ring and get paid, I think we'll let you go."

"Really?" Moeera asked. The statement caught her off guard.

"Yes," Ben said. "Kidnapping isn't our thing. We just like to be on our guard. You might have been there for the same reason we were."

"I definitely wasn't," she said.

"I'd like to believe you," Ben said, "but I've got too much riding on this ring being safely delivered. That's the only reason we're holding you against your will."

They rode in silence for a while.

Ben broke it with a question. "Why are you on your own, Moeera? Are you running away from someone in Sashan?"

He must be talking about the teensy-weensy town we just left, Moeera thought.

"I ran away years ago," Moeera told Ben. "I found the perfect place for me. People I loved who loved me back. There was a fire, though, and I lost them."

"That's horrible," Ben said. "I'm sorry to hear it."

"Yes, it all but destroyed my life. My grandparents died in that fire."

"I'm sorry about that too."

"Thank you," Moeera said. "I didn't meet them until I was practically an adult, but once I did, I found two people I dearly loved."

"It's a shame that you lost them," Ben said.

"Yes," Moeera said. She tried to put the memory of the attack and the fire out of her thoughts.

Eventually Ben switched places with Dominic and the latter took the opportunity to get dry.

Dominic was an inch or two shorter than Ben, but otherwise favored him pretty closely.

"Is he your brother?" Moeera asked.

"Yep," Dominic said.

"I thought so. He said you'll let me go after your business in Trappe."

"He told you about Trappe?" Dominic asked, surprised.

Moeera nodded.

"I guess we will then," Dominic said. He sat in the same spot his brother had.

"My name's Moeera."

Dominic nodded.

"Where do you stay when you're not working?" she asked.

"The wagon," he said.

"Oh," she said.

"What about you? Where do you stay?"

"Anyplace. I trade chores for a floor or bed to sleep on."

He nodded.

He doesn't seem very much older than I am, Moeera thought.

"It must be exciting being a treasure hunter," she said.

Dominic shrugged. "I guess it kind of is. It's hard work--lots of digging."

"I guess," Moeera said.

"You have to find things people want," he added. "If you just find some old money or gold, then someone who has a lot of both might not want to pay for more. You know? It's a challenging vocation."

"I bet," Moeera said. She wished he would untie her.

"At least we're going to get paid now," he said. "Landry and the wagon are almost all we have to our names anymore. Times are tight."

Moeera nodded. My ropes are tight, she thought. She said, "Landry's the woobacus then."

"Yeah," Dominic said. "Raised him from a little snart, we did."

"Lovely."

Dominic drifted off to sleep after a bit.

Moeera wished she could sleep, but she was still soaking wet and being jostled around on top of the trunk.

Instead of sleeping she worked on her bonds. She felt the ropes woven around her back and tugged with her fingers. They didn't seem to be very tight, but she couldn't reach any of the knots.

She flexed her hands which had lost some circulation, feeling for the knots holding the tightly tied twine. Her fingers reached the knots and began the slow process of making the twine move. It would take some time and patience to loosen her hands.

By the time the wagon stopped again the sound of rain was a memory and so were Moeera's bonds. Ben came around into the wagon and studied the scene with dismay. Both Dominic and the bedraggled prisoner were stretched out sleeping like babies. Her bonds lie in a heap by one of the

227

trunks.

"Dom!" Ben said.

"Huh."

"Ahem! Dom!" Ben snapped, nudging his brother's arm with his boot.

"Yeah, Ben?"

"Get up! So much for guarding the prisoner."

Dominic sat up, rubbing his eyes.

"Hey!" he exclaimed. "What gives! How'd she get untied?"

"Wake her up and ask," Ben said.

Moeera was already rousing from her sleep. She stretched and grunted.

"How'd you get loose?" Dominic asked.

"How do you think?" Moeera replied.

"You had a knife," he said.

"Your rope isn't cut; neither is your twine for that matter. The rope wasn't tight. The twine was tighter, but I wriggled out of both."

"Well," Ben said, frowning, "it sounds like you're better at knots than he is."

"Just desperate," Moeera said. "It was uncomfortable sitting on the trunk like that."

Ben smiled. "Listen: I want you to stay with us till we get our money for the ring. After that you can do whatever you like."

"It's important," Moeera said.

"It's very important," Ben said. "Can't have you blabbing to anybody about our nighttime dig."

"Can I hang around without being tied up?" Moeera asked.

"I suppose," Ben said. "Can we trust you?"

"To do what?" Moeera asked.

"To not rat us out," Ben said. "To not try to hurt us or escape."

"Hmm …," Moeera said, her hand on her chin as she thought it over, "what's in it for me?"

"Not being tied up," Ben said. "And if you're helpful we'll cut you in for a share of the money."

Dominic's eyes widened as he stared at Ben.

Moeera's eyes lit up. "You'll pay me? You're joking."

"Why do you say that?" Ben asked.

"Because I just got here," she said. "You kidnapped me! I didn't have to do any of the work."

"No, you didn't," Ben said, "but we stand to collect enough to set us up."

"Set you up?" she asked, not certain what he meant.

"Yes. Able to buy houses, build houses, hire servants, impress important people .... We could be part of the upper class--noblemen. We could be somebodies instead of nobodies."

Moeera stifled a laugh. "Okay, Ben, I'll keep it secret. Is this okay with you, Dominic?"

"I guess," he said. "You can share the work from now on, though."

Moeera nodded. "Sure. How helpful do you need me to be?"

Dominic smiled. "Can you cook anything worth eating?"

*   *   *

Two hours later Dominic stopped the woobacus and told the others where they were. It was a small town called Mountain Hollow. Trappe was still far away.

They built a fire to cook their breakfast. Everyone was hungry with growling stomachs. Dominic took care of feeding and watering Landry. Moeera rummaged through the chest that contained the food stores. She found eggs, bread, a bit of cheese, and a lot of vegetables.

"I can work with this," she said. "Where's your stuff like pans and knives and such?"

Ben got Moeera the supplies she requested. She worked furiously to get prepared. In short order she had her ingredients frying over the dying fire.

Moeera glanced at the grass and the trees. "Things are back to normal, at least."

"How's that?" Ben asked.

"The grass ... the foliage," Moeera said, "purple again."

"Sure," Dominic said. "It's always purple in Gillikin Country."

"Yesterday it was yellow," Moeera said.

"Yes," Dominic said. "Yesterday we were in the land of the Winkies."

"Mmm," Moeera acknowledged.

Inside she was aflutter. The Nebulous had taken her quite a way farther than she thought!

"We'll be hard-pressed to get there in time," Ben said anxiously.

Moeera rummaged around in their crate of cooking supplies. She pulled out a pair of tongs. With these she turned the roughly sliced bread toasting on a rock next to the cooking fire.

"Don't despair, partner," Moeera said, trying to sound cheerful. "Your toast and eggs will be ready to eat in two minutes."

"Now that's what I like to hear," Ben said. "I'm famished."

"Me, too," Dominic said. "I'm thrilled that Moeera's a good cook and all, but are we really cutting her in for a third?"

"Yes," Ben said.

"Do you want to marry her or something?" Dominic asked.

"No," Ben laughed. "Dom, we just met. Believe me, it's worth the third of our pay for her loyalty."

"Why?"

"Yeah, why?" Moeera asked.

"Imagine that she went to the constable of the nearest village and said those two brothers--the Whoosiwhatzits--desecrated a grave in Sashan."

"The townsfolk might come after us," Dominic said.

"Sure, and they might throw us in the clink," Ben said.

"Yeah," Dominic said, "that would be a problem."

Moeera was still practically floating on air upon hearing she might get an equal third of the reward. Ben's next sentence made her come back in a snap.

"I'll say," Ben said. "Mozik would probably hunt us down and kill us."

Moeera nearly spilled Ben's breakfast all over him.

"Whoops! Steady! There you are: eggs, toast, jam. Now ... Dominic, here's a plate for you."

When they were all three eating Moeera struck up the conversation.

"Are you enjoying your breakfast? Good, good. Tell me about this Mozik. Who is he and how'd you meet him?"

The brothers looked at each other. A wordless exchange took place ending with Ben nodding at Dominic and Dominic nodding back.

Dominic cleared his throat.

"We were searching out a treasure chest in the lost city of spirals. We had a site marked out and worked the dig. One day our innkeeper came to the dig with a visitor. He was this big, important-acting fellow. Said he needed to find this ring. 'I'll pay you a king's ransom if you bring me the ring,' he told us. We said sure."

Dominic took a long stick and stirred the coals in the fire circle. Ben took up the taletelling.

"We found the treasure chest of the lost city of Spirals that same day," Ben said. "Nothing major; nice little box full of coins and trinkets. No jewelry to speak of."

"We sold it to some king in the Northwest. Has a charming kingdom called Oogaboo? He paid us a fee, and we dove into this ring business."

"Mozik didn't live in the area where the spirals were. He told us that he'd find us again no problem. Said he was able to find people easily, but things like this ring were too tricky. We began searching."

"Two months later he appeared out of nowhere and demanded the ring. We told him we hadn't found it yet. That made him angry. He threatened us and told us to hurry up and find this ring."

"We followed what few clues we could find going from here to there to there and back again. Every time the trail seemed hot we came up empty. Mozik would check in on us again and again. Every time he got more and more angry we hadn't got the ring yet. When we told him we were on our way to check a burial site he said to meet him in Trappe. He'd have our loot for us."

"Yeah," Dominic said. "He was excited when we told him we'd found Carr's grave."

"Well," Moeera said. "Mozik sounds like a real treat. Why's he want the ring so badly?"

"Family heirloom," Dominic said. "Somebody stole it."

"Do you trust him?"

They looked at each other.

"Not really," Ben said, "but he's rich and promised a big payout."

"The treasure-hunting business isn't all it's cracked up to be," Dominic said. "Some things don't want to be found."

Moeera contemplated their story. She trusted they were honest. They hadn't any real reason to lie to her. She didn't trust Mozik, though. Family heirloom indeed.

She cleaned up the dishes and repacked them in the wagon. Then she squeezed into the driver's seat beside Dominic to get a look at the countryside as he drove. A couple hours later when they switched again she took a turn driving for a while. Ben navigated and their destination grew ever closer.

*   *   *

Mozik himself was expecting them at Trappe. He sat on a large, comfortable throne made of polished cedar wood and lined with satin cushions. He was a very large man, standing six foot, four inches. Muscles rippled over his entire body. Brown hair peeped through his shaved, tan scalp.

Mozik lounged on the Sour Serpent Inn's mezzanine. He had his own private view of Trappe's main street below, but he himself was shielded from prying eyes by translucent white sheers. He drank from an enormous mug of ale and contemplated the prize he was to receive in a day's time.

He would finally have the ring after all this waiting! If those two diggers were correct they should now be on their way to present it to him. Oddly, though, he could not pinpoint their exact location with his ability of biolocation. No matter! It reinforced his belief that they brought the ring. The ring itself must be interfering with his ability.

He smiled contentedly. The waitress entered, approaching him with trepidation.

"Would you like more ale, sir?" she asked. It unnerved her that this behemoth and owner of the inn had arrived in town. He rarely visited. She hoped he would not stay long.

"Yes, dearie, that would be splendid," he said. He emptied his mug and placed it on her serving tray.

"Could I interest you in some lunch?"

"What are those steaks the clientele rave about so fondly?" he asked.

"Moose, sir," she said.

"Moose. Bring me one of those. Tell Garner not to put a heavy char on it. I like mine rare."

"Rare. Yes, sir. I'll be back directly with your ale."

She disappeared into the side passage leading to the stairs.

Mozik continued staring at the main street below. People strode by as they moved about their business; here a few miners, there a couple ranch hands. A gaggle of nuns scurried toward the rectory. Children passed by kicking a metal can in place of a ball.

Across the way the Trappe town hall stood forlornly watching time pass. A wooden shutter hung crookedly from a second story window. Beside the

232

hall stood a smaller inn and saloon where the lunchtime crowd was just beginning to enter.

Mozik licked his lips, thinking about the glory awaiting him when he wore that tiger's eye ring upon his finger.

*   *   *

"That's it, Moeera," Ben said, "the sign for Trappe."

Moeera glanced at the wooden signpost by the roadside. It was surrounded by scrubby brush and stony soil. A dry wind blew from the Northeast, jiggling the two wooden legs ever so slightly.

"What a relief!" Moeera said. "After all that traveling we're finally coming to our goal."

"Yes!" Ben exclaimed. "We'll finally be done with our job for Mozik. We'll be rich!"

Ben's face beamed happiness.

Moeera wasn't so thrilled. She hadn't really been a part of this until now. Was that why? Or was something else bothering her?

"It all ends in Trappe, hmm?" Moeera asked.

"Sure," Ben said. "We'll be free from scrabbling around so hard for a living."

"That would definitely be wonderful," Moeera said.

Ben could hear the doubt in her tone. "What's bothering you?" he asked.

"Besides the town's name? Just that this Mozik is offering up payment so big that you offered me a third to keep mum about it. Plenty and to spare … for that one ring."

"It's extremely valuable to his family or people," Ben said. "Something like that."

"Why? He couldn't have just commissioned someone to make some new rings … or a good copy? Who are his people, anyway?"

"I don't know," Ben said. "He's a big, tall man--but in no way a giant. He never said where he was from."

"Hmm," Moeera mused.

"As for the ring itself …it beats me why he wants it so badly. I figured it went with some crown jewels or something."

"Maybe," Moeera said. "He must stand to get a lot of power from it."

Ben reached into his work vest and pulled the ring from a concealed pocket. "Look it over, Moeera. Go on. I didn't see any marks on it, but it wouldn't hurt to look again."

She scrutinized the ring in the sunlight. It was the same as before, a plain, but pretty, gold band thicker under the mount. The smooth tiger's eye stone was held in place by four golden posts. The ring had no marks or engraving at all.

Moeera slid it on her finger, smiling. "You're right; no marks anywhere. It is a nice ring."

Ben drove the woobacus on, clicking his tongue. "Not far now, Landry," he told it.

Moeera heard a voice come from the distinct vicinity of the woobacus. It said, "Why don't you take a turn pulling?"

She laughed nervously. "I sure can use a drink when we get there. I'm getting heat fever!"

Ben laughed.

Moeera sat with her hands on her lap. She felt the coolness of the ring between her fingers. Too bad it's being sold, she thought. It feels quite nice where it is.

"Don't worry, Moeera," Ben said, "I'll buy us each a drink as soon as we get there."

"Thanks," she said. "I feel jittery. I still don't trust that this guy means to pay you, though. Even with all that trouble the two of you went to finding it."

She looked at Ben who guided Landry ever on. He was calm, but no longer smiling.

"Whoah, Landry," he said suddenly. "Sorry, pal, but I need you to stop for a bit."

Landry did so obediently.

"What is it?" Moeera asked.

"I need to get something from the back," Ben said.

He returned a minute later with a piece of cheesecloth in his hand.

"Take this," he said, pushing it toward her with something shiny. It was a trowel.

Moeera took them.

"Go on," he said. "The sign makes a good marker. I'll wait here."

Moeera climbed down to the ground.

"Just a little insurance," Ben said. "We ought to be careful, oughtn't we?"

She nodded.

Chapter Eight

Finally, the wagon pulled onto Trappe's main street, flanked on both sides by buildings. It was a bustling, but small frontier town just south of the Great Gillikin Forest. Mountains and more wilderness lie beyond it. Its founders could have easily chosen the even more foreboding name of Last Chance.

Ben parked the wagon at the first building he saw.

"Don't worry, Landry," he told the tired woobacus. "I'll bring you some cold water to drink."

As Moeera drew aside the wagon's back flap she stared at Dominic. "What did you say, Dominic?"

"Nothing," he said, jumping to the ground.

"I could've sworn you said, 'Hurry up!'," Moeera said.

"No."

Dominic looked at the building. "The Dewdrop Inn," he read off the façade. "Maybe somebody here knows where Mozik is."

"Let's go in," Moeera said. "I'm thirsty."

Ben walked toward them with a bucket of water. He added it to the water trough Landry drank from.

*   *   *

Soon the three were sitting at The Dewdrop's bar eating a modest, but delicious lunch. Each had a generously tall glass of beeziwo.

Neither the barkeep nor anyone else there had ever heard of Mozik.

"I'm sure we'll find him before long," Dominic said.

After lunch they exited the inn to check on Landry and begin their search. The next place to check would be The Sour Serpent across the street.

Moeera sat on the bench near The Dewdrop's front door. She watched

Ben set up Landry with a feeding bucket as Dominic strapped on a gear bag.

A rough-looking group approached them from the street. They seemed to spring up from nowhere as they approached the covered wagon. Moeera counted five men wearing matching outfits of purple and blue. Two held clubs, the other three had an assortment of flails, daggers, and maces.

"Hello, boys!" the one with the iron mace exclaimed. "Fancy finding you here."

"Hello," Ben said.

"Hi," Dominic said. "Who are you?"

"Who we are isn't important," the speaker said. "What is important is that Mozik would have his prize."

"That's why we're here," Ben said.

The man was on the short side as were his comrades. None stood over five foot four. He smiled.

"Ah! So, you've brought the trinket."

"Of course," Ben said. "That was part of the deal. Where is he?"

"Very close," the man with the mace said. "Let's go see him now. He hates long waits."

Ben and Dominic fell in behind the speaker who led them toward The Serpent. His cronies flanked them, cutting off any direction they might choose for escape.

Moeera watched from the bench. She pulled her hand from under her leg and stared down at the ring.

"What's so special about little, old you?" she muttered.

She took a last look at her friends being herded into The Serpent. Then she stood up as casually as she could and went back in The Dewdrop.

Mozik stood behind the sheer curtains covering the front of The Serpent's mezzanine and smiled. His men had acquired the Delgy Brothers. The only witness appeared to be a young harlot hanging out at The Dewdrop. Almost perfect. Chances were she'd forget seeing the diggers upon finding another friend. His victory was assured.

*   *   *

Moments later Ben and Dominic stood before Mozik's throne, his henchmen stood in the shadows. Their master looked bored--not a care in the world.

"I thought we might have a hard time finding you," Ben said to the big man. "I imagined you might find us."

"And so, I have," Mozik said amiably. "Hello, Benjamin … Dominic."

"Mozik," Ben said, nodding.

"Sir," Dominic said.

Mozik's face lit up. "Don't keep me in suspense, fellows. Have you found the Tiger's Eye?"

"We have indeed," Ben said. "Exactly where we told you we would."

Mozik made a sound somewhere between a cry of exultation and a screech of victory. "Show me!"

"Not yet," Ben said, thrusting his hand in front of him.

"I'm not in the mood for games, Delgy," Mozik hissed. "Where is the ring?"

"In a safe place," Ben said.

"The only safe place for that ring is on my finger," Mozik growled.

"It's safe as can be," Ben said. "We're only too happy to hand it over. Thing is, we want to be paid."

Mozik glared with a look that could have killed. Then he grinned and said, "All right, boys, fair is fair. Follow me."

He strode past them to the rear wall. They followed him through it and gasped.

The room they stood in was small, windowless, and lit by a single lamp. In its center four big chests were stacked two deep. The top two were open, their lids flung backward. One had gold coins overflowing onto the floor. The other appeared to be full of uncut diamonds. They gleamed dully.

"Here you go, boys," Mozik said. He had the closest thing to a friendly smile he could muster. "Gold coins, diamonds, jewels, and a chest of royal regalia from the Uputcha Tribe. All yours if you deliver the ring."

Dominic reached out a hand to fill with gold coins, but Mozik seized it. "Ah, ah!" he said. "Ring first."

"Aw," Dominic said, "I wanted to make it rain."

"Really, Dom?" Ben asked. "Soon you'll be able to bathe in money." Dominic smiled.

"Sure, Mozik," Ben said. "We'll take you to it. It's not far."

They departed by way of the stairs with Mozik's five goons following closely. The lamp still burned in the treasure room.

A shadow fell across the room's contents. Moeera listened to the floor and steps creak under Mozik's imposing weight. She held her breath until they were downstairs. Then she slid out of the treasure room and crept toward the mezzanine's front. She stayed in the corner, peering between sheers to see her friends climb into a black and gold carriage pulled by a team of bachukkas.

Gotta hurry, she thought.

She passed by the treasure room doorway, stopping abruptly. The lamp was dying, but what light remained revealed an entirely new picture. She stepped in and picked up a gold coin.

It was no longer gold or a coin. It was a seashell--a flat, white seashell. She touched the pile overflowing the trunk. Every one of them was the same type of seashell. She glanced at the diamonds. They were pebbles, possibly quartz pieces. Their translucent innards caught the last of the dying light.

Moeera frowned. Just as she'd thought. Mozik was a lying cheat. And he had helpers that easily outnumbered her friends. She thought back to her conversation with Ben when they'd passed the Trappe signpost. It was a trap alright! She found the open window she'd used to climb inside.

*　　*　　*

"How much farther?" Mozik asked.

"We'll be there in a couple minutes," Ben said.

"Really, Ben, why not tell me exactly where it is now?"

Ben shrugged.

"No need," Dominic said. "There's the marker now!"

He pointed from his carriage seat.

"You didn't," Mozik said. He gazed open-mouthed at the sign for Trappe.

"Sure," Ben said. "I wanted it to stay safe. Who'd look for it there?"

"Anyway," Dominic said.

"It's buried to the left of the sign, wrapped in cheesecloth. You should be able to dig it out by hand," Ben said.

"Well!" Mozik yelled. "Kercar, get down there and fetch my prize!"

The chief of Mozik's goons yelled, "Maghyal, get down there and dig up his prize!"

The chain of command was used down to the last man. Five minutes later, Harthir began scraping dirt and rock aside and into a small pile. Ten minutes later he wasn't much further.

"What's taking him so long?" Mozik shouted at Kercar.

"What's taking him so long?" Kercar repeated to Maghyal.

"What's taking him so long?" Maghyal asked Snerl.

"What's taking him so long?" Snerl asked Dersas.

Dersas climbed down from the expensive carriage, walked over, and poked Harthir in the ribs. "Hey! What's taking so long?" he asked.

Harthir waved his dusty dagger, scowled, and said, "This is stupid."

Dersas paused and then whispered something to Harthir along the lines of "I know, right?".

Harthir whispered back the following: "Snob's so awful rich what does he want with some dumb ring?".

"Got me," Dersas whispered. "Now what?"

"Tell him this is stupid." Harthir shrugged.

Dersas looked at Snerl and said, "This is stupid."

"For the love of the Red Tower!" Mozik screamed. He pushed the carriage door open and hopped out.

His lackeys were still playing pass it on when he stomped up to Dersas and pushed him hard into Harthir. Both fell down.

"Give me the dagger," Mozik ordered. "I'll do it myself!"

He began stabbing and turning the dirt with gumption.

Scrape, scrape, scrape!

Dig, dig, dig!

Stab, stab, stab!

All the while he muttered about his men and their lack of initiative.

Ben and Dominic watched as best they could from the carriage. They were really beginning to enjoy themselves.

*   *   *

Moeera was in a true quandary. There was no treasure, and her friends didn't know. And that's merely the beginning of the problem, she thought, looking at the ring on her finger.

She'd switched the ring out for a plain sandstone when she buried it with Ben. She hadn't done it to swindle the brothers--she just felt it wasn't secure by the signpost. So, its true hiding place was known only to her.

Now Ben and Dominic were on their way to certain doom. Mozik would likely punish them severely. What could she do about it?

A thought crossed her mind. What was to stop her from getting out of town with Landry and the wagon, leaving by another road? She'd have the pretty ring, too. There was absolutely nothing to stop her.

She found that she couldn't do it. As tempting a scenario as it was she liked Ben and Dominic, considering them true friends. They'd trusted her. She had to help them get away.

Soon she and Landry were back on the road heading for the signpost. She urged the beast to go faster. The sun shone brightly overhead. The ring glinted and glittered on her finger.

Suddenly the woobacus stopped. Moeera groaned and said, "What's wrong with you, you stupid beast?"

She tugged at the reins, but Landry ignored her.

"Don't you understand?" she bellowed. "He'll kill them. They'll die for this stupid ring and it's not even their fault!"

Calmly, the woobacus turned its head to look at Moeera. As clearly as a person would speak it said, "It's you who doesn't seem to understand, Missy! I'm tired and need a proper rest! Who are you calling stupid by the way?"

Moeera recoiled as if she'd been slapped.

"What! You speak!"

"I always have," the woobacus replied. "How is it you're finally listening properly?"

Moeera's head spun. "You know what I'm saying?"

"Of course. You must love the sound of your voice you talk so much."

"Ben and Dominic are in danger," she said. "Please, Landry. Please take me to the edge of town so we can save them!"

"I wish I could," Landry said, "but I'm exhausted. Truly. Go save them yourself."

"Ooo!" she exclaimed. "I can't do it alone. How can I save them on foot and hopelessly outnumbered?"

A funny thing happened. Not funny ha-ha or funny tee-hee. Funny odd. Funny strange.

Thick, red smoke poured out from beneath the covered wagon. It rose up, blinding Landry and Moeera both.

Landry panicked. "What's going on?" he cried. "Fire! It's fire! I'll die for sure!"

Moeera was frightened. She scooched herself to the seat's edge and jumped to the ground.

As she rose from her knees a strange voice like tinkling bells asked, "Are you all right, mum?"

A figure emerged from the red smoke. It wasn't human; her best guess was it was a demon!

"Aaaah!" Moeera shrieked.

"Calm yourself," the purple-scaled being said in its lilting voice.

"Don't hurt me, please!" she cried.

"Hurt you? I'm here because you asked for my help."

It reached toward her with a small, clawed hand.

"Your help!"

"Indeed," it said. "You don't look like the master, but you called out in the same way 'I can't do it alone'. And you're wearing his ring. See that there."

It touched the tiger's eye stone with the tip of a claw. The stone flashed ever so slightly, almost imperceptibly.

"Yes, you are," the demon said. "You must be a new master."

Moeera stared down at the tiger's eye. She looked at the demon. "The ring! The ring calls a demon?"

"Demons," it corrected. "It commands enough demons to do the work of one thousand men. How do you not know that ..., Master?"

Moeera's mind was blown. As frightening as this demon looked it appeared that it was hers to order about.

"So, you'll help me?"

"Yes."

"Now?"

"Yes, what do you need?"

"I need to help my friends. They're going to be beaten, imprisoned, probably killed."

"Is that all?" it asked. Then it read her thoughts. "Oh, indubitably. Let's tip the odds, shall we?"

It snapped its dainty demon fingers and they disappeared in a puff of smoke.

Chapter Nine

Mozik knelt on the ground using the dagger like a shovel. "Where is it! Where is it? Where is my ring?" His voice rose in pitch becoming a hysterical scream. He had dug down twelve inches.

Ben and Dominic enjoyed every second of it, but now Ben was wondering what was going on.

Then Mozik spied a torn piece of cheesecloth and hurrahed gleefully.

"Yes!" he laughed. "At last, it's mine. The power, the glory. All mine."

He cupped the dirt around the cheesecloth in his large hands, pulling it out. He leapt to his feet and strode over to the carriage.

"As good as your word," he said to the brothers. "I had my doubts, but ...."

"You needn't," Ben said.

"Like we told you: found and safe," Dominic added.

Mozik unwrapped the cheesecloth carefully lest the ring fall upon the dirt. When the cloth's contents were revealed, however, rage and fury filled his eyes.

"What manner of deceit is this!" he roared.

"What!" Ben shouted. "What's wrong?"

"A piddly little pittance of a pebble!" Mozik exclaimed, flinging the pebble and his best alliteration at Ben and Dominic. He struggled for a breath. "I'm going to--"

"What?" a girl's voice called.

"Who!" Mozik exclaimed. He craned his neck to look beyond his luxury carriage.

Moeera stood there with Landry and the covered wagon.

"Move along, harlot!" Mozik shouted. "This doesn't concern a trollop like you."

"It does if you mean to hurt my friends," Moeera shouted back.

"Run, Moeera!" Dominic shouted. Snerl slapped him in the mouth and pushed down on his shoulders.

"Friends, huh?" Mozik called. "If these sad sacks are your friends, I suppose you know where the ring is!"

"I guess you aren't as stupid as you look!" Moeera yelled.

"Get them, boys!" Mozik shouted. "Get her and anyone else who might be over there!"

"Sure, boss!" Kercar said.

He, Snerl, Harthir, and Dersas charged over.

"This is your plan?" Landry asked.

"Certainly," Moeera said.

The frightened woobacus gulped.

Harthir walked around Moeera, pinning her arms behind her back. "Stupid girl."

"You said it," Kercar sneered. "Snerl, Dersas; check the wagon for anyone else."

"That's my cue," a voice that sounded like blended bells and laughter said.

As Dersas drew aside the cover a purple blur exploded at him and Snerl.

"What in blazes!" Snerl cried.

"That's exactly where you're going," the demon said cheerfully.

It grabbed Snerl and threw him. Snerl vanished into thin air.

Harthir said, "Come, girl. Mozik's waiting and I don't want to hurt you."

The next instant a loud crack sounded, and smoke rose from the ground.

"OWW! AAAH! OH!" Harthir screamed.

Moeera elbowed him and moved away.

She watched the demon rake its claws across Dersas's face.

"Do you like Hoppy?" it asked. "Every time one of these fools lies one of his toes pops into flame."

Kercar threw his arms around Moeera and began dragging her to the carriage.

The demon followed after like a tiger stalking its prey.

"Call it off!" Kercar hissed in Moeera's ear. "Tell your monster to stop."

He whirled her around to see Ben scuffling with Maghyal. Mozik stared at her and the demon. He dropped Dominic from a headlock and sputtered, "She's using the ring! How is that possible?"

"Diamond in the rough?" the demon replied.

It swung its hand in an arc to reveal a curved blade set on an ax handle. It drug this in an ever-deepening swipe into Kercar's body.

"LAAAH!" he shrieked in pain.

The demon pulled the blade free, and the thug fell to the ground dead.

"No! It wasn't supposed to happen like this," Mozik said.

Maghyal let go of Ben's wrists and dove from the carriage. He ran off into the bushes.

"Looks like it's you and us," the demon said.

"You're supposed to serve me!" Mozik snarled.

"Surprise!" the demon said. It advanced on the carriage, licking its lips.

Ben yelled, "Moeera! What in the Hell is that?"

"A demon," she said, shrugging. She went to the carriage, looking up at Ben. "It came because I'm wearing the tiger's eye ring."

"I thought we buried it."

"I know," she said. "I just really didn't trust Mozik. You know that treasure … the king's ransom."

"Yeah! It's beautiful!"

"It isn't real. It was just an illusion," Moeera said. "The coins were sand dollars; the diamonds were quartz."

Ben frowned. He helped his brother down from the carriage.

The demon climbed up nimbly to block Mozik's escape.

"No treasure," Dominic groaned.

"Magic ring, yeah?" Ben asked. "How about that, Dom? That one lady we talked to was right."

"You knew?" Moeera asked.

"No! Well, someone said it was, but she was nuts! She said it lets you talk to animals."

"Ben, Landry talked to me plain as day on the way here."

"Incredible! What did he say?"

"He's tired and the demon scares him."

"It scares me, too," Ben said.

"It scares me, too," Ben said.

He and Dominic walked away from the carriage as the demon moved closer to Mozik.

"I'm glad you're all right," Moeera said.

She felt a hand grab her from behind and hook around her throat.

"Call the bastard off," Dersas said. "Call it off, you devil woman!"

Moeera shrugged, trying to duck herself out from the man's grasp. She felt something then she'd remember till the day she died. The fingers of his other hand closing around her ring finger, working to pull it off! She twisted around, coming face to face with his shredded visage. The ring slid to her fingertip ....

"Help!" Moeera cried. She shook her head away from that bloody mess and stared into the sky.

Then Ben and Dominic were with her. Dominic tackled Dersas just as the ring slipped from Moeera's skin. It continued to move in midair as Dersas hit the ground.

On the carriage the demon seemed to stiffen a bit. It was bearhugging Mozik, and wherever the two made contact Mozik's flesh burned with fire. It turned to glance at Moeera, dropping the man on fire.

The demon watched Moeera who in turn watched the ring glide through the air. Then a dark shape swooped upon the ring and grasped it in hooked talons!

"An eagle!" Dominic shouted.

"Get it!" Moeera yelled. "The ring!"

She reached toward the gliding bird of prey, shouting, "Give the ring here!"

It was no use.

The eagle flew on, gaining altitude. It rose into the sky.

"No!" Moeera yelled.

She looked over at the demon. It shuffled off the carriage and scampered toward her. Then it stopped and asked, "Are you no longer possessor of the Tiger's Eye?"

"No," she said. "I lost it."

"Then you have lost my aid as well," it said. "A pity."

"Thank you for helping me," Moeera said.

"No thanks necessary ... girl," it tittered. "I will leave you now lest I am

246

tempted to bring a guest to supper."

"The ring!" Ben said. He watched the eagle glide in circles above them. "We have to get it back! There is no treasure--no reward."

"It's gone now," Moeera whispered.

"Hold," the demon said, turning to the three friends. "I am no longer your servant, but perhaps I feel up to some mischief of my own making."

It frowned and closed its eyes. It held up its hand and wiggled its fingers as if operating a marionette. Then it opened its eyes and pointed to the horizon.

"Look!" it cried. "Some creatures who live close by. Maybe they'll bring you luck."

With that the purple demon smiled and walked away vanishing into thin air.

"Goodbye," Moeera said.

The three of them squinted to see what the demon had spoken of. Two shapes in the sky came closer and closer beating powerful wings. As they drew ever closer they took on the shape of ... people? Winged people carrying ... snakes?

At last, they came in for a landing nearby and revealed themselves to be not people and not angels, but ... monkey?

"Monkeys with wings," Dominic said.

"How?" Ben asked.

"I don't know," Moeera said. "I've never heard of such a thing, but there they are."

Chapter Ten

The monkeys were looking around and sniffing. One saw Mozik beating himself with a rug to put out the demon fire and gave the carriage a wide berth. It cackled oddly, then scampered over to Landry and the covered wagon. The second one looked at the three companions and followed his friend. They hopped into the back of the wagon.

"Probably searching for food," Ben said.

"Can you still see the eagle?" Dominic asked.

"Yes," Moeera said. "It's circling over there; hunting no doubt."

"If we feed them," Ben said, "maybe they'll take us after that eagle to get the ring back."

"Just how do you expect we'll be able to do that?" Mombi asked.

Ben shrugged. "I don't know. If ever there was a good time to be able to talk to animals this would be it!"

"Ironic, isn't it?" Moeera commented.

"Life's ironic," Dominic said.

He dusted himself off and walked over to the wagon.

"Hello, monkeys," he said in a pleasant voice. "Where are the nice monkeys? Oh, there you are."

He got to the wagon and watched the winged monkeys watch him. They chattered and hopped up and down.

"No, you can't fly away," he said. "Not yet. Not in the wagon. Are you hungry?"

One monkey stamped toward him, agitated. It screeched.

"It's okay," he said. "I don't want to hurt you. You're so pretty. You can fly in the sky. That must be wonderful!"

The monkeys chattered at him nervously.

"I have some bread you can have," he told them. "And pears. We have a bundle of pears if you like. Do you eat pears?"

The monkeys voiced their concerns to the stranger. They were very nervous, but they did seem to expect some kind of food. Doubtless they'd encountered people before, and where people were; food was.

"Can I come in there with you?" he asked.

He started climbing into the wagon, but the monkeys started shrieking.

"I'm not going to hurt you, not you pretty monkeys. No, not you. I'll give you some pears to eat."

He motioned at his mouth. One monkey grabbed the other and pointed to Dominic.

"Eat," he repeated. "Food. Pears to eat. Do you like carrots?"

The monkeys were fascinated by this smooth-talking person.

"The pears and carrots and bread are in the trunk," Dominic said.

"Ooo eee, ah ah," the monkeys said.

"Don't be afraid, monkeys," Dominic said. "I'm not afraid of you. I'm getting you food now."

He lifted the trunk's lid.

"See what I have!" Dominic said cheerfully. He held out two pears. Then he placed them on the floor.

That was all it took for Dominic to befriend the flying monkeys. They took the fruit and sat down to eat.

"They're eating," Dominic said out the back of the wagon. "I think they like me."

"That's really wonderful, Dom," Ben said. "Do you think they look strong enough to carry one of us after that eagle?"

"Maybe," Dominic said.

Moeera climbed up. The monkeys were still eating. When they noticed her, they chattered and shook their wings.

"That's Moeera," Dominic told them. "She's nice. She's a friend. Have a pear, Moeera."

"Okay. Thanks, Dom."

"You gotta talk really friendly. The nice monkeys like it."

"Nice monkeys," Moeera said. "Who knew you were so good with monkeys, Dom?"

"Not me," Dominic said. "I'm just making this up as I go. That's right.

Have a carrot, monkeys."

Dominic handed each one a carrot. This time they took the offering from his hands.

"Seems like a snowball's chance in Hell that we'll get them to help," Ben said. He stood at the wagon's back peering in at the odd quartet.

"We're old friends now, me and these two flyers," Dominic said. He had some bread in his hands to follow the carrots which were disappearing fast.

"Don't give them all our food," Ben said.

"I won't. Just a snack."

"Question is ... do they like Moeera?"

"Sure," Dominic said. "They love Moeera. You want to feed them something, Moeera?"

"Won't they be full soon?" she asked.

"Maybe, but a growing bird-mammal needs to eat," Dominic said.

Ben laughed. The monkeys noticed and followed suit.

"Monkey see; monkey do," he said. "But seriously, Moeera's the smallest of us. They should be able to carry her if they work together."

"Me!" Moeera exclaimed. "Why me?"

"Weren't you listening?" Ben asked.

"Yes, but I don't want to be carried by two winged monkeys to ask an eagle for the ring back."

"Why not?"

"It's dangerous! What if I fall?"

"You won't fall."

"How do you know for sure?"

"I don't."

"It's crazy."

"We'll follow in the wagon. If you fall, fall onto the cover."

"Right. Anyone ever tell you that you aren't very reassuring?"

Dominic spoke up. "You want the ring back, don't you?"

"Of course, we all do," Moeera said.

"They won't drop you. They're fine monkeys. Right, you two are very great."

The winged monkeys had calmed down considerably since they first arrived. They seemed to have accepted the three humans as safe.

"What about Mozik?" Dominic asked.

"See for yourself," Ben said, looking toward the fancy carriage.

"Keep them busy, Moeera," Dominic said.

"How?"

"Show them my clothes or something."

"Okay."

Dominic climbed down to see the remains of Mozik and his lackeys. He and Ben walked past Kercar's lifeless body. They saw Harthir sitting on a rock, trying to splint his bleeding foot.

"Help me, help me, help!" he cried.

They kept walking.

"Didn't you hear me?" he bleated.

"Ben, did you hear something?"

"No, Dom, I didn't hear anything."

They climbed aboard the carriage and found Mozik where the demon had left him when the ring left Moeera's finger. He looked up at Ben and Dominic. His shirt was gone, replaced by charred, black tatters that wouldn't cover a doll baby. Vicious-looking burns covered his chest, stomach, and arms. The burned skin was black, too. It flaked away from his body in the wind. His hair was missing from the large tomato he called a head.

"My God," Ben whispered.

The connoisseur of the tiger's eye ring glared at them, but half-heartedly. He was dying plain and simple, and there was nothing to be done. A gurgle escaped his mouth followed by saliva covering his chin.

"Ohh ...," he moaned. "I salute you boys. I should have been ...honest and straight with you. That ... isn't the way ... I conduct myself, though. Now I'm going to leave this ... world and my ... life. I would have ... ruled ... my people, but ... ukh ...."

Mozik's body seized, and he convulsed for a minute. Just when they thought he was gone his eyes focused again and he grabbed Ben by his leg.

"Let the ring to the eagle," he said. "Such things always come with a ... high ... cost."

Mozik died. The light of the living left his eyes as he gave his death rattle.

"Well," Dominic said. "I guess that's the end of him."

"I guess so," Ben said. He turned to go.

251

"Ben! Look!" Dominic exclaimed.

Mozik was gone. Where he had just been a large, black-skinned creature with bat-like wings was. The human-sized bat was dead as a doornail and covered in burns.

"Is that what he really looked like?" Ben asked. "Creepy."

"You said it," Dominic said. "He was a monster all along."

They climbed down from the carriage. The lackey who pulled the ring from Moeera's finger--Dersas--came sprinting up.

"You blockheads!" he said. "Mozik was a turd but he paid nicely. "Why'd you have to mess it all up?"

"He didn't mean to pay us very nicely," Ben retorted.

"Stinks to be you," Dersas said. "Now you don't have a treasure or the ring."

He laughed.

"At least I have a face," Dominic said.

"Oh, yeah?" Dersas sneered. "I'm taking this carriage and the bachukkas, too! Might as well get something for the trouble."

"You mean in addition to an infection?" Dominic asked.

"Dingus!" Dersas spat. He climbed up to the driver's platform.

"Do you think he knows Mozik's actually a giant bat?" Dominic asked.

"No," Ben said. "But he'll know soon enough."

*   *   *

"You two can carry her up!" Dominic said.

The monkeys followed his pointing finger.

"Up into the sky. You know where that bird is flying."

They watched Dominic curiously. One flapped his wings.

"Right. That's right," Dominic said. "Like this."

He and Ben got on Moeera's sides and hooked their arms under hers. The monkeys watched them curiously. Then they tried doing the same.

Moeera felt their hands take her under each arm; firmly, but gently as if supporting a hurt friend. Then wings flapped and Moeera felt her weight drag against the monkeys' grip. Her feet lost contact with the ground and she was aloft! She held onto her wits for dear life as the wings beat and thrashed the air to either side.

Moeera screamed a bloodcurdling scream. The monkeys made odd sounds she thought must be laughter.

Despite her fear she felt astounding--the world was far beneath her! She had a bird's eye view of everything. The plains below, the forest surrounding the periphery, the two inns on the end of Trappe's main street. It was easily the most exhilarating thing that had ever happened to her.

She stared ahead to look for their target. Sure enough, the eagle was there circling in the air as it watched for prey. She wondered if it even still had the ring.

The monkeys flapped and flapped and flapped. Slowly, ever so slowly, they closed on the circling raptor. Moeera could hear the gentle puffs of their inhalations and exhalations. They were smaller than she, but very strong.

What would she do when she reached the eagle? If she reached the eagle. Would it let them come close? How would she get the ring? She hoped that Ben and Dominic would have the wagon nearby.

At last, they came to a point close enough to see the eagle's face, its dark--but intense--eyes, its curved beak, its sharp talons. There was the ring! It clung to the bird's foot by sheer luck, its circumference larger and then some than the eagle's toe.

The eagle's arc carried it close, but its speed exceeded that of the monkeys'. It went around, around, came toward them again.

"What are you doing in my prey circle?" the eagle asked. Moeera understood it perfectly.

The ring? Yes, it had to be the ring's power at work.

"Trying to get my ring back," Moeera called to the eagle.

It flapped its wings, changing trajectory to match the monkeys and their comparatively slow flight.

"This?" the eagle said. "Kindly take it, please."

He seized Moeera's right hand which hung loose around a monkey's shoulder.

"You have to pull it," the eagle said. "It's stuck. More trouble than it's worth."

Moeera felt the eagle cling to her back, its claws digging in. She felt with her fingers until she found the foot. Her fingers touched the ring's smoothness. Moeera seized it between her thumb and forefinger and jiggled it. It came away easily, sliding down the eagle's toe and claw. Then it was off. She held it as tightly as she could and watched the eagle fly away.

253

"Thank you," she said. "And that goes double for you pretty monkeys."

Now what?

She took a deep breath and flipped the ring onto her index finger. It slid on about an inch and she held her thumb against it.

"Can we go back to Dominic now?" she asked.

"Oh, yes," the monkeys said as clear as day.

"Do you think he has more good things to eat?" one asked.

"For you?" Moeera asked. "Always."

They flew around in a tight arc and headed back to the wagon. True to their word Ben and Dominic had brought the wagon as far along as they could. They encountered bigger and bigger trees, rocks, and brush, though. If Moeera had fallen at any time it would not have been onto the covered wagon.

"I sure am lucky that you're so strong," she said.

"We spend lots of time climbing as well as ... flying," the monkey said.

They carried her to the wagon and descended down, down, down, landing softly on the ground. Once Moeera was standing on her own they let her go. She transferred the ring to her ring finger.

"Moeera!" Ben said, smiling ear to ear. "You made it. Did you ...?"

"Get the ring--yes!" she said, holding her hand up to show him.

"All right!" Dominic said. "Can you understand the monkeys?"

"Yes," she said. "They understand me, too. It's amazing."

"Ask them where they live," Dominic said. "And how they like flying."

Moeera asked the questions.

The monkeys responded that they loved flying. It made them happy to move through the sky the way birds did.

"It's the best when you see a hungry tiger or lion prowling," the first monkey whose name was Jet said.

"As for where we live," the second monkey whose name was Stekig said, "it lies east of here; a lush forest full of trees and animals."

Moeera related this to the treasure hunters.

"Can I try talking to them with the ring?" Dominic asked.

"Sure," Moeera said, taking it off and handing it to him, "but you seem to talk well enough without it."

"It's not the same," he said, sliding the ring onto his finger.

"Do any other animals where you live fly with wings?" he asked.

The monkeys looked at him then at Moeera then back to Dominic.

"Anybody else fly in your woods?" Dominic asked.

The monkeys chattered a bit, but none of them could understand.

"Well, that's funny," Dominic said.

"Here," Ben said, "let me try."

He put the ring on and asked, "What do you do for fun?"

The same peculiar thing happened to him. He couldn't understand the monkeys, and they couldn't understand him.

"I don't get it," Ben said. He passed the ring back to Moeera. "You try again."

Moeera asked the monkeys about their forest. This time it worked fine.

Stekig told her that some bats and squirrels were also flying mammals where they lived. The forest was robust, though. Its trees were big enough to build luxurious dwellings in. They shared the forest with many, many animals including leopards, sloths, lions, tigers, bears, wild pigs, raccoons, badgers, and weasels.

Jet said that what the winged monkeys liked to do best was joke around and play pranks on each other and other animals.

"Cool," Dominic said. "We should visit them there. I'd love to see that forest."

"First we have to find a buyer for the ring," Ben said.

"Sure," Dominic said.

"You mean you're still going to sell the ring?" Moeera asked. "Even though it's magical?"

"Yes," Ben said. "All the time and effort we put in over the last couple years needs to amount to something."

"I suppose so," Moeera said. "But you might want to use the ring before you sell it."

"It doesn't seem to work for either of us," Dominic said. "What a gyp!"

"Yes," Moeera said. "I wonder why that is."

"Me, too," Ben said, "but you know what? It doesn't matter because it works for you, and we need to sell it."

The monkeys said their farewells. Moeera translated for them. They'd been glad to meet the three people, but now they had to get home to tell their parents.

Ben, Dominic, and Moeera watched them fly high into the sky and disappear into the distance.

"Let's go back to Trappe," Ben said. "Just to be sure we didn't leave any loose ends."

"Okay," Moeera said. "Maybe someone there knows more about Mozik or his 'people'."

They piled into the wagon. This time Dominic drove and Moeera talked to Landry who was still tired but believed he could make it back to town if there was food and rest involved.

Once again, they parked at the Dewdrop Inn. They saw Mozik's carriage parked in front of The Sour Serpent.

"Three guesses where Dersas and Harthir are," Dominic said.

"Do you think they're together?" Moeera asked.

"Probably," he said. "They all seem related somehow."

"And none of them has any brains," Moeera said.

Ben laughed. "That's for sure. I think we need to talk with them, try to find out if they know anything helpful."

"What could they know?" Dominic asked. "They're idiots and hooligans."

"Nevertheless," Ben said, "they worked for Mozik. Maybe he told them something important about the ring."

"It's going to be ugly," Dominic said. "Kercar and Snerl are gone because of us."

"I think it's more their own fault," Moeera said, "but it will be dangerous."

"That's okay," Ben said. "We have backup."

"The ring?" Moeera asked. "You want another demon running around?"

"No way," Ben said. "Still if the situation demands …."

Moeera nodded.

Chapter Eleven

They entered The Serpent to find Dersas tending to Harthir's foot. The latter winced in pain as his booger-faced friend bandaged his foot. A bowl of bloody water sat on a table. "What are you doing here?" Dersas growled.

Harthir looked up questioningly and recoiled as if burned. "No!" he shouted when he saw Moeera was there.

"Stop it, you idiot!" Dersas said. "You want my help or not?"

Harthir forced himself to sit still, but he looked nervous all the same.

"Hello," Ben said. "We were curious. Who are you, and how did you get involved with Mozik?"

"You never saw a Weeb before?" Dersas sniped.

"No," Dominic said. "What's a Weeb?"

"We're Weebs," Harthir said. "Mozik visited our Master Neel, said he needed some handymen."

"Handymen?" Moeera said, frowning.

"You! You stay away from me!" Harthir exclaimed. He looked as if he wanted to shrink away to nothing. If not for his foot wound, he'd have been out the door.

"I don't want trouble," Moeera said. "We just want to know what's going on."

Dersas backhanded Harthir across the mouth. "Get hold of yourself, coward. She's just a girl," he sneered.

"With a demon," Harthir gulped.

Dersas talked as he tended his partner. "Yeah, handymen. We fix things for people. We fix 'em real good." He tied off the bandage and reached for a flat piece of wood.

"You told us earlier that he paid you well," Ben said.

"Sure," Dersas said.

"What did he pay with?"

"What do you mean?" Dersas asked.

"Was it treasure? Money?"

"Nah, nothing like that. We prefer our earnings to be more … real," he said, wrapping another bandage around the foot and wooden board.

"I don't understand," Ben said.

"Money's useless if you go home to Weebton. Food, drink, lodgings … those are what make life possible. A harrowing tale of danger and bravery makes it worthwhile. Something to tell the ladies. Mozik gave us all those things."

Somehow Ben knew for a certainty that the ladies Dersas referred to wouldn't give him the time of day when they saw his wrecked face.

"Oh," he said carefully. "What will you do now?"

"We haven't figured it out yet," Dersas said, tying off Harthir's splint.

"What are these foofoos doing here?" Maghyal asked. He plopped himself down next to Harthir.

"Nice of you to show up, you cowardly plip," Dersas sneered.

"Thanks for running away and leaving us," Harthir said.

"Sorry, but if you haven't noticed there are two less of us now," Maghyal said. "Three if you count Mozik."

"Yes, well, Mozik never got his hands dirty," Dersas said. "Only at the very end there digging in the dirt."

"Hah hah!" exclaimed Maghyal. "'This is stupid.' Harthir, you crack me up."

"Yeah, that was classic," Dersas said.

Moeera stared at Ben and Dominic. It was hard to believe that these three 'smeats had been brandishing weapons much less could be expected to hurt anyone. The world was crazy.

Harthir piped up, "If you hadn't run off like that you could've made a distraction. We could have beat the demon!"

"With what army!" Maghyal admonished.

Ben saw an opening in the discourse and leapt in.

"Will you stay here in Trappe?" he asked.

"You're mighty nosy," Dersas said.

"You held us prisoner and tried to hurt us," Ben retorted. "I'm curious

258

about your future plans."

"Mozik bought the inn--or owned it for a while; I'm not certain how long it's been his," Harthir said.

"Really?" Dominic asked.

"Yep," Harthir said. "I don't know why other than having a place to hang out while he waited for you. I'm staying until my foot heals."

"Well, he doesn't own it anymore," Moeera said. "He's dead."

The man behind the bar almost dropped the glass he was drying. He plunked it onto the bar and hurried over.

"Mozik's dead?" he asked. He wore an apron over his modest suit.

"Yes," Moeera said. "You can go see for yourself in the black carriage outside."

"How did he die?" the bartender asked. He wiped his forehead with the back of his arm. Then he untied his apron and took off his jacket. Soon it hung over a chair.

"He got burned," Dersas said.

"No kidding?" The man beelined for the door.

"He is still in the carriage, isn't he?" Ben asked.

"Sure," Dersas said. "I wasn't about to touch that corpse. Didn't want to be cursed or nothin'."

A scream erupted from the front of the building. The Weebs laughed.

"Garner must've found Mozik," Harthir said.

"In all that monstrous glory," Dersas said. "Stank like the dickens, too."

Maghyal was confused. "What are you blathering about?"

"Wait for it," Dersas said.

The batwing doors at the front were battered aside as Garner charged in.

"What in the name of Wam are you playin' at?" the bartender asked.

"Who, us?" Maghyal asked.

"I don't see Mozik out there at all," Garner said. "There's a big, dead bat on the carriage. Looks like it got torched."

"Gruesome, isn't it?" Moeera said. "He was scary enough as a man; that thing on the carriage could give anyone nightmares."

"Thunderation!" Garner exclaimed. "Where did that thing come from? Are there more like it lurking in the shadows?"

"You're not going to believe this," Ben said, "but that bat-thing is Mozik!"

"The lies you tell!" the bartender said.

"It's true," Ben said. "Ask the Weebs."

Garner looked at Dersas. "Well?" he asked.

"It is him," the thug confirmed. "I didn't know he looked like that until he was dead."

"You ever seen anything ... anyone like that before?" Garner asked.

The Weebs shook their heads.

"How 'bout you three?"

"No," Dominic said. "We haven't."

"What did you plan to do with the body?" Garner asked.

"Don't look at us," Ben said.

"We should bury him," Harthir said.

"Naw," Maghyal said, "that'll take too long. He's burnt already--let's cremate him."

"Sure," Dersas said. "A nice, big funeral pyre. Folks love bon fires. The whole town will come out to see the big guy off."

"A spectacle, alright," Garner muttered. "Sounds fine to me."

"Yeah," Harthir said. "Obliterate the thing. Good riddance."

*   *   *

Moeera, Ben, and Dominic walked into The Dewdrop Inn. Landry was resting as much as he could outside.

Now there were more people sitting at the tables, talking, and creating a cheery atmosphere. The serving staff from the morning had been supplemented by evening workers. The three of them found a table to sit at. They pretty much collapsed into the chairs from all the day's excitement.

"Did anyone bring any money?" Ben asked.

"No, sorry," Moeera said.

"You, Dom?"

Dominic dug in his pockets and came up with some crumpled bills.

"Ben, it's the last I have," Dominic said.

"Here's what I have left," Ben said. He added a bill and some coins to the pile. "All together I think that should buy us supper."

"That's it, huh?" Moeera asked. "I understand why you were so excited about that treasure."

"Yup," Dominic said. "We're broke."

"You have our meal ticket right there on your finger," Ben said, pointing at the ring.

Moeera sighed. "How much do you think you can get for it?"

"Three hundred, four hundred, maybe," Ben said.

"Who's going to want it enough to pay that much?" Dominic asked.

"Don't know," Ben said. "We have to start looking at people and watching for a potential buyer."

"That could take weeks," Dominic said.

"Months," Moeera amended.

"What if we told them what magic the ring has?" Ben asked.

"Here," Moeera said, sliding the ring off and handing it to Ben. "Try it."

Ben held it in his hand but didn't put it on.

"It doesn't work for me," he said.

"Try again," Moeera told him. "It seemed to work for the eagle because it talked to me before it gave me the ring."

"That's right," Dominic said. "Try it, Benny."

"There aren't any animals in here," he said.

"Then go outside and check on Landry."

A woman walked up to them. She was young with dirty blond hair tied up in a green ribbon.

"Excuse me, you're new in Trappe, aren't you?" she asked.

"What gave us away?" Dominic asked, cheerfully.

"Trappe's small enough to spot a new face," she said. "That and your woobacus outside. Not so many folks have them around here."

"We've had Landry for years now," Ben said. "Since we left home in the Winkie Country."

"My name's Gwen," the woman said. "May I join you?"

Ben and Dominic didn't say anything so Moeera said, "Sure. May I call you Gwendy?"

"My nickname's Windy."

"Fine," Moeera said. "So, Windy, what do you do here in this fine town?"

"I wait tables over at The Sour Serpent."

Ben involuntarily spit out his drink.

"What's the matter?" Windy asked.

"We just had an unfortunate business dealing with the owner there,"

Moeera said.

"Oh?"

"He swindled us," Dominic said.

"You mean Mozik?" Windy asked.

"Mozik's the one, Windy," Moeera said.

"He doesn't own The Serpent anymore," Windy said. "He's dead."

"Dead? Really?" Moeera said.

"Yes, but his flunkies are still there. They're a rotten bunch of jerks. That's why I came over here."

The waitress brought the sandwiches then.

"Hiya, Windy," she said. "You drinking the same?"

"Winkie beer," Ben said in answer to Windy's questioning look.

"Yes, I am," Windy said. "Busy night, Patricia?"

"You could say that," the waitress said.

"You gotta love a good weekend," Dominic said, taking a drink.

"No, you don't," Windy said. "Can I get a grilled cheese, dear?"

"Coming up," Patricia laughed. "Don't you eat free across the road?"

"Yes, but the place is crawling with idiots," Windy said.

Patricia hurried off to place her new order.

Moeera pushed her glass to Gwen. "Here, Windy. Sounds like you need this more than I do."

"Thanks …."

"Moeera."

"Nice to meet you, Moeera," Gwen said. She downed the almost full glass in two big gulps.

Ben and Dominic exchanged glances.

"Ah! Thank you, Moeera!" Gwen said as Patricia brought a full glass.

"Here you go," she said, placing the drink on the table.

When she'd left again Moeera looked at Gwen.

"How bad are the jerks hanging out at the inn over yonder?"

"Mozik's friends?" Gwen asked. "The worst. They haven't any good manners."

"He was no better," Dominic said. "That louse!"

"How did he swindle you?" Gwen asked.

Ben recounted the story of finding the ring and the discovery that the reward was fake. He left out the parts about the demon.

262

"That's dreadful," Gwen said, her lips covered in foam.

"You got that right," Ben said. "You don't know anyone who'd want to pay a good price for a gold ring, do you?"

"Not in Trappe," Gwen said. "Maybe in Kimbaloo. There's a jeweler there who's known for his collection."

"Where's Kimbaloo?" Moeera asked.

"Not far," Gwen said. "It's southeast of here."

"Thanks," Ben said. "What's his name?"

"Noshtal."

"Noshtal," Ben repeated.

"Any wealthy girl in these parts wears his designs," Gwen said. "Pretty stuff."

"Thanks!" Ben said. "We'll have to go see him."

*   *   *

They could barely pay for the meal. Patricia got a mere klingkit for a tip. Gwen looked as if she might go to sleep at the table.

"What do we do about her?" Ben mused.

Patricia heard him and said, "Don't worry about her. I'll see that she makes it home safe."

Ben nodded. "Thank you."

"No problem."

They left.

When they reached the wagon, Ben tried to talk to Landry.

"It still isn't working," he said.

Moeera said, "Let Dom try."

So, Ben gave the ring to Dominic who tried starting a conversation with Landry to no avail.

"Here, Moeera, keep hold of it," he said, giving the ring to her.

She slid it onto her finger. "How are you, Landry? Feel any better?"

"A little," the woobacus said. "I'd really love to bed down someplace, though."

"We'll see if we can arrange that straightaway," Moeera said. "Landry?"

"Yes?"

"Do you understand anything that the boys say to you?"

"Not much. I know when they want me to pull the wagon or wait for them somewhere."

"Oh."

Moeera turned to the brothers. "We need to find a stable or paddock or something for Landry to sleep in tonight."

"Right," Ben said. "Let's check along the road here. Bound to be something."

They found a stable with some extra room and closed Landry in for the night. The three bedded down in a nearby field.

"I hope it doesn't rain," Moeera said. She rolled over on her blanket trying to get more comfortable.

"Come on, Moeera," Dominic said. "Our luck's not that bad."

"I hope you're right," she said. "I'm too tired to run for the wagon."

"You said it," Ben said. "I'm beat."

"Beat up, you mean," Dominic told him.

"You two sure you don't wanna drag yourselves to the Weebs' bonfire?" Ben asked. "It's sure to draw a big crowd."

"No, thanks," Moeera said. "I don't care much for big fires anymore."

And that said the three soon fell fast asleep.

Chapter Twelve

I t was nearly noon by the time they woke the next day. The sun hung high in the sky. Moeera stretched her arms, yawning. They stowed their blankets in the wagon and got a fire going. Moeera boiled some carrots and potatoes.

A little later Ben hitched Landry to the wagon, and they set out for the little kingdom of Kimbaloo.

"Now leaving scenic Trappe," Moeera said. She sat in the driver's seat, holding fast to the reins.

"Good riddance," Dominic said from the spot next to her.

"Just another stop on the road of life," she replied. "Just think--sell the ring for the really high price it's worth, come back, propose to Windy, have some kids--"

"Hold on, Moeera," Dominic said, raising his hand. "Let's not get ahead of ourselves."

"Well, sure, but I think she liked you."

"She got drunk at supper," Dominic said. "She would've loved anyone."

"If you say so."

                    *   *   *

They'd been on the road for some time and were about to stop and give Ben a chance at driving. That's when they spotted the huge tree lying across the lane.

"Stop, Landry," Moeera said. "We'll have to figure out how to get past."

"Yes, Miss Moeera, time for a rest anyway," he said.

The wagon rolled to a stop. Ben hopped out and came around front.

"Time to switch, right? I've been so bored back there!"

"Tree down," Dominic said. "Look." Gloom filled his voice.

Ben stared at the mammoth oak with dismay. "Whoah! That's huge!"

"Do you have an ax?" Moeera asked.

"Of course, we do," Ben said, "but maybe the two-man saw is the thing to use."

"Two-man saw?" Moeera asked.

"Sure," Dominic said. He pointed to the underside of the wagon where it was mounted with leather straps. "It lets two people cut together. You cut going back and forth."

"Oh," she said.

They took out the big, long saw which stretched about six feet.

Ben pointed to the tree. "Do you think the three of us could push half the trunk like we were spinning it--that is if we cut down the center?"

Moeera took in the size of the thing. It looked to be about three or four feet in diameter.

"No," she said. "I don't think we can move it. Do you?"

"Maybe if Landry helps pull," Dominic said.

"What about the ring?" Moeera asked. "Let me try calling for help."

"Doesn't the thought of demons scare you?" Ben asked.

"Sure, but the thought of being stuck out here and having no food because we don't find a buyer scares me more."

"When you put it that way," Ben said, "what have we got to lose?"

"Moeera, be careful," Dominic said.

She nodded and stared at the ring. "We need help moving a big, fallen tree in our path," she said.

Moeera glanced around watching for smoke. She looked at Ben and Dominic. They all focused on Landry.

"Don't look at me," he said. "I'm confused."

"Why isn't it working?" Dominic asked.

"I'm not sure," Moeera said.

She felt the ring on her finger, tracing the stone and the cold gold. She rubbed the tiger's eye slowly.

"We can't do it by ourselves," she said softly.

A tree to their left began smoking like a chimney afire. Purple smoke poured out, permeating the forest. The foul stench of brimstone filled Moeera's nostrils.

A scaly, yellow demon emerged from the smoke and walked up to Moeera. She was very scared but resisted the instinct to flinch.

"Hello, Mistress," it said in a deeper voice than the previous demon. "You're new."

"So are you," she said. "To me, anyway."

"Yes," it said, amused. "Beezer helped you recently. And then you lost the ring."

"I got it back," she said, "and I need your help to move a tree that's fallen across the road."

The demon looked at the tree. "What if I don't want to move the tree?" it asked.

Moeera stared at him mouth agape.

The demon laughed in its baritone that didn't seem to fit its appearance. "I'm joking," it said. "I think we'll need more than me, though."

It whistled the mellow drone of a clarinet. Familiar red smoke poured from underneath the wagon and the first demon appeared.

"Hello, Master," it said, smiling at Moeera; or so she thought. Its voice was just as high as she remembered.

"Hello," Moeera said. "Thanks for sending the winged monkeys our way."

"No problem, Master. It worked I see."

"Yes," Moeera said. "Now I have another problem."

"She wants us to move that fallen tree," the other demon said.

"I see an ax," the purple demon said. It walked over to Ben. "May I?"

"Of course," Ben said. He handed the ax over and stepped away.

"I'll chop," the purple demon said to the yellow one. "You stack."

"Fine," the yellow one said. "It's better with two."

The purple one attacked the downed tree with an army's gumption. It stretched its arms out swinging the ax so fast it blurred. As fast as that one tore chunks free the yellow one dashed in, grabbing the logs and dashing out again. It was a blurry thing of motion as it stacked an enormous cord of wood to the side of the dirt lane.

Moeera watched fascinated as the demons made mincemeat of the tree. They moved so fast--faster than the eye could see--it was hard to see them actually working.

Ben made a face at Moeera. She stepped next to him and he said, "Sure, I could've done that."

"Oh, certainly," she said, all mock seriously.

"Not bad, Moeera," Dominic said. "Not bad. It still scares me that they're demons but look what they can do for you."

"It's a little disconcerting," Moeera commented. "All it takes to make it happen is this funny little ring."

"We're lucky the ring works for you," Dominic said.

Moeera glanced at the two demons. They were two thirds of the way to having the way cleared.

"What did that woman say about the ring being magic?" she asked.

Ben shrugged. "She told us it had magic on it--'divine magic'. She didn't say what it could do, though."

"What was that name she mentioned, Benny?" Dominic asked.

"Huh? Oh, yeah. Said it belonged to someone named Solomon."

"Solomon," Moeera said. "Who's Solomon?"

"I never heard of Solomon before," Ben said. "But that's whose ring she said it was."

"Curious," Moeera murmured. "It has strong magic. That much is true. As for the rest of it ... who knows?"

"Solomon must've lost it somehow," Dominic said. "Carr took it to his grave."

"Maybe," Ben said. "Maybe someone hid it in the coffin before Carr was buried."

"Why?" Dominic asked.

"I don't know," Ben said.

The demons chopped and stacked the last of the wood. Now there was a nice access way between the tree roots and the upper trunk. They made short bows to Moeera and vanished in a puff of red and purple smoke.

"That's that," Moeera said. "Now we can be on our way."

"As soon as Landry calms down," Ben said.

Moeera turned to the woobacus. "Don't worry, Landry. They've gone. Nothing to hold us back now."

"Are you sure they're gone?" Landry asked.

"Sure," she said. "They finished clearing the road and disappeared back to wherever it is they go."

"Okay," Landry said. "They have me nervous as can be. I still feel like something's watching us. Something terrible."

"Ben, Dom," Moeera said. "Come pet Landry. He's so shook up ...."

She stopped in mid-sentence as strong hands grabbed her under the armpits and pulled her off the ground!

"Whaaaat!" she yelled.

"Moeera!" Ben cried.

Moeera soared up and up into the air.

"Hey!" she exclaimed. "Is that you monkeys again?"

Ben, Dominic, and Landry were mere specks on the ground below.

"Do we look like monkeys to you?" a creature from nightmare asked in an oddly toned voice as it flew up beside Moeera.

It was a woman--a red-skinned woman, but she seemed just as much bat as human. Unlike Mozik, who'd been black-skinned, she was the color of blood from head to toe. She glided through the air on her red, leathery wings, keeping pace with whoever--or whatever--carried Moeera. Her black and brown clothes clung skintight to her body.

They flew above the treetops at a frightening speed. Moeera imagined they were moving quite faster than the flying monkeys had the day before. Ben and Dominic were some distance behind them.

Chapter Thirteen

Darkness had fallen by the time Ben woke up. He found he was still lying on the road. Fingers tugged at the ropes where his hands were bound behind his back. "Dom," he said. "Dom's still out," a voice said.

"Patricia?"

"Yup."

"Boy, am I glad to hear your voice," Ben said.

"Happy to hear that, Ben," she said, "but I'm not a boy."

"Of course not," he muttered.

"I followed you into this cursed forest because *you're* a boy, ironically."

"That may have been a mistake."

"You're damned right," Patricia said. She undid the knot above his wrists and unraveled the ropes.

"Thank you," Ben said, feeling the circulation returning to his hands, arms, and legs.

"I gave those two that chased me the slip, Ben," she said. "I decided to cross my fingers and wait for dark to bust you loose."

"Thanks."

They both got to work on Dominic and Gwen's bonds.

"Where are the witches now?" Dominic asked as Ben untied him.

"There's a big bonfire in a clearing over there," Patricia said. "Can you hear them? They're singing."

They listened and sure enough heard a song being sung by the witches.

"Let's get the hell out of here!" Gwen exclaimed.

"Quiet," Patricia said, "Do you want them to hear you?"

"What about Landry and the wagon?" Dominic asked.

"You crazy?" Patricia asked. "This might be our only chance to escape."

"Did you hear that?"

"Hear what?"

Then they both saw some nearby brush moving.

"That! Someone's coming."

"Do you think it's more bats?"

"Don't know," Ben said.

Twigs snapped and voices permeated the underbrush.

"Quick, Dom! You flush them out!" Ben exclaimed.

Dominic dove into the bushes, trying to follow the rustling witch hazel and other shrubby trees to the source of the voices. Suddenly he heard a high-pitched shriek.

A woman's voice cried, "Run! There's a bear or something coming!"

Ben's muscles tensed; his fingers tightened around the club he held. What was going on?

"Ben!" Dominic shouted from the bushes. "They're running further into the woods!"

The rustling in front of him stopped and a voice asked, "Who's there?"

"Dominic," he replied.

Cautious footsteps came toward him, twigs crunched. The bushes parted revealing ….

"Windy!" Dominic shouted. "What are you doing here?"

She smiled.

"What about me? Don't you recognize me?" the other woman asked.

Ben came running up. "Patricia? What are you and Windy doing here?"

"What does it look like? Following you!" Patricia retorted.

"Come on," Ben said. "Let's get back to Landry and the wagon. You can explain why you're following us!"

Patricia smiled slyly.

"Sounds good," Gwen said. "By the way where's Moeera?"

"Who knows," Ben said.

They followed him out of the brush to the dirt lane.

"So …," Patricia began, "you guys left town pretty quickly. You really want to meet Noshtal bad, huh?"

"Yes," Ben said.

"So?" Dominic asked.

"So, we didn't get to say goodbye," Gwen said. "You guys bought me dinner, and then you split without another word."

"We just barely bought you dinner, Windy," Ben said. "Really. What's the big deal?"

"Your brother is cute! That's the big deal!" Gwen exclaimed.

Ben was stunned. He'd never seen this coming. In hindsight, he thought, Moeera was correct about Dom's chances with Gwen. He smiled. Even now life didn't cease to amaze.

"You guys seemed pretty smart and all. You're going places," Patricia added.

"And we've never been very far out of Trappe," Gwen said.

"Right. We've never even been to Kimbaloo … to the buttonwood," Patricia said.

"We want to come with you!" Gwen exclaimed.

The brothers exchanged glances.

Ben laughed. "No, you don't."

"Yes we do," Gwen said, nodding her head.

"Let's make it a double date!" Patricia added.

Dominic froze.

"As nice as that sounds, ladies," Ben said, "Moeera was carried off by monsters. What's to stop the same thing from happening to you?"

"Monsters!" Gwen yelped. "Monsters got Moeera?"

"Yes," Dominic said. "They flew down, grabbed her, and flew away again!"

"Oh, God!" Gwen cried.

"Relax," Patricia told Gwen.

"How can you say that!"

"Ben and Dom won't let that happen to us," Patricia said.

"Why not?" Gwen asked.

"They just won't. Have a little faith."

Dominic looked like he wanted to slap his hand over his face, but he didn't. He looked at Ben. Ben looked at him.

"All right," Dominic said. "Climb in the back. We're going to Kimbaloo."

"Yay," the others said.

"Moeera's in trouble," Dominic said. "We have to figure out how to get her back."

"As for us making something of ourselves," Ben said, "we may get stuck as button harvesters--we're broke."

"No worries, honey," Patricia said, producing a small purse. "My life savings."

"No way," Dominic said.

"Did you think I wait tables for my health?" Patricia asked. She slid the purse into her blouse and nodded.

*   *   *

Dominic was fuming as Landry pulled the wagon in search of Kimbaloo's castle keep. "I just don't know what we can do, Benny!" he exclaimed.

"It'll be all right, Dom," Ben said. "We'll find some way to find Moeera."

"How?" Dominic asked. "Those things carried her off, and we don't even know what they were!"

"I don't know," Ben admitted, "but every day brings something new."

"What?"

"We might not find the answer today to help her, but maybe tomorrow. Maybe Patricia or Gwen will think of something."

"Humph," Dominic said. He didn't know how that could help, but it was something.

Landry pulled the wagon along the cobblestone road. They must be getting close to their destination if its good condition was any indicator.

A figure appeared in the road. He approached the wagon with determination.

"Fresh buttons!" the boy cried. He walked up to Ben's side, thrusting out a round box filled to the brim with buttons of all colors and sizes. "Collar buttons! Blouse buttons! Cuff buttons! You name it; freshly picked today in the kingdom of Kimbaloo!"

"Ho, boy!" Ben cried. "Is this the way to Kimbaloo?"

"Fastest way there is to hand me a coin, mister," the boy said. He looked about eight years old.

Ben reached into his pocket, searching around with his fingers. He had to have something left. He had to! Grasping a tiny nooknek he pulled it out and handed it to the boy. The coin had indeed been his last.

The button boy dropped the coin into his button box, smiling. "What do you require, mister?"

"Directions …," Ben said. "Does this road lead to Kimbaloo?"

"Oh, yes! Or my name's not Hem."

"Very good. Thank you, Hem."

"You're very welcome," Hem said. "Don't forget to take a button."

Ben reached down to the button box and selected a pretty blue shirt button.

"Wise choice, wise choice," Hem said, bowing. "Now I must continue my selling."

With that the boy fastened a lid over the box and dashed off the way they had come.

"A button," Dominic said. "We could have made better use of the coin."

"Yes," Ben said, "but at least we know we're going the correct way."

"Mm-hmm," Dom said. He snatched the bright disk and pocketed it.

They traveled another few miles when they spied a plume of smoke rising from the road ahead.

"Now what?" Dominic asked.

"Be ready to turn back," Ben said, frowning. "Just in case."

The scene they encountered was enough to make the bravest man turn back.

Chapter Fourteen

A group of black-clad women encircled a traveler they had tied to a widow maker by the roadside. The tallest woman wore a tall, conical hat. She held a book in front of her from which she read strange words. The man tied to the tree began screaming.

"Help me! Don't let them have me!"

Landry stopped dead in his tracks. About thirty women turned to look at the newcomers.

"I think we should turn around," Ben muttered.

"Darn tootin'!" Dominic said.

As Ben directed Landry to turn left the woman with the book pointed at them. Eight of the women dashed over to surround them.

"Please, if you'll excuse us we'll just go back the way we came," Ben said.

"Right," Dominic said. "We don't want to interrupt."

The woman just in front of them hissed. "You've already done that."

"We'll get out of your way," Ben said.

"The Mother wants you to stay where you are," the woman said.

"The Mother?" Dominic said. "Surely she's no mother. She looks like a witch to me."

Hearing this the ring of women burst into laughter.

The woman to Ben's side said, "You could call The Mother a witch. She's very powerful. She's training us to be the caretakers of these woods."

"Oh," Ben forced out. His mouth had gone very dry.

"Finally!" Gwen shouted, leaping from the back of the wagon. "I thought we'd never get to--"

"Windy!" Dominic shouted.

"What's going on out here?" Patricia asked. She too had left the wagon.

"These ladies are blocking our way," Dominic said. "The one with the book is a witch!"

"Oh, dear," Patricia said softly. She saw one of the women break the circle and stride toward her. A dagger glinted in her hand.

Patricia knew they were as good as captured and that death would probably come next. She bolted back the way they had come.

"Patricia!" Gwen screamed.

"Seize them!" the voice of The Mother came.

Then everything was chaos.

Patricia was still sprinting down the trail. Two of the women gave chase, but she had a nice lead.

A black-garbed woman grabbed Gwen's arms and pinned then behind her back. "No!" Gwen screeched.

Dominic leapt from his seat beside Ben and ran to help Gwen.

Several women tackled Dominic.

The Mother turned toward the wagon, eyes flashing. She closed the book which vanished from her hand. She reached toward Ben, closing her fingers. In the driver's seat Ben felt as if a giant's hand had grasped him tight. His hands were pinned to his sides.

"You'll see there is no escape," The Mother said in a voice like water steaming off a burning log. She pointed to the man tied to the tree.

As he screamed in terror his body began fading away. It took but a few seconds for him to disappear completely as a person's shadow does in the shade. Ben would have sworn that his scream lingered in the air.

The Mother and her women laughed. Then they pulled Ben from the wagon. He, Dominic, and Gwen were tied up and left on the road like sacks of potatoes. The witches looked through their few possessions in the wagon. Then they moved off beyond the tree with the loose ropes tied around it to palaver in privacy. Before long the two who'd chased Patricia returned empty handed and joined their fellows.

Soon one of the women appeared standing over Ben. The position he was trussed up in only allowed him to see her sandaled feet. Then she knelt down next to him and he could see black leggings and tunic.

"I am the spider," she said, "and you are the fly. You must be a stupid person to come into The Mother's woods."

"I didn't know they were her woods," Ben said. "Please let us go."

"Ignorant or not you belong to us now," she replied. "We take what we wish to sustain ourselves. You will make us stronger, and it will take but a small bit of pain."

"Let us go!" Ben shouted.

The woman laughed. "Our numbers will grow until we seize everything that is."

She ducked down till her face was beside his. He thought her pretty for a blackguard. She held her hand toward him and blew a powder in his face.

"Sleep," she said.

And Ben did.

Chapter Fifteen

Darkness had fallen by the time Ben woke up. He found he was still lying on the road, back stiff. Fingers tugged at the ropes binding his hands behind his back. Someone was untying him.

"Dom," he said.

"Dom's still out," a voice said.

"Patricia?"

"Yup."

"Boy, am I glad to hear your voice," Ben said.

"Happy to hear that, Ben," she said, "but if you've noticed I'm not a boy."

"Of course not," he muttered.

"I followed you into this cursed forest because you're a boy, ironically."

"Thank God for you, lady."

"You're damned right," Patricia said. She undid the knot above his wrists and unraveled the ropes.

"Thank you," Ben said, feeling the circulation returning to his hands, arms, and legs.

"I gave those two that chased me the slip, Ben," she said. "I decided to cross my fingers and wait for dark to bust you loose."

"Thanks."

Now that he was free they both got to work on Dominic and Gwen's bonds.

"Where are the witches now?" Dominic asked as Ben untied him.

"There's a big bonfire in a clearing over there," Patricia said. "Can you hear them? They're singing."

The others strained their ears and sure enough heard a song being sung by the witches.

"Let's get the hell out of here!" Gwen exclaimed.

"Quiet," Patricia said, "Do you want them to hear you?"

"What about the wagon?" Dominic asked. "And Landry--we can't just leave him!"

"Are you crazy?" Patricia asked. "This might be our only chance to escape."

Then they were silent because they all felt paralysis holding their bodies still.

"Didn't expect anybody to be watching the prisoners, did you?" the witch hissed.

Ben stared at her. He could be mistaken, but he thought she was the one who'd put him to sleep.

"What do you want with us?" he croaked.

She smiled. "Maybe we'll kill you tonight, sacrifice you to the wood spirits."

"That's awful," Dominic said. "Isn't there something we could give you to let us go?"

"What do you have?" the witch asked.

"The woobacus and the wagon," Ben said. "Keep them."

"They already belong to us," she said. "Well, they belong to The Mother."

"What about information?" Dominic asked.

"Information?" the witch spat. "What do you know that I'd care anything about?"

"There are demons around," Ben said, "in these very woods."

"What do you know of demons?"

"That we've seen two between here and the town of Trappe," he said.

"Go on," the witch said. "Who summoned them?"

"Our friend Moeera did," Dominic said.

"Where's this friend now?"

"Some bat-people carried her away," Dominic said.

"Bat-people, eh? With wings?"

"Yes! They flew off with her!"

"That is interesting," the witch said, "but not enough for me to let you go."

279

"We have a special jar," Ben said. He'd been wracking his brain for anything that might distract her.

"Ah!" the witch said. "What's in it?"

"Something very dangerous," Ben said. "It's yours if you let us go."

"Where, pray tell, is this dangerous item?"

"In a trunk on our wagon."

"You mean our wagon," the witch said. "Mine and my Mother's!"

"You don't know how bad the thing is that's in there," Ben said. "If one of your sisters opens it--you could all die."

"Well! I've heard you out," the witch said.

"Will you let us escape?" Gwen asked.

"Nah-ah," she said and blew sleepy sand at them in a billowing cloud.

It put them back to sleep--all except Patricia. She hadn't slept before and she didn't now either--she merely pretended to sleep. You see, Patricia held her breath and finding she was able to move again clapped a hand over her eyes and nose. It worked.

So, when the witch skipped off to look for the magic jar Patricia began waking her friends. It wasn't as easy this time, but finally they were all awake.

"Thank goodness! Now we can vamoose!" Gwen said.

"We have to get that jar back," Ben said. "It's important."

"More important than our skins?" Patricia asked.

"It might be," Ben said. "Moeera said a wizard put something very bad in there."

"Why?" Gwen asked.

"He trapped it in there to keep it from harming anyone."

"Why did you tell her about it then?" Patricia asked. "How do we get it away from them?"

"And get away," Dominic added.

"We'll think of something," Ben said.

As they sat there thinking and speaking, they could hear the singing becoming raucous chanting as the women cavorted around the fire.

Chapter Sixteen

Where are we going?" Moeera asked when she summoned up the courage. "Whoever you are, I'm afraid of high places. I'll heave all over if you don't tell me where you're taking me."

The bat-lady smiled and said, "Far away."

Moeera cried out, "I need--"

As quick as that the bat-lady flew to her, covering her mouth.

Moeera's heart raced.

"None of that," she crooned. "We saw you at the blocked road, and we know you can summon the demons."

Moeera felt the frightening sensation of the ring being slid from her finger. Now she was truly helpless.

*   *   *

Moeera didn't know how much time had passed when they landed. It seemed as if it had taken forever. During the long flight the sun had fled the sky.

The rough, strong hands deposited her on a marble balcony. She stumbled on her sleeping feet and crumpled to the hard floor.

"Not so tough a woman without the ring, are you?" the bat-lady teased. She squeezed Moeera's chin between her long fingers and gave the girl a shove.

"What did you expect, sister?" another of the bat-people asked. This one was a young male.

A third, larger bat-man moved to the other two. He must be the brute who flew me here, Moeera thought. Muscles covered his red-brown body.

"I expected much more from the woman who bested Mozik for the ring," the bat-lady said.

Double doors opened behind them revealing more of the creatures. Moeera glanced up and realized the doors led into a mountainside, the marble balcony clinging moth-like to the red rock face.

"Take her," the bat-lady commanded the newcomers. They brandished obsidian-tipped spears.

Moeera's hands were tied behind her back with a cord.

The bat-lady held her hand up, letting light from mounted torches catch the gold of the ring now residing on her finger.

"Won't mother be pleased to see you," she commented.

The guards herded Moeera down red stone stairs into a room of opulent decorations. A dais dominated the room's center, and upon this reclined a bat-lady dressed in fine gossamer and satin. Her hair of gold fell in ringlets around her crimson face. She watched the entourage enter with mild curiosity.

The trio who captured Moeera approached the dais and knelt before the regal figure.

"Children," the reclining figure said in a relaxed yet imperious voice. "What gift have you brought me?"

The younger bat-lady remained kneeling and held out her arm. "Oh, mighty queen and mother of mine, I present to you the ring of the ruler of the hosts."

Upon hearing this the queen rose quickly, moving to stand before her daughter. Her eyes beheld the ring as a wolf beholds a rabbit.

"Britust! Can it be so? Is this the ring your uncle sought so fervently?"

"Yes, Mother," Britust said. "It has powerful magic as the ring of the ruler of hosts would. It summons demon slaves."

"Give it to me, child," the queen said. Her gossamer robe flowed in a draft making as if to flutter from her lithe body.

Britust stood, sliding the ring from her finger and passing it to the older woman.

The queen smiled, admiring the gold ring. "Nakeim, honor me by placing the ring on my finger."

"Yes, Queen Stagust," the bat-man who had borne Moeera to this strange place said. He strode up beside the queen, taking the tiger's eye ring from her hand. He towered over the woman; his great batwings folded against his back smartly.

Queen Stagust extended her hand and Nakeim slid the ring onto her ring finger. "Thank you, dear," she quietly said. She held out her hand, admiring her new ring. She seemed to memorize every aspect of its look upon her hand.

"Mother?" Britust inquired.

"Yes?" the queen asked, still staring at the ring.

"What of the other matter?"

"What matter is that?" Queen Stagust asked.

"This girl I found," Britust said, nodding to Moeera.

Queen Stagust wasn't looking, however. She was still lost on her new piece of jewelry.

"Girl?" she asked.

"The one who had the ring. She must have taken it from Mozik."

"Really?" The queen glanced at Moeera. "She doesn't look like much." Moeera frowned.

"What's your name, girl?" the queen inquired.

"Moeera."

"Moeera. How did you come upon the ring?"

"I found it, your majesty," Moeera said.

"Did you steal it from my brother?"

"How would I even know your brother, highness?"

"He's hard to miss," Stagust said. "Mozik is a big, overbearing, loudmouthed fup."

"Mozik's your brother?" Moeera asked. "I don't see the resemblance."

"Half-brother, girl. Believe me, I got the looks from our mother."

"Yes, highness," Moeera said. "I found the ring. He tried to steal it from me."

"Where's Mozik now?"

"Dead, your majesty."

"Well." Stagust stepped back onto the dais, glowering. "I should have known! The fool. No wonder I was suddenly blinded to him."

"Blinded, highness?" Moeera asked.

The queen stuck up a hand. "Enough," she said. "How does one summon the demons?"

Moeera didn't answer.

"Bragust!" Stagust snapped at the young bat-man standing by Britust.

"Run her through!"

"Yes, mother." He took a spear from a guardsman and aimed its point at Moeera's midsection.

"Now wait!" Moeera screeched.

"For what?" the queen asked. "You tell me my dear brother is dead, yet you won't advise me in the use of my new trinket?"

Bragust pulled the spear back. He flexed his muscles anticipating the forward thrust.

"No!" Moeera screamed.

Stagust raised her hand, the ring gleaming in the torchlight.

"Hold a second, Bragust," she commanded. "What, Moeera? Do you have some staggering last words for us?"

"All you need to do is tell the ring you need help," Moeera said. "Just say: 'I can't do it myself'."

"No magic words!" the queen exclaimed. "Do I look like I was born moments ago? Kill her, Bragust."

"It's true, Mother," Britust said. "I saw her summon the demons that way."

"That's different," the queen said slyly. "Don't run her through, Bragust."

"What do I do with her?" he asked.

"Whatever you want, dear boy," Stagust told him. She turned her gaze back to her ring. "Throw her in the dungeon. Now leave me. I wish to play with my new toy."

*   *   *

Moeera sat huddled in a corner of the dungeon. The guards didn't bother to put her in irons. They just chucked her into a cell and slammed the heavy door shut. Before their torchlight grew dim she caught a glimpse of several people hanging on a far wall across the corridor. They resembled insects pinned to a collector's display.

Tears streamed down Moeera's cheeks as she sat in the darkness. Her friends were gone. The magic ring was gone. She was gone.

Eventually she fell asleep.

When she woke up she realized to her horror that time had little meaning in this dark dungeon cell. She could feel the cold, hard walls and floor. She felt around for something ... anything, but there was nothing at all. She retreated to her corner and sat there, thoughts running blind through the fields of her mind.

What of Ben and Dominic? She expected the bat-people let them alone once they had her. The ring was what they wanted--what everyone she met seemed to want.

What would they do with her? She was alive, but what would her fate be? Would she rot away in this dark, cold prison? Would the queen send the demons to kill her ... or worse?

She wondered about her mother and father. They were probably fine without her. Her father would undoubtedly laugh if he could see her now.

Moeera imagined what she might be doing if she hadn't been captured. Seeing the uncanny Forest of Kimbaloo renowned for its buttonwood. She imagined Dominic, Ben, and herself presenting the ring to the collector for inspection. He would smile happily and pay them handsomely.

She and her friends would go on the ultimate treasure hunt. What would they find? A golden palace? An ivory cask containing directions to the Forest of Burzee where the fairies lived? Maybe a tomb filled to the top with jewels. Despite her predicament she smiled at the thought.

None of that could happen while the bat-people had her under lock and key. Why put her in the dungeon? Why not turn her loose?

She wondered if it had something to do with the queen using the ring. Perhaps she was insurance, and they would keep her only long enough to be sure the ring worked for the queen.

Her face darkened. That could be it. The ring hadn't worked for Ben or Dominic. Maybe it wouldn't work for the queen either.

Then what? Would they force her to command the demons? What would they want done? What in the world did they want?

I have to get out of here, she thought. There must be a way.

After what seemed like a very, very long time she heard the heavy door open. A hard voice said, "Mealtime," and was followed by a bowl being thrust into her hands. Then the guard shut the door again.

Moeera wanted to scream. The darkness continued without so much as a sliver of light. Her captors obviously didn't need light to function.

She drew her knees up against her chest and wrapped her arms around them. She rocked front to back. Whatever the bowl contained didn't have a very inviting smell.

Chapter Seventeen

Finally, Moeera reached out to pick up the bowl. Her fingers searched the floor in the dark. They encountered hard, cold rock and dust. Then she heard a sound like tinkling bells. Moeera's heart raced.

"Let it go," a high-pitched voice said.

Moeera pulled her legs back up and listened.

"If you want me to help you out of here, then don't eat any of the food they give you."

"Who is that?" Moeera asked, knowing already.

"You know my voice, don't you, silly?"

"You're the demon."

"Yes, and you're the master …, but you let the ring get lost."

"Those bat-people took it from me," Moeera said. "I don't have it--why are you here?"

"Can you keep a secret?" the demon asked.

"Sure," Moeera said. "I have no one to tell anyway."

The demon giggled. "You're funny," it said. "The fact is I like you."

"You like me?"

"Yes, you're nice. And curious. And you're polite."

"Oh."

"My first master who commanded me with the ring was fine, but he didn't seem to see me as a person."

"He didn't?"

"No, I wouldn't say he did. He didn't even think of me as a slave. I was his worker, but he saw me as a tool."

"That's depressing," Moeera said.

"Tell me about it. The ring wielders who came after him weren't better.

Most were bad people."

"You don't like bad people, then," Moeera said.

"Hell no!" the demon exclaimed. "Pardon the expression, but I have quite enough of bad people at home. They pop up everywhere--a never ending infestation."

"If I'm not your master how can you help me?" Moeera asked.

"The same way I did when I convinced those monkeys they really wanted to fly in your direction."

"What about your new master?"

"New master ... oh, you mean the High Roller Queen."

"High Roller?"

"Queen Stagust. She's in line for the top throne of her people. They're called High Rollers."

Moeera grimaced. "That must be what Mozik was talking about."

"He was a High Roller, too," the demon said. "Now he's in a place where his actions are chaperoned morning, noon, and night for eternity."

"She wears the ring now," Moeera said. "Shouldn't you be here to kill me?"

"She'll have to have someone else do that," the demon said.

"Why?"

"She won't be my master until you're dead--if at all."

Moeera inhaled sharply.

"It's true," the demon said. "That ring came from the Lord of Hosts. It was meant for his chosen and his chosen only. Since leaving that first master the ring has worked for others, but there have been many who wore it never discovering its purposes."

"Why can I use it?" Moeera asked.

The demon shrugged its scaly shoulders in the dark. "Who can say?"

"You must have an idea!" Moeera gasped.

The demon tittered. "You're a diamond in the rough. You have importance that you can't even consider, yet."

Moeera shrank into her corner, thinking. How could she be important? She felt insignificant.

The demon sighed. "Don't tell a soul I told you this, but even the most important individuals--the shapers of destiny--begin small."

"How?"

"Everyone is born small and helpless. Everyone. They grow and grow much like a caterpillar. Some become moths, some butterflies, and some become the most beautiful butterflies you've ever seen."

"Sounds like nature," Moeera said.

"It is. Everyone finds their path. Yours could be really special since you can wield the ring."

Moeera considered this. She wanted to do magic. Up until Carrie and Charles's house had burned she wanted to be a witch or a sorceress. Maybe she still would be.

"You'll help me get out."

"Of course, mum. Remember, don't eat anything they bring. I'll do the rest."

"I'll try."

"Try hard."

Moeera felt a draft for a moment. Then she was alone again.

*   *   *

"Moron!" the guard said later that day through the pitch blackness. If you don't eat you'll die of starvation."

Moeera shuddered. By now she was very hungry, but she didn't move.

"Please," she said. "Please let some light in. I can't see."

"You don't need to see to eat," the guard said. He stalked off, slamming the door shut behind him.

Moeera sat against the wall and twiddled her thumbs.

*   *   *

Queen Stagust watched her daughter moon over her latest crush in her throne room. Britust was a couple years older than Moeera but couldn't be more different.

"We could fly to the Lake of Leisure tomorrow if you're off duty," Britust told Studly. "Those crystal-clear waters--the only ones around that clear--would feel so good, don't you think?"

"You wish to swim then," Studly said stiffly. He wondered if being a palace guard and the object of the princess's affections would work.

"Yes," she said. "That and other things." Her fingers brushed the buttons of his uniform shirt.

"Very well," he said. "We shall fly there at first light."

Britust smiled and quietly giggled.

288

"Now if you'll excuse me I must get back to my commander," Studly said. He bowed to the queen and kissed Britust's outstretched hand.

After he'd left Bragust said, "Truly, dear sister, must you initiate your shenanigans here in front of Mother and I?"

Britust shot him a cold look.

Bragust stood at a table making careful alterations to a heavy stone ball. Tink, tink, tink went his chisel as he carefully hit it with a hammer.

"Mother, can you make him mind his manners?"

"Bragust," Queen Stagust said. "What vexes you?"

"She's just so obvious about her liaison with Studly," Bragust whined. "It's hardly tasteful."

"Darling," his mother said. "Your sister is approaching the time in her life when she must find a suitable mate. Soon I'll be ruling all of our people from the Red Tower. One of you will take my place ruling this third of the High Roller Hegemony."

"Yes, Mother," Bragust said. "Which of us do you think it will be?"

"Hard to say," Stagust said. "Your sister is older and a fine roller. She's one of the best ever."

The queen smiled.

Bragust frowned.

"Very well, Britust," her brother said. "You're a shoe-in."

Britust giggled. "She's pulling your wing."

Bragust put his tools down, his jaw hung open. "Is that true, Mother?"

The queen cackled and said, "You know you're the best roller nowadays. Why so nervous about it? Your sister's good, you're good. Either one of you could lead with my blessing."

Britust's face brightened. It would have turned quite red in the cheeks if it hadn't been red already.

"Thank you, Mother," he said.

A tall guard appeared.

"What is it?" the queen asked.

"The prisoner isn't eating, your majesty," the guard said.

"She's been in the dungeon for a short time. I wouldn't worry."

"Yes, my queen," the guard said, bowing before he left.

"Why is she still alive, anyway?" Britust asked.

"We have yet to see any demons appear to serve us," the queen said. "I think we should keep her around a bit longer."

"Just in case," Bragust said.

"Exactly," his mother replied. "If there wasn't more to her than we know your Uncle Mozik would be using the ring right now to challenge my ascendancy."

Chapter Eighteen

Moeera's hunger prowled her mind like an angry tiger. She had no idea how long she'd been locked up. She hadn't seen the demon or the guard in what seemed to be forever. She was living a nightmare.

"Mee?" a familiar voice asked.

"Yes, Mama!" Moeera said. "I'm here. Is that really you?"

"Hold on, dear," she heard her mama say. "Be strong. God is with you."

It was all in her mind. Wasn't it? Nevertheless ….

"Where is he?" Moeera asked. "I've prayed for help, but aside of a creature more afreet than angel I'm alone!"

Silence reigned.

"Mama, can you hear me?" Moeera asked.

Silence. Darkness.

"Mama!" she cried. "I'm sorry you died. I miss you."

"What did you need?" asked another voice.

"Papa?"

"Yes, it's me," his voice said. "How did you get locked in this dungeon?"

"I found my grandparents, Papa, but I lost them again. I've been involved in one adventure after another since then. Now I'm trapped in this awful place!"

"I wish I could help you, Moeera," he said, sounding depressed. "I'm in a bad place too."

"I never wanted to leave you, Papa!" Moeera cried. "We should have fought the bad witch together."

"I know, Mee, but we would have failed."

Moeera's heart raced; her body shook. "Why?"

Suddenly she heard something moving at the door to her cell. A bolt snapped aside.

"Papa," she moaned.

"I'm no relation to you, wretched girl," the guard muttered. He grabbed the untouched food bowl from the floor. "Here's a loaf of jitoe. If you starve to death you do the queen's work for her."

He tossed the jitoe near Moeera and moved away.

"I almost forgot," he said. "I brought you a lumi stone."

A faint glow assailed Moeera's eyes. After repeated blinking she could see the apricot-sized stone in the guard's outstretched hand.

"Take it," he said. "You said you wanted light. It's the best I can do."

She took the glowing stone from the guard.

"Thank you," she croaked.

"You're welcome," he said. "Eat something."

With that he stepped out, shut the door, and slid the bolt into place. SNAK!

She sat there alone, but hopeful in the pale, blue light.

*   *   *

The next morning Queen Stagust sat pondering on her throne. Bragust was at his table, polishing the stone ball with a translucent oil.

The queen tapped her fingers on the throne arm. Her long fingernails made a tap, tap, tapping sound.

"Is everything all right?" her son asked.

"Just wondering about something."

"What about?"

"What do I require help with?"

"What?"

"Help," she replied. "To summon the demons. I need to have a task so big as to require their help."

"Oh," he said.

"Can you think of something?"

"How about the Hie Canyon?"

"What about it?"

"It's not used as much as the Tower Canyon. Why not ask for help chasing out those pesky Hammerheads?"

292

"Oh, yes!" she said. "Let's try that!"

She twirled the ring on her finger. Then she took a deep breath and said, "I can't do it alone. I need help!"

Nothing happened.

She and Bragust looked about for demons, but there wasn't so much as a fang, claw, or scale.

"There was smoke before they appeared in the woods," Bragust said. "Try again, Mother."

Stagust held her other hand on the ring and said, "I need help! I can't possibly do this by myself."

Again, nothing happened.

Stagust gnashed her teeth.

*   *   *

Moeera sat in the dungeon holding the lumi stone. She was hungry enough to eat a bear. The light spilled over her cell revealing the loaf of jitoe.

I mustn't eat it, she thought. The demon told me not to.

It sat on the floor.

Ugh! Just a bite? Could one bite of that thing hurt? Where is my friend the demon anyway?

She inched toward the jitoe. Stretching herself toward it she grasped it with her free hand.

Just a bite, just one bite, just ....

"Aaangh!" she cried, flinging it through some bars where she could not reach it.

"Hey! Jitoe!" the demon's voice exclaimed. "I haven't had this in forever!"

"Get me out of here," Moeera begged.

"You're in luck," the demon said. It pushed the bolt back and opened the door. "Come on. I'll take you out of here--or die trying."

"Can you die?"

"Wouldn't you like to know?"

Moeera got off the floor and followed the demon through the dungeon. The lumi stone was the only source of light.

"This way," the demon said. "Through here."

They finally emerged into a lit corridor. Sconces lined the walls.

"Quietly," the demon whispered. "I think I can fool anyone into seeing us as two high rollers."

They walked the hall looking for a way out.

*   *   *

"I don't understand it, Bragust," Queen Stagust said icily. "I've called for help half a dozen times now. Where are the demons?"

Bragust shook his head.

"Well," the queen said. "I'll try it one more time." She grasped the ring, thought about the Hammerheads, and said, "I need to get the Hammerheads to leave the canyon. I can't do it myself. I need help!"

It was at that very moment that Moeera and her demon friend passed by the throne room. Their search for a doorway had led them up and up increasingly steeper passages.

The queen had just made her seventh call for help. The demon heard her as they passed the entrance. Stagust noticed them pass by, but all she saw were two royal guards.

The demon yanked Moeera aside and said to her, "Keep walking and watching for an exit to the outside."

"What about you?" she asked. "We're not even outside; will you leave me now?"

"The queen's getting suspicious," it said. "I need to calm her down, so you have time to get far from here. I'll be quick. Keep walking the hall like you belong here with them."

Moeera nodded.

The demon twirled about. Smoke began enveloping it as it dashed into the throne room.

"What do you require, Master?" it asked in its ringing voice.

"Well!" the queen exclaimed. "Now that's more like it."

"You have a job for me, don't you?" the demon asked.

"Indeed," Stagust said. "I need you to banish the invading Hammerheads from the Hie Canyon."

"Consider it done, Master," the demon said, saluting. It twirled around again producing so much smoke and brimstone that the queen and prince began coughing. It nimbly danced out unseen to follow Moeera.

"Help me clear out this smoke, Bragust!" his mother ordered. She waved a fan around the dais.

Bragust opened a couple windows.

294

Moeera walked quickly down the series of hallways she encountered. She kept an eye on the doors for a familiar stairway; one like that which led from the balcony to the throne room. At some point the walls had become plain rock rather than plaster.

A bat-man approached from behind her. She was about to panic when she heard the lilting voice of her friend.

"It's me, mum," it said.

"Thank Heaven," Moeera said.

"No need for talk like that, mum."

"I can't find the stairway from before."

"Keep looking," the demon said. "I'll look, too."

They followed the hall, and before long she heard the demon snap its fingers.

"I see it," it said.

"Where?" Moeera asked. She saw rock walls; nothing more.

"There," the demon pointed.

"Are you kidding?" Moeera asked.

"No, it's there I tell you. Feel along the wall."

Moeera went to the rock wall and nearly fell into an opening between the wall and the floor.

"Ah!" she cried. "Careful, demon, there's no floor here!"

It sidled up for a closer look. "Right you are!"

"So, where's the stairway?"

"Nearby," the demon said. "I'm not completely sure. You see, they use this big shaft that runs from deep in the Earth up through the mountain. It's perfect if you have wings."

"Almost like it was made for them," Moeera said.

"That's why you aren't finding stairs. We know they have at least the one set, though."

Moeera nodded. She kept an eye on the gaping hole in the floor and began feeling around again. She saw the rocks begin to move in front of her. She did a doubletake.

"What?"

"You found it!" the demon said.

It turned out she had, in fact. Where the rock seemed to move she

295

discovered an alcove that turned back on itself, and there was the stairway.

"I hadn't even noticed this," she said.

"You had other things on your mind, didn't you, mum?"

"Yep."

They slipped into the alcove and mounted the stairs. You could have heard a pin drop. And at the top of the stairs ....

"The balcony!" Moeera cried joyfully.

"A way out," the demon said cheerfully, "but a treacherous climb down."

"Oh, no," Moeera said. She looked over the side into oblivion.

"What to do," the demon said. "You need to escape. The longer you stay here, the more a chance of them discovering you're not in the dungeon."

"Look how steep that is!" Moeera exclaimed, feeling dizzy. "I'll never make it!"

"But they'll probably kill you," the demon said.

"Yes."

Moeera closed her eyes and exhaled sharply. She climbed over the railing and tried to find a jutting rock or anything else that would provide a foothold. The demon scrambled over the railing and was soon standing on its hands with its feet leaning against the railing.

"There's a rock just to the left of your left foot, mum."

Moeera tried feeling around for it with her shoe. "I can't find it," she said.

"It's a few inches farther down," the demon said. "Stretch yourself silly. There you go."

Moeera felt a wave of relief wash over her. She'd taken the first step. Now for the next thousand or so more. She watched the demon whose eyes seemed luminous in the night. It jabbed its fingers against the rocks, sliding claws into the tiniest of cracks. Then it inched farther down and did the same with its toe claws. Moeera watched in amazement.

"You're very good at this," she said.

"Oh, well," the demon said. "Perhaps I'm just built for it." It tittered; the tinkle of bells standing in stark contrast to the dark, craggy rock--not to mention the demon's frightening visage.

Moeera was terribly afraid of the climb. She'd never done anything like it before. Finding a safe place to cling to with her fingers was hard enough,

296

but it was next to impossible to find solid places to put her feet. The sensation that she would fall back toward the open air terrified her and filled her with dread.

"Hold on, mum," the demon said.

"I'm trying," she said.

The demon scrabbled around until it was facing the same way as she was. It held onto the mountainside next to her.

"I can help," it said. "I'll climb down first and tell you where your footholds are."

"Okay."

It crawled downward along the rock face till it was out of sight. "Now let's see. What have we got as far as footholds go?"

The demon scanned the rocks and directed Moeera as she descended. Even with its help the going was hard. She couldn't shake the sensation that she would fall back into the open air. She remembered her childhood when she saw Wecks the Wizard float like a feather from the town hall roof to the ground.

"Move your left foot down about half a step," it said. "Yes, there's a hold there--feel for it. Just an inch lower."

Moeera did and had to stretch her body to the farthest she dared.

"Help," she said.

"Easy, mum," the demon said. "There's a rock below--you're going to move your right foot down."

"I can't let go with my hands! I'll fall!"

"Oh, torches! You have to want it, mum! Are you going to just roll over and die?"

"Augh!" Moeera exclaimed. "I don't want to fall!"

"Take that step, mum! You can do it. Grab at the wall as you step."

Moeera wanted to cry. She tried breathing easily, but her heart raced a mile a minute. She took her foot off its hold and gravity began pulling the rest of her downward. She sucked the cold night air in through her teeth. Her fingers fell away from the cold, hard rock. She felt the sickening feeling of falling as her foot sought an outcrop to land on. Her hands slid on the rock, wet.

At last, her foot landed on something solid--small, but solid. Her hands felt for crevices or grooves around the rock, anything to hold firmly. The best it seemed she could find was a spot where the rock bulged outward. This really didn't present much to hold onto.

"Don't over think it, mum," the demon said. "And whatever you do don't look down--I'll tell you where to step."

"How can you climb ... so easily?" Moeera demanded.

"I'm light, wiry, muscular," it said. "I have claws. All of this helps. Being a demon helps, too."

"I'm sure it does," Moeera said.

"Now, mum, there's a rock a step down from your left foot. Reach! It's further over."

She followed its directions lowering her foot, leaning ... leaning. It was excruciating.

"So close, mum, so close. Mere speck of space to go."

Moeera stretched, straining her muscles. She felt her foot make contact with the rock. She wriggled her body over to set her center of gravity.

Then she slipped.

Chapter Nineteen

The Mother's face was flickering orange in the firelight as she listened to her "daughter" babble about the jar she held in her hand. The jar itself was a well of blackness absorbing every stray ray of light.

"What makes you believe a word those mongrels say?" The Mother asked.

"If it's true, then this jar contains power," the witch said.

"I already possess power," The Mother said. "I intend to teach you and your sisters to make that power grow."

"If I open this jar I could be more powerful than you!"

"Shel, you're quite deluded," The Mother said. "Perhaps you're not the apprentice I'd hoped."

A couple of shouts interrupted the conversation. Patricia and Gwen were thrust into their midst by some of the witches. Ben and Dominic came immediately after, held fast by two witches.

"What do you mean interrupting our revels!" The Mother demanded.

"We want to join you," Gwen said defiantly. "We want to be witches, too."

"That's right," Patricia said. "We're trading our men here for a place in your circle."

The Mother grinned with the whitest teeth they'd ever seen.

"A trick?" The Mother asked. "You seek to deceive me?"

"No," Gwen said. "We wish to rule the land with true power."

"Shel speaks of this jar. How did you come by it?"

"We took it from The Pip."

"The Pip, eh? Is this 'Pip' still drawing breath?" The Mother asked.

"No," Ben said.

"Silence, dog!" The Mother exclaimed.

"If you truly wish to join our order, you'll have to pass a test."

"Name it," Patricia said.

"Dance with us around the fire tonight," The Mother said. "Let yourself go wild."

"Sounds good to me," Gwen said.

Patricia nodded.

"But first: Shel give the fair-haired one the jar."

"What? Why!" Shel stuttered.

"I want her to open it; right here, right now."

"No!" Dominic yelled.

One of the witches slugged him in the gut. He doubled over.

"Don't open it," Ben said.

"So afraid, my rabbit," The Mother said. "You should be more afraid of what we'll do to you later. Go ahead, daughter. Open it."

Gwen took the jar from Shel who scowled menacingly at her. Her chance at greatness had gone to a new recruit.

"Don't do it, Windy!" Dominic moaned.

Gwen swallowed hard and held the jar in both hands. She twisted the lid.

All eyes were on that jar.

POP!

The lid came free and ...nothing at all happened.

"What's in there!" The Mother rasped. She grabbed the jar away from Gwen, raising it up to look in.

Ben didn't know what was going on. Where were the horrors Moeera had warned him about?

"Shel!" The Mother bellowed. "Are you satisfied? This jar contains nothing more than simple preserves!"

Shel's face went pale. Her expression twisted into one of hate as she speared Ben with her eyes. "Liar!"

Ben was silent.

The Mother threw back her head and laughed. "Oh, my. It's worth the disappointment to see you thoroughly embarrassed, Shel."

Sniggers came from the surrounding witches.

Shel shrieked and ran at Patricia. She produced a knife from under the folds of her tunic.

"I'll kill you!" she yelled, stabbing at the woman.

Patricia screamed, trying to leap back. She didn't move far, though; her way was blocked.

Shel drove the knife at Patricia's breast, but before it landed the blade shattered in midair.

"Enough!" The Mother commanded. "Don't compound your mistake by challenging my will. Treat your new sisters with respect!"

"Yes, mother," Shel murmured meekly. She glared at Patricia.

The Mother grinned at Patricia. "Your name's Patricia, is it?"

"Yes," Patricia said.

"And you are …?"

"Windy."

"Neither of you have any need for your men anymore?"

"No," they said.

"Then you may call me Mother from this moment forward. Come dance with us around the fire of fertility. You're home, dears."

Gwen and Patricia smiled.

Chapter Twenty

The witches tied Ben and Dominic to trees and spent the next few hours whooping and dancing in the clearing. The brothers could see the women dancing around the fire from the corners of their eyes.

Then they let the fire burn down to coals plunging the woods into pitch blackness. Silence blanketed the trees around the two brothers.

There they hung. Hanging there, backs crushed against tree trunks, they wondered what had happened with the jar Moeera had been so serious about. That and if they would ever leave this forest with skins intact.

After an excruciating forever Ben heard footsteps.

"Ben?" a voice asked.

"Right here," he rasped.

"Oh, Ben," Patricia said. "We're going to get you loose and get the hell away from here."

"Thank God," he said. "You acted pretty convincing before in front of the witches."

"Trappe doesn't have much to do for fun other than playing pretend or playing tag," she said.

She and Gwen worked on his bonds together.

"Hold him," Patricia said. She sawed at the ropes with a wicked-looking knife.

Ben pulled away from the tree. "I don't get it," he said.

"What about?" Patricia asked.

"Moeera's jar," he said. "It was full of wriggling things before that looked like grubs. How could it be preserves now?"

"Oh, that," Gwen said. "I brought along some food in my purse. Shel grabbed the jelly by mistake."

Ben's eyes bugged out of his head. "But that means ...."

"Moeera's jar is still closed--and it's safe, too!" Gwen exclaimed. She pulled her long skirt up to reveal the sack with the jar shape within tied to her calf.

Patricia started untying Dominic, but Ben was dumbfounded.

"The jar is in that sack?" he asked.

"Yes," Gwen said.

"How?"

"After the dancing I snuck inside the wagon," she said. "They caught me after I climbed back out, so I said I was checking to see if there was any booze."

"Thank you!" Ben said excitedly, hugging Gwen.

"No worries, Ben. We'll keep the thing safe."

Once Dominic was free they abandoned the camp of The Mother. It proved hard backtracking the road in the dark, but they were determined to get as far away as they could.

None of them noticed when they veered off the road to Trappe and headed West.

At the first signs of dawn, they came upon an earthen mound larger than The Dewdrop Inn, wider in fact. They were exhausted and wagon-less, so they decided to investigate the single wooden door in the mound's front center.

"Go on, knock," Gwen said.

Dominic rapped on the old, wooden door. It was the only feature that gave the mound the look of civilization.

No answer.

Dominic knocked again.

After several minutes Ben yawned and said, "Try it."

Dominic did and the door opened easily. A musty smell greeted them.

"What is it?" Gwen asked, holding her nose.

Patricia scrunched her face and said, "It smells like death."

"Maybe it is death," Ben said with his nose crinkled. He stepped past Dominic.

"You're not actually going in there!" Patricia admonished.

"The witches will be mad when they realize we're gone," Ben said. "It's almost light as it is."

"We'll take our chances in the mound," Dominic said.

"Eww!" Gwen said. "I'm going with you."

She stepped inside.

Patricia followed reluctantly. "You realize we're going to have to pull the door closed if we don't want them to find us," she said.

"Yes," Ben said. He tugged the old door shut behind them.

"Now what?" Patricia asked. She took Ben's arm, leaning into him.

"Scary story time?" Dominic asked.

Gwen flicked the back of his head with her index finger. "Not funny, Dom!" she exclaimed.

"Let's see how far back this passageway goes," Ben said.

"We won't see much of anything," Patricia said.

They walked slowly into the musty, cool darkness. The way was clear of obstacles.

"Hey!" Ben said. "There's a light up ahead. I can see the tunnel's outline."

Part of the tunnel had collapsed about twenty feet in front of them, letting light shine in through the mound.

"That's as far as we're going," Ben said.

"I'm glad for the light," Gwen said. "I wouldn't make it much longer in the dark."

"Me either," Dominic said.

"It looks like the tunnel splits here," Patricia said, pointing at the right side of the pile of dirt and rock.

The others saw that she was right. Another passage led right. Ben walked over to it, carefully treading around the fallen debris.

"It's just a short thing," he said. "It leads to another door."

He stepped around the corner. When the others followed they found him staring at the new door.

"This one seems so out of place," he said.

"I see what you mean," Patricia said. "It looks new."

The new door differed greatly from the entrance door. There were no signs at all of aging or weathering. Where that one was plain, crude even, this one had been sanded smooth and painted a rich hue of dark blue. Gold filigree formed a picture on the surface that was embedded in the wood. It depicted a sun shining its rays upon an island in a sea. The sea was capped by waves, glinting in the bit of light that reached from the roof collapse.

They all gazed at the door's golden ornamentation in awe.

"What do you think it means?" Patricia asked.

"Our problems are solved," Ben said.

"How do you mean?" Gwen asked.

"It's gold," Ben answered. "We can bring it wherever we go and finally make some money."

"Sure, I guess so," Gwen said.

"That's not what I meant," Patricia said. "This mound probably holds tombs."

"Did the smell give it away?" Gwen asked.

"Quiet," Patricia said. "The artwork on this nice, clean door. What do you think it means? Does it tell who's buried here?"

"It might," Ben said. He looked at the design thoughtfully. "It looks like an island."

"Yes ...," Patricia said.

"That's all I can tell," Ben said. "I don't know what it refers to."

"Me neither," Dominic said.

"We should take the door down and take it with us when we leave," Ben said.

"Now you're talking," Gwen said.

"But Ben ...," Dominic said.

"What Dom?"

"We'd be stealing from the dead ... again," Dominic said.

"I guess so," Ben said.

"I thought that time with the Tiger's Eye ring was the exception."

"So did I," Ben said. "Then the ring got stolen by monsters. We need to get paid somehow."

"It doesn't feel right," Dominic said.

"You know, we aren't certain there's a tomb here in the first place," Ben said.

"We should check behind the door at least," Dominic mumbled.

"Dom's right, Ben," Patricia said. "Try the door."

"I will," he said.

He took the latch in his hand and pushed downward on the handle. It moved without so much as a squeak. The catch holding the door to its

305

frame went up and released from the frame. Ben kept the catch raised and pushed the door inward.

The passage beyond the door was seemingly empty, save for the sconces along the walls.

"I can't see to the end of this one," Ben said, "but if we light the torches …."

He rummaged in his pockets for a tinder box.

When he lit the first torch it flared to life. Soon several more had been lit. Ben and Dominic each removed one to carry further down the passage.

They found a second door twelve feet past the first one. It was similar but lacked the sun in its ornamentation.

"No sun," Dominic said.

"But why not?" Patricia asked.

"Who knows?" Ben asked.

This time Dominic opened the door. The scene on the other side was identical to the passageway they'd traversed so far. Twelve feet further revealed yet another door.

"I think we're safe taking the first door," Ben said. "This place seems to have plenty!"

"Curious," Patricia said. "They all seem to open to the same place-- further along the passage, anyway."

"And this one's plain," Gwen noted.

This latest door sported the handsome blue paint of the previous two, but it had no ornamentation--gold or otherwise.

"I wonder if we're getting close to the edge of the mound," Ben said.

"We must be," Patricia said.

"There's something scratched on it," Dominic said. "Looks like writing."

Gwen tried to look past Dominic's shoulder. "Let me see."

"Can you read it, Dom?" Ben asked.

"It's really small," Dominic said. "It says 'Serendipidoor'."

"What's that?" Patricia asked.

"What in the world is a serendipidoor?" Ben asked.

"Who knows!" Dominic grasped the latch and opened it, pushing the door open.

The space beyond the door flooded the passageway with blinding light.

It felt as if the world had turned on its side. All four travelers experienced an overpowering sensation of wooziness as they slid into the doorway and the light. All four closed their eyes instinctively to keep from being blinded.

*   *   *

They opened their eyes to a most unexpected sight. They faced an enormous lake stretching past the far horizon. A cold breeze whipped through the air. If he didn't know better Ben would have thought he was facing ....

"The ocean!" Gwen cried.

"It can't be the ocean," Dominic said. "We aren't anywhere near it!"

"Look!" Gwen exclaimed. "How do you explain that then?"

"Mirage?" Dominic asked.

"It's no mirage, Dom," Ben said. He scuffed his shoe on the rough, hard rock underneath him. He heard the wailing of shore birds seconds before they flew overhead. Patricia knelt near him to examine the windswept rocks. She picked up some scattered pebbles from the boulders.

"Look," she said, standing up with her findings cupped in her hand. She picked one object from the bunch and handed it to Ben.

"No way," he said in astonishment.

"What do you have?" Gwen asked.

"Let me see," Dominic said.

Ben spread his palm flat to display the small, white shell.

"How did we get here?" Patricia asked. "Magic?"

"I think so," Ben said. Speaking of magic .... "Gwen, do you still have the jar?"

She felt her calf and said, "Of course."

"Good," Ben said. "That's good."

"It's windy here," Patricia said, "but so beautiful." She took Ben's hand and laced her fingers in his.

"Wherever here is," Ben said. Then on impulse he leaned in and kissed her.

She kissed him back. She turned to Gwen and Dominic, smiling. "Shall we look around?"

Gwen smiled and nodded.

Dominic took a last look at the water. "Good idea, Patricia."

They crept over the rocky shore with the sun shining brightly overhead.

Soon the landscape became green with lush grass and trees of differing sizes.

"Which way?" Patricia asked. "Further inland or follow the coast? There doesn't seem to be a path."

"Let's follow the coastline," Ben said. "That should bring us to something … if there's anything around that is."

Chapter Twenty-one

It was the worst feeling Moeera had ever experienced--worse even than the harrowing flight with the High Rollers. For a few seconds she felt she had the ability to fix it--to grab on and jam her foot onto something. She grabbed and she kicked ....

Then all hope changed to utter despair. She was falling faster now.

"Help!" she shrieked.

"Mum!" the demon cried. It scrabbled around, practically hanging off the mountainside backward.

Moeera dropped like a rock. She saw the rocks below rushing up to meet her. She squeezed her eyes shut tightly.

She didn't see the air below her filling with red smoke; nor did she see herself vanish once it enveloped her. All she saw was red.

*　　*　　*

She landed with a hard thump that felt like more of a smack!

The wind had fled her lungs. She fought to breathe in more life sustaining air. I'm alive, she thought. How am I alive?

She sat looking around herself, but saw only red, billowing smoke.

A hand grasped her shoulder.

"Yi-I-I!" she exclaimed, jumping.

"Only me, mum," her demon friend said.

"How'd you keep me from going splat on the rocks?" Moeera asked.

"I brought you with me," it said.

"Brought me where?" she asked fearfully.

"Hell, mum ... the underworld."

A chill rushed down Moeera's spine. How could she feel more afraid than she did on the mountainside? Her purple-skinned benefactor had just made it happen.

The smoke drifted, dissipating as an updraft caught it. Moeera saw rock walls that flickered as if lit by candlelight. She heard an inhuman shriek echo through the cavern from somewhere down the line.

She turned to the demon and said, "Hell! You brought me to Hell?"

"I didn't want you to die!" the demon exhorted. "I was prepared to return here as I always am, so I did. And you came along."

Moeera shuddered. The demon had saved her life, but at what cost? This must be a most awful place!

The demon reached out, grasped Moeera's hand, and pulled her after it.

"Hurry, mum! Stay quiet and follow me. We'll be out in the terrestrial world in no time."

Moeera complied as best as she could. She followed the demon through narrow passageways. It seemed so cramped the walls might close in and crush them, but Beezer knew the way.

As the demon yanked her along on his mad dash she found her mind returning to unanswered questions. Was the demon male or female? Who did the demon work for? Why did the ring give the wearer power over demons? Could she really trust the creature?

Suddenly the rock passageway led into an enormous cavern. It was black-walled and dark, but she could see because pools of liquid magma glowed with orange and yellow light. There were people all around--every one of them were part of one horrid tableau or another. Most didn't even look quite human.

There was a muscular man trapped on the ground by a trio of great cats. Each cat's fangs were the length of Moeera's forearms. The brutish-looking man screamed in agony as the cats tore into his flesh.

She saw another man with similar features to the first--powerful muscles, a low and slanting forehead, and a long, narrow skull--being made into a sort of pin cushion by a horde of demons. They stabbed him one after the other with sharp spears. Each would force the spear point in and lean with all his weight. The man's face twisted in agony.

The smell of burning hair and flesh assailed Moeera's nostrils. Demon laughter clashed with the sounds of wailing, begging, and crying. She turned her head in disgust.

"Watch your step, mum," Beezer said. "I'll lead you around the pools."

"Should I close my eyes?" she asked.

"If you do that you'll fall for sure."

"But this place is terrible!"

"It is, Mum; it's supposed to be."

Moeera looked frightened, but inside she was terrified.

The demon named Beezer held her hand and said, "I have to report to the King before leaving again. I'll get you out of here if you're brave."

"What about them?" she asked. She stared past him.

"They deserve their punishment ... they earned it in life. You won't be hurt while you're with me."

She nodded. This was a hopeless place, but at least she wasn't alone.

"Hope comes here to die," the demon said. It had plucked the thought from her mind easily.

She followed Beezer across the black, jagged rocks--most of which were lost in the darkness. Behind them the six demons with the spears continued torturing the brute. He screamed and screamed.

A slapping sound assailed her ears. Beezer led her to a curving rock wall, and they ascended a stepped path upward. She caught sight of a woman's figure floating just below the surface of the glowing magma. The female shape glowed hot--perhaps less so than the ensconcing magma. The body splayed out in the appearance of a dead woman floating. Just before Beezer led Moeera along a rocky ridge she saw the arms move and the head rise ever so slightly.

"She's alive," Moeera breathed.

"She is--they all are," Beezer agreed. "But they had to die to arrive here. Now they feel pain and damnation for the rest of their days."

The demon itself shuddered as it pulled her through an opening in the cavern wall. "We're leaving the Primordial. The next area has quite a few sinners as black hearted as they come."

Moeera squinted in the daylight. The land on the other side of the "Primordial" looked for all purposes to be outside. It was a vast plain covered in mud and people. More demons--these quite a bit larger and sporting horns on their heads--tramped through the masses. These people appeared to be average, run-of-the-mill human beings. The men wore only loincloths, and the women wore simple skirts and cloth brassieres.

The demons lashed the people with long whips causing them to push and shove and move about like cattle or sheep. Moving through the mud in close quarters forced every third person to slip and fall into the muck. Many of the people were encrusted head to toe in the dark brown slop. The sun overhead made it hot and grueling. She imagined the people must be dying of thirst.

"They won't die, mum," Beezer whispered, "not anytime soon anyway." She shivered.

"Come on. We'll soon be there."

He led her along a wooden bridge jutting from the opening to the Primordial. It swayed like it was alive, a dizzying thing. Out on the plain people moaned and shrieked. If one fell and didn't get back up he or she was trampled until a demon arrived to whip them.

Beezer pulled her through an opening in the black stone. More rock tunnels beckoned. These were smoother, and the rock color was lighter.

After a run through the tunnels, they emerged into a small space very much like the inside of a house.

Moeera saw five demons sitting around a table playing cards. Two were purple like Beezer, one was orange, one was blue, and the fifth was red.

"Look who's back!" the red demon said.

"Beezer!" the blue demon said. "Hey! Who's that?"

"Never mind," Beezer said in that ever-cheery voice.

"Don't you tell me to never mind!" the blue demon huffed. "It looks like a human. Are you bringing your work home with you again?"

"Crazy is what he is," the orange demon drawled in a scratchy voice.

He? Moeera thought. So. Beezer was male. Demons had genders after all.

"This is Moeera," Beezer said happily. "I have to return her to Earth. Can you keep tabs on her while I report to the King?"

"The King!" the two purple demons cried in unison.

"Earth?" the red demon asked in a voice that made Moeera think of birds of prey. "Is this girl alive!"

"What's going on?" Orange asked.

"The ring of the Lord of Hosts has found a new master," Beezer declared. "I'm one who gets summoned for service. I've been to Earth three times now--I have to report on what I saw there."

"What did you see there?" the blue demon demanded.

"You know I need to tell the King first."

"Very well," the blue demon whose name was Bash said. "Be quick about it."

"I will," Beezer said. He turned and looked into Moeera's eyes.

She studied his bloodshot, red, terrifying eyes feeling as if she stared into a wolf's eyes.

"Stay here and stay quiet, Moeera," Beezer told her. "I can't take you to my meeting with the King. The experience would be too uncomfortable for both of us."

"What will I do?" Moeera asked, not at all comfortable where he was leaving her.

"If you must do something, chat with my fellows here," Beezer said. "Bash especially enjoys hearing voices. Ta."

He disappeared through a door that wouldn't budge when Moeera grabbed the knob. She pulled and turned, but it held fast. She let go and glanced back at the table. The demons were watching her intently. She turned back to the door, crying out in anguish.

There was no door.

What she now found immediately before her was a painting upon a wall--nothing less; nothing more. She stared hard at the image of two warriors locked in combat. One was human, but the other was scaly and reptilian. In fact, it had a tail resembling a snake's rather than legs.

Moeera's face screwed up, and tears began flowing down her cheeks. It was too much. She was in Hell with demons. None of them was even the demon who claimed he was her friend.

"Dearie, you can't follow him; it's just a painting to you," the blue demon said in a voice that grated her already frayed nerves.

"Oh, kid, don't cry," the orange demon drawled. "Beezer's very clever. He'll visit the boss and take you back to Earth in no time at all."

"Who are you?" Moeera asked them. "Who are you to him? And you," she addressed the orange demon, "just moments ago you called him crazy!"

"He is!" Orange said. "He brought you here to Hell."

"You don't belong here," the purple demons said.

"You're alive," the red demon said. "You shouldn't be seeing this. You have to die first."

"I hope I don't come here when I die," Moeera said.

"Likewise," Red said. "You're not evil; I can smell the goodness from here. Bad enough we have to deal with all these wretches."

Bash made a face. "Ugh. Good ones are the worst! Bad is bad, but good makes me vomit. No offense."

"Beezer seems fine around me," Moeera said.

"Like I said: crazy," Orange growled, gnashing his teeth. "If you sin enough in life, then you'll get to spend more than enough time here."

"Quiet, you!" Bash admonished. She looked at Moeera with eyes from nightmare. "I'm Bash. We're all from the same family as your friend."

"Beezer seems nice," Moeera said. "How can a demon be nice?"

"We were all angels once upon a time," Bash said.

"Angels?" Moeera said. "What's an angel?"

"What's an angel?" Bash asked, grabbing at a chair for support. "Do you live under a rock? How is it you know of demons, but not angels?"

She shrugged. "Everyone learns to behave and listen to her elders," Moeera said, "lest demons carry them off."

"Correct," Bash said, "and angels?"

"I don't know," Moeera said. "I don't remember ever hearing of anything called an angel before."

The demons began whispering amongst themselves excitedly. After they'd finished Orange stood up from his chair and said, "Name's Itzer, girl. We'll tell you all about angels. You came to the right place."

Chapter Twenty-two

Meanwhile, Beezer stood before the throne of his true master, the king and overlord of Hell itself, known by many, many names. Old Scratch, Beelzebub, Satan, Mephistopheles, The Devil ... Beezer knew him as:

"Cloot! Oh, great master and mighty king! Pillager of the vain, destroyer of the invulnerable, spoiler of the wholesome! The impervious crumble before thee. I bring news of the terrestrial sphere."

"What is it faithful one?" the Devil asked. He had a loud, but surprisingly calm voice. His breath moved visibly in the air.

The greatest irony in Hell, Beezer thought, was that the chamber of King Cloot was freezing cold. The small demon shivered from the icy temperature and the fear he felt in his heart. He must tell everything he knew, but not expose his new friend as any kind of danger to the underworld.

Beezer stared up, up, up at the gargantuan figure. Cloot--we will stick to Beezer's method of address--sat on the vast throne adorned with skulls. He was four times the size of an average human being. He wore of all things a white toga clasped with a golden apple. A segmented, golden wrought belt encircled his waste resembling a serpent. His skin was a light peach color except for his cheeks which were rosy. His hair was bronze-colored, his face handsome. The most fearsome aspect of his being were his eyes. They glowed red; no irises, no pupils--just a red that filled each watchful eye. In his right hand he held a golden trident.

Beezer resolved to get his report over with so he could be about his business.

"I have been to Earth not once--three times in the last two cycles!"

"Tempting souls, no doubt," Cloot said, smiling. "I suppose you wish a reward for this moonlighting."

"No, King Cloot. I was merely answering the summons of the ring of the Lord of Hosts."

Cloot's smile vanished, replaced by a frightful scowl. "That accursed trinket! It's been lost for generations. Surely you lie, my loyal demon!"

"No, Mighty Cloot!" Beezer exclaimed. "That which was lost is found. Once again a human is able to command the ring and with it one hundred demons."

"Gah!" Cloot raved. "I'd thought His little device for enslaving our brethren was gone."

"Yes," Beezer agreed. "But it was known and sought after. Now one who never knew it existed is its master."

"How did this mortal come by it?"

"Purely by chance, your magnificence!" Beezer exclaimed. "A High Roller prince uncovered it to use in his bid for power. He was prideful and careless, though. The ring is worn by another."

Cloot ran his left hand over his face, tracing his lips with perfect fingers. He shook his head. "The proud fall the hardest. Do you know how angry I am that the blasted thing is back?"

"No, King Cloot," Beezer said.

Cloot stood up, holding out the trident which he thumped against the floor. It clanged on the black obsidian rock. His face twisted into a look of pure fury.

"I could turn every ... last ... tormented ... soul in this place to stone, I'm so ANGRY!" he roared. His appearance shifted as skin darkened and became rougher. Horns resembling those of a goat erupted from his temples. Coarse, thick hair sprang from the edges of his toga. It blotted out his chest and enveloped his arms and legs. His sandals disappeared revealing cloven hooves.

Beezer watched this transformation and involuntarily gulped. The Prince of Lies could create an endless series of tortures for those he hated. Would he punish Beezer because of the news he brought?

As Cloot's illusion of splendor faded away the chamber grew larger. The obsidian floor became an immense lake of ice. Cloot himself grew larger and larger until Beezer resembled a toy in comparison. Huge wings sent an icy wind blowing throughout the cavern. Beezer shivered.

Finally, the Devil appeared as he truly was--the enormous, terrifying, heart stopping monarch of Hell trapped waist deep in the frozen lake of Cocytus. Beezer stared upward from his vantage point which was now a narrow rock arch halfway above the surface of Cocytus and halfway below his master's three faces. Each mouth held one of the Earth's most treacherous sinners: Brutus, Cassius, and Judas Iscariot.

Beezer heard a voice which combined all the best qualities of roars, gurgles, and screeches.

"AND YOU'VE BEEN SUMMONED THRICE!"

"Yes, Mighty Cloot! I'm bound to the ring!" Beezer called to the enormous Devil. He couldn't get the notion out of his mind that the Master was speaking with his mouths full.

Please don't be reading my mind right now, he thought.

"THIS MORTAL WASTES NO TIME AT ALL WITH THE RING. PERHAPS ... YES! IF YOU ARE SUMMONED AGAIN YOU MUST INFLUENCE THE RING WIELDER TO USE IT FOR DARK PURPOSES!"

Beezer didn't know if it was the freezing cavern or Cloot's words that sent shivers scurrying up and down his back. He bowed his head. "Of course, Master."

"NOW GET OUT! I DON'T WANT TO DESTROY ONE OF MY FAVORITES JUST BECAUSE MY MOOD'S GONE FOUL!"

"Going, Master," Beezer said. He turned to walk out of Cloot's chamber.

Below him the worst sinners of humanity--the traitors to their lords and benefactors--hung suspended in the frozen lake. These were the truly evil. None of them moved a muscle because they were fully encapsulated. Most were in a supine position. He saw one exception in a jackknifed position. He couldn't make out the man's eyes, but he was sure they were open and seeing the ice in front of them. How long would the man be forced to hold that position? He didn't know.

There was an old crone in a natural floating position, her arms splayed to the sides, her head looking down, and her feet sinking downward. Like all the others she was immobile--frozen in that moment of time. She had an excruciating eternity to consider her betrayal, Beezer thought.

Hundreds upon hundreds floated frozen in the Devil's lake. All the while Cloot's massive wings fanned forward and back keeping the lake frozen solid.

Beezer met the next demon coming to converse with Cloot. It was Feverdog. The pus-ridden, green-skinned being nodded curtly as they passed, then involuntarily shivered.

"He's worked up today, isn't he?" Feverdog muttered. "All his illusions laid bare. Mordred whimpered for mercy as I passed him, the son of a--"

"Tread lightly," Beezer said in his ever-cheery voice. "He has the worst mad-on I've seen in …."

"What?" Feverdog laughed. "Three days? Two?" He passed Beezer by.

Beezer nodded to himself and quickened his pace. He hated entering Cloot's presence when he wasn't casting illusions. It was bad enough when he resembled a twenty-two-foot-tall Archangel Michael. Trinity-headed, bat-winged, and the size of Mt. Ebal scared the evil right out of him. It was true.

Behind him he heard Cloot roaring at Feverdog. Poor Feverdog. He stepped lively to get beyond his master's sight.

Eventually Beezer passed all the traitors he'd avoided on the way in. There were traitors to their guests, traitors to their countries, and finally traitors to their kindred among whom he spied Mordred--still making puppy dog eyes. He had a sudden urge to kick the prisoner's head but resisted it. Letting the bastard cool his heels was punishment enough.

* * *

Moeera was dealing the cards when Beezer returned to "the kitchen".

"Do you think you can best me this time, or will I wind up owning another of your souls?" he heard Moeera ask as he shut the door.

His family and friend looked up at him as he stepped into the room, the door once more becoming the battle painting.

"What's going on?" he asked.

"We're playing blunderbuss," Moeera said. She seemed happy enough.

"Sounds like you're winning, mum."

"I am," she said.

"I gotta admit, Beez, this little spitfire of yours is smarter than most mortals," Itzer said.

"That she is!" he replied.

"How'd your little meeting go?" Bash asked. She looked up from her fan of cards.

"Not too bad," Beezer admitted. "Feverdog came in after me, though. He's a goner."

The two purple demons burst out laughing.

"What's funny about that?" Beezer asked.

The one whose name was Creepy grinned and said, "Feverdog got Lilith sick with the Black Plague. Even though she's deceased and a longtime resident here he got her sick."

"She probably deserved it," Beezer said. He'd met Lilith. The woman gave even the worst demon the willies.

"What did his vileness say?" Bash asked.

"You know. Thanks for all you do. Keep corrupting those souls. Great job, pal."

Moeera shuddered when all the demons laughed. The discord made her bones numb.

"As long as it went better than the time you let Jesus Christ cast you out of that woman," Bash murmured. "It took two hundred years to chip you out of Cocytus."

Beezer shrugged. "Cloot takes every half-win and every failure as a personal betrayal. I tried to hold my post, but I was overpowered. Sue me."

"Your king isn't very forgiving," Moeera said.

"He's the total opposite of that," Red said. "What a hot temper."

"Thank you one and all for looking after Moeera," Beezer said. "I have to get her back to Earth now."

"You're welcome!" Bash said.

"Our pleasure," Itzer growled.

The rest said their goodbyes to the human and went back to their cards.

Beezer led Moeera back to the passageways.

Moeera followed him on another harrowing walk around Hell. He spirited her through the Evil Ditches where once more she witnessed the large, horned demons whipping the inhabitants.

"They spent enough of their time alive lying," Beezer told her. "Pandering, seducing … now they're scourged and driven about like livestock."

This time they avoided the Primordial by sneaking through the narrow track of the hypocrites.

"Whatever you do, don't step on anyone's robe," Beezer warned Moeera.

She glanced at the robed prisoners who looked exhausted and ready to topple over at any moment. She didn't want to know what happened if they fell down.

"There's a secret way in the shadows over there," Beezer whispered. "We'll go to that."

She followed him around the track almost stepping on the face of a man crucified to the chamber floor. There was no way around him. She stepped on his chest to get over him.

"Caiaphas," Beezer addressed the crucified man in mock attention. He stepped on his groin, and then was past.

"Be ready," he whispered to Moeera. "When I say so, veer to the right."

A few minutes later Beezer signaled, and she turned into the dark cavern wall. Beezer held her arm tightly and pulled her into the rock which gave way in a spongy sort of way. They pushed through a wet, mossy substance in the dark for the next fifteen minutes or so. Then they came upon a lit alcove where the rock walls were a tan color. A sigil was painted on the wall in red. It was circular with three wavy lines intersecting it. A long diagonal line entered it from the lower left and exited again from the upper right.

"What is it?" she asked.

"This is your ticket back," Beezer said. "I'm going to chant the activation spell, and you're going to pass through the wall and be back on Earth."

"Aren't you coming with me?"

He shook his head. "No, I have things I must take care of here. Hopefully, I can avoid the king while I do them."

"Thank you for saving my life," she said.

He nodded. "You're welcome. You're all right for somebody who can use the ring."

He began chanting and his voice filled the candlelit alcove. Moeera stared at the red symbol painted on the rock. It started to drip as if the wall bled. The red pattern expanded until it blotted out the tan rock.

Beezer uttered the final phrase of the activation spell and pushed her into the wall which seemed as solid as smoke. She felt the red liquid cover her wetly. The rock alcove fell away around her. Wind swirled and blew. She heard sounds of chaos: voices raised in anger, resentment, fear, and confusion. Then the sounds hit a crescendo. She screamed.

The world exploded.

Chapter Twenty-three

Silence. Moeera found herself lying prone in the yellow grass of a field. Unlike her journey using the Nebulous she felt good. Her surroundings seemed utterly silent in comparison to the cacophony she'd heard leaving Hell.

She sat up, checking herself over. Everything seemed to be working ....

"Where!" she called to no one, not certain her ears worked after that horrid noise.

"Pshew ...," she breathed.

She appeared to be in Winkie Country again. If that was true, then Kimbaloo must be quite a distance away. Ben and Dominic were on their own again, she thought. Broke, too.

She'd lost Beezer to whatever obligations he had in the underworld. She'd lost the tiger's eye ring to Mozik's sister. She'd lost Ben and Dominic to distance. She'd lost Carrie and Charles to the blood witch and the fire.

Thinking about Carrie made her want to cry. She'd obviously perished with the blood witch when the burning roof collapsed. Now she had no one to finish teaching her the witch arts. All she had left was ... a jar?

The jar! She scrambled to her feet as the knowledge dawned on her: Ben and Dominic had the jar! She'd left it wrapped in her kerchief at the bottom of an old sack. The sack that she carefully packed beneath the cooking gear in the wagon.

What if they opened it?

She wondered if that would happen. They'd asked her about the jar's contents thinking the wriggling critters were fish bait.

She'd explained it to them the best she could. About Pandora. About the tribulations and plagues. About hope and the fact that Charles had recaptured at least one of the hardships. It currently existed as the icky creatures in the jar.

They seemed to believe her story--at least that she believed it was true. Did they believe her enough to resist opening the jar? Sure, as long as it didn't muddle their minds the way it had with her.

Moeera focused on breathing. In out. I-n; ou-t. She hoped her friends did not open the jar.

*   *   *

After walking for a long time and noting the sun moving across the sky Moeera found a few houses. They were small, one-story affairs with peaked roofs and warm color schemes. Two sat on the left side of the winding dirt lane, and the third sat on the right. Each had a tidy yard of grass with inlaid steppingstones. Two of the houses had corrals. She saw pigs, sheep, and even a few buppuses.

"Hello," a man greeted when she walked by his house. He was short-- about four feet tall--wearing overalls and a blue shirt and hat.

"Hello, sir," she replied. "I'm Moeera. Do you know of anyone who has a tavern or a room to let?"

"Name's Hendry Munkick," he said. "If you continue on down this main road you'll eventually find a tavern called the Merry Kitten. As for a room, I'm not sure."

"I just need a place to rest for a night and collect my thoughts. Yesterday was a really hard day for me."

"Tired, huh?"

"Exhausted."

"I think Val has an extra room. He's my neighbor. Let's go see."

"That would be so nice," Moeera said.

It was weird looking down at him. She felt as if she was talking to a child, but Hendry was no child. Gray hair ran through his otherwise dark locks and bristly beard. He picked up the carved walking stick leaning against his front door and stepped onto the dirt lane.

"With a little bit o' luck we'll catch him before supper. His Sarah is a first-rate cook."

"I don't mean to impose myself on anyone," Moeera said.

Hendry looked at her. "Don't be ridiculous, Moeera. You could use some help. We might live simple here in Slippakanu, but we try to help our neighbors."

323

"Slippakanu? That's the name of your town, hmm," Moeera said.

"It is," Hendry said, ambling across the lane to the closest house. "It's named for the critters that live along the river."

"There's a river nearby?"

"Yes, the Great Winkie River. It has a really big otter community living alongside it. They do a lot of slipping and sliding."

"If this is Winkie Country," Moeera said, "then what are you doing here?"

"Pardon?" Hendry asked.

"You're a Munchkin, aren't you?"

"Yes," Hendry said. He grinned a mischievous grin.

"Then what gives? What are you doing in Slippakanu?" Moeera asked.

"I helped build it--that's what. Everyone in Slippakanu used to live in Munchkin Country ... except some of the kids, of course."

"Why come here?"

"Because it was here, that's why. We got together one day and asked: 'Is there something more?'"

"Weren't you happy in Munchkin Country?"

"Some of us were, some weren't. I was, but I was curious, too. You're a traveler; have you ever felt the desire to leave home and find something new?"

"Yes," Moeera said. "I know that feeling well. It's why I'm here today."

"We all felt that, too. It was enough to make us organize ourselves to explore the other countries of Oz."

"Now you live here."

"Yes," he said. "Gillikin Country was really wild; thick woods and rocky hills that blocked our wagons and carriages. So, we visited the green area, saw the king's castle, kept heading West. We liked Winkie Country so much we stayed. That and everyone was tired of traveling."

"It must have been an adventure journeying cross-country."

"It was. Enough for my lifetime. We built a quaint, but fine town here."

"How many?"

"We left with about eighty-nine pilgrims. Seventy-eight of those are here now with an additional thirty-two born since we left the East. Two were born on the way."

"Goodness!"

"Adventure doesn't come close to describing it," Hendry laughed. "If Val doesn't have room, you can sleep at my place. Long as you don't mind the floor."

"You're very kind, Mr. Munkick."

"No use for formality with me, Miss Moeera. Call me Hendry."

He accompanied her across the lane to Val's house.

*   *   *

Val and Sarah were even friendlier than Hendry. Moeera was promptly invited for supper and to spend the night at least. They were eager to hear her tales of traveling and promised to tell her some of their own. She washed her hands and arms in a water basin out back before joining them at their table.

Moeera attacked the plate of food with no distraction; she'd been hungry for quite a while.

"Look at that," Val said to Sarah. "Your cooking is irresistible even to a giant."

Sarah smiled. "She has good taste, I see; but she's hardly a giant. Just a bit tall."

Moeera stopped to glance at the couple watching her. "It's delicious," she said. "Best home cooking I ever ate."

"Now who would want to eat a home?" Sarah joked.

She and Val laughed.

"How long has it been since you had something to eat?" Val asked.

"I honestly don't remember," Moeera said. "I've been running for my life so much I lost track."

"Running!" Val exclaimed. "Running from what?"

"Bunch of fiends that burned my house down ... flying bat ... High Rollers ... you name it--it's been chasing me."

"Lordy!" Val said. "Where was all this?"

"Gillikin Country. The house was in the forest," Moeera recalled. "One second things were fine. I lived with my friend Carrie and her husband. The next I was driven away by robbers."

"What of your friends?" Sarah asked.

"The robbers set fire to our home. I tried to help Carrie get out, but she was still in there when the roof fell down. So, I ran."

"Oh, no! Terrible, terrible," Sarah gasped.

"You're lucky to be alive!" Val said.

"Yes," Moeera said.

She was alive; that much was true. As for luck she wasn't so sure. Now that she'd thought about it some more she felt quite at loose ends.

She was half-trained in witchcraft. Or was she? She had no idea how much knowledge Carrie had had. Or how Carrie compared to other magic users. Moeera could do a few big things, a few little things, and what else?

"Are you all right?" Sarah asked. "Seemed like you were someplace else."

"I was," she murmured. "I mean my mind wandered."

"You've been through a lot," Val stated. "You're welcome here until you've recouped your energy."

"Thank you," Moeera said.

"Are you tired?" Sarah asked.

"I'm exhausted," Moeera answered.

Sarah stood up, patted Moeera's hand. "Come with me, Moeera. We have just the thing."

Chapter Twenty-four

Sarah ushered Moeera into a teeny, little room along the back of the house. "Here's our spare bed," she said. "It's yours as long as you need it." The little bed had a fluffy pillow and a patchwork quilt. Every color of the rainbow had a place in that quilt.

Moeera smiled. "Thank you. It's really nice. I'll probably be out of your hair tomorrow."

"No need to rush, dear," Sarah said. "It's what extra beds are for-- visitors. You've been through a hard experience. Rest."

"I will," Moeera said. "Anything I can do to help out around here, let me know."

"Of course," Sarah said. "There are a couple cloths and towels in those drawers there. Feel free to wash up if you like. The spring house is down the hill out back. The outhouse is a right turn between here and the barn."

Moeera's head churned with all the new information.

"Sleep well, Moeera," Sarah said. With that said she left Moeera to it.

Moeera sat on the small bed. It looked so comfortable she wanted to douse the lamp and go right to sleep. Would she fit in it, though? It had been constructed with a Munchkin-sized person in mind.

It was the nicest bed she'd ever seen. She tried it and found that she just barely fit if she lay corner to corner. She tried to roll onto her back, but she became scrunched in an uncomfortable position.

Oh, well.

She crawled out, pulling the covers with her. She spread them on the wooden floor and rolled herself up in them.

This is probably their children's former room, she thought. She would have drifted off right then, but she had to extinguish the lamp. It was on top of a chest of drawers by the door. Like the bed and the little dresser, it was miniature. She unrolled and stood to put the light out. Then she found the covers in the dark and rolled up once more.

She slept.

*   *   *

Moeera missed breakfast the next morning; she slept soundly until about eleven. She crawled from her cocoon of bedcovers and grabbed washcloth and towel from their spot. Then she left the little bedroom to visit the outhouse.

She took stock of the memories that the child's bedroom stirred in her. Thoughts of bedtime stories, learning to sweep up and dust, playing make-believe with her dolls.

It struck Moeera that if she never married she would never bear children of her own. Funny. She'd never given it a thought before. Seeing these people here, though; these nice transplants from the Munchkin Country she couldn't help but wonder if her choice was wrong. Maybe someone waited out there somewhere for her.

No! she thought. She was not willing to risk becoming her mother for love. She couldn't imagine there had been a time when her parents had been close and warm with each other the way these people were. What chance did she have?

She watched the sunlight shining through the tiny window near the outhouse roof. When she tucked washcloth and towel under her arm and headed for the spring house she heard grunting. The buppus chewed the weeds from the other side of its fence. Everything here was calm and slow. She breathed.

After washing the best she could at the spring house she thought about her next move. She planned to leave as soon as possible but didn't think she could get back to Dominic and Ben. She thought of the Nebulous but wondered about another run-in with the High Rollers. She needed to figure things out.

She found a large rock, too big to move from the back yard, and sat down to wrack her brain. Not coming to any helpful conclusions, she wandered till she found Sarah watering the kooblecots.

"Good morning," she said.

"Good morning, Moeera," Sarah said. "Did you sleep okay?"

"Very well. Thank you."

"I noticed you on the floor. You looked so comfortable I didn't have the heart to wake you."

"I was comfortable actually," Moeera said. "I was really beat, so the floor didn't bother me."

Sarah smiled. She put her watering can down and brushed her hands against each other.

"What chores can I help you with today?" Moeera asked.

"Oh, nothing," Sarah said. "Or maybe you can help with lunch. How's that sound?"

"It sounds fine," Moeera answered, "but I could do more."

"You've been through a lot," her friend said. "Take today at least to relax."

That gave Moeera plenty of idle time to search her memory. Could she use the Nebulous to return to the lane between Trappe and Kimbaloo?

She probably could because she could vividly remember the part of the lane with the downed tree. Still, she would need to be well-prepared. Another night of rest might help. Would the High Rollers be watching the lane waiting for her to return? Maybe.

Moeera sighed. She felt lost.

A man's voice said, "You must be the visitor Hendry told me about."

Moeera looked up to find a well-dressed man of the typical Munchkin stature holding his jacket lapels. His tall stovepipe hat sat atop his ancient, wizened face.

"That's me," Moeera said, standing up to shake the man's hand. Even with the hat he was shorter.

"Hendry tells me you come from Gillikin Country."

"Yes. I'm Moeera," she said, smiling cheerfully.

"Smollie Gurt," he said. "I'm the mayor of Slippakanu."

"Pleased to meet you, Mr. Mayor."

"You can call me Smollie," he said. He made a harrumphing noise. "Let me cut to the chase, Miss Moeera. Did your friends perish in that fire?"

Obviously, Hendry hadn't held anything back when discussing her with Gurt.

"Yes, sir," she said. "The house caught fire and they died when the roof fell in. It was thatched and the forest was bone dry. It never stood a chance."

"I see. Who were the ne'er-do-wells that set the house ablaze?"

"Excuse me?"

"Hendry said a mob was involved, that they attacked you."

"Yes," Moeera said, swallowing. "They came to our house like an army. We locked them out, but they set the place on fire."

"Terrifying," Smollie said. "Do you know who they were?"

"I'm not sure. Maxwell, the man leading them, had visited us just days before."

"He did? Why?"

"My friend Carrie made woods remedies for illnesses. He brought his mother who had pain in her leg. Carrie sold them a salve for the soreness. It seemed friendly enough."

Smollie blinked a couple times. "And then he brought a mob to your house. Strange."

"I think I'd call it diabolical myself."

"How did you escape?"

"I climbed out a back window," Moeera lied. She wanted to keep the part about the magic to herself. She was certain that was the reason the mob had attacked.

"But your friends …."

She looked him straight in the eyes. "They didn't make it. The smoke was thick, and the roof collapsed before they could climb out, too."

"I'm sorry," Smollie said. "That's terrible. You ran all the way here, Hendry told me. Amazing."

She nodded. "I was scared for my life."

"You managed to put a lot of distance between you and them. You're sure there wasn't any law breaking involved to make them try to cook you?"

Moeera looked at the mayor and said, "Would I tell you if I had broken the law?"

"Good point," Smollie said. "Let it be said that Slippakanu is a peaceful town. It's not very big therefore everyone knows each other. Keep that in mind."

"You'll have no trouble from me, Mr. Mayor," Moeera said.

"That's what I like to hear, my dear," he said. "Call me Smollie."

They shook hands.

"I'm pleased to have met you, Moeera. I'm sorry for your losses. Have a nice stay here among us. Until we meet again."

"Till we meet again," Moeera said.

She watched the elderly gentleman saunter down the lane. Curious man, she thought. Despite his nosiness he seemed to be a likable chap. She'd met more nice people in the past day than ever in her life.

Chapter Twenty-five

Moeera stood in the little bedroom's center, her head nearly touching the ceiling. She listened to her breath as she inhaled and exhaled, inhaled and exhaled. Her mind was calm. She closed her eyes, turning her sight inward.

"Ah so suh," she began chanting slowly. "So suh sun ba nay ... yay ba nay oh ... oo pa hay oh."

Her spell had begun. She continued chanting the activation words. Her mind focused on the task at hand. This time she had a mental picture in her head of where she wanted to go.

She made passes with her left hand all the while picturing the road with the cut tree to either side. She danced her left hand up the side of her body to the top of her head. Then she brought it down the other side. She felt herself warming as from a great fire.

*　　*　　*

Moeera surveyed the sight before her from her knees. There was less pain and fatigue this time, but her breath caught in her throat.

She was alone in the forest at the site of Carrie's house. The only recognizable thing left of the house was the boulder that used to stop the door. It stood in place, blackened from the fire that had taken the house and her teachers. She shuddered as a wave of nausea hit her.

When the feeling passed she rose from the forest floor. A few steps brought her to where the front wall used to be. She leaned on the boulder for support and ventured into the ruins.

The ground was littered and uneven. Here and there were shapes under the ash and dirt: the stove, the fireplace, not much else. The tiny chimney had collapsed; stones lie scattered all about.

Moeera dug through the ashes with her fingers. Had anything survived the flames?

A rock here, a pot there. She must have wandered into the former kitchen. She oriented herself by the hearth to aim for the living room. She began crying choked sobs at first, followed by a torrent of despair. There was nothing left. Absolutely ....

Wait. What was that?

She had tread on something hard. It rolled beneath her foot.

She probed through the debris with her fingertips, coming up with something small and slender. She pulled it from the dirt, gazing at it. It was about the thickness of her middle finger, blackened with an ever so slight curve.

The Wand of Murr. Somehow it had survived.

She wiped her eyes with her sleeve and walked out of the ruins.

She felt around until she found an invisible bench. She collapsed onto this and let the tears and anguish pour out.

*   *   *

Later she performed the Nebulous again to return to the Munkicks' spare bedroom.

Twice in one day, she thought. She frowned though. Why hadn't she arrived at the road to Kimbaloo?

She'd gone back to the most important place in her life, she guessed. She was still very much grieving the loss of Carrie and Charles. She sat on the tiny bed and held her legs up against herself.

Tomorrow she'd try again. This time she'd home in on Ben and Dominic themselves. It would work, too. The Nebulous would deliver her right to them.

Chapter Twenty-six

Ben and his friends hiked along the coast. The first day in this curious locale was spent just inside the tree line. They'd slapped together a crude but satisfying shelter. It dulled the breeze and protected them from the bright sun. The four piled into it and slept the day away.

When they woke up night was setting in, so they built a small fire and ate what food Gwen had in her purse.

"Do you still have your savings on you?" Ben asked Patricia.

"Yes," she said. "I'm more prepared for this excursion than you, love."

He laughed.

The four of them talked for a while. They decided to take turns watching the fire. Dominic first, then Gwen, then Patricia, and finally Ben.

Ben headed to the shelter, but Patricia said, "I don't know about you, love, but I'm sleeping under the stars tonight."

"Where?" he asked.

"Over there looks comfortable," she said. "Come on."

He followed her past a stand of young oak trees where they retired to the soft ground covered with fallen leaves.

*   *   *

The night watches went as well as they could for being lost in a strange land. Dominic watched for two hours by his estimation--he'd added wood to the fire three times. Then he'd woken Gwen who he told about his timekeeping system and went to sleep in the shelter.

Gwen didn't make it the full two hours. She was nodding off so much she woke Patricia early. She found her cousin nestled in Ben's arms just past the stand of oak.

Patricia walked Gwen to the shelter. Then she sat down by the fire.

Before too long she would need more wood. The bigger pieces were running low.

We didn't gather enough, she thought.

The embers beneath the burning logs glittered in the hot coals.

What a strange couple of days it had been. Good though considering she'd met Ben and Dom and Moeera. She shivered at the thought of Moeera being carried away by bat-people. Monsters and witches. God only knew what they'd find here--wherever here was.

Ben walked out of the shadows carrying an armload of branches. He deposited them on the remaining wood pile.

"Join you for your watch?" he asked.

"Sure," she said. "I'd love the company."

"Good," he said, sitting next to her on the cold ground.

She glanced at the sky. "Tonight is so romantic: moonlight, stars, the ocean just over there ...."

She leaned over and they kissed passionately.

When the kiss finally ended he said, "Being lost isn't so bad with you."

She smiled warmly. "Do you say that to all the girls?" she asked.

"Just you."

They kissed again.

"Your boss at the inn is going to hate me," he said.

"Why?" she asked.

"I stole his best waitress," Ben said.

"You didn't steal anything," she said matter-of-factly. "I came along of my own free will."

"How will they manage without you?"

"They'll get another server, silly," she said.

"What about your parents?" he asked.

"They'll probably worry," she said, shrugging her shoulders, "but they know I'm a big girl. Besides Gwen's my cousin, and she told her folks we were visiting Kimbaloo."

"Yes," Ben said.

"You're smirking."

"It's just that your intentions were good, but now we aren't in Kimbaloo."

"You've never been there before," she said.

"No."

"Then how do you know this isn't Kimbaloo?"

"No button trees," Ben said.

"None yet," Patricia amended.

"You're absolutely right," Ben said.

"So, what do you want to do tomorrow?" she asked.

"Keep following the coastline," he said.

She nodded. "That's what I thought you'd say."

"Any other ideas?" he asked.

"No," she said. "That sounds okay to me."

He added some wood to the fire which quickly caught. He found a nice tree trunk to sit against.

"Come here," he told her.

"Is that your best come hither look?" she asked.

"Yep."

"Alright."

She went over and sat between his legs, leaning back against his chest.

They sat there cuddling near the fire, both excited; both with hearts beating fast. It was comfortable enough that both drifted off to sleep as the fire turned to ashes.

*   *   *

Ben woke before dawn with a stiff back. He felt Patricia's weight pressing him back against the tree. He looked past her brown hair into the last vestiges of nighttime. All was calm.

Birds twittered in the treetops and the bushes. He noticed a red flash in the weeds that became a fox when it stood still. Then it disappeared again as it resumed its way home.

Ben stretched his arms out as far as he could, yawning. Patricia stirred, but didn't wake up. She snored softly.

"Let me up, hon," Ben said.

"Mrrmmm," she murmured.

"I have to get up."

"Why?"

"You know."

"No," she said.

"I need to pee."

"Oh," she said. She opened her eyes. "Oh, God, it's cold."

"That's because we let the fire go out."

"Mm-hmm."

Patricia got off of Ben and stood up, stretching. She held herself while he dashed into the woods to relieve himself. When he returned she said, "Let's go cuddle in the shelter."

"But the watch," he said.

"No one's about," she said, "and I'm cold."

"Okay."

They went to the shelter where Dominic was practically sleeping on top of Gwen. Patricia picked a spot in the leaves and reached out for Ben. He hugged her close and they slept.

* * *

A bit later Dominic woke Ben and Patricia. Morning had dawned with a multitude of birdsong and the pleasant fragrance of honey. Gwen was up foraging for berries. They started hiking again.

The hills sloped downward bringing them back to the rocks. They smelled the salty surf washing the land continuously. An hour's walk brought them to an established road which led them inland. Cottages dotted the countryside. Pastureland and fields stretched into the distance separated by low rock walls. Sheep grazed in the pastures by the hundreds.

The picturesque scene gave way to a bigger surprise. A small band of riders mounted on magnificent creatures that moved with speed and grace came toward them from the distance.

"Should we be afraid?" Patricia asked.

"They're beautiful," Ben said. "Look at those animals!"

"Who are they?" Gwen asked.

They'd soon find out. The riders slowed the majestic beasts to an easy canter.

"Ho, strangers!" the lead man called. He was large, blond-haired, and fair-complexioned. He wore a light blue, tight-fitting coat, tight-fitting trousers, and a striped cloak.

"Hello!" Ben called.

The animals came to a stop in a small cluster. The man slid from his saddle, approaching the travelers.

"I am Jarlath," he said. "Ye are visitors here, are ye not?"

337

Patricia stepped up to him and said, "We are. We seem to have gotten lost."

The man winked. "I daresay ye couldn't choose a finer place to be lost in, lovely lady."

Introductions were made. Jarlath's fellow riders included two men named Aengus and Ewan; and two women named Fiona and Shannon. All were extremely fair-haired, fair-skinned, and tall.

"So where are we anyway?" Dominic asked. "We didn't expect to find ourselves by the sea."

"Yer in the Land of the Young," Shannon said with a mischievous grin. "How do ye not know where ye are?"

"We were in the forest near Kimbaloo," Gwen said.

"I know of no land called Kimbaloo," Fiona said. Her long hair cascaded down around her shoulders reaching almost to her feet. She had a very calm look about her as she studied the newcomers.

"We found a big mound of earth by the roadside," Ben said, "and we went through some doors inside. The first two were decorated with a picture of an island."

"The Land of the Young is an island," Aengus said.

"I believe yer coming here had some magic involved," Ewan added. "What say ye, Fiona?"

She looked at them in a puzzled sort of way. "Yes," she said, "it could very well have been magic that brought ye here."

"Perhaps Fi can look into it further," Jarlath said. "She knows the ways of magic."

She nodded.

"Come with us," Jarlath said. "We don't live far away--just over yonder. Ride with us."

"We don't have ...," Dominic said, trailing off.

"Horses?" Jarlath asked.

"Is that what they're called?" Gwen asked. "They're so beautiful."

"Ye never saw a horse before?" Shannon asked incredulously. Her red hair was decorated with bright combs.

They shook their heads.

"We'll have to help ye up then, aye?" Aengus said.

Gwen and Patricia rode with Aengus and Ewan while Ben and Dominic

338

rode with Fiona and Shannon respectively.

"These horses are amazing!" Ben cried as they galloped toward the largest grouping of houses.

Fiona laughed and threw her head back, her hair tickling his face.

Chapter Twenty-seven

Moeera tried once more using the Nebulous to find Ben and Dominic. This time she held the Wand of Murr as she chanted the activation spell. The blackened stick glowed faintly its light building in intensity as she performed the spell. Alas, this time she didn't journey anywhere. She held the two brothers in her mind's eye, but when the lightshow ended she remained in the little bedroom.

Strange, she thought. What could I have done wrong?

She didn't know. She sighed, slipped the wand into her bodice, and pondered the matter.

It was then that she had a personal insight. Her life as a witch was over no sooner than it had begun--a depressing conclusion. She no longer had Carrie to teach her. She knew magic, but not very much, she thought.

She decided to put the past behind her and stay around Slippakanu. Maybe she could get some help and build her own quaint house. It needn't be near as large as the Munchkin houses--maybe higher ceilings. Maybe she'd like living there.

She stayed with Val and Sarah for three more days during which she helped tend the crops, bake the bread, and care for the (always hungry) buppus. After that she thanked them deciding it time she ventured farther down the road to explore her options.

The people of Slippakanu were primarily farmers. She found only farms the first day. That night she kept to herself sleeping in a hammock.

The second day following the main road she encountered blacksmiths, a miller, carpenters, masons, woodcutters, and more farmers. Finally, she came to The Merry Kitten.

The Merry Kitten turned out to be more than the local watering hole. It housed the town's general store, too. The town depended on it for trading goods and supplying any materials the farmers couldn't manufacture or grow themselves.

Moeera inquired with the bartender, Ninj, if they wanted any help.

"What's your story?" Ninj asked. She was a thin stick of a woman with brown hair and an equally thin nose.

"Chased out of my old home," Moeera told her. "Friends died. I'm trying to start over, and this town seems like a nice place to put down roots."

"You don't mind the absence of any men your size?"

"I welcome it," Moeera said. "I don't need to be partnered with a man."

Ninj frowned. "No women your size either, honey."

"I meant that I'm willing to stay alone. Fate can decide if there's an adequate mate coming my way."

"Well! Fate can be funny, and fate can be fickle. You realize you're the first big person I've seen since settling here by the river."

"You moved here?"

"I helped found the place," Ninj said proudly. "I followed Smollie on his trek to build a new colony free from some of the rules we didn't care for."

"So Slippakanu is brand new," Moeera said.

"Almost, yes," Ninj said. "We've been here nearly twenty years. The town's growing, too. Had another wedding ceremony last month for a couple who came here as children."

"Was one of them Val and Sarah's?"

"The Maises? Yes. You met them?"

"Mm-hmm. They put me up when I got here a few days ago," Moeera said.

"How's that going?"

"Very nicely," Moeera said, "but I said goodbye yesterday. They're nice people. It was just time to move on."

"So … now what?" Ninj asked. "You sleeping out on the ground?"

"In a hammock actually."

Ninj shot Moeera a wry grin. "We can do better than that if you'd like. How long you going to be around?"

"I think I'd like to stay in the area permanently. The people I've met so far are nice," Moeera said.

Ninj looked thoughtful. "Do you have any money?" she asked.

"A halfscrot is all."

"Well!"

She drummed her fingers on the bar.

"Can you sew?"

"Of course," Moeera said.

"With any skill?"

"Yes, I believe so."

"One job here that isn't filled at all is that of tailor. We could use one."

Moeera thought.

Ninj added a crucial bargaining chip: "Of course it's repairing we really need; not necessarily new clothes production."

"I suppose I can do that," Moeera said.

"The farmers' wives will be thrilled to hear that. No more making do by themselves. And no more trips outside town to visit a tailor."

"Okay."

"Tell you what. You can set up shop in my backroom. We don't need all the space we have back there. It'll work. We can put in a couple extra walls so you can live there, too. At least till you save some money."

"Who's the boss 'round here?" Moeera asked.

"Me," Ninj said. "I own the place. Welcome aboard."

Ninj stuck out a hand. Moeera took it and shook.

"Thanks, Ninj," she said, smiling.

"You're welcome," Ninj said, "but you may not feel it's a good thing when you see all the repair work you're going to get."

"Bring it on," Moeera said. "I have nothing else to do."

*   *   *

The wives of the town did bring it on. They brought Moeera baskets of clothing with rips, tears, holes, and frays. She mended and darned and patched until her fingers ached. The clothes pile to fix grew taller and taller and kept her busy.

She thought of it as job security and imagined the pretty little house she might have built soon.

*   *   *

"How'd it go?" Ninj asked after the second day Moeera was officially a tailor.

"Unbelievably," Moeera muttered. "For such a small town there sure are a lot of damaged clothes!"

"You did say they should bring it on," Ninj chuckled. "But, hey! You're employed. You're new, but you're already an important part of our community."

"I guess."

"Aw. Have a drink? Eggs is prepping for evening service. Why don't I take my break and we can chat?"

"Fine," Moeera said.

"Great," Ninj said. "I'll order us some grub from the Egg-man."

She handed Moeera a tall, cold glass of Munchkin beer. Then she strode into the kitchen.

Moeera sat on a stool and sipped her beer.

"Hard to believe that not so long ago this place was wilderness, isn't it?" the man sitting a few stools down asked. He was a Munchkin like everyone else thereabouts.

"I guess so," Moeera said. She looked at the short man. He wore the typical Munchkin fashions excepting the coloration. Instead of blue from head to toe he wore gray pants, a black waistcoat, and a conical, white hat.

"You're new in Slippakanu, aint'cha?" he inquired.

"What makes you say that?" Moeera asked.

He smiled. "There's no girls as big as you are here."

"Oh, so you think I'm fat?" she asked, unable to resist fooling with the nosy man.

"No, no," he said. "You're not fat--you're knee-high to a poplar is all." He turned from his drink. "Name's Gormib."

"Moeera," she said, "and I am new here. I've taken a job here at the Kitten mending clothes."

"You're the new tailor then."

"Yes, she's the new tailor, Gormib," Ninj said, climbing atop the stool next to Moeera. "Don't scare her away!"

"Now why would I do that?" he asked as if it was a joke. "I was just being neighborly is all. Taking an interest."

"Being nosy," Ninj said.

"I'm not nosy, Mrs. Avann," Gormib said.

"Really?" she asked.

"Yeah," he said. "Oh, Mrs. Avann, do you want to hear a new song I wrote?"

Ninj looked at him with feigned surprise. "You wrote a song? No kidding! Moeera, Gormib wrote a song! Isn't that crazy?"

Gormib didn't give Moeera the chance to reply. He blurted out, "It's called 'Rolling in the Hay'!"

Ninj's jaw dropped a mile as he sang:

> Rolling in the hay in the barn
> On a hot, sweaty night
> With my gal.
> Rolling in the hay with my love
> Our hearts beating awful fast
> We kiss each other's lips
> While we're in the hay.
> My lady fair holds me tight
> While we're rolling in the hay.
> She whispers in my ear....

At that point he began coughing, trying to clear his throat. When he could speak again he said, "That's what I have so far, uh, I'll sing you all of it when it's finished."

Ninj painted such an amiable smile on her face that Moeera wondered if she'd had a stroke.

"Wow!" Ninj gushed. "You wrote that? I'm impressed."

"Yeah, Mrs. Avann, I uh wrote it for you."

"Can you believe it?" she asked Moeera, who was trying very hard to not burst out laughing.

"I have other songs, too," Gormib said. "I'll sing--"

"No!" Ninj commanded. "You skedaddle now and finish the rest of that song."

"But I can write it later," he said. "I can sing you other songs."

"No, I want to hear the rest of that one. Go on now. Git!"

Dumbfounded, Gormib downed the last of his beer and headed out.

Ninj closed her eyes. "Thank God!"

"What's his story?" Moeera demanded.

"He's a crackpot," Ninj said, "but he's mostly harmless."

"Mostly, you say."

344

"Yes," she said and laughed. "The only danger is letting him corner you; he runs his mouth infinitely."

"He likes you."

"Me and others I'm sure," Ninj said. "He's a pain if you have to listen to him too long. Especially when he's feeling amorous."

"Something has to be wrong with him," Moeera said.

"Oh, yes," Ninj said. "He claims he's a wizard."

Moeera nearly spilled her drink. "A wizard!"

"Yes," Ninj said. "He didn't help found Slippakanu--he followed after us a few years later after the hard work was already done."

"Does he do magic?"

"He says he does," Ninj said, "but I've never seen any."

"Oh," Moeera said.

"He has a pretty high opinion of himself, the shrimp," Ninj said. "Said he was compelled to come here for some important reason. He's just a weird guy who likes to babble."

"Right," Moeera said.

"Order up!" Eggs called.

Ninj went behind the bar to grab two plates of steaming goodness.

"Here we are," she said, placing one in front of Moeera. "You hungry?"

"Yes," Moeera said. "Thanks."

"You're welcome," Ninj said.

They began to eat.

"So, what did you do before you came here, Moeera?"

Moeera contemplated what to say. "I lived in the woods," she said, "learning woodcraft and all about plants and animals. I learned a little bit about herbs and healing plants."

"Interesting," Ninj said between bites, "maybe you could teach me about some of the plants here."

"Maybe," Moeera said. "With the river nearby, I bet you have jewelweed."

"What does jewelweed do?"

"Helps to cure poison ivy rashes," Moeera said.

"That sounds useful."

"Yes."

"We could fabricate some of this cure to sell here," Ninj said.

"Sure," Moeera said. "It wouldn't be hard to do."

Chapter Twenty-eight

Moeera stayed happily in Slippakanu for half a year. She did her best to fit in despite being the tallest person around. Her fingers grew strong and nimble from all the mending she did.

Hendry Munkick helped her make arrangements to get a small cottage built on a plot of land not far from The Merry Kitten. She gasped when she saw the tiny house finished. It was beautiful.

It stood one story high with ceilings to suit her height. The peaked roof was made with wooden shingles that looked much stronger than the thatch she lived under before. She had four rooms: kitchen, bedroom, living room, and mud room. Nunn the blacksmith installed the kitchen woodstove that very day.

Ninj and her children Joseph and Robert helped paint the house a cheery yellow with white window frames and flower boxes. Moeera had never been so happy before in her life. She'd found a place where she fit in, truly fit in. Now she had the digs to prove it. It didn't include magic, but at least she felt safe and loved. She had friends--true friends.

*   *   *

She wondered on and off about what Ninj told her about Gormib's claims he was a wizard. She encountered him a few times at The Merry Kitten, but she didn't draw his attention the way Ninj did. The little Munchkin didn't seem very magical, but she wondered all the same.

About a week after her house was finished she had the day off from work. She was outside in the pleasant sunshine hanging laundry when she heard singing. It was off-key and coming from the lane. She looked over to see Gormib strolling past in The Merry Kitten's direction.

"Hello there, Mr. Whitecap!" she called out.

The small man ceased his singing, looked her way.

She waved.

He strolled over the yard.

"What's that you called me?" he asked.

"Mr. Whitecap," she said, "because you wear a white hat, that's all. I don't know your last name."

He nodded. His small, black eyes gazed piercingly at her. "I remember you. You're the tailor."

"I am indeed," she said.

"You can call me Gormib," he said. "You're Moeera, I believe."

She nodded. "What are you about this fine day?"

"Nothing much," he said. "Business is slow today."

"What do you do?"

"Peddler," he said. "Odds and ends, tools, things I make, things I find. I left my pushcart at home today, though."

"That's a shame," Moeera said. "Maybe I could use something. "I'm running short on clothespins."

"Oh ... er ... I suppose I do have some of those--not with me, though."

"Mine seem to fall off the line and get lost."

"That's too bad," he said. "Next time I'm by I'll bring some along."

"Good," she said. "I'll hold you to it."

"If you'll excuse me," he said, "I'm on my way to get a new canteen. Then I'm going to visit the river."

"The river?" Moeera asked.

"Sure. Yeah. Lots to look at there. Sliders, turtles, frogs .... Maybe I'll do a bit of fishing."

"Do you swim in it?"

"Yes, if it's hot enough, and it's hot enough today."

"Have an excellent time then," Moeera said.

"Thank you," he said. "I shall."

"Watch out for sorcerers," she said firmly as he turned away.

He stiffened as if he'd been burned. "What did you say?"

"Watch out for sorcerers."

He looked back at her questioningly.

"Ninj told me you're a wizard."

"I was," he said slowly. "Everything around here seems to work fine without magic, though."

"But you do know magic?"

"Of course," he said. "Look there. At your line."

She looked to see new clothespins materializing before her eyes.

"Hmm," she said. "Neat trick. What else can you do?"

He traced lines and loops in the air with his left hand while he muttered an incantation.

Moeera felt the wind blow by, saw it ruffling her clothes. They flapped against the line like birds ready to move skyward.

Moeera clapped her hands. "Why are you a peddler?"

"No one really needs magic around here," he told her. "Fellow has to make money."

"I guess, but why not find a place where the folks need magic?"

"I like it here," he said. "Plenty of people my size. Being a Munchkin is easier when you're not surrounded by tallers like you."

It made perfect sense, but ....

She focused her mind on the little man. What was he thinking about?

A mosquito buzzed at her ear.

Slap!

She held the dead insect against her neck and reached to touch Gormib's hand. Just the briefest contact flooded her mind with images. Tall beings in cloaks in the shadows. Wands glowing with power. Snakes. Blades. Fire.

"Hunh!" she gasped. "You're hiding! Hiding here amongst your own kind."

"How do you know that!" he snapped. He saw her brush the mosquito from her neck.

"You!" he gasped. "You know magic. But you're so young! How old are you?"

"Eighteen," she said.

"How?" he asked. "Who taught you?"

"Is that important?" she asked. "They can't teach me anymore--they're dead."

"How did they die? That's important," he said.

"Angry mob and a horror called a blood witch."

"A blood witch," he said, sliding to the ground. "How is it you're still

349

breathing?"

"My teacher made me flee using The Nebulous."

"I see," he said. "And the blood witch?"

She shook her head. "The house we were in collapsed on her. It was burning. She should be dead."

"Hmm," he said. "She should be dead. I hope she is. Blood witches are evil beings. They destroy the living--in ways worse than killing."

Moeera shivered. "Are you hiding from other blood witches?"

"If any are after me I am," he said. "There are bad people who are after me. I'm most definitely hiding from them."

"Who are they?"

"I thought you read my thoughts," he said.

"Just a few vague images," she said. "I saw tall, cloaked people and snakes."

"That would be them," he said. "You're better off not knowing any more about them."

"Maybe you can tell me more about them next time," she said.

"What next time?" he asked.

"The next time you come by," she said matter-of-factly. "We can talk about this sort of thing. Far as I know we're the only two around involved with magic."

He frowned, but she could tell he was thinking. After several minutes he said, "It would be nice to speak to someone else without having to guard what I say. You're right about that."

She nodded.

"Would you like to go walking with me to the river?" he asked. "We could get to know each other better as fellow conjurers."

"I'd like that very much," Moeera said, hoping he wasn't as annoying as Ninj had led her to believe.

"Come along then," he said.

Moeera locked her house, pocketing the key. She strode on down the lane with the small wizard.

"I was always bored in Munchkin Country," Gormib said. "I was assigned to The Lollipop Guild as an apprentice. I had no interest in that whatsoever. After doing a lackluster job for a while they drummed me out."

"I joined a barbershop quartet--got drummed out of that too. Joined

350

the carpentry alliance--washed out before building my first neighborhood. You notice the pattern."

Moeera nodded.

"I didn't know what to do," Gormib said. He kicked some stray pebbles on the lane.

"I decided to visit my cousin Lotty who lived several towns away. She had her life together and could be intelligent without saying 'I told you so'. I'd find out her opinion about what I might do to be productive, but keep myself amused, too."

"What did she say?" Moeera asked.

"I didn't make it to her," Gormib said. "I got about halfway there and fell into a trap. Someone had dug a pit smack in the middle of the road."

"I hollered and yelled at the top of my lungs, but no one came by. It got dark. An animal or two peeped over the edge at me, happy to see it was me down there and not them, I guess. I sat down in the dirt to wait."

"Finally, when I'd half fallen to sleep I heard a voice say, 'Now what have we here?'"

"I didn't say anything on account of being kind of scared, you know. The voice said, 'Come here.' I rose into the air like a balloon. Now that was scary!"

"I got my feet on the road by the pit and looked up at this man waiting for me. He was tree-sized, gaunt, and dressed all in black. His dark beard was close-shaven. He wore a tall hat that looked more like a crown than a Munchkin-style hat."

"He asked me who I was in his deep, commanding voice. I reluctantly told him. Then he wanted to know why I was abroad."

"I said, 'I'm just from that way and going to visit family I have in Kooble.'"

"He told me that sadly I would be doing no such thing."

"'Why not?' I asked him."

"'Because I'm enslaving you,' he told me. 'Good help is hard to find.'"

He took me to his hideout then using The Nebulous or a similar thing he called 'The Fool's Rainbow'. He was a warlock or sorcerer, I never figured out which. He cast a spell that bound me to the plot of land his residence was on and treated me like a slave."

Moeera listened with rapt attention. "How'd you get away?"

"He didn't count on my paying such close attention to his incantations. I carefully memorized all I could and kept track of what they were for. One night when he visited some friends I dug into his largest book of magic and found the charm to release me from bondage."

"I quickly brewed up the odorant that should let me pass beyond the spell's barriers. It worked, I got loose, and I ran as far as I could. But I couldn't find my way home again! I was lost."

"I wandered here, there, everywhere. I eventually discovered I was by a river, so I wandered alongside until I found the docks of folks from Slippakanu. They had left my own town years before so I decided I might be safe here."

Moeera nodded. "I see," she said. "What about what's his name?"

Gormib stirred the dirt with a long stick. "Up to no good somewhere, I'm sure."

"Perhaps he's forgotten you," Moeera said.

"Probably not," Gormib said firmly.

"Oh?"

"The images you saw in my mind are the fears I have that he and his fearsome friends are looking for me."

"He probably caught someone else to help him by now."

"Sure, maybe …."

"What did you do?" Moeera asked, intuition blazing.

"I … stole his bird," Gormib said.

"Stole his bird!"

"Yes. His raven!"

Moeera clutched at her forehead. Ugh! This guy is stupid, she thought.

"Why'd you do that?" she asked.

"It's magic, the raven is …."

Her voice got loud. "Of course, it is! So why did you take it?"

"Really!" Gormib exclaimed. "He stole it from someone else, and then when I escaped I stole it from him!"

"Why!" Moeera demanded.

"It tells the truth."

Moeera was speechless.

"I couldn't leave it--it would've helped him track me down. It answers questions, and it always tells the truth! But now when I ask it if he's

352

searching for me it tells me he most certainly is. He and all his friends."

Moeera shook her head. His tale was so preposterous, but he seemed truthful. Why would he say he learned his magic while a prisoner if it wasn't true?

They arrived at The Merry Kitten. She waited outside while he bought a canteen. After what seemed like an eternity he came out and filled the vessel with water at the hand pump.

"That's better," Gormib said cheerily. He pointed to a trail on the other side of the road. "That's the quickest way to the rocks."

Gormib led Moeera down the trail humming as he went. It appeared to get heavy use, the ground was packed down firmly in its center and the weeds and shrubs began about six inches to either side. It took them through a woody area where it descended easily, but purposely till they emerged near the riverbank.

The Winkie River is big and wide and deep. Moeera watched the water roar along, diverging around a small island not much more than a few boulders topped with dirt, leaves, and a single small aspen tree. Close to the shore on the side they were on was a shallow area formed by a kind of sandbar. To their left all along the bank was a boulder field.

"Let's take a break over on the rocks," Gormib said.

"Okay," Moeera said.

She carefully followed him over the rocks until he sat down on one. She chose a long, flat boulder next to his.

He stared at the river with his beady, little eyes.

"It's very impressive," Moeera said.

"Yes," he agreed. "They plan to build a mill near here soon right at the river. They actually started it, I guess; it's a bit farther up."

Moeera nodded. "That's a great idea."

"Yes," he said. "Did you know that there's a section of the river way before it gets here they call The Trick River?"

"Nope," she said.

"It changes direction from time to time," he said, grinning.

"It overflows? Changes course?"

"No, it reverses direction entirely, then switches back, then reverses."

"It certainly sounds tricky."

"Hey, what do I see?" he commented. "The show's about to start."

"Show?" Moeera asked. "What show?"

"Look there!" he said, pointing to the edge of the boulder field.

Moeera saw a brown creature moving toward the water in a serpentine fashion. It had a long neck and a sleek, furry body. She watched it dive into the churning water.

"What's that?" she asked.

"A slider," he said. "Great swimmer. They live in nests all along the riverbanks. Spend most of their day hunting and fishing, but they know how to have fun, too! Watch!"

The slider swam across the river to the far bank which looked steeper and bereft of boulders. Once there it was joined by half a dozen others that seemed to appear from nowhere. Moeera smiled when the animals scrambled to the top of the incline and ran down launching their bodies at the water. They slid down the lower bank like missiles darting into the river.

Splish! Splash!

Moeera laughed to see the streamlined critters sliding into the water, diving under, and then popping up to scurry up the slope again to repeat the process.

"They are something else, aren't they?" Gormib asked.

Moeera nodded. "They're so comical … and cute!"

They watched the sliders for a while by the river. At one point their numbers grew to include as many as thirty of the water-loving mammals. A few even ventured up onto the rocks watching the pair with inquiring, curious eyes. They rose up, sitting on their hind legs while "standing" balanced by their tails and hind feet. Their long bodies and stubby whiskers made them resemble little people. They sat near the lady and the Munchkin as if to await being invited into a conversation. Then they scampered off to rejoin their companions at play.

"Amazing," Moeera said.

"I never get tired of watching their antics," Gormib said. "You don't know any spells to communicate with animals, do you?"

"No, I don't," Moeera said, thinking of the lost ring that let her talk to Landry and the flying monkeys as plain as if they were people.

Chapter Twenty-nine

Months passed. Moeera put down her roots so-to-speak. She toiled away at her little tailor shop in the Kitten, even beginning to fashion some clothing from scrap. She constructed a weaving loom that she used at her little house, and she brought some of the prettiest woven fabrics she made to work to please her clientele.

She talked to Gormib once in a while but found him conceited and shallow. She could easily see why Ninj found him so annoying.

Sometimes she would explore by the river and watch the sliders at play. Some of them became so familiar with her they would walk along with her, watching her pick jewelweed and cattails.

Ninj was Moeera's best and truest friend so sometimes when the need arose Ninj would leave her in charge of things at The Merry Kitten. It was on just such an occasion that the mayor arrived with work for the tailor.

"I have a tear in the lapel of my favorite suit," Smollie Gurt told Moeera as she poured him a glass of beer.

"That's a shame, Smollie," Moeera said.

"Could you take a look at it, put it on the top of your work pile?"

"I don't know, Smollie," Moeera said. "That wouldn't be fair to everyone else, would it?"

"I thought you might say that," he said, sadly. He looked ancient as ever. The mayor of Slippakanu had probably known God shortly after He created the world.

Moeera smiled. "Oh, Smollie! Of course, I can bump you to the top of the list. No worries, sir!"

He grinned. "Thank you, dear. I appreciate it."

"Anything for you, old dad. After all, if it hadn't been for you starting your own town here I wouldn't have a place to live."

"You'd have found somewhere," he said between sips.

"Not so nice as this," she said.

"So where is Mrs. Avann?" Smollie asked.

"She had some things she wanted to trade for in Treetop Town. I'm minding the tavern for her. Me and Eggs anyway."

"Speaking of Eggs;" Smollie said, "see if he can make me a grilled cheese, pretty please."

"I'll check," Moeera said.

She walked to a window and called out, "One super grilled cheese sandwich, please!"

Eggs's voice echoed the order back.

"Thanks," Smollie said.

"You're welcome!" Moeera replied.

*   *   *

The sun was setting in the hills when Ninj returned that evening. She and her boys parked the wagon by the Kitten and gave the giant buppus a bucket of feed to work on. Then Ninj went inside to check on Moeera.

"How'd it go?" Moeera asked.

"Very well," Ninj said. "The folks in Treetop Town were happy for the food supplies I took them. They traded me some very nice things. Wine, jam, tea, berries, wood, and handmade crafts. How was the bar?"

"Fine," Moeera said. "The usual crowd. If you call them a crowd, that is. Nothing hard at all."

"That's good," Ninj said. She pulled a tall blue and white candle from her big belt pouch. "I brought back this candle for you."

She retrieved a glass saucer with her other hand which she set on the bar. Then she set the candle firmly on the saucer. Moeera examined it, smiling.

"Thank you; it's nice."

"I saw it and thought you might like it."

"I do," Moeera said. "So now what? No one's here right now. Eggs left. It's been slow."

"In that case I think we can close early tonight," Ninj said. "Would you like a ride to your place?"

"Sure."

After the tavern was closed up and Moeera was at her front door she heard the sound of the buppus tramping down the lane pulling the wagon behind.

She let herself in and lit the lamps. She was tired, but she sat at her kitchen table and lit the candle. It gave off a pleasant scent of spruce trees.

Nice, she thought, studying the candle which had the look of the blue and white colors being entwined.

The glass saucer had a mark she expected was the craftsman's seal. A sentence was painted on the saucer, but it was all Greek to Moeera.

Thoughts flooded her head. Ben and Dominic chasing her in the graveyard. Meeting the winged monkeys. Being abducted by the High Rollers. Falling into Hell. Finally, she thought of her narrow escape from the burning cottage in the Gillikin Woods. Her eyes closed and she shook her head side to side to banish the memories.

I'm putting time as well as distance between me and that, she thought.

She opened her eyes again. Life here was good. She knocked her hand on the table.

The candle burned silently casting its cheery warmth across the kitchen table. Moeera watched for a few more minutes. Then she focused on the flame. She whispered a single word, and the candle was out.

She outened the lamps and went to bed.

*   *   *

"I experienced the strangest thing on my way to work this morning," Ninj was telling the morning cook Scott as Moeera walked in.

"Oh, what was that?" Moeera asked.

"Good morning, Moeera," Ninj said. "I said hello to Starchus Vay, and she flat out ignored me!"

"That's very strange," Moeera agreed, frowning. "Are you certain she heard you?"

Ninj waved her arm in exasperation. "She looked right at me! Then she turned around and walked away!"

"Goodness!" Moeera said.

"What'd you do to her?" Scott asked.

"Nothing I can think of," Ninj said. "I'll tell you what, though; sister-in-law or not I'm mad."

"Something similar happened to me this morning," Moeera said.

"Really? What?" Ninj asked.

"Bishop Mark was unlocking the church door, so I said, 'Good morning'. He nodded to me and said, 'Good night'."

"Well at least he said something," Ninj said.

"It was weird, though," Moeera said. "He seemed totally off, like he was asleep."

"Bishop Mark?" Ninj asked. "He's the most outgoing man in town!"

"Not today," Moeera said. "He seemed exhausted."

"Oh, dear," Ninj said. "I wonder if he's sick."

"I don't know," Moeera said. "I only know Smollie should be along soon to have his jacket lapel mended."

"Smollie and his dapper ways," Ninj said. "Sometimes I think his entire reason for starting a colony was so he could be a fancy-dressing mayor."

Moeera started toward her miniature tailor's shop in the back room.

"Wait, Miss Moeera," Scott said. "Could you help me pull down some supplies that are high up?"

Moeera threw Ninj a look as she headed into the kitchen. Scott liked to enlist her help in completing vertical tasks.

Ninj wiped the bar and counter tops, whistling as she did so. Her mind drifted. It still bugged her that Starchus had ignored her like that. She didn't understand it.

Oh, well, she thought, everyone had an off day here and there. Even Bishop Mark according to Moeera.

She put it out of her mind and worked on preparing for the day's customers.

*　　*　　*

At ten o'clock that morning Mayor Gurt shuffled in with his favorite suit jacket. He left it in Moeera's care and departed with the shortest of conversations.

Moeera was dumbfounded. Had the townspeople gone off the deep end? First Bishop Mark; now Smollie behaving out of character. Smollie never passed on the chit chat. Was it just an aspect of the Munchkins she'd missed seeing before? Did they get moody this time of year?

Scott and Ninj both seemed normal enough. Although now Ninj was miffed about her sister-in-law's snub. Moeera listened to her whistling. It sounded cheery enough.

She sighed and took out a needle and thread to fix the jacket.

*   *   *

Smollie Gurt speed walked from The Merry Kitten. The old man moved with a gait that belied his advanced age. He didn't appear to even see anyone else.

Eventually he reached the Church of the Believers. His hand didn't even connect with the door before it opened, and a calm voice bid him enter.

Bishop Mark pulled Smollie inside and shut the door. He said nothing more, turning away from the old man and walking into the sanctuary. The bald man headed for the altar avoiding the beams of sunlight shining through the side windows.

Smollie followed him in the same manner. Wherever a beam of sunshine shone down he stepped around it.

Parishioners sat in the first row of pews staring blankly ahead at the golden cross on the altar. Starchus Vay sat like a lump concentrating on the cross. Next to her sat her wife Ginj. Farmer Toby sat sweating away covered with dust and bits of hay. Arnie Potts held his pipe in his hand, but it wasn't lit.

And there were others: Fred the Blacksmith; Fred's cousin Hoops of the Lollipop Guild who had brought a hay wagon load of candy, beer, and goods from Munchkin Country; Tiffany the squealer who kept everyone informed (she wouldn't be informing anyone about this clandestine meeting or about anything else anymore for that matter). Seven kids also sat there-- far too still for children.

"Well," a blood-chilling voice said from the altar, "the gang's all here."

The figure that came strolling forward flanked stiffly by Bishop Mark and Smollie Gurt wore dressings of white gauze that flowed from her arms like wings. She looked less nightmarish than she had in Carrie and Charles's small house. In the dimly lit church her white, flowing raiment made her resemble an angel from the Bible.

The blood witch towered over the Munchkins. Instead of the animalistic woman whose mouth spilled blood down her front this aspect of the woman walked straight and tall. Her raiment was neat and complete, quite regal-looking with her posture. The white clothes and skin made her blend into the elaborately decorated sanctuary, a statue.

359

She surveyed the gathering, noting the many faces. She had taken control of each and every one of these people. More than twenty slaves were married to the darkness to do her bidding. Delightful.

"Now that we're all together I'd like to make my needs clear," she said.

She walked up to Fred. He was big and burly even for a Munchkin. She reached down, sliding a finger under his black beard to scratch his chin. He sat there stupidly, unable to move.

"You desire to serve me, don't you?" she crooned.

Fred nodded, staring sappily.

"That's good," she said, enunciating each word crisply. "As I said I have certain … needs."

She stepped back to the center aisle where everyone could see her. "My friends, there is one who has come among you that must answer to me. Therefore, you will go amongst your fellow citizens and families spreading the gift I bestow upon you now. You are all my family."

The Munchkins stared at her blankly. With an extra bit of effort, they said "yes" in a chorus.

"Now line up for communion," she said.

They stood as one, filing into a line that led to her in front of the altar. Starchus Vay was first in line, stepping up to the witch who took her by the shoulders. She stood oddly still as the witch leaned her head in as if to kiss the lady's lips. The pale white being's mouth bypassed Starchus's and sought her neck instead. The blood witch bit quicker than lightning and her lips affixed to skin.

Starchus didn't flinch or struggle. She let the creature suck her blood for several minutes. The witch smiled at Starchus and nodded at the pews. The wife of Ninj's sister sat down with a thump.

The process repeated time and time again; male and female, adult and child. They all communed with their master. After she sipped twenty-three Munchkins' blood the witch's face took on a pinkish complexion. Her lips shone red as cherries.

"When all have come to meet me here they will receive my special blessing," she told them. She held Bishop Mark's hand tightly. Then she released him, and he sat down with the others.

She smiled; her eyes were flames. "We shall be a family--a family of blood! When we are all a family the fugitive will feel my vengeance."

360

Chapter Thirty

M
r. Munkick was in the field planting more kooblecots. Folks couldn't seem to get enough of the snappy fruit. He wiped his brow with his sweat rag and looked at the sun. It shone hotly until it passed behind some clouds.

"Ah," he said. "Finally, a break from this heat."

He pulled a barrel from the wagon, sliding it down a wooden ramp. As wood scratched wood thunder rumbled loudly. He stuck his head up to scan the sky.

"That was quick!" he said to himself, gaping at the ever-darker sky. It looked like this would be the last barrel of seedlings he planted.

How right he was!

The full-grown buppus harnessed and tethered to the wagon made a lowing noise.

"What is it, Bessie?" Hendry asked.

"Merrrooo," the buppus lamented.

"Just this last barrel of seedlings," he told her. "Then we'll stop planting kooblecots."

"Rooo!" Bessie groaned.

Hendry looked at the beast. "Storm, yes. We'll get to shelter in a minute."

Raindrops the size of teabags began falling.

"Yee gads!" Hendry cried. "Time to go home, Bessie!"

He never heard her groan a reply because a large shape sprung at him from out of nowhere.

Wolf!

But it wasn't a wolf. The attacker grappled him to the ground and pinned his arms underneath him in a very un-wolf-like manner. Hendry looked into the face of Fred the Blacksmith!

"Fred!" he said in shock. "What's wrong? Why?"

Fred said nothing. He leaned down over Hendry until the farmer could feel his hot breath.

Hendry tried to push his body up off the ground, but Fred was too heavy.

"Fred! I'm sorry!" Hendry cried. "Whatever I did to offend you--I was wrong!"

He blubbered underneath the bigger fellow.

Fred seemed to neither notice nor care. He struck his friend's neck, impaling his blood vessels with newly grown fangs.

Hendry screamed. He slipped into unconsciousness as the blacksmith sucked the blood from his veins.

* * *

"What are you doing here, Bessie?" Val asked the buppus. It sat at his gate still hitched to the wagon. A barrel of seedlings rolled around on its side.

He walked to it in the pouring rain.

"Where's Hendry?" he asked, frowning.

No answer. Well, what did he expect? He wanted to lead Bessie back over to Hendry's, but not in the drenching storm. Instead, he unhitched her from the wagon and led her into his own pen. She wandered into the barn to safety.

Val went inside the house.

"Strangest thing, Sarah," he said. "Bessie wandered over all hitched up for planting, but no sign of Hendry. I hope he's all right."

Sarah stepped out of the kitchen. She looked pale and tired. Behind her was Ginj Avann.

"Oh, hello, Ginj," Val said. "When did you get here?"

Sarah came up to Val, taking his hand in hers. Ginj circled around in back of him.

"Is everything okay?"

They set on him as one. Val was momentarily terrified as two pairs of fangs broke his skin. Then he was gone.

* * *

The door to the Merry Kitten banged open. Ninj glanced up to see Hoops

362

walk in.

"Hiya, Hoops," she called. "What'll ya have?"

He didn't answer--just stared at her intently. A little too intently.

"One of these days you're going to have to tell me why they named you Hoops," she laughed.

Silence.

She stopped what she was doing and stared back. She placed her hands on the bar and leaned against it, her elbows bent.

"Hoops, what gives? Are you sore because I didn't take more pops off your hands? The back room's full of 'em."

He continued staring with that dull look.

"Okay, so don't talk to me, fella," Ninj said. "Don't expect me to cry over you and your lollipops!"

He edged toward the bar ever so slowly.

Maybe he fell and hit his head, Ninj thought.

A tremendous clatter rang out from the kitchen. Ninj ran to the window and peered through.

"You all right, Scott?" she shouted.

He wasn't.

Pots and pans were all over the floor. Scott was struggling with someone.

"What the ...!" Ninj roared.

She turned to run back and help Scott, but Hoops had made it to the bar. He reached over, seizing Ninj by her belt.

"Excuse you!" she exclaimed. "Leggo, Hoops!"

He held fast so she cocked her fist and caught him in the chin with a right hook. Her punch landed true, sending him sprawling. His body thudded on the wooden floor.

Ninj shook her hand in pain as she ran back to help Scott. Whoever was in the kitchen with him was strangling him it sounded like.

She found a familiar form bent over him and forcing him back against the counter. Dismay and surprise flooded her head.

"Ginj?" she asked with trepidation.

The figure didn't move or speak; it leaned over the cook making slurping noises.

"Ginj Avann! Is that you? What the Hell are you doing?"

The figure released Scott's body which fell on the counter. Then it turned around to face Ninj.

Ninj felt sick to her stomach. It was indeed her twin sister Ginj, but at the same time it wasn't. The lady looking at her had Hoops's exact same blank stare. She had blood running from her mouth, dribbling down her chin to the floor. Even in her shocked state Ninj could hear the miniscule splats as the drops met the floor.

"Ginj, what's happened to you!" Ninj exclaimed.

Ginj's blank stare seemed to freeze. She raised her hands ever so slowly to touch the wetness on her face. Her fingers danced a moment over the blood.

Then she smiled.

"Ginj!"

Ginj reached out toward her sister longingly ... hungrily. She had a lover's smile that seemed to say, "Come to me; I want you". Her hands reached, stretched and her feet followed.

"No, Ginj! Snap out of it! Please."

Ninj backed up slowly the way she had come. Ginj staggered after. She made a noise as if trying to talk, but there were no words, just a choking sound.

Ninj turned to run from the kitchen and the hellish vision that was her sister. She lurched right into Hoops.

She screamed the loudest, most blood-curdling scream of her life.

Still emotionless, Hoops grabbed Ninj in his arms and leaned in as she kicked and struggled for dear life. He held her arms against her sides like a vise. His breath came hard and labored and heavy.

"No," she pleaded. "Leave me be."

Hoops struck as Ginj watched jealously. His head snaked around, seeking the best angle to strike.

Thuk.

Ninj felt the fangs sink through her skin. She was terrified. What was wrong with Hoops and her sister? Were these fiends really them? She was going to die.

THWACK!

Ninj felt her entire body shudder as Hoops pushed her hard into the kitchen's island. At least his mouth was off her neck. Then she heard a voice that brought a sudden sense of elation to her.

"Let her go!" Moeera exclaimed.

Ninj saw her tall friend lift the hoe she carried and bring it down hard onto Hoops's skull. He released his iron grip and crumpled once more to the floor.

"What in blazes is happening here!" Moeera demanded.

Ginj shrieked. Moeera looked into the bewitched Munchkin's face. She saw the blood-covered mouth and chin, the pale white skin, and she heard the gurgling from Ginj's throat. In that moment it was as if she was in the little cabin again watching the blood witch challenge Carrie.

"No," Moeera said. "This isn't happening."

Ninj screamed in anguish as her sister reached out to embrace her.

"Ninj!" Moeera yelled. "Get behind me!"

She sidestepped to allow the woman room. Ginj--or what had been Ginj--followed right behind, grabbing at Ninj. Moeera felt a sense of déjà vu as she interposed herself between her friend and Ginj. She pictured Carrie's house and the blood witch and Carrie defending her.

This wasn't the blood witch, Moeera thought. She flipped the hoe over and tried to knock Ginj out the way she had Hoops. Ginj had more life in her than Hoops it appeared. She grasped Moeera's shirt, blocking her ability to swing the hoe.

Moeera looked down at the bewitched twin. The little woman held her by the shirt front and lunged at her with those blood-covered fangs. Moeera twisted her body around, but Ginj had a firm grip.

"Ninj! A little help here!"

Ninj was in shock and slow to react. Ginj got up close to Moeera.

Moeera jostled the hoe back and forth, but Ginj straddled the blade and stepped on it. She was too short to reach Moeera's neck, but she was trying.

Ninj moved behind her sister and grabbed her around the waist. But as Ninj reached, Ging struck Moeera's chest at just the spot above her top shirt button. She raked her teeth across, sinking her fangs into the soft flesh above her left breast.

Moeera gasped.

Ninj put some oomph into her actions, yanking Ginj back hard. Ginj fought, but her fangs slid away from Moeera and her sister pulled her back. Ginj hissed and snarled.

"Moeera, are you all right?" Ninj called. She had Ginj in a headlock.

"No!" Moeera shouted. She brought the hoe crashing down on Ginj's head.

"She's out," Ninj gasped.

"Thank God," Moeera breathed. She held a dry washcloth against her breast to stop the bleeding. "Check on Hoops."

Ninj checked Hoops half fearing he would spring back to consciousness and try to bite her.

"He's still out cold," she said. "I think you put him out for a while."

"Here's hoping!" Moeera said.

"Moeera, what's happening?"

"I'd like to know that myself," Moeera whispered.

"We need to talk," Ninj said, "and I need a drink."

She stepped over her sister's unconscious body and shuffled to the bar. She set two glasses on the bar and brought out a bottle of Munchkin whiskey. Hoops had delivered it just a couple days earlier.

"Want some?" she asked.

"Yes!" Moeera replied. "Is that the good stuff?"

"It's the new stuff."

"Any stuff should do the trick right now," Moeera said.

Ninj poured them each a fifth.

"To us," she said, raising her glass.

"To us," Moeera echoed. She knocked back a swallow.

"Now," Ninj said. "What in God's name is wrong with Ginj?"

"I'm not sure," Moeera said uncomfortably.

Ninj watched Moeera's eyes closely. "If you took a wild guess, what would you think is wrong?"

"I've seen someone act the same way before," Moeera said. "It was a blood witch that came to fight my friend Carrie."

"A blood witch?" Ninj asked, frowning. "I've heard of witches, but what in the world is a blood witch?"

"A witch that consumes blood to empower itself," Moeera said. "It gains power over those it drains, too. It can drain a little blood and leave the victim for all appearances normal; it can drain more which makes the victim more dazed, or it can feed repeatedly and make the victim like itself. Once it feasts on your blood it forms a bond allowing it to control your actions."

"Lordy!" Ninj said. She looked back toward the kitchen. "Is my sister a blood witch?"

"I don't know. She's acting like the one that I saw."

Ninj shivered. "So, she wants to suck my blood, eh?"

"Yes."

"And Hoops?"

"Under her control or someone else's. If Ginj isn't the blood witch, then there's one somewhere around here. Very powerful; very evil."

"Why did a blood witch come after your friend?" Ninj asked.

"Carrie was a witch," Moeera said. "She defeated and killed some blood witches during The Magic War. This one wanted revenge, I guess."

"You don't even know for sure?"

"No, when she attacked she seemed like an animal--like Ginj did."

Ninj covered her face with her hands. She slowly pulled them down again. "We need to check on Scott."

"Yes," Moeera said.

"How do we cure my sister?"

"If she's a thrall of another we kill it," Moeera said. "That's the only thing I know for certain."

"What if Ginj is a blood witch now?"

"I don't think she is," Moeera said.

"Why not?"

"She came here during the daytime," Moeera said. "Blood witches have an aversion to light. Most of them can't stand it."

"Hmm...." Ninj thought.

"Let's tie her and Hoops up," Moeera said.

Ninj brought a coil of thick, braided rope from the store's supplies. Before long they had the two trussed up tightly as could be. When they went to check on Scott, though, he was gone.

"You say Ginj sucked his blood?" Moeera asked.

"I couldn't see very well," Ninj murmured, "but that's what happened."

"He must be fleeing back to the blood witch," Moeera said. "I didn't think your sister could be the one behind all this."

"I don't know," Ninj said. "She married Starchus so anything's possible." She laughed, but her face showed no mirth.

"The only way to help them," Moeera said, nodding at Hoops and Ginj,

367

"I believe, is to find the blood witch and overpower her."

"You believe, huh."

"Yes," Moeera said. "I only apprenticed to be a witch. My training ended when a mob and a blood witch killed my teachers."

"Is it the same witch then? She followed you. Then it's your fault she's here."

Moeera took another drink of whiskey, wincing as it slid down her throat. "Probably, Ninj."

"What are you going to do about it?" Ninj demanded.

"Plan," Moeera said. "It's the only way to get out of this mess alive."

Chapter Thirty-one

Ninj did her best to stay calm despite her own sister being tied up in The Merry Kitten. She and Moeera went to Moeera's house where they sat at the kitchen table. Moeera retrieved the Wand of Murr from its hiding spot under her pillow and laid it on the table between them.

"So, what's the plan?" Ninj asked.

"If I was the blood witch, where would I hide?" Moeera asked.

"If she's so powerful, why would she hide at all?"

"Maybe she thought if she just appeared here sticking out like a sore thumb the townsfolk would flee," Moeera said.

"Maybe," Ninj said. "Do you think there's a limit to how many she controls at one time?"

"There must be," Moeera said. "Scott up and left with us still in the other room. He didn't try to attack us. And Ginj seems completely under her thumb."

"Hoops wanted his fangs in me," Ninj said, "but he was a pushover compared to Ginj."

"It's daytime, too," Moeera said, shivering. "She's lying low. When it gets dark she'll be braver."

"Why send Ginj and Hoops after us?" Ninj asked. "There're more important folks in town."

"Like Smollie Gurt? It explains why he wasn't his usual talkative self. Yet he did still talk to me about his repairs. He was still him in that head of his."

"Neither of the ones who attacked us had anything to say," Ninj said. "Not a word."

"Ginj was ferocious," Moeera said, checking her wound with a wince. "Big, big teeth, too. Smollie's weren't big that I could see."

"Neither were Starchus's," Ninj said. "I'm betting that her snub earlier was a sign of this craziness."

"Who else acted weird today?"

"Arnie Potts."

"Farmer Toby."

"Fred the Blacksmith! Ordered a drink and forgot to drink it--idiot!"

"Because he was already being controlled!"

"Bishop Mark!"

At the rate the blood witch was affecting the townspeople their chances of finding any allies at all seemed hopeless.

Ninj grasped the large ax she'd brought along from the store. "I'm ready for them. I doubt they're ready for this!"

"Interesting choice of weapon," Moeera said.

"Yes!" Ninj exclaimed. "Now where do you think that bitch is hiding?"

Moeera looked her friend in the eyes. "I don't know. She could be holed up anywhere."

"She's taking over the town," Ninj said. "Wouldn't she want to start from the center?"

"Yes," Moeera said. "I guess so."

"The Merry Kitten's the center of town," Ninj said, "but she wasn't there."

"So … the stables are closest," Moeera said.

"I doubt she'd hide there," Ninj said. "The constable's office, maybe."

"Let's check there," Moeera said.

"What? Just us two?"

"Who do we trust?"

"I see your point," Ninj said. "Our odds seem lousy, though."

"I have an idea," Moeera said, staring at the wand.

"Oh," Ninj said. "That makes me feel better. Is it a good idea?"

"I don't know."

*   *   *

Constable Gee was a slim, young man who'd grown up in Slippakanu. He'd traveled across country with his parents as a young boy, and once grown became Constable Beck's deputy.

Now he was the constable of a peaceful, little town where the most exciting thing to happen was the seasons changing. That and the time a giant skinny-dipped in the river,

He was yeeting axes at a wooden target set up behind his office when Ninj Avann and Moeera arrived.

"Haa-ah!" he yelled, letting a powerful hatchet leap to the target to land near the center.

"Hello, Danny," Ninj said.

"Constable Gee," Moeera said.

"Hello, ladies," he said, retrieving the hatchet from the target. "What are you about?" Then he noticed Ninj's ax.

"Are you here to yeet with me?"

Ninj shook her head. "No, we have other things on our mind. There's a dangerous witch in town."

"What!" Gee exclaimed. "We've never had a witch here!"

"You do now," Moeera said. "A blood witch. She's using her power to control our townspeople."

The constable looked at the two women in mild disbelief. "What's a blood witch? We don't have any witches in our town."

"My sister's bloodlust says otherwise," Ninj said as calmly as she could.

"Bloodlust? Your sister? What?"

They explained their suspicions to him as quickly as they could, making certain to describe the bizarre behavior of Hoops, Smollie, Bishop Mark, and Starchus.

Constable Gee hadn't seen anything strange all day. "Are you sure about all this?"

"Yes," Moeera said. "This witch is turning your people inside-out to make them her slaves."

He was silent for a while. Then he said, "She certainly isn't here. Where else might she hide?"

"You don't believe us, do you?" Moeera asked.

"Not really. Where's your proof?"

"Hoops and my sister are both tied up right there in The Merry Kitten," Ninj said. She'd just about lost her patience.

"Tied up?" Constable Gee asked. "Are you nuts?"

"Come see for yourself," Moeera said.

"Very well," he said, holding the hatchet by his side. "Take me to see them."

The two women walked across the way with purposeful strides. Constable Gee followed them, keeping a wary eye on Ninj's ax.

Moeera followed Ninj inside as the church bells rang, marking the hour. She glanced in the church's direction but wasn't able to see it.

Ninj crept along with her ax at the ready. When they arrived at the spot where Ginj and Hoops had been left they found neither people nor ropes.

Constable Gee relaxed, his shoulders dropping. He smiled, warily. "That was some joke you ladies told me," he said. "I really felt nervous coming here."

"They were there, Danny! I swear!" Ninj exclaimed. "What's going on?"

"Come on now," he said. "Fool me once ...."

"Constable," Moeera said. "We didn't make it up. Hoops and Ginj were bewitched."

"Oh, really?" he laughed. "I'm going home now for supper. Don't the two of you have work to do? This is the only saloon in town!"

"You'll see," Ninj said. "We aren't making it up."

"Good day."

He left, slamming the door.

"Of all the stupid!" Ninj ranted.

"Right," Moeera said. "Ninj, I think I know where she is."

"Where?"

"The church."

"The church?" Ninj asked, startled. "That's a holy place. Why would a witch pick there to hide?"

"She's just smart, I guess," Moeera said. "Bishop Mark was acting weird, though. So, I think she's there."

"Let's go then," Ninj said. "Do you still have your stuff?"

"Yes," Moeera said, patting the satchel she carried over her arm.

Chapter Thirty-two

They walked outside to find the sun getting low over the treetops. Soon all of the enslaved townsfolk would be prowling. Ninj swallowed and cradled her ax in her arms. She hummed nervously.

"Courage, Ninj," Moeera said. "We can do this."

"Murder somebody," Ninj said.

"Someone who's destroying our home," Moeera said. "She means to wipe us out."

"Why?" Ninj asked as the church came into view.

"That's what blood witches do."

They strode toward the church, the largest building in the center of town, with its tower and pointed steeple. A crowd milled about the front door.

"Where is she?" Ninj called to the people she saw.

No one answered.

The crowd began moving out toward Ninj and Moeera.

Hoops, Scott, and Eggs approached them. All three had blank stares.

"Get back, boys!" Ninj ordered, hefting her ax. "I don't want to hurt you."

They halted. Others bumped into the three men from behind.

"Where is the blood witch?" Moeera asked.

Still no answer.

The crowd moved forward a step.

"Stop it!" Ninj yelled. "I'm warning you!"

The crowd rushed her, surging forward. Ninj swung her ax in a wide arc, catching the blade on Hoops, Scott, and Constable Gee. The constable sported the same blank look as the others. The three of them fell to the ground. Ninj shrieked as six more blank-faced Munchkins rushed her. Her ax landed on the schoolteacher's shoulder, cleaving through her collar bone, but the others overran her while she pulled the ax head free.

Moeera recited a spell, pointing the Wand of Murr at Ninj's attackers. The wand glowed in her hands. The five grabbing at Ninj froze in place. Ninj pulled herself off her knees, standing once more.

The remaining Munchkins numbered seven. They circled Moeera and Ninj. Three were children, four were farmhands. All looked on, blankly.

Moeera recited the spell again, locking the seven Munchkins in place.

"Unbelievable!" Ninj said. "You can do all that?"

Moeera nodded. "It took some practice--it's lucky I remember how."

Ninj shook her head. "Let's get in there, Moeera."

They squeezed between the statue-like Munchkins. Moeera grasped the handle on the door and pulled. It creaked open. Ninj entered with her ax and Moeera followed. The door swung shut.

The inside of the church sanctuary was dim and gloomy. In the shadows they could see people sitting silently in the pews. They walked further in.

That's when Moeera spied the blood witch lounging across the altar, watching them. She made eye contact with Moeera from halfway across the room.

"There she is," Moeera said quietly.

"That's her," Ninj said.

"Yes, that's who killed my teachers."

"And now she's eating her way through Slippakanu," Ninj said.

The blood witch slid down from the altar, white dressings billowing around her to settle at last revealing a svelte figure.

Moeera and Ninj stopped walking when they got to the fifth pew. The first four pews held most of the townspeople. They stared sideways at the two women.

"Welcome," the witch said in a calm, comforting voice. "I'm so glad you could join us this evening."

"Why are you here?" Moeera asked. "What do you want?"

"Your friendship, of course," the witch said, a single drop of blood flowing down her lips. "Your love and devotion and service. The Pip broke you in. Now I can teach you the rest."

"No," Moeera said.

"No?" the blood witch echoed. "What do you mean 'No'?"

"Exactly that," Moeera said. "You either release these people and leave, or I'll destroy you."

The witch laughed. "You have confidence. I like that. As for your demands ... they come off as unrealistic. I'll have servants. If not you, then certain of these people have tasted of my veins. They would make suitable apprentices."

"No," Moeera said. "I won't allow it."

The blood witch glowered at her and began striding forward. "Watch your lip, girl. I'll have your blood, but if you can't behave with courtesy, I'll see you in the dust."

Moeera's thoughts raced. She recited the spell again, the wand glowed, and ... the witch strode up and lifted her by the neck.

"Foolish," the blood witch said. "That won't work on me." She looked at Ninj. "It will work on your friend."

Ninj froze in place. The witch slid the ax from her hands and dropped it on the floor. Moeera gasped for air, struggling with the vise-like grip. The witch tossed her to the floor.

"Now what will it be, dear Moeera? Death or the chance to live forever?"

Moeera coughed. She reached into her satchel and pulled something out, gripping it in her hand.

"What have you got there, little girl?" the witch asked.

"Nothing," Moeera lied. "I want to live forever."

"Come here," the witch said.

Moeera got to her feet, keeping her right hand closed.

"Come here," the witch repeated. "I need but a taste, and then you'll see things my way."

Moeera walked to the witch. As the witch leaned down to bite her neck Moeera thrust her hand against the witch's chest smearing mud against her.

"So that's your game!" the witch screeched, backhanding Moeera. "Trying to thwart me with mud?"

Moeera scrambled up and away. She ran as fast as she could toward the door.

"Stop!" the witch screamed, pointing at the fleeing woman.

The Wand of Murr, still clutched in Moeera's left hand, glowed white hot. Moeera ran out the door.

The blood witch shrieked like a Hell-condemned soul. She stalked after Moeera, stopping only once to say, "She is yours."

As the witch exited the people in the pews walked to Ninj's paralyzed body. Ginj reached her first. With a wild animal's ferocity, she tore into her sister's neck and began slurping the blood. Starchus also found a spot on Ninj's neck. As did Farmer Hendry. The rest surrounded them, waiting their own turns.

Chapter Thirty-three

Moeera was hysterical. Her spell to immobilize the blood witch didn't work and neither had the mud. Now she'd abandoned Ninj to the horror within the church walls. She looked around wildly. What could she do? Where could she go?

The people she'd immobilized out here were beginning to get loose. Eggs, some kids, and some other guys--farmhands she thought--began staggering about. As the spell wore off entirely, they shuffled straight toward her.

The church door flew open so hard it broke a hinge. The blood witch followed the blank-eyed people, stalking toward Moeera floating on rage.

"We aren't done, Moeera!" she cried. "Not by a long shot!" Her arms hung by her sides; hands balled into fists.

Moeera fled around the left side of the building. If she could stay out of the witch's sight, she might have a chance. She spoke five magic words and vanished.

The blood witch beat the others around the corner. When she didn't see Moeera she gnashed her teeth together. She lifted her right hand into the air, making a grabbing/pulling gesture.

Moeera watched her from behind her screen of invisibility. The ground shook beneath her feet and a wrenching, smashing sound rumbled all around. Part of the church's side and rear walls was moving away from the building, pulling away from the connected roof and foundation. It moved counterclockwise to rush straight at Moeera.

Moeera dropped her cloak of invisibility and tried to put an air charm on her feet. It didn't work. She had never mastered it during her practice with Carrie. The stone wall rammed into her, knocking her to the ground.

"That was easy," the blood witch said. "You really have no idea what you're doing, do you?"

The blood witch's slaves moved to surround the prone form of the apprentice witch.

Moeera's head ached, her body ached, and even her insides ached. She sensed the Munchkins getting closer. She murmured the words of the Nebulous. Her mind focused on the rocky bank of the river and what she liked to watch from there. She repeated the magic words and continued her inner vision. A faint shimmer coalesced around her body.

"What do you think you're doing!" the blood witch sneered. "I'm not letting you escape that way again!" She focused on Moeera, reciting a spell of her own.

Meanwhile, Moeera continued reciting the words of the Nebulous. The glowing outline rose from her body and launched into the sky. Moeera continued her chanting while she watched the light disappear into the sky.

"Get her up off the ground and bring her to me!" the blood witch commanded. "Her blood shall be the sweetest, yet."

The enslaved Munchkins did as they were told. Eggs and the farmers hauled her still throbbing body up. Eggs held her arms behind her as the blood witch came to whisper in her ear.

"I, Izzpalin, now add you to my servitude. You'll follow me forever, doing exactly as I wish; that is how deep the bond of blood will tie us." She leaned toward Moeera's neck with fangs flashing.

"Ow! What!" the blood witch cried in surprise.

A rainbow-hued ring of light sprang up around the blood witch, Moeera, and Eggs. Half a dozen dark shapes scurried all over the blood witch.

"Impossible!" Izzpalin cried. "You can't even make a proper magical escape; you certainly can't summon wraiths!"

They weren't wraiths.

They were long, slender, brown-haired, otter-like animals called ....

"Sliders!" Moeera yelled, her head throbbing.

The blood witch screamed and bit and kicked and hit at the dog-sized mammals. They slid around and about her, a whirlpool of living motion. All six of them bit at her repeatedly. Their long claws raked her exposed

378

flesh and easily shredded her white gauze dress. She shrieked and screamed and cursed, but the sliders were on a mission. Her curses changed to pleading. She begged anyone who would hear her for help, but no one lifted a finger.

As Eggs held Moeera she watched the sliders drag Izzpalin toward a buppus trough. They harried and bit at her until she backed right into it and went ass over teacups.

SPLASH!

She was under the water with the sliders piling on top of her, holding her under the water's surface. They appeared to dance atop the frothing, splashing water of the trough.

And then it was over.

Eggs released Moeera who fell to her knees, her head and the rest of her still hurting from being smacked by a building. The townsfolk began muttering and mumbling as their minds shrugged off the blood witch's influence. They were confused, but at the same time seemed to remember they'd been pawns of the unholy blood witch.

The sliders ran over to Moeera, but instead of biting and harrying; they kissed her with their whiskery muzzles. They dashed off in the river's direction.

Moeera breathed softly. She forced herself to walk over to the trough. Looking into the water she saw that the witch was absolutely, positively dead--drowned by a foe she'd never expected, the simple animals who in their own way were a part of the town. One pale, thin arm hung out of the trough lifeless.

Epilogue

More than a week went by before Moeera did much venturing outside her house. She barely managed to drag herself the short distance from the churchyard--her physical and emotional pain had been that great.

She'd called out to the waking Munchkins of Slippakanu begging anyone whose head had cleared enough to check on Ninj. Eggs stumbled into the church to help his boss only to find her lifeless body sprawled on the aisle floor. She'd been drained of blood so entirely that she'd perished. He'd told Moeera the devastating news, and she'd bawled for her best friend. Her true friend who'd been like family to her was gone. She blamed herself.

The blood witch orchestrated Ninj's demise, but Moeera had run out on her friend during the fight. If she'd stayed, would Ninj have made it out alive?

Ninj hadn't been the only one to die. Hendry Munkick had died soon after regaining his senses. So had Smollie Gurt, Bishop Mark, Ging Avann, and Starchus Vay. The town had reeled upon finding the corpse of their beloved Mayor Gurt. Word had it they were debating on some special way to honor his memory.

About a week after the carnage Moeera ambled to the river to watch her saviors at play. She sat upon a boulder, even managing some giggles, watching the Sliders perform their antics and their daredevil sliding routine.

She heard an odd, rasping bird call. Gormib approached her with a large, curved cage hanging from his hand. In it was his stolen raven.

"Hello, Miss Moeera," he said, sitting on an adjoining rock.

"Gormib," she said. "How are you?"

"Alive," he said. "I hear that's thanks to you."

She nodded toward the brown, splashing creatures in the river. "Thanks to them, actually."

"Oh?"

She recounted her story of what went on inside and in front of the church.

"How'd you make them do that?" he asked.

"I didn't. I mean I used The Nebulous to fetch them from the riverbank, but they did all the rest. They attacked the blood witch."

"I'll be darned," he said.

"I brought them to be a distraction; I thought one or two might do that. And I thought if it frightened them that one might even bite her, but I didn't expect them to fight her."

"Well, it worked," Gormib said.

"Yes."

"I'm leaving town," he told her.

"You are?" she asked.

"Yes. Would you like to come with? I could share my magic knowledge with you."

"No funny business? No rolling in the hay kind of songs?"

"Of course not!"

"He's lying!" the raven croaked.

Moeera stared at the bird. Then she looked at Gormib and said, "At least I know one of you will tell me the truth."

About the Author

Christopher Schmehl lives in Laureldale, Pennsylvania with his wife Eileen, their two sons, and their lovable diva of a Chiweenie Molly. He enjoys reading, writing, swimming, and a good flick.

Made in the USA
Middletown, DE
26 August 2023

37411547R00225